About

Rachael Thomas has always loved reading romance and is thrilled to be a Mills & Boon Modern Romance author. She lives and works on a farm in Wales—a far cry from the glamour of a Modern Romance story—but that makes slipping into her characters' worlds all the more appealing. When she's not writing or working on the farm she enjoys photography and visiting historical castles and grand houses. Visit her at rachaelthomas.co.uk.

Andie Brock started inventing imaginary friends around the age of four and is still doing that today; only now the sparkly fairies have made way for spirited heroines and sexy heroes.

Thankfully she now has some real friends, as well as a husband and three children, plus a grumpy but lovable cat.

Andie lives in Bristol and when not actually writing, could well be plotting her next passionate romance story.

Tara Pammi can't remember a moment when she wasn't lost in a book—especially a romance, which was much more exciting than a mathematics textbook. Years later, Tara's wild imagination and love for the written word revealed what she really wanted to do. Now she pairs Alpha males who think they know everything with strong women who knock that theory *and* them off their feet.

£19 185, 18

The Italian Mavericks
COLLECTION

January 2019

February 2019

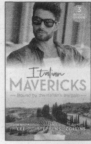

March 2019

April 2019

May 2019

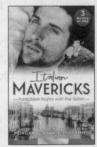

June 2019

**Watch out for the Greek Mavericks
collection coming soon!**

Italian Mavericks: Carrying the Italian's Heir

RACHAEL THOMAS

ANDIE BROCK

TARA PAMMI

MILLS & BOON

First Published in Great Britain 2019
By Mills & Boon, an imprint of HarperCollins *Publishers*
1 London Bridge Street, London, SE1 9GF

ITALIAN MAVERICKS: CARRYING THE ITALIAN'S HEIR
© 2019 Harlequin Books S.A.

Married for the Italian's Heir © 2016 Harlequin Books S.A
The Last Heir of Monterrato © 2015 Andie Brock
The Surprise Conti Child © 2016 Tara Pammi

Special thanks and acknowledgement go to Rachael Thomas for her contribution to the *Brides for Billionaires* series.

ISBN: 978-0-263-27604-6

0519

MIX
Paper from
responsible sources
FSC
www.fsc.org
FSC˘ C007454

This book is produced from independently certified FSC™ paper to ensure responsible forest management.

For more information visit: www.harpercollins.co.uk/green

Printed and bound in Spain
by CPI, Barcelona

MARRIED FOR THE ITALIAN'S HEIR

RACHAEL THOMAS

For Mum

PROLOGUE

Two months ago

PIPER LOST ALL sense of reason as his kiss seared her skin and his accomplished touch brought her body to life in a way she'd never known. The pain and grief that this day held for her were blotted out as he whispered words of Italian that sounded romantic, but she had no hope of understanding them.

She gloried in his embrace, for the first time in many months feeling treasured, wanted and needed. What would come after this moment she couldn't think about now. She didn't want to face the emptiness. All she wanted was to abandon herself to this man and his passion, to yield to his kisses and give herself utterly and completely to the moment—and to him.

She gasped in frustration as he stopped kissing her. He pulled away and looked down at her, his sinfully dark caramel eyes full of desire—for *her*. Empowered by this, she smiled at him, unable to hide the longing that was tearing through her faster than lightning. She'd never been desired by any man, and had certainly never been kissed the way he had just kissed her. But, more than that, it was the way she wanted him to kiss her again and again.

This man was a skilled lover, and the way he was looking at her now, with raw lust that vibrated through the semi-darkness of the hotel room, she knew there was no turning back—not that she wanted to. The attraction between them had been too fierce, too strong, even before he'd suggested they leave the party.

Tonight she would give herself to this man. But she was well aware there wouldn't be a tomorrow. She might be an innocent woman discovering the pleasure of a man's touch, but she knew not to expect more. She'd worked as a waitress at many society parties in Sydney and in London and she had recognised him as a playboy—a man who wanted one uncommitted night of passion, who loved and left women. Tonight she didn't care about her dream to settle down with the right man. Tonight she wanted the wrong man.

She wanted to drown her sorrow in the passion even she couldn't deny, which had ignited between them from the very first moment their eyes had met as he'd arrived at the party. It had arced between them as if they were meant to be here together, caught up in a moment of passion which would surely change her...change her life. How, she didn't know. She just knew that this moment was one she had to explore.

He touched her face, tracing the pad of his thumb down her cheek, and she closed her eyes as her knees threatened to give way. He pulled her closer, holding her tightly with one arm, keeping her body pressed against the hardness of his, making her virginal body pulse so wildly with unquenched desire it was as if the conclusion of the kiss was already sealed. As was her fate.

'Before we go any further, do we need protection?' His husky and heavily accented voice shimmered over her, and her senses were so confused by the desire which burned through her Piper couldn't think straight.

'Protection?' The whispered word sounded so seductive she could hardly believe it was *her* voice. How had the sensible and shy woman she usually was become such a seductress?

'I intend to make love to you, *cara*.'

He slipped off his suit jacket in a purposeful way which made her heart race as much as his words did. All sensible thought vanished from her as she watched him turn and toss it onto a nearby chair. His white shirt was bright in the partial darkness of the room.

She quivered with anticipation as he stepped back to her, excited and terrified about what would happen next. With deliberate slowness he took her in his arms again and kissed her. Then his hand moved down her neck and along her shoulder, slipping under the strap of her dress, sliding it away. As his lips followed the blazing trail of his hand she let her head fall back and gave herself up to the abandonment of the moment.

'Sorted…' She gasped the word as his kisses moved down her neck, hardly able to think straight because of the fire each kiss ignited within her.

'Then there is nothing to stop us.'

With unnerving ease he pulled the zip at the side of her dress and the black silk slithered down her body. The heat of embarrassment rushed over her, and she watched his face as he touched her breast, his fingers concentrating on the hardened peak of her nipple, making her gasp with pleasure. Then he lowered his head and teased the other nipple with his tongue until she thought she might explode with pleasure.

'That is so…' She closed her eyes as heat seared within her, unable to say anything else.

'Do you want me, *cara*?'

His warm breath increased the sensation of delirium as his tongue teased her nipple.

'I want you…' She struggled to say the words as he continued to work his magic. She entwined her fingers in his thick hair, not wanting him ever to stop. 'To make love to me.'

He laughed softly against her breast, the sensation making her writhe against him.

'I can think of nothing better, you little tease.'

His accent thrilled her as much as his words, intensifying this new and exciting need inside her, pushing the real Piper further away.

'Now.' She pulled him close against her, wanting to feel his body, to taste his skin. 'I want you *now*.'

A soft, sexy laugh escaped him and he let go of her briefly, putting her at arm's length. The black silk of her dress slithered to the floor in a pool around her feet, leaving her in skimpy black panties and strappy sandals.

His dark gaze roved over her near nakedness and the air between them sparked with desire. A flash of her usual shyness threatened, but she pushed it back, refusing to allow it into this moment, and reached for him. Her need to see more of him and touch him made her pull so hard at his shirt buttons they popped off.

His feral growl of pleasure pushed her on, making her want him, want *this* even more. She couldn't stop now—couldn't be her usual cautious self and spend the rest of her life wondering *What if?* Tonight she would experience 'What if?' She couldn't let this moment go by without responding to it.

In a movement so swift, so decisive, he pushed her back onto the bed, pulling off his white shirt and exposing his muscled torso, dusted in dark hair. Then, with a wicked gleam in those devil-may-care eyes, he removed every last scrap of clothing from his glorious body.

She watched, entranced and excited, as he stepped towards her, towering over her. She trembled in anticipation as she lay there, his gaze never leaving hers. Her heart pounded so hard she was sure the whole of London could hear it, and a sigh of pleasure escaped her as he lowered himself over her, the hardness of his arousal almost too much.

He spoke again in Italian as he kissed down her throat and she ran her hands over his strong back, pressing her nails into his skin. But still it wasn't enough. Still she wanted more.

Driven by a powerful need she no longer had any control over, she slipped her hands between their bodies and he lifted himself slightly, allowing her to touch him. She wanted to feel him, to torment him as he'd done her. But still it wasn't enough. She wanted to remove the last barriers of clothing and feel him touch her intimately before possessing her completely.

Urgency took over and she clung to him, raising her hips, her body begging his for release and the oblivion of passion. She wanted him so much. It was as if she'd been waiting for this moment—for him.

'*Dio mio.* You are a goddess sent to torment me.'

His guttural voice together with his insistent kisses up her neck was almost too much, and she knew that it had to be now—that they had to come together, that there was no turning back.

He moved, clasping his hands around her wrists and pinning her arms either side of her head. The wild look in his eyes was as terrifying as it was exciting. His breath was coming hard and fast as he fixed her with those dark, sexy eyes. She lifted her hips, clasping her legs around him as her need to be one with him increased.

Another curse left his lips and he let one of her arms go as he raised his hips and ripped her black panties from her. Her shocked gasp only encouraged him further, and he barely paused as she pressed her nakedness against him, feeling the heat of his erection intimately.

'Per Dio.'

The words rushed from him as she moved, bringing them together. He thrust into her, her startled cry making him stop. She glanced up to see a furious frown on his handsome face, but she couldn't let it end there. She wanted total possession. She wanted him to take her, make her his. Even if it was only for tonight.

'Don't stop.' She lifted her hips, taking him deeper inside her as she raised her head and pressed kisses against his chest, tasting the salty tang of desire on his skin.

'You're a…' he whispered hoarsely.

But she pressed her lips against his, hiding the truth as she used the unrelenting need in her body and lifted herself up to him, making his possession deep and powerful, forcing him to surrender to the moment too.

Another feral curse left him as he joined her in the frenzied dance of sex. It was so exquisite, so much more than she'd ever dared to hope it could be, that as she hovered on the brink of oblivion she cried out, holding him tight against her as several tears escaped, sliding down her face. She buried her face against his chest, inhaling the sexy scent of him, knowing it would be etched in her memory for ever.

As would the moment she'd lost her virginity, becoming a real woman with a man whose name she didn't even know.

As her heart rate slowed and his body relaxed she moved, but he caught an arm around her, pulling her close against him. 'You are not going anywhere yet, *cara.*'

Those sultry words made her mind spin—as did the reality of what she'd done. Through the fog of desire rational thought was finally becoming clear. She'd lost her virginity and jeopardised her new job— all for a man who hadn't even bothered with the pleasantries of an introduction. His kisses and soft words had seduced her on a day when she was at her most vulnerable, a day when she needed to know she was alive, prove she could be a woman in charge of her life.

His breathing deepened as he slept, and even though her body was held tightly against his Piper knew she had no option but to leave. She might have experienced the most wonderful night, but this wasn't who she was.

She slipped carefully from the bed and quietly gathered her clothes, dressing in the near darkness. He stirred and she looked at him—at his handsome face, his lean body partially covered by the white sheet— committing it all to her memory, because this was a man who didn't want anything other than casual affairs. Despite her naivety, she knew this.

Quietly she left the room of the man whose name she didn't even know—the man she would never see again as she returned to being the shy woman who'd arrived in London from Australia only a year before.

CHAPTER ONE

FURIOUS AT THE way his life had begun to unravel over the last two weeks, Dante Mancini pushed back the effects of too much whisky at last night's impromptu meeting. He tried not to think of the outrageous solution Benjamin Carter had proposed to counteract the damning article *Celebrity Spy!* had run.

The scandalous piece—naming himself, Ben Carter, Sheikh Zayn Al-Ghamdi and Xander Trakas as the world's most debauched bachelors—had done untold damage to their favourite charity, The Hope Foundation. Now those who ran it had demanded they clean up their acts or step aside as patrons. To make matters worse, a business deal he'd been working on was in danger of collapsing because of the damage to his reputation—he was a bachelor who played the field and now everyone knew it.

Could Ben's idea work? Would taking such drastic action as marriage divert unwanted attention from the charity *and* secure his most lucrative business deal yet? Possibly. But was he prepared to take the gamble…?

Dante pushed open the door to his office building, not bothering to remove his sunglasses and definitely not ready to admit that the copious amount of whisky he'd drunk whilst being told he needed to find himself a wife was the reason for his fierce headache and foul mood.

He stabbed at the button to call the elevator and inhaled deeply as he waited, still fuming that Bettino D'Antonio was pulling out of the deal because he, Dante Mancini, and his company didn't uphold family values.

As the doors to the elevator swished open he walked in, desperate for a moment of solitude before he entered the suite of offices which served as the headquarters for his self-built global business empire dealing in renewable energies. In a bid to bring back some control and chase away the threatening headache he inhaled deeply once again.

The doors closed and instantly his senses were on alert. His memory rushed back to an illicit night of hot sex in a London hotel with an unknown redhead who'd haunted his dreams and stalked his thoughts each day ever since.

She had been wild and passionate, and yet as he'd made her his he'd realised she was a virgin. A fluid curse left him as the elevator doors closed, trapping him inside with a memory which only added to his unaccustomed bad mood. It irritated the hell out of him that those gorgeous green eyes continued to haunt him and that, despite the alcohol still in his system from last night, his blood heated at the memory and a shot of lust hurtled round him.

'Maledizione.' He *never* thought of a woman once their affair was over, and the redhead encounter had been two months ago. Well and truly over.

He clenched his hands into tight fists at his sides. Now was *not* the time to become embroiled in memories of one meaningless night. He had to remain in control—focus on the matter in hand. He couldn't allow that piece of gossip in *Celebrity Spy!* to jeopardise one of the biggest deals he'd ever gone after, or to tarnish the work of the charity he helped to fund. But neither was he about to be dictated to by Benjamin Carter. He had absolutely no desire to settle down in that very elusive state of marital bliss just to salvage his reputation. There had to be another way and he'd find it—of that he was sure.

Not a moment too soon the elevator doors opened and he left the memory-evoking scent of perfume and marched into his office. His head thumped mercilessly from last night's excess of whisky and his temper was frayed from the latest developments on the deal.

His secretary jumped up eagerly as he stormed in but he refused to indulge in his usual morning pleasantries. He didn't have the stamina for niceties right now. All he wanted was total silence and coffee—strong and black.

'I don't want to be disturbed.' He snapped the instruction at her as he strode past her desk, desperate for the solitude of his office with its sought-after views over the old quarter of Rome.

'Signor Mancini…' she began, overriding his instruction, and he stopped and looked at her, about to open his office door, glad of the sunglasses he still wore.

The last thing he wanted his secretary to know was that he was suffering from an uncharacteristic overindulgence of alcohol. After his meeting with Ben and the others he'd managed to catch an hour or two of sleep during the overnight flight back to Rome on his private jet, but that hadn't helped dull the effects of the whisky. All he needed was to be left alone.

'No calls. No meetings. Nothing.' He threw the words at her and as she took a breath to protest turned from her and burst into his office. He slammed the door and closed his eyes, taking a deep breath. The world had gone mad. Everything he'd worked so hard to achieve seemed in danger of falling to pieces around him.

He muttered a curse and strode across his large office, pressed the button on his coffee machine, then stood at the windows looking out over the city that had at first been a hard and demanding mistress but was now one of only two places in the world where he felt completely at ease.

As the welcome aroma of coffee filled his office he heard movement behind him and tensed. He turned slowly to see just who it was in his office, aware now that his secretary's unusual insistence on speaking to him must have been to warn him that he had someone waiting for him.

What he *didn't* expect to see was the flame-haired siren who'd haunted him since that night two months ago, when she'd slipped from his bed in the early hours, long before he'd woken. *Not* something he was accustomed to.

'I hope you don't mind that I waited in here for you…' The redhead's soft voice wavered with uncertainty and, dressed in jeans and a navy knitted poncho, she certainly didn't resemble the glamorous self-assured beauty he'd bedded that night. But then she hadn't been all she'd pretended to be that night, had she? She hadn't been an experienced seductress. She'd been a virgin. A fact she'd kept from him until it had been too late.

He pulled off his sunglasses and looked at her. How had she found him? How did she know who he was? Those few hours in his hotel room had been so passionate, so filled with lustful need that they hadn't even exchanged names, let alone phone numbers.

Icy-cold fingers of dread clutched at him. Was she

here to use that story in *Celebrity Spy!* for some kind
of blackmail? Did she want to sell a kiss-and-tell story?
Was that why she'd come to Rome unannounced? To
demand money from him for her silence?

'As a matter of fact I do.' The angry bitterness in his
voice barely concealed his disappointment at this realisation. He'd placed her on some kind of pedestal since
that night, his thoughts constantly returning to her like
a lovesick teenager. She'd got to him in a way no other
woman had come close to doing. Even now his blood
heated at the knowledge that she was so close, just as it
had when he'd smelt the lingering trace of what he now
knew to be her perfume in the elevator moments ago.

She stood up and he let his gaze travel quickly down
her jean-clad legs, remembering how they'd felt as she'd
wrapped them around him. Savagely he dragged his
mind back to the present. Dwelling on one night of sex
was not in his nature.

'What do you want?' He fired the question at her.

'I just have one thing I need to say and then I will go.'

Her voice still held uncertainty and her face looked
pale. Was that just because she wore hardly any make-
up?

She looked totally different from the seductress
who'd tempted him from the party that night, and she
stood before him now looking every bit the innocent
and inexperienced virgin she had been when he'd taken
her to his hotel room. But she wasn't a virgin any longer. He had been her first lover and he wanted to know
why she had kept that from him. The question wouldn't
come. As she looked at him he sensed something much
bigger, much more threatening.

'How much?' he demanded, narrowing his eyes as
he tried to gauge her reaction, angry that he'd put him-

self in this position, that he hadn't exercised his usual caution where women were concerned.

Her delicate brows flew together. 'How much what?'

He stepped closer and the scent of her perfume teased at his memory again. He closed his mind to the images which threatened to engulf him. The woman who stood before him now was very different from the woman who'd teased him until he'd all but lost his mind as well as his control.

He sighed and walked towards his desk, tossing his sunglasses down before leaning on its solid wood, fixing her with a hard glare. 'How much do you want? For your silence?'

'I'm not about to tell the world,' she snapped back at him, her voice full of injustice.

He only just managed to stifle a smile. The fiery redhead had briefly surfaced from behind the façade of unassuming inexperience she had adopted.

'Then why are you here, *cara*? And, more to the point, how did you find me?' Already he was bored with this conversation. His head thumped cruelly and he wanted nothing more than to sit down in silence. He had a deal to salvage and he didn't need Little Miss Shy adding to the mix of hurdles he had to power over.

'There was an article…' she said softly as he walked back towards the windows.

He turned to face her and noticed how she followed his every move, turning herself slightly to maintain eye contact with him. It made him suspicious.

'I'm more than aware that there was an article,' he growled back at her, the tension in his head reaching almost breaking point. This tedious conversation should have ended when she'd named her price—right before he threw her out. So why hadn't she? More to the point, why hadn't he thrown her out?

'That is how I got your name.' He raised his brows as she blushed before continuing. 'We didn't exactly have time to exchange details.'

Exchanging details had been the last thing on his mind. All he'd wanted was her naked and beneath him. He'd been rash and uncontrolled. Hell, he'd even taken her word that she was on the pill. Something he'd *never* succumbed to, no matter how deliciously tempting the woman.

'True, but we had much more fun that way, did we not, *cara*?' He smiled at her, allowing himself to remember her eagerness, her insistence which had so turned him on, testing his control beyond its usual limits.

'Piper.' Her eyes narrowed as she glared at him, the green depths of them sparking wildly.

'Piper?' he repeated, his mind still not able to function as it should. Hell, he hadn't even had an espresso yet to banish the remnants of whisky, even though the welcome aroma now filled the office.

'My name is Piper. Piper Riley.'

He nodded. 'And now that we are both in possession of each other's names, perhaps you'd tell me exactly why you are here.' Once again he moved across his office and glanced at the woman who'd been just the redhead in his mind until today. As before, she moved to face him. Now she had a name would she continue to linger in his mind so temptingly? He hoped not.

'I needed to see you because…' She faltered and he folded his arms across his chest, becoming increasingly irritated by the conversation.

'*Dio mio*. Just say what you have to say and leave. I don't have time for games.'

'Very well.' She stood taller, lifted her chin a fraction and looked directly at him. 'I'm pregnant.'

Dante had thought the previous twenty-four hours had been filled with nothing but trouble, swallowing up his usual cavalier attitude. He had never expected—or wanted—those words to be said to him. He couldn't be a father—not when he'd already proved his inability to look after anyone.

'How?'

The word shot from him before he had time to think, time to compose himself, but she stood resolutely before him. Even the heated redness which rushed over her pale face for a second time didn't alter the fact that she had suddenly become bolder and more confident— much more like the woman he'd made love to that night.

Piper held her ground, remaining rigidly still, focusing her full attention on the man whose baby she was carrying. A man whose reputation had been plastered all over the tabloids in recent weeks, one of the world's most eligible and debauched bachelors. He was far from ideal father material, but she couldn't deny him the knowledge that he was going to be a father—much less deny her child the right to a father.

She watched him as he prowled around his office, oblivious to the fact that the coffee he evidently needed was ready. He looked as immaculately stylish as he had the night of the party. The only difference was the hint of stubbly shadow at his jaw and the lines of tension on his face, which stirred her sympathy. But she couldn't let sentiment get in the way. Not now she knew exactly who she was dealing with.

'I think we both know how.'

She couldn't believe the seductive purr which wrapped around those words as she looked at him, wondering just what kind of effect this man still had on her. Her heart raced wildly and her stomach somersaulted. She wasn't at all convinced it was just her nerves at the situation. It was the darkly passionate man she'd lost her virginity to—Dante Mancini. A playboy and exceedingly proud of it, if the article she'd stumbled across in *Celebrity Spy!* was to be believed.

'What I mean is how, when you allowed me to believe that the protection I wanted to use wasn't necessary?' His words were slow and his accent heavy, as if he couldn't take in what she'd told him—or the implications.

Yes, that was the question she'd asked herself as she'd done the first pregnancy test—and the second. It had changed to the question of how she could have been so stupid as she'd done a third, and by the time she'd torn the packaging from the fourth and final test it had changed to words she never usually used, followed by panic at what she was going to do.

Being a single mother was *not* what she wanted. She'd grown up with a doting father and had always wanted that for her children. And now she was pregnant with this man's baby.

'In case you weren't aware, I had never been in such a situation with a man before. I assumed when you mentioned protection that it had been dealt with.' She hurled the words at him, furious at herself but even angrier that he'd balked at taking such responsibility.

He walked towards her, suspicion in his dark eyes, and she fought hard against the memory of them being full of desire for her, full of need for her and overflowing with passion. It had been a moment out of time that she'd wanted to remember for ever. Now, thanks to the legacy of that night, she had no choice.

'And how do I know you didn't go straight from my bed to that of another man? How do I know the baby you claim to carry is mine?'

She gasped in shock at his fiercely cold words. She'd played out many scenarios in her head over recent weeks, but none had been as brutally attacking as this. In a spur-of-the-moment decision she'd booked a ticket to Rome, because all she'd wanted to do was tell him, face to face, that he was going to be a father. She'd never anticipated anything more. The close bond she'd had with her father had made it impossible for her to do anything else but tell Dante Mancini personally. She'd foolishly believed that he'd want to know that those wonderfully passionate few hours together had created a new life. His child.

How wrong she'd been.

Defeat washed over her, followed by tiredness. She hadn't even booked a hotel. Once she'd made up her mind all she'd wanted was to get to Rome as soon as possible and to do what she considered the right thing before her confidence deserted her.

'There are tests that can determine such things.' She ploughed her fingers into her hair, pulling it off her face, holding it before letting it fall back. She was too tired to deal with this now. She'd felt sick for the duration of the flight, going over and over how to tell him. Trying to second-guess his reaction.

'Then there will be a test carried out as soon as it is safe to do so.'

The harsh words focused her mind acutely.

'I have no intention of taking your word for such a claim.'

'In that case you may be interested to know it can be done in a few weeks' time.' She couldn't help the rush of triumph as he glared at her. Had he expected her to flounder, to back away and leave without fighting her corner—her child's corner? As the battle of what to do had waged in her mind she'd done her research on the internet, and she knew that, within two weeks if he demanded it, she could confirm that he was the father.

He moved towards her—so close that she could see the flecks of black in the caramel-brown of his eyes, almost obliterating their colour. She could also detect the faint hint of alcohol and wondered if he had left another woman's bed that morning, after a night of sex and champagne like the one *they'd* shared. The thought sickened her and nausea rushed over her again. Her knees threatened to buckle as the reality of her shattered and foolish dreams sank in.

'You sound very convinced that the child is mine.'

He sounded indifferent to her distress, his accent intensified, and being so close to him brought back memories of their night together, increasing the almost overwhelming nausea. She gathered herself quickly. She couldn't break down now. Not here. Not in front of him.

'You are the only man I have ever slept with. That night we spent together was totally out of character for me.' She pushed down her reasons for acting on the undeniable attraction which had sparked so outrageously to life between them. She'd tried to continue working, but with his hot gaze all but stripping her naked right there in the middle of the party it had been almost impossible.

'So why did you do it?'

He walked slowly round her and she turned, needing to keep him firmly in her line of vision, and inwardly she cursed the lack of sight in her left eye that she'd been born with. She wanted to tell him to stand still, but she hated people knowing, and thanks to the operation she'd had as a child and the contact lenses she wore there wasn't any need to explain endlessly any more.

She took a deep breath. Honesty was the best way, and if he wanted to know why she'd gone hand in hand with him to his hotel room she would tell him. 'It was the first anniversary of my father's death, and I guess I wasn't my normal self.'

His penetrating gaze slid down her body and she swallowed down the nerves that were threatening to get the better of her. 'And is *this* your normal self?'

'Yes,' she snapped, hurt by his scathing tone.

She knew she looked nothing like the woman he'd taken to his hotel room. Not only that, she knew she was far from the self assured woman who'd carried out her job dressed up to the nines in borrowed clothes and fresh out of the beauty salon. That woman had been so far removed from who she really was it was almost laughable—except Dante Mancini didn't look the least bit amused.

'*Va bene*. That can easily be sorted.' He reached towards her and pushed her hair back from her face so gently it might almost have been an intimate and loving gesture—*almost*.

Shocked by the heat of his fingers as they grazed her face, she stepped back. 'What do you mean, that can easily be sorted?'

'The woman I met in London exists. She was very real as she smiled at me, enticing me with her beautiful green eyes. She was also very real as I undressed her, kissed her and made love to her.'

She bit down on the urge to tell him that woman had never really existed. That night she'd been someone else, driven by the need for physical contact and the spark of sexual attraction which had exploded as they'd first made eye contact. Since that night she'd lost her job because of her dalliance with a client and discovered that she was pregnant. The woman he remembered would never be able to exist again. Already she'd changed.

'That may be so, but I have no intention of being that woman again. All I came here to achieve was making you aware of the fact that you are to be a father.' Inwardly she cursed her impulsiveness at coming to Rome. What had she been thinking? That love and happiness would follow?

'And now that I *am* aware we will do things my way.'

He strode back to the windows and stood looking out over Rome as the early winter sunshine danced on the rooftops of a city she'd always longed to visit.

'We will do no such thing.' Again she questioned her motives for being here. 'I want nothing. You can go back to your wild lover-boy existence. Goodbye, Dante.'

She took a deep breath as he squared his shoulders against her verbal attack, then walked briskly to the door of his office. All she wanted was to escape. To run away and hide so she could nurse her wounds and rebuild her damaged dreams of a happy-ever-after. How stupid she'd been to harbour any hope that he would stand by her, take on the role of father. What she'd read in *Celebrity Spy!* should have been enough to extinguish those hopes long before she'd boarded the plane.

She heard his curse before she saw him as he put

himself between her and the door, and she wondered if he'd guessed she couldn't see him from her left side—or anything else, for that matter. Was he exploiting the weakness she took such great pains to conceal?

'Let me pass,' she demanded as anger and disappointment collided inside her, making her voice sharp and fierce.

'You are not going anywhere. We have things to discuss, things to settle.'

'Such as?' She folded her arms beneath the knitted poncho she'd opted for early this morning as she'd left her small flat in London.

Dante looked at Piper and fought the urge to step back and let her go. He knew she was capable of walking away with something he'd never wanted—a child. But his business mind had worked overtime as she'd spat fury and fire at him. Piper carried his child—the one thing that might now be the answer to all the problems which had erupted since that damn article.

'My child.'

He couldn't and wouldn't think any further about the plan that had formulated in his mind.

'The one you tried hard to deny could even *be* yours until I mentioned the paternity test?'

The accusation in her voice cut deep, touching a part of him he hadn't known existed.

'You are carrying my child, my heir, and no matter how that has come about I will support you. Of that there is no question.' Outwardly he was in control…inwardly his past mistakes rushed at him. But he couldn't turn his back on his flesh and blood. He might have got it wrong in the past, but this was his child. 'But naturally there will be conditions attached.'

'I don't want your grudging support, Dante. I want more than that from you for my child—or nothing at all.'

The indignation in her voice reverberated around the office and her green eyes looked so fierce he actually wanted to kiss her. To feel her lips against his once more and kiss away all that fury, replacing it with the passion he knew only too well existed within her.

'I don't care what you say you want. You wouldn't have come all this way to tell me you are carrying my child if you didn't want *something*, Piper.' He liked the feel of her name on his tongue, but still suspicion niggled at him. 'Perhaps I was right the first time. Is it money that will buy your silence?'

Her green eyes blazed with fury and anger emanated from her in palpable waves. 'I want no such thing, and I can see I have made a very big mistake in thinking you would be even remotely interested in our baby.'

She turned and grabbed the door handle, pulling the door open, but his reactions were quick and he pressed his palm against the door, slamming it shut before she'd even opened it wide enough to walk through.

'You are not going anywhere until this is sorted, *mia cara*.' He leant close to her left ear and whispered his warning, surprised when she jumped away, turning to glare once more at him. The threat in his voice had made her look vulnerable, and his proximity made her as nervous as a kitten, but still she pulled herself together and prepared to fight.

'I am not your *mia cara*.' She all but spat the words at him, like a wild cat which had been cornered. 'And I want nothing from you. Forget you ever saw me.'

How could he forget her when ever since that night in London she'd been in his thoughts? An unnamed lover who'd given him her virginity and a night he would never forget.

Benjamin Carter's suggestion floated once again on the periphery of his thoughts. Piper's arrival at his office couldn't have been more perfectly timed. Her news—unwelcome at any other time—fitted perfectly into his rapidly forming plan. He needed a wife and she carried his child.

'That will not happen—not when you are carrying my child.' He held her arms gently, preventing any further attempts to flee. 'Marriage is the only option.'

CHAPTER TWO

'MARRIAGE?' THE WORD spluttered from Piper and she blinked at Dante, acutely aware of his hands holding her and scorching her skin through the layers she wore, setting free memories she'd rather not deal with right at this moment.

'If you didn't come here for money then it must be for a ring on your finger.'

The callous tones of his accented voice were splintered with bitterness, shattering any faint and futile hopes that what they'd shared in London might have been the start of something. That his rash proposal was for real.

Who was she trying to fool? She had been nothing more than an amusing diversion from a dull dinner party. And wasn't that precisely why she'd slipped from his bed in the early hours, stealing a last lingering glance at him as he'd slept? She'd hoped to save her job and her reputation by leaving before the hotel had come to life, but even that attempt had been in vain.

'Have you *any* idea how arrogant you sound?'

Where had the considerate and charming man she'd left that dinner party with gone? Was this the real Dante, or was he just shocked at the news she'd brought?

The idea of being pregnant after a one-night stand

with a man she'd known she'd never see again had been a complete shock to her. So much so that she'd bought all four pregnancy tests in stock at the small pharmacy near her flat in an attempt to convince herself that she'd got it wrong, that their one night of non-committal but passionate sex hadn't resulted in pregnancy. Each time she'd used a test she'd become more panic-stricken.

'Do *you* have any idea how ridiculous it was for you to come here, tell me such news and expect me to stand aside while you leave?' Anger laced his accented words. 'You might have left me once, but it will not happen again, *mia cara*.'

'But *marriage*?' she protested, desperate to make him see how impossible such an idea was. All she'd wanted was for him to know, to be told to his face that he was going to be a father. It would have been what her father would have wanted her to do. 'We don't know anything about each other.'

'I know where you like to be kissed and how very sexy you look when you are naked. I think that is a good enough start, no?'

He smiled a slow, seductive smile and her heart almost stopped beating as she remembered how he had kissed her, how she'd all but begged for more, not wanting him to stop, wanting only to lose herself in the oblivion of the passion he'd showed her.

'Exactly the kind of answer I'd expect from a man like you.' Her temper fired and she drew in a deep breath, challenging the charm he seemed so incredibly capable of even in such a situation.

His eyes darkened and his brows furrowed together. 'A man like me?' His accented words were filled with suspicion.

'There must be *some* truth in that article in *Celebrity*

Spy!' She faltered as his eyes narrowed and she knew she'd touched a raw nerve. But hadn't he charmed her, seduced her, all without them even exchanging names?

'Do you normally believe everything inside such magazines?'

He moved fractionally closer and she resisted the urge to step back, to keep him from invading her space with the power of his masculinity.

'No, of course not.' She snapped the words out quickly, and judging from the smile which lingered on his lips he knew he too had hit the target.

'I would also suggest you change your reading material to something more…how shall I say it?…salubrious.'

Thankfully he stepped away, and she let out a breath she had no idea she'd been holding, but the urge to justify herself was too great. 'I don't normally read it. I was flicking through it whilst waiting at an employment agency.'

'Employment agency?' He turned his attention back to her instantly, those incredibly sexy eyes full of mistrust.

She bit down hard, inwardly cursing her wayward tongue. The last thing she wanted him to know was that she was no longer employed because of their night together, but she'd walked into a trap of her own making.

'I no longer have a permanent contract. The dinner party in London was a one-off.'

'So,' he said, and there was a hint of triumph in that one word. 'You are without a job and pregnant?'

She looked at him warily and corrected him quickly. 'Between jobs.'

'And will you easily find another job as your pregnancy progresses? I think not, *cara*.'

The undeniable self-assurance in his voice irritated

her more than she cared to admit—because he was right. Hadn't that been her worry as she'd tossed and turned every night since discovering she was pregnant? Maybe if she was still living in Sydney, where she'd grown up, she'd be able to find a job. But she wasn't in Sydney. She'd come to her mother's city of birth, London, and she knew nobody. And, as much as she wanted to return to Australia, she needed to stay with her mother.

'That is for me to worry about.' And worrying was just what she would still be doing when she left here. She'd had such a strong bond with her dad that she couldn't imagine bringing a baby into the world and it not knowing its father. It was her experience of a father-daughter relationship which had convinced her that seeing Dante was the right thing.

She hadn't told her mother about the baby yet, afraid to disappoint her, afraid she'd use her father's memory to make her feel guilty. Would he have been disappointed? No, she silently answered herself, but he would have wanted her to do the right thing.

The need to clear her conscience, to tell Dante personally, had fuelled hopes that he would at least acknowledge the child and hopefully want to be part of its life. But marriage? That was something she hadn't considered. And even if she had that article in *Celebrity Spy!* would have smothered that dream completely. Dante Mancini was a charmer—a playboy with a ruthless disregard for any kind of commitment.

'You will not have to worry about work now you are to be my wife. I will provide you with everything you and my child can possibly want—and more.'

He stood with his back to the amazing view of Rome, with the winter sunshine sliding in around him, making reading his expression difficult. But she had no doubt how fierce the darkness of his eyes was.

'I do not want to marry you.' She injected attitude into each word, desperate to push home her point.

'It's not negotiable, *cara*. I am in need of a wife and you are carrying my child—which makes you the perfect choice.'

He walked towards her, away from the sunshine which had temporarily concealed his expression, and the determination she saw on his handsome face made her heart sink. She had very little energy left to fight with.

'In need of a wife?' She stumbled over the word 'wife', hardly able to believe he wanted *her* to become his wife. How could a self-professed playboy—a man who had the wealth, power and looks to have any woman he wanted—want to marry *her*?

'I am in negotiations for a business deal which I can only pull off if I am seen to be a man with family values. I need a wife—a woman I can be seen publicly with, and one who can be discreet. Because that untimely piece in *Celebrity Spy!* has made those negotiations somewhat difficult. What better way to prove I am a man of family honour than to stand by the woman who is carrying my child?'

'You make it *all* sound like a business deal.'

'That, *cara*, is precisely what it will be. You came for money and support and you will now get both—providing we are seen out in public as the perfect couple. The world must believe we are madly in love. In return you will have the honour of being the woman who tamed Dante Mancini.'

Dante looked at her, saw her face pale and watched her eyes close, provoking images of her beneath him as passion had driven her wild and he'd unwittingly claimed her as his. Now she would pay the price of acting the part of a seductress when she'd been nothing more than an innocent virgin. She'd pay the price with two words. *I do.*

When her eyes opened, seconds later, the spark of annoyance was back within their sea-green depths. With her shy blushes and understated clothes she certainly didn't look or act like the kind of woman he would date, let alone fall for, but she had on that night in London. He might have scoffed at Benjamin Carter's suggestion last night of using the discreet agency run by the American matchmaker Elizabeth Young to find him a suitable wife, but now he would definitely call upon the agency's services. He needed to transform the Australian redhead who carried his child back into the woman he'd met in London.

'Honour? You overrate yourself, *signor.* If it is to be a business deal and not a true marriage I will accept— with one condition.'

'*You* do not make the conditions.' This was not something he was used to. Women dictating to him. It was unheard of. He was always in control, always laying down the rules.

'I will make all the conditions I want.'

Her flippant tone almost pushed him too far, reminding him just how much his head throbbed with alcohol-induced pain.

'It is obvious that your need of a wife is far greater than my need to tell you that you are going to be a father.'

'*Molto bene.* Name your terms.' Angrily he crossed the room and sat behind his desk, leaning his arms on its clutter-free surface and fixing her with a warning glare.

'The *marriage* will be in name only and it will be ended after an agreed time. Once you have duped the world into thinking you are a reformed character and have secured your business deal, I assume.'

She stood in the centre of his office, her long legs snagging his attention, making him think things he had no right to be thinking—especially as he was negotiating a deal with her. A deal that would save his reputation and enrich his business—*and* claim her as his.

'Va bene.' He nodded his agreement. So far she spoke sense. He didn't want to be married and had never contemplated it. All he needed right now was to change the way the gossips thought of him, prove he could be a family man if he chose to be and ultimately finalise the deal that would put his company at the top of the renewable energies industry. He also needed to calm the fears of their charity and fix any other negative impact of that damning article.

'And you will play an active part in the child's life.'

Her words fell into the suddenly large gap which separated them, highlighting how very different they were.

His brows rose. How could he play an active part in the child's life when he'd been solely responsible for his younger brother's untimely death? He wasn't fit to be a brother, let alone a father. He couldn't commit to giving his son or daughter anything other than material things. His emotions had frozen and shut down the day his father had walked out on them. Alessio's death was proof of that.

She must have sensed his reluctance because she stepped closer. 'I want nothing more than that. If you cannot agree then we do not have a deal and I will leave right now.'

He took a deep breath, forcing back the guilt and regret from the past. He had to think of this as just another deal. One like the many he made each year. He couldn't open the wounds of his past. But as he looked at Piper he suspected it was already too late. She was the key that had turned in the door he'd long ago slammed shut.

He'd never longed for a woman once his desire had been quenched, but Piper had changed that and it was a change he wasn't happy about. Reluctantly he admitted he would have to accept her terms. If he didn't marry her and took another wife she'd have an even bigger story to sell and more damage to do. Worse than that, he would be guilty of turning his back on his child, and he'd pay any price not to do that.

'We have a deal. I will have it drawn up into a contract by tomorrow.'

For a moment she looked lost, as if she'd expected a big battle. Little did she know that was just what it was for him—but it was his battle and he would fight it alone. He didn't need anyone—least of all a woman who threatened everything he'd turned his back on after the revelations exposed by Alessio's death.

'Then, as we have concluded our business, I will go to my hotel.' She picked up a bag from beside the chair she'd been sitting in when he arrived. If that was all her luggage she really hadn't intended on staying in Rome long. *Long enough to turn my world on its head.* If she thought she could just walk away now, she'd got it all wrong.

He sprang from the seat. 'You are not going anywhere except to my apartment—with me.'

'That is totally unnecessary,' she said, and pulled the somewhat battered bag, which bore no resemblance to the designer bags his women usually had, onto her shoulder. She moved towards the door and once again he found himself needing to stop this woman from leaving.

'We are lovers, are we not?' He lowered his voice, smiling to see the blush which crept over her face at the way he spoke. 'And if we are to be believed as such you will not stay in a budget hotel.'

'How do you know it's a budget hotel?'

Indignation flared to life in her voice and her eyes and he knew he'd scored a point in this particular battle.

'I merely assumed.' He shrugged and looked at her, liking the way her lips pressed together tightly as she fought to hold back her retort. A fight she soon lost.

'Well, don't,' she snapped at him, then lowered her gaze briefly before meeting his once more.

'This is a business deal—one which will legitimise my child. A child that will be the heir to all I own. You will have every luxury, Piper, and my word that nothing else will happen between us.'

Piper gulped back the disappointment. *Nothing else would happen between them.* She should be pleased. It was exactly what she'd asked for, what she'd wanted, but a part of her ached with the pain of it. She wasn't his type. The article in *Celebrity Spy!* had left her in no doubt of that. But the passion which had ravaged them that night in London must have meant something.

'That is all I want,' she lied, desperate that he wouldn't detect even a hint of her dismay. She had to remain strong and firm. He couldn't know she'd often thought of those few hours which had changed her life even before she'd known she was pregnant.

'*Va bene.* It is settled. I will escort you to my apartment now—you look tired and in need of rest.'

As he looked at her she could almost believe he was

genuinely concerned, but to fall for such an idea would be her undoing and she had to remain strong.

'I think it would be better if I booked into a hotel.' Her words faded to a whisper at the black look on his handsome face, which appeared more severe due to the shadow of stubble he was sporting.

'How can we be seen as lovers, about to become engaged, if you are not living in my apartment and, as far as the world is concerned, sleeping in my bed?' He shrugged in that nonchalant way which had attracted her the first night she'd seen him. 'It would not be very convincing, *mia cara*.'

Piper pushed her fingers through her hair, trying to control the emotions which were running riot inside her. Emotions she knew full well were intensified by her pregnancy. Why did she feel so let down, so disillusioned? He'd offered to stand by her, support her financially, and most importantly to be a part of their child's life even if he wasn't a part of hers. So why was she fighting the urge to cry? She had what she'd come for—and more.

She dragged in a sharp breath and looked up at him as he approached from her left side—her blind side— startling her when he touched her gently on her arm, as he had done several times already.

'I didn't mean to startle you,' he said softly.

Too softly. Her urge to give in to tiredness and tears intensified.

'Come. You need to rest. You must have left London at an early hour this morning.'

She allowed herself to be guided to the office door, and with his arm lingering around her waist he walked to his secretary's desk, issuing a flurry of Italian instructions which were met with curious gazes directed at her from the shocked older woman, unsettling her further. Was she so far below the kind of woman he usually dated that even his secretary was shocked?

Everything seemed to take on a glow of unreality as he escorted her out of the offices and to a waiting car. Moments later they were ensconced in the car, moving quickly through the streets of Rome as car horns sounded insistently around them. She wanted to see the sights, but the ride in the car was making her feel unsteady, and all she could do was sit back in the soft leather seats.

On her right, she felt Dante watching her. She could feel the scrutiny of his gaze and almost hear his unspoken questions. Everything about being with Dante again was unlocking all those emotions she'd hidden away as she'd left that hotel in the early hours.

As she got out of the car the tall buildings of the old town towered over her and blocked out the winter sun. She looked up at an impressive building which must have seen many things through history, unable to believe what she'd agreed to.

He took her bag from her. 'This way. My apartment is on the top floor and offers stunning views of the city from the roof terrace. Have you been in Rome before?'

The light and easy way he spoke was in complete contrast to the way her heart was thumping. What had she done to herself? What had she agreed to? Marriage, be it in name only or not, to a man she barely knew?

'No. Europe always seemed too far from Australia to think of.'

It had been a trip her mother had wanted to do. She'd tried to convince her father, but he'd never wanted to leave Australia, saying he didn't need to go so far when he had all he needed at home. As he'd said those words he'd looked at her, and now Piper questioned if her mother's need to return to England had been the start of their marriage problems.

Dante held the front door open for her and she walked into the cool shade of the old building, trying to leave the memories and questions she'd never have answered outside.

'Yet you were in London when we met?'

'I'd only been there for a year. My mother wanted to return to her native country after...' She floundered for a moment, thinking of the day her father had suddenly died. Exactly one year to the day when she'd met Dante. 'My father was Australian, my mother British, and after he died she wanted to be with her elderly mother so we left Sydney. Sadly, Grandma passed away a few months ago.'

Dante scrutinised her as he waited for the elevator and she wondered if her true feelings were showing clearly on her face, despite the calm and matter-of-fact way she'd imparted the story of her beloved father's death.

'And you were brought up in Sydney?'

She was glad when the elevator doors opened, diverting his attention. She'd never known anything *but* Sydney. It was not only where she'd grown up, but where she'd been happiest. But all that had changed when her father had been killed in a car accident. The senseless accident had happened not even a year after he'd been told he was in remission from cancer. The injustice of it made her gulp back the tears which threatened.

'Can't you tell from the accent?' She laughed off the pain of those memories, wanting to move the conversation away from her. This wasn't about her any more. It was about what was best for the baby. Her father had stood by her mother when she'd fallen pregnant and they'd been happy together. But obviously it hadn't been enough for her mother, because she'd started to make plans to return to London soon after the accident.

'It's a nice accent.' He smiled at her and she wondered if he'd sensed her unease, but his next words obliterated that thought. 'And very sexy too, when you are consumed by desire.'

'You should keep such comments for the women you date.'

The words left her before she could stop them, let alone think about what they meant to her. The thought of him dating other women made her heart heavy, but she had to push that aside. Their marriage was to be nothing more than a business deal.

He walked from the elevator, pulling out a key, and turned to look at her as he stopped outside his apartment door. 'Exclusivity is something I will demand from you if this deal is going to work for us.'

That wouldn't be a problem as far as she was concerned. Her one spontaneous and totally out of character affair had already caused her more trouble than she'd ever bargained on.

'I should impose the same on you, but I doubt a man like you can be exclusive to *any* woman.'

Dante didn't miss the crisp tartness in her voice. The subject was something he'd already given thought to on the drive to his apartment. He would have to be faithful to his new fiancée and, given that his body still heated at the memory of hers, it wouldn't be a challenge. The biggest problem would be to ensure he didn't repeat what had happened in London. She had made it clear this was to be only a business deal.

If he portrayed himself to the world as a caring and faithful man, in love with the woman who was to be his wife, he would not only clinch the deal he'd almost lost but wipe out the reputation that for years he hadn't cared about. If he didn't, the future of The Hope Foundation, the charity he wholeheartedly supported, would hang in the balance.

The three other businessmen who supported the charity were about to do the same. Zayn and Xander had agreed that Benjamin's suggestion that they settle down was the only way. He'd watched on, uncharacteristically drowning his misgivings in a bottle of whisky, as the ghosts of his past had taunted him that he'd never be able to be responsible for another person without hurting them, forcing them to leave him.

Now he was responsible for a woman who should have been his for just a few hours of mind-blowing sex. Not only that, he was responsible for the child she carried—*his* child. Could he put himself through that? Could he engage the emotions he'd switched off and risk losing everything again?

'You will have my full and undivided attention at all times. We are in love, no?' As he looked down at her that spark of lust, a sexual chemistry too strong to deny, arced between them. He saw her eyes darken, watched her lips part, and his body responded in the only way possible to such a blatant invitation.

'Nothing can ever happen between us again, Dante.'

Her whisper cracked with desire, and in normal circumstances he would have laughed softly, pulled her against him and kissed her into submission. But these were not normal circumstances. This wasn't just a meaningless affair that would end as soon as the sun rose the next morning.

'I have agreed to our terms.' He unlocked his door and stood back for her to enter, smiling down at her in an attempt to hide the conflicting emotions warring within him. 'A marriage in name only that will give us both what we want.'

'More than that, Dante.'

She stood outside, as if crossing the threshold to his home was the last thing she wanted to do. To have her permanently in his life was not what he wanted, but he had his reasons for making this deal. Just as she had hers.

'It will give our child what it deserves.'

The mention of the baby shocked any response from him and he turned and walked into his apartment—a place he'd never taken a woman before, preferring the anonymity of hotel rooms which he could leave when he was ready.

'Tomorrow you will sign a contact.' His irritation at the situation he found himself in sounded in his words—even he could hear that.

Not only was he inviting a woman into his home and his life—permanently—he was giving himself the biggest challenge of all. One he wasn't sure he could master. He would have to invest himself, his emotions, in a child. How could he do that when the pain of Alessio's loss, the guilt of his inability to be what someone else needed, still festered in his dormant heart?

'Until then you will have to trust me when I say that I will be the perfect gentleman, and that you may sleep soundly in my bed.'

'In your bed?' The few hesitant steps she'd taken into his domain faltered to a stop.

'Alone,' he added.

She really was adamant that they would not be repeating those hot, sultry hours in London. So be it. He didn't want the added complication of lust becoming more than that.

'We've settled this. As my lover you need to be seen here, at all times of the day and night. What the outside world will never know is that I will sleep there.'

He gestured to the second bedroom, which served as his office. Last night, if one of the other three men had suggested he'd be taking a woman into his life and sleeping in his spare room in order to salvage his reputation and that of his supported charity, he would have laughed.

'I'm not sure... I'll find a hotel.'

'That is not an option any longer, *mia cara*. You should not have come all this way, imparted such news and then expected me not to put my terms on any arrangement made.'

The late night and early start were finally catching up with him, and all he wanted was to shut the door on the world and relax. But first he had to contact Elizabeth Young and ascertain if her agency offered the services he required. He needed to transform the plain and ordinary woman before him into a fiancée that would bring the gossips to a tongue-tied halt.

'I can't take your bed.'

'*Va bene*, then I will share it with you if it makes you feel better.' He stifled a smile at her shock.

'No,' she said, and she all but flounced past him into the apartment, her attitude hinting that the woman he'd met in London was still lingering inside her, waiting to be drawn out. If he dared to find her.

'Then at last we understand one another. I suggest you make yourself at home. I have work to continue with.'

Never had he ever thought he would be inviting a woman into his home, into his life, and telling her to make herself comfortable. The idea was unnerving, but reluctantly he knew it was necessary.

It would make him part of his child's life. It was a child he'd never wanted, but despite that he already knew he would do anything for it.

CHAPTER THREE

PIPER WOKE THE next morning, the soft sheets caressing her skin as she stretched, and then realisation hit. This wasn't her bed. She sat upright quickly and looked around the room, momentarily not recalling actually getting into bed. In fact she couldn't remember much after arriving yesterday with Dante.

She'd been so tired. The confrontation with Dante had sapped any remaining strength she'd had—which had been very little after weeks of barely sleeping because of the situation she'd found herself plunged into. But right now her biggest worry was the fact that she was in bed, wearing only her underwear, and had no recollection of getting there.

As if her thoughts had summoned him Dante knocked lightly on the bedroom door. *'Buongiorno.'*

His deep and undeniably sexy voice came through the door and the image of him that it conjured in her mind was immediate and vivid—but she had to remember the man she'd confronted yesterday was the same as the one described in *Celebrity Spy!* He'd also been suffering the effects of alcohol, probably from partying the previous night with glamorous women. It had shocked her that he was so far from the loving man she'd met briefly in London.

'Come in,' she said, far more boldly than she felt, and tugged the sheet tighter against her. Had she undressed in a tired trance or had he removed her clothes?

The door clicked open and Dante entered. The hint of stubble which had coloured his face yesterday was gone. The clean-shaven look reminded her of the man she'd lost more than just her virginity to.

'I trust you slept well, *cara*?'

'I did—thank you.' She wasn't going to give him the satisfaction of asking if he was the one who had undressed her and pulled the luxurious sheets over her instead of leaving her lying on the bed. Her only memory from last night was of lying there for just a few minutes.

'Good. We have a busy day ahead of us.'

He walked closer, his expression bland and unyielding, and try as she might she couldn't help but admire the way his shirt was all but moulded to his body. A body she remembered clearly and a body she wanted to know again. Except that would be too dangerous— now that she knew who he really was and what he was capable of.

'We do?' She hoped the flush that crept over her cheeks wouldn't give her away.

'*Sì.* I have the necessary paperwork for our deal, awaiting your signature, then we can go shopping.'

A hint of mischief sparked in his eyes as he turned his full attention to her as if he knew she was being a tease but refused to rise to it.

'Shopping?' she asked casually as she sat back against the soft pillows. If only she didn't feel as if she'd walked into the pride leader's den. 'Why do we need to go shopping?'

'For the single most important item, if this deal is to achieve its aim. A ring.'

He moved towards the bed and she had to work hard to resist the temptation to pull the sheets tighter still against her—whether to hide her state of undress or protect her heart as it fluttered at his increasingly dominating presence, she couldn't tell. Either way, she wouldn't do it—wouldn't give him the satisfaction of knowing just how much he could unbalance her with one look.

'Of course.' Her nonchalant tone was a total contrast to the racing of her heart and the flutter of the butterflies which had taken residence in her tummy. 'I will join you shortly.'

'Breakfast is waiting for you.' His dark eyes fixed her intently to the spot and instantly she was back on that bed in the hotel room in London as he'd stood and looked at her, desire and passion so tangible in the air that she hadn't wanted the moment ever to end.

'Thank you.' She dragged her mind back from that night. She would have to put such notions well and truly to one side if she was going to survive this deal she'd struck. Dante didn't have feelings for her. She was merely a means to an end. A way to seal his deal. He was exactly the inscrutable businessman *Celebrity Spy!* had portrayed him as being.

The trouble was she also knew he was a skilled lover—which was what had earned him such a scandalous reputation with women—and a rebellious part of her yearned to experience that man again. After all, her current situation couldn't get much worse. She was pregnant, jobless, and being forced into marriage as part of a business deal. It was ludicrous when all she'd wanted to do was make him aware of his child and ease her conscience.

She watched as he turned and left, unable to pull her gaze away from the broad shoulders covered in a pale blue shirt that somehow emphasised every last muscle her fingers annoyingly remembered tracing on his back.

Once the door had clicked closed she slid out of bed. Although her tummy protested its emptiness she headed for the shower, determined that when they went out later she would look at least a little bit more glamorous and like the women he'd been pictured with throughout that article as proof of his Casanova lifestyle.

The problem was she didn't really know how to achieve such glamour—that was why she'd been sent out to the hairdresser's and lent a dress that day she'd been told she would have to stand in for a colleague for one night and be hostess for a dinner party in London. Whilst she'd enjoyed feeling so different, it hadn't really been *her*. It was a different Piper who had gained the interest of Dante Mancini, one of the world's most debauched bachelors, but it was the real Piper who'd fallen for him right there and then.

Dante stood on his terrace, looking out over Rome as the city became its bustling usual self. Sounds of the street drifted up while he sipped his coffee and waited for Piper. On the table inside, which he'd instructed to be laid for two, was the contract. Once that was signed there would be no going back. He would be responsible not only for Piper, a woman who intrigued him more than any other, but for a child. A responsibility he wasn't sure he could meet when the demons of Alessio's death still plagued him.

'I'm sorry I kept you.'

Piper's sexy voice, with its delicious accent, dragged him from his dark thoughts.

'I took the liberty of arranging an assortment of choices for breakfast,' he said.

'That sounds wonderful.'

She smiled up at him and he instantly remembered the moment he'd first seen that smile directed at him. He'd walked into the party, not really wanting to be there, and he'd seen her. Despite the fact that she'd been working she'd looked glamorous and very sexy in a black silk dress which had caressed her curvy figure, making him want to touch her, hold her.

He'd wanted her from that moment and had used his charm to achieve just that. Little had he known that his usual sense of control and self-preservation would fail him the moment they first kissed.

'Is it not usual for women to feel ill in the mornings when they are pregnant?' He couldn't keep the scepticism from his voice as the thoughts which had invaded his dreams last night clouded round him once more. He had no proof that she was pregnant. He'd taken her word not only for that, but for the fact that *he* was the father. He would take the advice his legal team had given him when drawing up the contract and have his own doctor confirm the pregnancy.

'Yes.' She smiled at him again, apparently oblivious to his suspicions. 'Thankfully I don't seem too troubled by that and I hope it stays that way.'

'*Bene*. First we eat—then we will deal with the contract.' He pulled out a chair for her and waited for her to sit, but knew instantly that had been a mistake as the scent of her freshly washed hair mingled with her perfume, invading his senses so fast he wanted to lower his head, kiss her hair and inhale her, then scoop her up and take her to his bed.

He'd forced himself to walk away from her last night, but could he do it again?

He stepped back. Away from such temptation. Nothing could happen between them. This wasn't a fling. Nothing about this was casual at all, and the last thing he needed was to complicate it further and get involved. He could never be involved.

He watched her as she ate, realising he hadn't ever had breakfast with a woman he hadn't slept with the previous night. In fact he rarely even had breakfast with women, preferring instead to leave the bed and give a very clear message. So why did sitting across the table from a woman who'd been so tired he'd had to help her to undress before tucking her into his bed and then gallantly leaving her alone feel so inviting?

'I'm sorry about last night,' she said, her shyness returning as she blushed. 'Falling asleep like that, I mean. You must think I'm very rude.'

'I think you were tired from travelling in your condition.' He poured fresh coffee and tried hard not to allow the image of her asleep on his bed, hair splayed out around her, to return to his mind and torment him. She'd looked so vulnerable, so beautiful, and all he'd wanted to do was look after her. But could he do that? He hadn't been able to look after his own brother, so how could a woman he'd just met be any different?

'Well, I'm refreshed and feeling much more myself today, thank you.'

'Prego.' He pushed the black thoughts away and picked up the contract which he'd seen her glance at several times, as if it was a dog that might bite her at any moment. 'This has been drawn up according to the terms we discussed yesterday, and once signed it will bind us together in our deal for a minimum of two years.'

'And the baby?'

Her question rocked him but he kept his focus, portraying outward control even if inside he was far from controlled.

'I will be a part of my child's life for ever.'

The firmness and passion in his voice shocked him—as did the realisation that it was what he wanted. His child wouldn't be born illegitimate, with the odds stacked against him. His child would have everything he could possibly give it to succeed in life.

'But we will both be free to end the marriage in two years and during that time we can live separately—once the main objectives of the deal are achieved, that is.'

'The main objective for you being to secure a business deal?'

The accusation in her voice hit its mark, making his requirement seem insignificant in the face of hers. The deal *had* been his initial motivation, but as the implications of their few steamy hours together that night had sunk in he'd known he would do anything for his child. There was no way he would walk out and never look back. He was not his father.

'Di preciso.' Briefly English failed him as the truth of his thoughts penetrated deep into him. 'Exactly. But if I do not secure my business deals then I will not have the means to give my child much.'

'You could give it love.'

Her words smarted in the wound she was opening. One he'd long since thought healed.

Love was the one thing he *couldn't* give. Anyone he'd given that to had gone from his life. His father, his brother... With the exception of his feelings for his mother, love was one emotion he could not do, because by doing so he'd risk everything. Love hadn't stopped his father walking away when he and Alessio were young. It hadn't stopped his brother from falling in with those gangs, and it hadn't helped at all when for years he'd not even known where Alessio was. It certainly hadn't helped when he'd discovered the truth of his brother's death.

Love was a futile and wasted emotion.

'My child, my heir, will have everything it needs—of that you can be assured.'

She looked at him, those green eyes smouldering with doubt—a doubt which beat wildly within him right now. Did she have any idea what she was asking of him with those words?

'That is all I want for my child, Dante. The love and security of knowing its father, of being able to have a good relationship with him as I did with mine.'

Piper tried to push thoughts of her father aside. Now, in the face of Dante's scepticism, was not the time to remember just how much she missed her father. The grief of losing him was still raw after all these months. It was why she'd sought solace in Dante's arms that night, why she'd given herself to him—that and the powerful attraction which had sparked between them.

'This is the contract.'

He pushed the papers across the table to her, his hand lingering on it as if he wasn't sure he actually wanted her to have it. She saw the gold of his signet ring gleam in the lights above.

She sighed, not sure she should be signing anything, but she couldn't stay like this, in limbo from reality, not knowing what was going to happen. At least this way her child stood some chance of having a father who was around. He passed her a pen and she looked again at his ring. It was engraved with the letter A. Was that the initial of a past lover?

'One signature on each copy,' he said firmly, pulling her back from her thoughts.

'There,' she said as her name sprawled across the line. 'It's official.'

'*Bene.* Now we will need to purchase a ring.'

His words brought her crashing back to the present.

'Is that necessary when it is only an engagement for show and a marriage on paper?'

'*Sì, cara,* it is. As are a few other changes.'

'Changes?' Trepidation filled her. What else did he have planned?

He walked towards her, his eyes seeming to devour her, sending sparks of awareness all over her body, just as they'd done that night in London.

'You have changed, *cara,* since we met in London.'

She frowned, taking in his words. Was she not good enough for him? The spiteful rejection from her days at school rushed back at her. Then, her lack of vision in one eye had been all too obvious, and some of her classmates had thought it amusing to taunt her. Now, after the operations her father had insisted she have, her disability was not so obvious. Although the ability to see with her left eye would never be possible, it was far less noticeable.

'This is who I am, Dante, not the woman you met in London.'

'I disagree. But right now I need to buy you a ring— one that will announce to the world that you are my intended bride.'

'And make you look like a man with *true family values*?' She couldn't keep the barb out of her voice.

'*Di preciso.* Now, if you are ready, we shall go and make our purchase.'

* * *

Half an hour later Dante's car arrived in the centre of Rome, in an area which thronged with locals and tourists alike. The winter sun was warm and for a moment she relished it after having spent the last few months experiencing her first British winter.

'This way,' he said as he leant close to her ear, and his words sent a whisper of tingles down her spine as he spoke.

At least this time he was standing on her right side and she'd known he was there—although that wasn't entirely a good thing if the way she'd reacted to his nearness was anything to go by.

'I have arranged a private consultation with one of Rome's most renowned jewellers.'

To her surprise he took her hand as they began walking through the crowded streets. When had he arranged that? With a sinking heart she realised that the father of her child, the man she'd agreed to marry, moved in a very different world from the one she was used to. He could just make a call and demand what he wanted.

Nerves skittered inside her tummy like erratic butterflies as he stopped outside a shop whose windows were a source of curiosity for quite a number of people, and she blushed as some glanced their way when Dante pushed open the door. Instantly they were greeted by a member of staff, but the fast-flowing Italian became too difficult for her very limited knowledge of the language.

'We are honoured to be of service to you, *signorina*.'

The man's English proved to be better than her Italian and made her feel a little less apprehensive. At least she would know what was being said.

'If you'd like to come this way, Signor Mancini?'

Dante stood back and waited for her to follow the

older gentleman, and within minutes they were in a small but elegantly furnished room.

'I have followed your instructions, *signor*, on what the *signorina* prefers, and have arranged a selection of rings for you to view.'

Piper tried hard to keep the smile on her lips, to appear as if this was real instead of the nightmare it had suddenly become. She had to remember this wasn't an engagement in the true sense of the word. Just as the contract she had signed that morning reminded her that their marriage would not be a real one. Putting a ring on her finger was no different from putting her signature on the contract he'd so insistently laid out on the breakfast table.

'Piper?'

Dante's voice, close to her left side, startled her again. 'I'm sorry,' she said, trying to quell the racing of her heart—which she suspected had more to do with the man himself than with being startled. Quickly recovering, she gestured to the table and the array of rings set on a deep blue velvet display tray. 'I've never seen anything quite like this.'

'This is just the beginning,' he said softly.

The darkness of his eyes shone with unwavering adoration and for a moment she was almost fooled—almost believed that he did love her and wanted nothing other than to make her his.

The harsh reality was quite different. It was not for any kind of sentimental reason and certainly not out of love.

'This is enough for now.' She blushed beneath his practised charm and when his brows flicked suggestively her stomach tied itself in knots and her breath caught audibly in her throat.

'We should choose the ring now, *cara*, before I forget why we are here and kiss you.'

He looked at her, the intense blackness in his eyes smothering the caramel-brown she found so attractive. She could smell his aftershave and found her lips parting of their own free will as her breathing quickened and her pulse raced. Shyly she looked up at him as he moved closer still. Panic skittered through her. He was going to kiss her—here, in public.

A polite cough from the older man thankfully diverted Dante's attention from her and for a moment she couldn't get enough breath into her lungs. She focused on regaining her composure and took a seat at the desk, giving the glittering array of rings her undivided attention. She looked from one large stone to another, hardly able to believe she was sitting there, within touching distance of so many valuable and beautiful gems.

She felt Dante move behind her and her whole body heated from his nearness. But when he placed his hand on her shoulder and leant over her she thought she might pass out. Why was she behaving like this? He didn't want her for anything other than to make him look good in a business deal. She would stake everything on the fact that he didn't want to be a father. His reaction to her news had been cold and detached. Marriage had been the last thing she'd expected to hear him demand as she'd sat in his office yesterday, waiting for him to arrive, having been assured by his secretary that he wasn't usually late.

'Select whichever one you want.' His voice was close to her left ear, but from the heat of his body against her back and the scorching of his hand on her shoulder she knew he was there. How could she not when her whole body had come to life?

'They are all beautiful.'

She turned her head to try and look at him, and in doing so found his face very close to hers. So close that he could kiss her, press his lips to hers, with only the slightest effort. His gaze locked onto hers and she couldn't look away. Not even when he lowered his head and very gently brushed his lips over hers.

Her eyes closed and her lips softened beneath his before he pulled back slightly and with endearing tenderness brushed his fingers over her cheek. 'You outshine them all.'

Don't be fooled. The voice of reason fought to be heard inside her head as that kiss, that gentle and brief feel of his lips on hers, unlocked everything she'd been trying to deny since that night in London.

Piper turned away and tried hard to focus on the rings before her as their gleam blurred and tears threatened. Now was *not* a time to give in to emotions.

She reached out and picked up a ring. 'I like this one.'

Dante took the ring from her, then moved to her side, took her left hand and slipped the ring onto her finger. It glinted as it sat, a perfect fit, on her third finger. She was so stunned by the sight of it she couldn't speak, couldn't say anything, and she certainly couldn't look up at Dante—not when tears threatened to spill down her cheeks like a waterfall.

'I think my bride has made her choice.' His voice was deep and accented and so sexy—just as it had been that night in London. It had haunted her since he'd whispered such beautiful words in her ears as they'd made love that first and only night.

Piper couldn't function, and she sat in a state of bewilderment as the older man fussed around them and then packed up the ring in the most elaborate box. All she could do was watch as Dante produced his credit card and paid for the ring, which effectively meant he'd paid for *her*, a bargaining tool for the deal he just had to win.

But to her the price was much higher. To her this was all about her child—the only reason she'd accepted such a deal.

CHAPTER FOUR

IT HAD BEEN three days since Dante had bought the ring, which had sealed the deal far more conclusively than any contract she'd signed. Each night she'd slept alone in his bed, and not once since that light but lingering kiss in the jeweller's had he tried to get close to her again. Neither had he done anything to suggest he wanted their arrangement to be more than a marriage on paper. He'd made it clear that whatever had exploded into life so spectacularly between them in London was over as far as he was concerned.

That kiss as they'd chosen the ring and those gestures had all been for the benefit of the jeweller. Her shock at the disappointment that knowledge had brought still weighed heavily on her as she stood in the apartment while Dante finished a call.

She felt as uneasy and out of place as she had that first morning as she listened to him, and then registered that he was talking in English.

'Xander will also call you,' he said, and glanced up, seeing her for the first time. He ended the call and turned his full attention to her. *'Buongiorno, cara.'*

The sensual depth in his voice did little to assuage her disillusioned mind-set.

'Buongiorno,' she replied, testing his language and

liking the feel of it almost as much as the approval which showed clearly in his sexy dark eyes.

Don't go there, Piper, she silently warned herself, determined to remember why she'd flown to Rome in search of a man whose name she hadn't known until she'd seen that article.

'I trust you slept well.' As usual he was the epitome of charm and courtesy.

'I did, thank you,' she replied, and her guilt at keeping him from his bed made looking at him as they sat at the table almost impossible.

'Bene.'

He poured her coffee, but for the first time since she'd discovered she was pregnant the aroma made her feel queasy and she opted for a glass of water instead. She looked up at him as he spoke again.

'You have a busy day ahead of you.'

She tried to work out what it was she should be doing. For three days she'd been cooped up here in his apartment, more like a prisoner than a guest. She'd called her mother, who had wanted her to go straight home, as had Katie and Jo, her friends in Australia, when they'd emailed. But where *was* home? In London with her mother? In Sydney with her happy past? Or here in Rome with the father of her child?

Confusion added to the feeling of nausea. 'I do?'

'Sì. I have arranged for someone to help you select a new wardrobe of clothes.'

She watched as he drank his coffee, oblivious to anything else except what *he* wanted. He certainly hadn't noticed she couldn't face any food this morning.

'I don't need new clothes.' She forced the words out, trying to focus her mind and not show this man any weakness—something she'd learnt long ago shouldn't be done.

'You are now my fiancée, Piper, and whilst you looked every bit the kind of woman who would ensnare my interest when we met in London, you would not convince many people now. For you to fit in with my world there need to be some changes.'

'Well, I'm sorry to disappoint.' She couldn't keep the spike of hurt from her voice, especially after she had already been making an effort. 'I don't happen to have a wardrobe of party clothes with me. It's not what I had in mind when I came to Rome.'

'No, I am aware of that—which is why I have arranged for some help.' The firm tone of his voice brooked no argument.

'Oh.' The croissant she'd just taken one small piece from in the hope of settling her stomach became like dust in her mouth. So she wasn't good enough for him as she was? Retaliation surfaced. 'I hardly see the point when I'm not going to fit into things in a few months.'

'The *point*—' he fixed her with those intent eyes '—is that our engagement be believed genuine, and presently I do not think it will be. I have arranged for Elizabeth Young, a professional matchmaker from America, to come to Rome and assist you. Every woman loves shopping, and with my name and funds at your disposal I'm sure you will too.'

So she was to be groomed into shape—moulded into the kind of woman who would fit the role of fiancée for the notorious Dante Mancini? And wouldn't that be for the best, no matter how *used* it made her feel? If she played the role so convincingly that his business acquaintances believed that she and Dante were in love, that she was the woman who'd made him want to settle down and be a father, she would have done her part in their deal. It would leave him no option but to do his and be there for their child—long after their marriage had ended. As stipulated in the contract she'd signed, he would then pay his price.

'Very well.' Her voice was starchy and she saw a smile spread over his lips as she looked across the table at him, trying to remind herself why she'd agreed to this charade. Dante could never be the father figure her own father had been, but could she trust him to take even the smallest amount of interest in his child? If he didn't there was no point in her being here now. 'And when will we be putting this glamorous fiancée to the test?'

His dark eyes sparked dangerously at her last words. 'This evening. We shall attend a party here in Rome. And at the weekend we have been invited to Tuscany by Bettino D'Antonio, which will be the biggest test of our *engagement*. He is the man I intend to seal the business deal with, and this weekend will be the time to reassure him I am a reformed man with family values. He must know you are expecting my child, and that we are in love and engaged to be married.'

She raised a brow haughtily at him, the feeling of being controlled and manipulated uncomfortable. 'So my duties are very clearly defined? I am to look the part of one of the many women you've been pictured with this year alone, while at the same time convincing everyone that what is between us is enough for you to give up your scandalous playboy reputation and settle down?'

The angry glitter in his eyes left her in no doubt that she'd hit the intended mark and was now in control—of this evening's outing at least.

'Elizabeth is the matchmaker Benjamin Carter used.

She is currently in Rome and will meet with you this morning.'

'Benjamin Carter?' Wasn't he also one of the bachelors named and shamed? She tried to recall the others.

'*Sì*, he was featured in that article, along with Zayn Al-Ghamdi and Xander Trakas.'

'And are those men also marrying to save their reputations?'

Suspicion filled her. They couldn't *all* be chasing a big deal, so what was it all about? If her memory served her right, one of them was the ruler of a desert kingdom.

Exasperated with herself for not paying more attention to the piece simply because she'd stumbled upon the identity of the man whose baby she carried, she rebelled against Dante. 'What if I don't want to be turned into one of your women? What if I don't want to change?'

'It is not negotiable, Piper. Elizabeth has my list of instructions on exactly what I want.'

'What *you* want? What about what *I* want?' Already she had lost the small triumph of being in control. How had she ever thought a woman like her could be in control of a man like Dante Mancini? He was ruthless. Just the fact that he was prepared to marry in order to secure a business deal should have set alarm bells ringing. Worry crowded in on her. If Dante was so ruthless, what did this far-fetched situation make *her*?

The answer came instantly. *A mother trying to do the right thing by her child.*

'You gave up that privilege when you signed the contract, *cara*. Right now this is all about salvaging my reputation so that I can seal a deal I've wanted to make for several years.'

'This is not what I intended at all. I should be back in London now, having informed you that you are to be a father—something I felt should be done face to face. I had not for one moment thought you would put forward such a preposterous deal and flaunt me like a trinket, luring someone into a business deal with exactly the kind of man he doesn't want to do business with.'

'Next time you read an article about me in a gossip magazine perhaps you will believe it when I am depicted as a mercenary businessman who lives hard and plays even harder.'

He moved closer to her, his eyes hardening and she knew if she was sensible she'd heed the warning in them.

'I have no scruples, Piper. I will always do whatever is necessary without a thought for anyone who stands in my way.'

'This isn't about *you*,' she gasped, feeling her emotions boiling over in a way she now recognised as part of her pregnancy. 'Or about your barbaric deal. This is about our baby. Your *child*.'

'A child I had no intention of creating.' His denial flew back at her, and the accusation in his voice was clear. 'But right now you are due to meet Elizabeth. This discussion will have to wait.'

He pulled his phone from his pocket and dialled, almost instantly giving instructions in Italian while he picked up papers and put them into his briefcase. He ended the call as he turned back to her, putting on the sunglasses she was beginning to understand were far more than just protection against the sun. They shielded him from everyone, hiding his cold, emotionless eyes.

'My car is waiting.'

The silence in the car as they negotiated the busy streets of Rome was intense to the point of being explosive. The brief conversation that had leapt unwittingly to life between them this morning had exposed all that was wrong with the deal she'd made with this man. They might have shared the most wonderful night of sex, and she might have given him her virginity in a spontaneous act of rebellion against the hand life had dealt her, but she had also fallen just a little bit too hard for him—and she would have to get over that quickly. Having any kind of feelings for a man such as Dante went against all her hopes and dreams for the future. The happy-ever-after ending her father had always promised her was out there, waiting…

Dante was incredibly attractive even now, and his brooding presence dominated the interior of the car as they sat together in the back, where she was powerless to resist the temptation to glance at his handsome profile. How was it possible that *she*, an ordinary girl who'd led a sheltered, protected and happy life in Sydney until her father's death, could fall under the spell of this undisputed pleasure-seeking billionaire bachelor?

Dante could still feel Piper's scrutiny as the car pulled up at outside a boutique he knew first-hand was visited by women from afar. Elizabeth had suggested it when she'd contacted him by email after Benjamin Carter had put the wheels in motion.

Dante hadn't been able to hide his pleasure at Benjamin's shock when he'd called to tell him about Piper and how very convenient it had been that she'd chosen that very day—the day he'd accepted that he needed a wife—to wait in his office, saving him the trouble of selecting a woman. But not only did Piper possess information about him that could destroy him professionally, she was carrying his child. He hadn't told Benjamin he would do anything to protect that child—even give up his bachelor lifestyle.

He got out and went round to Piper's side, aware that opportunistic photographers might be at such locations but hoping against it—at least until his fiancée had assumed again the identity she'd very skilfully used in London. Once she was that hot redhead again, and wearing his ring, he intended to give the press every opportunity to photograph them and spread the good news.

He took her hand, and the hesitation in her step was obvious as they walked into the shop, which he'd instructed would have to be closed to any other shoppers for the duration of their visit.

'Buongiorno, signor...signorina.' If the assistant was surprised at his presence in the shop she hid it very well. 'Signora Young is in my office. Please, this way.'

The assistant's use of English proved that his every request was being followed to the smallest detail. He looked down at Piper, at the glorious red hair which had been piled luxuriously on her head in London but which now fell loose around her shoulders, and felt a moment's hesitation at trying to change her. She was different from his usual choice of woman, enticingly different, and hadn't he become bored with the women of his circle?

He pushed that thought aside as quickly as it had formed. Didn't every woman like to be dressed up, styled by experts and then whisked away to a beauty salon to be pampered? She had a role to play in this deal and he intended she would play it properly.

'I will leave you in the capable hands of Elizabeth.'

He saw her swallow, the movement of her throat giving away the nerves she was trying to hide. It made her look vulnerable and tugged at his conscience—until he remembered the role of confident woman she'd played in London. She had looked confident and comfortable then.

'And what are your instructions for this transformation of your fiancée?'

The spark of fury in her voice only served to bring a smile to his lips, and from the flash of defiance in her eyes it was not a smile she wanted to see.

'Elizabeth has instructions for exactly what is required and she will ensure you know all that is necessary for an evening dinner party. I have seen you poised and elegant, Piper, so I am sure it will be easy for you to act that role once more.'

Before she could formulate any response he knocked on the office door and opened it. The woman who stood and greeted them was dressed simply, in a tan leather jacket over a white blouse and short skirt, and yet had an understated elegance about her. First impressions were important to Dante, and this time he was happy with Benjamin's suggestion to utilise all that Elizabeth Young's company, Leviathan Solutions, could offer.

'Signor Mancini... Ms Riley, good morning.' The woman's smile was warm and friendly as she stepped from behind the desk to greet them.

'Buongiorno.'

'I have all your instructions, Signor Mancini, and Piper—may I call you Piper?' She directed the question at Piper, who Dante thought now seemed remarkably relaxed. Was she resigned to the situation she was in? Maybe her insistence that it wasn't needed had been a ploy.

'Yes, of course,' Piper replied, and looked up at him and smiled.

He was shocked to realise it was a genuine smile,

one which lit up her eyes, taking him right back to the moment he'd first seen her at that dinner party in one of London's top hotels. He'd known in that instant that he wanted her—and had set about making it happen, using the champagne and the anonymity of such an evening to achieve just that, with his usual disregard for social proprieties.

'*Bene*, then I shall see you this evening. My car will be at your disposal all day, and will return you to the apartment later this afternoon.'

He had no wish to spend the day judging dresses, shoes and handbags. There were far more important things for him to do, such as finding a way to convince Bettino D'Antonio that making a deal with his business would be beneficial to both of them.

Piper relaxed as the door closed behind Dante and she heard him saying goodbye in the shop. At least nobody else would witness her so-called transformation as his fiancée other than Elizabeth Young, a woman with warm eyes and a friendly smile whom she couldn't help but like instantly, despite her part in all this.

'We should get started,' Elizabeth said, picking up a notepad and pen, and left the office.

Piper, wishing she could achieve that effortless chic style, followed her through the shop into a large changing room adorned with many ornate mirrors.

'Dante's list is extensive. I had already selected several gowns for this evening's dinner party, but the moment I saw you I knew there was one that was perfect.'

Elizabeth's enthusiasm was infectious, and Piper found herself excited as an assistant appeared. She watched in an almost dreamlike state as Elizabeth signalled to a member of the boutique's staff who held up a long bronze dress, adorned with sequins. The assistant held it across her arms as she stood in the dressing room. Piper had never seen such a dress before, let alone worn one. How could Elizabeth think it was perfect for her?

'Bronze will look amazing with your hair, and the dress will accentuate your gorgeous figure.'

Elizabeth's flurry of words held a hint of excitement which transferred itself to Piper. None of this was for real, but it was happening, and she *did* have the role of fiancée to play. Would it be so wrong to get carried away with the fun of all the glamour?

'It's beautiful.' Piper touched the delicate fabric as the assistant held it for her, wondering how it would feel to wear such a dress. Should she tell Elizabeth that her so-called gorgeous figure would be short-lived? 'It's *very* beautiful. But I'm not sure it will be suitable.'

'Just try it,' encouraged Elizabeth as she ushered Piper behind a changing screen.

Piper looked at her reflection in the large gilded mirror moments later, not even sure if the woman who gazed back at her was real. How could one dress make her look and feel so different?

'It's perfect.' Elizabeth's no-nonsense tone halted any further objections and Piper had to admit it fitted beautifully, as if it had been made for her.

'Then I will be guided by you.' She had no idea what else this evening's dinner party would require, but Elizabeth's air of confidence was reassuring.

'I wish all my clients were so easy to please.' Elizabeth smiled as she signalled to a member of staff that the bronze dress was to be packed. 'Next I have a black gown by the same designer. Perfect for a night at the theatre.'

For a second time Piper looked at her reflection, saw her body encased in the most gorgeous black silk. Was this really happening? The elation of the moment quickly faded as reality crept in. She was paying a high price for this Cinderella moment. She might be about to go to the ball, dinner parties or the theatre, but she certainly wouldn't find her Prince Charming.

From what she'd seen of Dante Mancini, Prince Charming didn't exist in the man she was now engaged to. For two months she'd lived with the hope that after that wonderful night together he might be her very own knight in shining armour. Now she had to accept that such fairytale ideas were impossible. Dante Mancini was ruthless in business and, it seemed, in love. Did he even know what love was?

'No time for daydreaming.' Elizabeth smiled at her in the mirror and Piper couldn't help but smile back, despite the unusual situation and her downward spiralling emotions. 'We have lots more to choose.'

'We do?'

'But of course. You've a weekend in Tuscany, and many events to attend in the coming weeks, and then there are outfits to select for when your pregnancy shows—ones that will accentuate your happy news, as Signor Mancini requested.'

She knew about the pregnancy? Dante certainly hadn't spared her blushes or embarrassment. Hearing it said plainly and so practically that he wanted people knowing that particular detail hurt more than she cared to admit.

'I wasn't aware you knew...' Piper began to stumble over her words, as she always did when she was anxious. 'It's still new to us at the moment.'

Elizabeth stopped and looked at Piper, her friendly

smile defusing the agitation brewing in Piper. 'I'm in full possession of the facts regarding the arrangement between you and Signor Mancini—of his need to appear to settle down in order to salvage the damage done by salacious gossip to their charity.'

'Their charity?'

Piper was confused. Wasn't all this in aid of Dante's business deal? She thought back to the day in his office, when he'd talked of the deal he was on the brink of losing. He hadn't mentioned a charity.

'Of course their charity. That article in *Celebrity Spy!* nearly destroyed the good work all four of them have done.'

'All four of them?'

'Yes—Dante, Zayn, Benjamin and Xander. It's almost as if *Celebrity Spy!* deliberately set out to destroy them and The Hope Foundation.'

Confusion made thinking difficult as Piper digested this new information. Why would Dante want her to believe this was all for his business deal? Why hadn't he told her about the charity, that it was the real reason, instead of letting her believe it was completely mercenary?

'And are all four to be married in order to give the appearance of having settled down in life and abandoned their bachelor existence?'

'Benjamin, Dante and Zayn will be, yes.'

Elizabeth couldn't quite meet Piper's gaze as she straightened a pale pink coat over a dusky pink wrap dress. She wondered where she would wear such an outfit.

'This will be perfect to travel to Tuscany and meet with Dante's clients. Take a look.' Elizabeth's voice held a hint of forced enthusiasm, and she still couldn't meet Piper's eye as she turned to look at her.

Piper walked from the dressing room back to the mirror she'd stood in front of so many times that morning already. The outfit looked and felt expensive, as had each and every one she'd tried on, but it was the turn of the conversation which had unsettled her.

'Are you sure? You seem worried.' Piper's precarious confidence was rocked at the sudden change in Elizabeth's demeanour. She seemed unsettled by the conversation.

'Of course. It's exactly what Dante requested.'

'Dante has mentioned that you arrange marriages. Are you finding brides or inventing fiancées for Benjamin, Zayn and Xander too?'

Piper looked at Elizabeth in the mirror and for a moment thought she saw a look of panic cross her face, but she continued to talk, unable to stop prying into things. This might be her only chance to find out what was really going on, so she continued quickly before Elizabeth changed the subject.

'Each one of them, along with Dante, was named and shamed in that article as the world's most debauched bachelors. Are they *all* your clients?'

'This bag finishes it off perfectly.' Elizabeth handed her a small bag the same colour as the dress and stood and looked at her, a light crease of worry showing on her forehead. 'Benjamin and Zayn are my clients, yes.'

'And is Xander going to follow their lead?' Piper continued to press, aware that maybe Elizabeth shouldn't be divulging such information but, she was part of this charade and had a right to know exactly what was going on. To her, this was for her child, but for Dante their marriage seemed to be about many things—except the duty of fatherhood.

'So I believe.'

'It does make it better, knowing it is also for a charity.' Piper recalled the call she'd interrupted that morning, with Dante unusually speaking English. 'I think Dante did tell you Xander would call you too.'

'Then I shall await his call.' Elizabeth ticked the last item off her list with great flourish. 'We are finished here—but hair, make-up, manicure and pedicure are next.'

'All this for one evening out?'

'You are in a very different world now, Piper. One many women dream of.'

'I'm not one of those women,' she said, and the sensation of losing control of everything, including her destiny, filled her.

CHAPTER FIVE

ELIZABETH'S WORDS HAD stayed with Piper as she'd been made over in a beauty salon. Her nails had been polished and her hair curled until she didn't recognise herself any more. Now as she stood with her hand on the doorhandle of the bedroom, ready to go out and face Dante, wearing a dress that revealed but somehow concealed her body, those words replayed again and again.

She *was* in a different world. One where money bought you anything you desired—including, it seemed, a wife. It didn't help that she wasn't the only woman being groomed for such a role by Elizabeth for the four men in the article. She was acutely aware that she was part of a damage limitation exercise that was more far-reaching than she'd ever thought possible. Worse still, she was his choice only because she carried his child and had come to Rome at precisely the time when he needed a convenient wife.

Piper took a deep breath and looked down at the full-length gown adorned with gold and bronze sequins, wondering if she'd ever truly come up to the standard Dante very obviously desired.

Desired.

That word sizzled in her mind. Last time she'd thrown caution to the wind and worn a gown that wasn't her own she'd ended up in a hotel room with Dante, making passionate love like long-lost lovers who'd been reunited. That night any awkwardness she'd felt about being with him, about giving herself to him, had melted like ice beneath the warmth of spring sunshine as each kiss had pushed her further to the point of no return.

But would he desire her now?

She shook her head, the soft curls making her hair bounce in an unaccustomed way. She couldn't let such thoughts into her mind. This was a deal, not a love affair, and she was adamant she wasn't going to make the same mistake again.

With a determined defiance she opened the door— and the sight which greeted her almost evaporated that self-made promise to ignore the man who made her tremble with just one look. She didn't want to find Dante attractive, but standing in the doorway to his terrace, resplendent in a tuxedo, he took her right back to that night in London. He'd stood out from all the other men that evening—and not just because he'd seemed so captivated by her.

Now he looked even more devastating, and definitely more dangerous than he had then. And he was. He was a danger to her foolish heart, which was thumping so hard in her chest. As he moved towards her his eyes grew dark and intent and swept down her body, making every limb tingle as if he'd actually touched her. And she hated herself for wanting that touch.

'*Mia cara*, you are beautiful.' His voice was rough with desire, and she stood beneath his appraising gaze and knew that every hour she'd spent with Elizabeth and then later in the salon had been worth it. He desired her—even if it was for tonight only.

Right at this moment it was as if the clocks had been

turned back. She felt shy, and yet as completely driven by the sizzle of attraction as she had been that night in London. Just as she had then, she wanted him to take her in his arms and kiss her.

'I trust you are happy with all that Elizabeth has done?' She wouldn't let him know how nice it felt to be told she was beautiful, or how it made her remember things that could never be again. How had he made her feel so desired, so beautiful as they'd made love? Already she knew that moment of passion could never happen again. Not if she wanted to retain her emotional detachment—and her sanity.

'*Sì*, I am very happy, and now I am about to show the beautiful woman who is to be my bride to all of Rome.'

His voice was soft and seductive and it sent a warm tingle sliding down her spine. He took her hand lightly in his fingertips, lifted her fingers to his lips, and without breaking that mesmerising eye contact brushed his lips over them. She wanted to close her eyes as pleasure darted around her. But that would show he affected her, would let him know that he had power over her. Her only weapon in the face of his captivating charm and practised seduction was indifference. She had to remember this was all an act, even if they were not yet in public. It was part of his plan.

'Maybe we should keep the act of being lovers for when we are in the company of tonight's guests.' She forced herself to believe those words but he paused, head bowed slightly over her hand, and raised his brows at her sharp words.

'A man should be able to tell a woman she is beautiful wherever they are.'

There was a playful glint in his eyes and a hint of a mischievous smile. He was toying with her, amusing himself, but it reminded her of his true character. He might be about to fool the rest of the world with his intention to settle down to married life and fatherhood, but she knew the truth—and she had to remember it too.

'Shall we go?' She pulled her hand slowly from his and stepped away from him, needing the space to think, to put her mind back in order. She couldn't fall for his charm—not again. Look what had happened last time the evening had started with a simple kiss of the hand and a seductive smile.

Dante smiled, pleased to know that the act of indifference she'd shown him so far since arriving in Rome was just that. Underneath all that cool composure she was still the hot, sexy woman who had driven him wild with desire. The same one who had lingered in his mind ever since, leaving him with a sense of something unfinished about the whole night.

He'd tried to tell himself it was because she'd left him without even a goodbye, slipping away before dawn, but now he suspected it was a little more than that. For the first time in many years of one-night stands and brief flings he still wanted a woman. More to the point, he wanted *this* woman. The need burned within him to touch her, kiss her and make her his once more.

This insistent need had only been intensified by the attention Elizabeth had given her all day. The bronze dress, alluringly diaphanous, shimmered with bronze and gold sequins which gave the fine fabric its modesty, although it clung to her body as if it had been poured over her. The swell of her breasts which, given the backless design of the dress, had to be braless, was clearly accentuated. As was her slender waist and her hips. The sexy creation hugged her hips, then flared out, but any more detail was lost on him. All he could do was think about her legs and how they had once wrapped around him as he'd thrust into her when he'd been the man to claim her as his—and soon she really would be.

'I have a mind to take you straight back into the bedroom and remove that dress.' He struggled to stabilise his hoarse voice and bit down hard against the rise of hot, throbbing desire which pulsed through him at the thought of doing just that. How had he thought he could keep things neutral with this woman when she'd been in his mind ever since he'd woken to find her gone?

'Is it not suitable?'

Her soft voice wavered anxiously and she brushed those sexy tousled curls back from her face. *Maledizione!* Did she know what she did to him?

She was stunning, beautiful—and the mother of his child. She was now his fiancée. Less than a week ago he had been a single man, a carefree bachelor to whom marriage and commitment had been very much avoidable.

Now he had the responsibility of his child. That thought briefly sobered his desire-infused mind, dredging up his past for inspection once more. He pushed the sabotaging thoughts aside and looked again at the beautiful woman who was to be his wife.

'It has achieved all that I hoped for, *cara*, and I am certain that I will not be the only man to want to do just that this evening.' His voice remained hoarse with desire, just as desire lingered in his body, not quite extinguished.

As she frowned in confusion he crossed the room to her, unable to resist the urge to touch her, to feel her soft skin beneath his fingers, his lips. *Dio mio*, he wanted her more than he'd ever wanted any woman—even more than he'd wanted her that first night in London.

He saw the moment she realised his intention, saw her step back, saw the blush spread over her face and it made him want her more. He'd never been so hungry for a woman and he'd never had to control such desires. He was used to getting what he wanted, and right now he wanted this Australian redhead—badly.

'No.' That sharp, short word cracked through the sexually charged air and she stood in glorious defiance, her chin lifted, her shoulders back and those lovely green eyes sparking icy fury at him. 'We made a deal, Dante, one that doesn't include such things. We are not a real couple.'

'*Sì, cara*, you are right. *Mi dispiace*.' English mixed with his native Italian as he fought for control over his response to seeing her like this.

One thing it did prove was that she was definitely unfinished business. Would the deal he'd struck with her be enough to keep him at a distance? It should be—as should the fact that he never wanted to care for anyone again, never wanted to be responsible for another person's happiness. He was done with caring, done with losing a piece of himself when a person left, and Piper had made it clear that she intended to leave once the minimum term of their marriage had been completed, taking with her his child. No, he mustn't allow emotions to cloud this deal.

'Just as long as we understand one another.'

Her deep and fast breathing told him she was far from unaffected by what had almost happened, even if her words were cold and to the point. She might not want to be his wife, but she wanted him as much as he wanted her.

'Very clearly, *cara*, and now we should go. I have timed our arrival to create maximum impact and so begin the talk of our engagement within the media.'

She looked down at the ring on her finger, her curled hair sliding off her shoulder in a way that was so sensual it almost undid all the control he'd fought hard to regain. He knew what she was thinking as she looked at the symbol of their deal. The platinum band set with a single large diamond would certainly be noticed. There would be no doubt that they were engaged.

'Yes, you're right,' she said, with a new strength sounding in her voice. 'The sooner you achieve your aims, the sooner we can return to something resembling normal. I can go back to London and you can continue as if this never happened.'

'That may not be possible for a while. It is going to be hard to prove to Bettino D'Antonio that I have reformed my ways without you at my side, but there is time later to discuss this—the car is waiting.' The thought of her returning to London so soon unsettled him, but he wasn't ready to explore why.

All too soon they were ensconced in the elevator, and her perfume brought back memories of that morning at his office a few days earlier. Then he had thought his imagination was playing tricks on him when the lingering scent in the elevator had brought her so quickly to his mind. The scent was evocative of that night in London, of the passion they'd shared, and now as they got into the car it reminded him far more than he could tolerate.

He studied her as she sat, determinedly staring forward while the car made its way through Rome's traffic, and wondered if she too felt the zing of electricity which connected them, gaining strength each day.

'Goodness,' she gasped and looked at him, her green eyes vivid and wide. 'So many cameras. I don't think I can do this.'

He took her hand and looked into the depths of green which reminded him of the forests of Italy in summer. 'You can. I'm with you.'

Her gaze held his and the connection between them intensified, sending off sparks around them. He had to kiss her—had to feel her lips beneath his and the soft swell of her breasts against his chest as he held her. He had to wrap his arms around her and feel her pliant body melt against his. He couldn't resist her any longer.

He leant closer. She didn't pull away, didn't move back, and her eyes darkened until they resembled the deepest ocean. She wanted him too. Despite the icy indifference she was hiding behind, she wanted him. A pulse of lust hurtled through him as she nervously moistened her lips with her tongue, the movement taking his gaze from those dark desire-filled eyes. *She wanted him.*

'I can't do any of this...' Piper whispered as Dante leant closer. He was going to kiss her. Instinctively she recognised the inky blackness which had filled his eyes, obliterating the brown completely, and she was powerless to resist. She couldn't move—couldn't do anything except wait to feel his lips on hers and hate herself for wanting that kiss, *needing* it.

He whispered something so seductive-sounding it could only be Italian, and she closed her eyes as his lips touched hers, sending shockwaves of tingles throughout her body. Then his hands held her face, imprisoning her as he pressed a deep and scorching kiss to her lips. She sighed softly when hot desire sparked to life within her, just as it had that night in London—as if nothing had changed. She sighed again and responded, and her breathing quickened as the kiss deepened.

What was she doing?

'No.' She pushed against him, her breath coming hard and fast. Every nerve in her body sang with awareness for him but she couldn't let it happen again, couldn't give in to it. 'I can't.'

He smiled at her, so sure of himself, completely convinced that just one kiss would have her tumbling back into his bed. 'You just did, *cara*.'

'I don't mean *that*.' She adopted a dismissive tone, as if being kissed to within an inch of her sanity was a perfectly normal occurrence. 'I mean all those photographers out there. I can't be who you want me to be.'

'You can and you will. We have a deal, no?'

His eyes narrowed and she looked out of the window, not relishing the idea of parading around for what appeared to be nothing short of a pack of wolves in such a tight dress when her body was on fire from his kiss.

'What if I get it wrong?' She turned and looked at him to see his brows rise in question. Then he smiled and her attention was drawn to that smile, to those lips which had just kissed her into a heady state of euphoria. She couldn't allow that again and would have to be on her guard.

'Do not worry, *mia cara*, I will be at your side all the way.'

That was precisely what she was worried about. But as she got out of the car and the cameras flashed Dante was true to his word and stayed at her side, the act of loving fiancé in full swing.

She smiled shyly as they stood briefly for photos and Dante put his arm around her, his fingers pressing possessively into her waist as he pulled her closer, giving her no option but to lean against the length of his body. The spark of desire which had just been reawakened hummed relentlessly through her until it was almost impossible to smile at the cameras.

If she'd thought the kiss had been potent then she'd definitely got it wrong. It was as if she was going up in flames of desire right there on the streets of Rome. His masculine and powerful musky aftershave weaved its way through her senses and the firmness of his thigh against hers brought images to her mind of them naked together.

Then Dante spoke to the press, turning her towards the hotel as he did so, and she focused all her attention on walking the short distance in heels she was far from used to. Anything was better than focusing on the feel of his body against hers and the heady pulse of desire which beat within her.

'Is it always like this?' she asked as they entered the peace and safety of the hotel.

'You will get used to it.'

He guided her through to the function room, where tables were laid with precise attention to detail. At least that was *something* she was familiar with after spending so many hours setting such tables and waiting on them as the rich and famous of first Sydney and then London dined while she remained invisible. She wholeheartedly wished she could do that right now—but dressed as she was, with a man like Dante at her side and desire coursing within her, that wasn't an option.

'I'm not sure I want to.' She was painfully aware of the curious glances and bold stares and didn't like it at all. It played too much into her insecurities, reminding her of childhood taunts.

'That sounds distinctly like you want to back out of our deal, Piper.' He took two flutes of champagne and handed her one, but she shook her head in refusal and instantly he sent for a more suitable drink.

'I'm not backing out of anything,' she said with a smile on her lips and a sweetness in her voice that she hoped would convey her annoyance. 'I'm going through with this deal for the right reason.'

'Which is…?'

How could he even ask that?

She paused as a waiter approached with a single glass of juice on a silver tray. Dante took it with thanks and handed it to her.

She looked straight into those sinfully dark eyes. 'Our child.'

'And I am not?' How could he boldly stand there and say that when he'd been the one to make such a deal?

'No, you are doing this for a business deal—although you'd like everyone to think it's for a charitable reason. But if there is one thing I know about you now, it is that you couldn't possibly want to marry—even for your child. Everything I read about you in *Celebrity Spy!* is true. So far I have found nothing to make me think otherwise.'

'At least you are well informed about me, whereas I know very little of you.'

She bristled as the conversation turned in a way she hadn't expected. 'There isn't much to tell.'

'I'd like to know why you were the hostess at that dinner party in London—"stepping in", I think you called it. What exactly *is* your profession?'

She tried to suppress the urge to shock him, but it was too great. 'I'm just a waitress.' It wasn't her choice of job—wasn't what she'd hoped for as she'd started university in Australia—but circumstances had conspired against her.

She watched as he clenched his jaw and a surge of triumph rushed through her. He had certainly never envisaged marriage and fatherhood, and she was completely sure that if he had he wouldn't have wanted his wife to be a mere waitress.

'And that is enough for you?'

'It's had to be,' she said, without realising she was opening the door to a discussion about herself she'd rather not have. She didn't want to talk about her beloved father, about the emptiness in her life where he had been. She was an ordinary girl—but to her father she'd been a princess, and he'd been the most important person in her life.

Thankfully at that very moment other guests joined them, and after that there wasn't much chance to talk— at least not about anything private, and especially not her past, nor the events which had changed her life. That was something she had no wish to share with a man incapable of any kind of emotion. He would never understand.

Dante unlocked the door to his apartment and for the first time since he'd been relegated to the small room which usually served as his home office he was glad of it. At least there he would be away from the temptation to kiss Piper, because after spending the evening being tormented by her body in the bronze creation Elizabeth had selected he was in danger of giving in to the lustful desire which pumped through him.

Never before had he had to restrain himself. He *always* got what he wanted, be it women or fast cars.

Holding back was not a comfortable sensation, and he didn't know how long he could go on being tempted so enticingly by her without acting on it.

'Piper…' He spoke softly as she placed her purse on the antique table in the living area. He wanted to tell her again how lovely she looked, and how much he wanted her, but instead decided that keeping to the terms of their agreement was better—for both of them. He couldn't allow himself to care, knowing she would one day walk away. Just as she had done the night after his baby had been conceived.

She looked at him, her big green eyes full of uncertainty, and when she bit her lower lip he clenched his hands into fists at his sides. Now was not the time to remember how those lips had felt beneath his just hours earlier, how they'd responded so willingly. Nor was it the time to remember that if they had been here instead of in the car when he'd kissed her they would never have left for the dinner party.

'Is something wrong?' she asked tentatively.

Everything was wrong. He was falling under a spell he was beginning to think she had no idea she was casting. She seemed oblivious to what she did to him. Tonight he'd seen her smile and laugh with people she didn't know, seen them warm to her in a way which had made pride fill him as she visibly blossomed.

'I just wanted to say you made a good impression this evening. Thank you.'

'I did it for my baby.'

She flung the words at him instantly and he bit back his retort. It was late, and now was not the time to be getting embroiled in a discussion he didn't want, no matter what the time of day. The way she'd said *my*

baby cut deep into his hardened emotions, more painfully than he'd thought possible.

'Tomorrow we will be leaving for Tuscany, where
you will do it all again—this time for me and my deal.'

CHAPTER SIX

PIPER SAT IN the sports car as it sped along the road towards Tuscany, glad that the threat of morning sickness she'd experienced earlier in the week seemed to have dwindled. Beside her Dante drove with clean precision, and she couldn't help but glance at him as he drove, embarrassed when he caught her out. His sunglasses hid the truth in his eyes and probably, after the burning look of desire he'd had in them when they'd returned from the dinner party last night, that was for the best.

She had no wish to fall even harder for him than she had already, and certainly didn't want to repeat their encounter in London. This was all about their child. Nothing else mattered other than giving her son or daughter the experience of knowing both parents.

'We are almost there,' he said, and quickly looked at her. 'Tonight we dine with Bettino D'Antonio at his new villa, so it would be best if we exchanged a few details about each other before this evening, no?'

'Is that in the interests of making our engagement believable or out of a genuine need to know more about the mother of your child?' He'd caught her off-guard with his callous disregard for her feelings and she'd risen to the challenge he'd inadvertently given. They would never be a real couple, but he would always be her child's father, and she intended to remind him of that duty as often as possible.

'Such attention to detail is necessary whatever the reason.' He slowed the car and turned off the main road onto a narrower road which twisted through a small and sleepy village before heading out into the countryside once more. 'This weekend will be make or break after months of negotiations between myself and D'Antonio. He has also invited Gianni Paolini, my rival in this deal, so I fully intend to use our newly announced engagement and the baby to maximum benefit.'

The tension of several hours in the car with Dante, being excruciatingly aware of every move he made, got the better of her and she couldn't help but continue to aim for irritation. 'And by that you mean I shouldn't elaborate on what I know about you, but paint a very different picture?'

'It is what we agreed, Piper.'

He swung the car into a driveway lined with mature cypress trees and, knowing he was right, she looked away just in time to see a large villa come into view.

'That's so beautiful...' she breathed, more to herself than to Dante.

'It pleases me to hear you say that,' he said as he stopped the car outside the old stone villa. 'This is where I come to get away from everything. Except for this weekend, it is the one place I am able to completely relax. Bettino D'Antonio has recently bought a villa in the next village, which he intends to use during the winter months, and despite the fact I'd rather not conduct business from here, it suits me well.'

Dante got out of the car and she watched him walk around the front of its sleek black bonnet. He looked up at the villa as he did so and briefly she thought she saw his face relax, as if this was a place where he truly was at home.

When he opened her door she slid round in the seat and tried to get out in as elegant a fashion as the tight-fitting skirt would allow. She failed miserably, if the raising of his brows was anything to go by, as her skirt rucked up, exposing her legs. With a wicked and suggestive expression on his face he held out his hand to her and helped her out of the low car.

'I have arranged for lunch to be served on the terrace. We can talk further on things we should know about each other, and after that you should rest before this evening's dinner.'

Piper didn't know if she wanted to talk to Dante at all. She had no wish to share her past with a man who cared for nothing other than getting the next deal. But if he *did* get that deal she would have honoured her side of their bargain. Would he then keep *his* promise and be there for his child? She was in no doubt that her son or daughter would not have the kind of relationship she'd had with her own father—the kind that had driven her to board a plane for Rome, convinced she was doing the right thing to seek Dante out. She hadn't wanted to deny her child the chance to have what she'd had, but as each day passed she was more certain than ever that Dante was nothing like her father.

'If we are going to convince people that we are engaged for real then I suppose we do have to at least know a little of each other.'

She followed him into the villa, taking in the luxurious interior. It looked far more like a home than the sleek modern style of his Rome apartment, and her curiosity was aroused by the paintings and antiques she glimpsed.

Dante opened two doors which led out onto a terrace covered in wisteria that would be beautiful in the summer. 'We *are* engaged for real, no?'

The tone of his voice left her in no doubt that he was taunting her—and enjoying it.

No, they weren't. If it was for real she would be helplessly in love with him, and he would definitely be in love with her. She couldn't deny there was an attraction, but it wasn't love. Was it?

'Not in the true sense of the word, no. We are not in love.'

'But to look as if we are in love is what we have agreed on, *cara*, is it not?'

'For very different reasons, yes, it is.'

'Then I suggest we relax and enjoy our meal and the winter sunshine Tuscany has to offer before making sure it does appear to anyone we meet that ours is very much a real engagement.'

He sat at the table, looking far too relaxed and comfortable with the whole situation, whereas she was nothing but jumbled nerves. Was that the deal she'd struck with Dante, or the man himself? She couldn't even consider the answer to that question.

'You look tired,' Dante said as he sat back.

The sought-after calm that usually settled over him after arriving in Tuscany wasn't quite so easy to come by today, but then he'd never been here to do business before—and that business had never been so important or so wanted. He *had* to win this contract, and it was that sentiment, together with the way the charity would view him, that had forced him to accept that Benjamin's suggestion of settling down was the answer to many issues—including, it seemed, a night of amazing but careless sex with a gorgeous redhead he hadn't even bothered exchanging names with.

'I am a little tired. Can we sort these things out now, so I can rest before taking a shower?' She pushed her hair behind her ear and looked at him, the vivid green of her eyes holding a hint of unease.

He pushed aside the guilt that he was making her uncomfortable and tried to banish the image which had suddenly sprung to mind of her in the shower. It wouldn't do to think of her naked beneath jets of water—not when he knew just how amazing she looked naked.

'When and where we met will remain the same—at least there is little chance of getting that wrong. However, we will say we have been seeing each other secretly since.' Briskness crept into his voice as he set out all that was supposed to have happened between them.

'Why secretly?' Her delicate brows furrowed in genuine confusion, making her look every bit as innocent as she had been—unknown to him—before he took her to his hotel room in London.

'To protect you from press attention, of course—except that it didn't go according to plan, as the *Celebrity Spy!* article will prove, giving me the perfect opportunity to refute its claims.'

'And where will these meetings have taken place?' She spoke in an efficient manner and might have been conducting a business meeting.

'London and Rome. What do you like doing? Where would you have wanted to go?

She looked at him, the hardness in her eyes softening slightly. 'Art galleries.'

'Art? I had no idea.' He was genuinely surprised, but couldn't allow himself to get sidetracked now.

'Why should you have? Neither of us expected the night we shared to become anything more than one night. We didn't even exchange names.'

She strolled across the terrace, folding her arms about her as if trying to keep every detail about herself protected from him. He watched as she stood and looked out across the rise and fall of the landscape he loved so much, interspersed as it was by clusters of ancient villages.

He hadn't expected anything from those few hot hours in bed with her, and certainly not to wake up alone the next morning. Was that why she'd lingered in his mind, teasing his memory with the passion of that night? Now, as he watched her, his gaze taking in her petite and slender figure showcased to perfection in another creation suggested by Elizabeth, he really did want to know more about her. What did she like? What was her favourite music and food? Questions raced through his mind.

'And what of your family?' He had to know at least something of her family background.

'My family?' She looked at him, suspicion in her eyes. 'It is just my mother and myself. We moved to London, her place of birth, after my father died.'

A jolt of something akin to sympathy raced through him. She knew what it was to lose someone she loved too.

'But you grew up in Australia?' He walked over to her, conscious of her watching him carefully, keeping her attention fully focused on him, just as she had done that first morning in his office.

'Yes, in Sydney. Anything else about my childhood you feel it's necessary to know?'

The scathing tone of her voice should have warned

him off, but knowing she too had lost her father drew him to her, as did a strange urge to talk of something he'd long since buried.

'You at least knew your father, had a bond with him, which is more than I ever experienced.'

'I'm sorry.' The sympathetic look in her eyes as she looked up at him, placing her hand on his arm, conveyed her shock at the unexpected revelation which had come from him.

'Don't be.' He shrugged off her touch and focused his gaze into the Tuscan countryside. 'I barely knew my father, which is just as well. He wasn't a man I would have wished to know.'

'Don't say that.' Her shock rushed over him in waves. 'Every child needs a father.'

'Not one who walks out on a woman, a young boy and a newborn son. No child deserves a father like *that*.'

'That happened to you?' Her gorgeous green eyes were filled with sympathy and he gritted his teeth against it. He didn't need sympathy from anyone—least of all her.

'*Sì.*' His overpowering anger made functioning in English briefly impossible.

'Where is your brother now?'

Piper's question rocked him to the core as memories of the time when that had been the only question he'd wanted an answer to flooded back faster than a high tide.

'He died.' The hounds were after him again, dragging out the horror of those years when he and his mother had had no idea where the teenage Alessio had gone. He couldn't do this now. He didn't want to share any of this with anyone, and definitely not a fiancée acquired through a deal. 'He was missing for several years before I discovered the truth of his untimely death.'

'That makes all *I* went through as a child seem so trivial.'

He turned to her just as she looked down, as if ashamed of even admitting such a thing. 'What *did* you go through?'

She still didn't look at him. 'I was born without sight in my left eye, and before I had an operation to make it look normal I was teased mercilessly by other children. Then I was knocked down by a car when I was seven. I didn't see the car, which thankfully wasn't going fast, but after that my parents—especially my father—wrapped me up and tried to keep me from all harm. I just wish I could have done the same for Dad. Maybe then he wouldn't have been killed when a car he was a passenger in crashed.'

Before Dante could think what he was doing he'd taken Piper in his arms and hugged her. Her willing body moulded against him and he stroked her hair, inhaling the scent of her shampoo, wanting only to make her pain go away.

'I had no idea,' he said, thinking again of what she had first said, and the way she always kept her focus on him, especially in his office that first morning. It made sense now.

'I don't like to talk of my father.' She looked up at him and he studied her closely.

'I meant about your sight.'

Before she could drop her gaze he caught her chin with his thumb and finger, forcing her to look at him. 'Nobody would ever know.'

She pulled away from him, a flush of embarrassment

colouring her cheeks. 'We can talk more later. I'm not feeling too good.'

He watched her go, wanting to call her back, to hold her to him again and give her comfort. Because, strangely, just having her in his arms gave *him* comfort. It was a sensation he was not at all sure about and so, feeling like a child learning to swim, enjoying the warm water and yet finding it terrifying, he moved swiftly to the water's edge and out of danger. Sentiment was something he'd never dabbled with, and now was not the time to start.

Piper's nerves were almost frayed as she and Dante entered the villa of the man he wanted to do business with—the man *she* had to convince their relationship was real.

She'd put on the emerald-green dress that Elizabeth had selected for the dinner, still ruffled by the fact that Elizabeth had known more of what was expected of her than Piper had. But that indignation had melted away when Dante had first seen her, looking at her not with the scrutiny she'd expected, but with genuine pleasure. And if she wasn't mistaken there had also been a hint of something else which had sent a shiver of anticipation through her...

But now was not the time, and she focused herself. She had a role to play—her part of the deal they'd struck a week ago in Rome.

'Dante,' Bettino said as he met them, taking Dante's hand and shaking it firmly. 'I confess that I was sceptical about the news that you had become engaged, but now I can see exactly why a man such as yourself would succumb to the need for marriage.'

Piper smiled graciously at Bettino and tried to ignore

the frisson of tension which had transferred itself from Dante to her at the other man's words.

'Bettino, meet Piper Riley—my fiancée.' Remarkably Dante supressed the tension and pride shone out in his voice. Piper felt her stomach flip over with nerves, still unable to believe she'd actually agreed to this charade.

She wanted to shy away from Bettino, despite his friendly smile and grandfather-like eyes. All she wanted to do was step back from his scrutiny and the limelight to a place where she felt safe, but this was part of the deal she'd made with Dante and she would do it so well even *he* wouldn't question her authenticity. She had to if she stood a chance of Dante being any kind of father to their child.

She smiled at the man Dante wanted to secure his deal with and harnessed all she'd been told about being in the public eye—first by the company she'd worked for in Sydney and then in London, and finally by Elizabeth, who had instructed her in the art of being the kind of woman a man like Dante would need at his side.

'Thank you for inviting me to your lovely home, Signor D'Antonio. It's a real pleasure to be here with Dante.'

As she spoke Dante slid his arm around her back and she breathed in slowly against the heat his touch sent scorching through her. She glanced up at him, thankful he'd at least stayed on her right side so she hadn't jumped when he'd touched her. Maybe telling him about her lack of sight hadn't been such a bad idea. Even if it *had* come out before she'd been able to stop it—something which never normally happened.

'I am pleased Dante has brought you. It is always a pleasure to meet a beautiful woman.'

'The pleasure is, of course, all mine, Bettino.' Dante's voice positively dripped with desire and admiration as he looked down at her, and the smile on his lips would have fooled anyone. As would the soft, desire-laden darkness of his eyes.

'My other guests will arrive shortly,' Bettino said, turning his attention back to Dante. 'And after this evening I will make my decision as to whom I do business with. But for now I want you both to relax and enjoy the evening. I want to see the real Dante Mancini, just as I want to see the real Gianni Paolini.'

'A very astute way of doing business,' Dante said, and Piper wondered if it was only her who noticed his jaws pressing tightly together.

Bettino laughed and they followed him into the villa, where they were offered a glass of champagne by a waitress—a role Piper felt far more suited to.

'Piper would prefer juice,' Dante said, and pulled her close again, looking down at her. 'We're looking forward to being parents.'

Bettino laughed and clapped a hand on Dante's shoulder. 'So not only are you to be married, but you are to be a father too?'

Piper blushed furiously at Dante's not so subtle way of informing Bettino of their news, but all thought was swept away as Gianni Paolini arrived with his wife.

He was an older Italian man who was nearer Bettino's age. Beside her she felt Dante's presence, and that unmistakable aura of power he'd had on the night they'd met in London. But would it be enough? Suddenly it mattered to her.

As the meal began the men talked around the subject of the deal, and Piper listened as Dante spoke passionately about his business. Her interest was aroused when

Bettino asked him why he'd started his own business, and she watched as he seemed to square his shoulders.

'I started as a teenager, clearing building sites of off-cuts and soon it became a large and expanding company—one which I hoped would make things better for my mother, who'd brought me and my brother up alone.'

'You have a brother?' Bettino asked, and Piper held her breath, hardly hearing the meaningless talk of the other women.

'My brother died.' Silence hung in the air, suspended on an atmosphere that might have been sliced with one swipe of a sword.

Thankfully the two older women had begun to talk about the various regions of Tuscany and Piper joined in, eager to divert attention from Dante. 'There are many parts of Tuscany I'd love to see.'

'Then you must ask your fiancé to take you,' said Gianni Paolini's wife.

Piper thought her tactics had worked—until suddenly and inexplicably the spotlight was turned on her.

'What do *you* do, Piper?' Bettino's wife asked.

Piper felt as if she was about to be tripped up, tricked into saying she was just a waitress—an unemployed one at that. Determined not to be outwitted, she drew on her career dreams. 'Art is my passion. I studied it at university for a time.'

'You didn't finish your course?' The question, full of conjecture, hung in the air, and to make matters worse she could feel Dante's gaze on her now.

'No, I didn't. I moved home to be with my parents when my father became very ill.' Saying it aloud brought all the pain back.

'What would you have done with your degree in art?' In stark contrast to his wife, Bettino's voice was full of interest and, as always, she blossomed beneath such genuine interest in her subject.

'I would have set up my own business as an art curator.' She pushed back the agony of losing her father and focused on the one thing she'd always been passionate about. Art.

Bettino sat back and looked at her as their main course arrived. 'We should talk later. I am looking to commission someone to bring this place to life with art.'

'Thank you, but I couldn't—not with a baby due in the summer.'

'Nonsense.' Bettino's voice softened. 'We'll sort something out.'

Piper almost couldn't keep the fizz of excitement at such a prospect under control, but she had to. She had to remember this was Dante's deal, not hers. With a smile she was unable to hide she looked across the table at him, and the irritation or annoyance she'd thought would be there after that little exchange was missing. In its place she saw the same desire he'd had in his eyes as they'd arrived, but somehow it was more intense. It seemed to smoulder, and she could feel the heat across the table.

She blushed and looked down, hoping the conversation would take a different turn.

'Do you plan to spend a lot of time here?' Dante asked Bettino, and Piper wondered if that had been a deliberate ploy to rescue her. Whatever it was, she was glad that she was no longer the centre of attention.

As the hour moved towards midnight Dante placed Piper's coat over her shoulders, pleased the evening had gone well. Piper had been amazing—she'd become the confident and vivacious woman he'd met in London.

She'd held her own as they'd asked her questions which, from their earlier talk, he knew would cause her pain. He'd found himself drawn to her in a way he'd never known, eager to discover more of the woman beneath the sexy exterior, but he'd quickly dismissed that idea.

That night they'd first met in London he'd experienced mind-blowing sex with her, unwittingly taking her virginity and creating a child that would bind them together for ever. But that didn't alter anything. No matter where she was or who she was with she would always be his, and even though he didn't want to tonight he would have to watch her close the door to her bedroom and shut him out.

It was for the best. He didn't want commitment and emotion. It was something he couldn't do, because the few times in his life that he had, it had forced away those he'd invested in emotionally, locking them out of his life for ever. He'd sworn after Alessio's death never to become emotionally involved with anyone ever again.

But with Piper that pledge was difficult to keep. She entranced him, made him desire her with just one of those coy looks she often gave him when she thought he wasn't looking. When she'd admitted her lack of sight in her left eye he'd wanted to hold her and show that it made no difference to him at all, that she was the most desirable and sexy woman he'd ever known. He wanted more than ever to care for her, protect her always.

After the way she'd had Bettino D'Antonio practically eating out of her hand he wanted her even more. She'd been marvellous tonight, her beauty subtly shinning in a way that the vain women he usually dated could never have achieved. It had made him want her again, in his arms and in his bed. Before their marriage ended and they went their separate ways he wanted her—completely.

He lowered his head to her left ear, about to whisper how well she'd done, when she jumped and turned abruptly to face him, a spark of annoyance in her green eyes. It quickly faded as she remembered her role and she smiled sweetly at him just as Bettino joined them in the large hallway. He berated himself for not remembering what she'd told him earlier, but the need to be close to her had become overwhelming, just as it had that night in London when nothing else had mattered except making her his.

'You startled me,' she said softly, before looking again at Bettino. 'Thank you again for such an interesting evening, and I'd be honoured to help you locate any items of art you require.'

'Thank you. I will definitely contact you regarding this matter,' Bettino stated firmly, and for a moment Dante wondered what was coming next.

Had something been said or done this evening to jeopardise the deal? He'd thought Piper's love of art might have clinched the deal, maybe forcing the older man to make up his mind before the end of the evening.

The genuine look of shocked joy on Piper's face at Bettino's words was so unexpected that Dante laughed gently at her innocent pleasure.

'I will wait to hear from you, *signor*,' she said.

'Goodnight, Mancini,' said Bettino as Dante put his arm possessively around Piper—not for show, as he expected she thought it might be, but because he wanted to.

He needed to feel her close, to inhale the heady scent of her perfume and feel that gorgeous body next to his. The thought of saying goodnight to her once they returned to his villa was not one he welcomed—not when the insistent throb of desire was alive in his body. He wanted her more than he'd ever wanted any woman.

'Goodnight, Signor D'Antonio.'

Bettino turned to Piper and took her hand, bowing over it as if he would kiss it in a gesture suited to another century, sending a spark of jealousy hurtling through Dante as she blushed and smiled shyly at him.

'Goodnight, Piper. I'm very pleased to have made your acquaintance. Your presence here this evening has been most welcome.'

'Thank you,' Piper said softly, sending a thrill of desire sparking through Dante.

She was a beautiful woman, inside and out, and a woman like that wasn't right for him. But that knowledge didn't curb the need which was pulsing through him.

That need and desire, which he doubted he could suppress for much longer, formed a potent cocktail as he drove as fast as the narrow roads would allow back to his villa, aware of her watching his every move in a way which added to the sexual tension swirling around them.

Did she feel it too?

There was no way out of it now—no way of avoiding it. He wanted Piper and he wanted her tonight. *Now.*

CHAPTER SEVEN

PIPER WATCHED DANTE as he strode across the high-ceil-inged living room of the villa. The look on his face was intense her heart beat a little faster. He looked as if he wanted to devour her there and then. The same expression he'd had as they'd entered his hotel room in London.

'You made a good impression this evening.' He stopped striding and stood, leaning one arm along the cream stone of the fireplace, and she fought hard against the dark and passionate look which filled his eyes—and the way her body responded.

She couldn't want him—not after he'd shown his true colours, shown himself to be a sharp and driven businessman who would stop at nothing to achieve his ultimate aims. He was using her and their baby. How could she find such a man attractive when all she'd ever dreamed of was a caring, loving man? He was so wrong for her, and yet being with him felt so right. Just as before, she wanted to be with him in every way possible, to risk everything and feel his kiss, his touch.

She certainly hadn't been fooled by his subdued and grief-laden voice as he'd spoken of his brother at the dinner table. He'd spoken of how difficult things had been for his mother, bringing up two young boys. Such a revelation had come as a shock, but she hoped she'd hidden it well. After all, as his fiancée she would have known such things.

'I did my best,' she said now, and sat down on one of the large, comfortable sofas. She couldn't stay in the middle of the room, watching him as if she were waiting for something to happen. She was certain that at any moment the tension around them would snap.

'You were utterly brilliant and you won D'Antonio over. He loved you. He practically melted each time you spoke and you know it.'

There was a caustic edge to his words as they sliced through the atmosphere in the room and she knew right there and then that something had changed. It felt different between them, and she didn't know what it was.

'Telling him of your passion for art was a clever move.'

'It is real, Dante. It is what I would have done if I hadn't given up university when my father became ill.'

'A well-played move, no?'

'I should go to bed.' She got up. The need to escape both the brooding man who dominated every bit of space in the room and the way her body yearned for his touch and his kiss was overwhelming. She definitely had to go.

'Tell me about your father's illness.'

Dante's words froze her to the spot and she looked at him, still standing without a care in the world, so casually leaning on the mantelpiece of the fireplace.

'There's nothing more to tell.' She fired the words defensively back at him as grief assailed her, rushing back so strongly her legs felt weak. She wanted to sit down, but doing so would mean staying beneath his scrutiny.

'It would have helped me to know of such a detail

before spending the evening with D'Antonio, trying to convince him we are a couple in love—a couple about to marry and share our lives—which means sharing our pasts.'

'That's something you too are guilty of.'

He pushed firmly away from the fireplace and came towards her, but she couldn't move, even though she knew she should. The fierce intensity in his eyes struck fear into her heart, closely followed by anticipation. For what, she didn't know.

'But we are not really sharing our lives, are we, Dante? We are engaged to be married, and it is merely for the convenience of your business deal.'

Now all the worries she'd had about the future over the last week pushed forth and she couldn't stem the flow of words.

'What will happen when you get your stupid deal? Will you walk away from me, from your child, as if we never existed?'

Dante closed the distance between them, coming to stand very close to her, making her heart pound in a way she'd only experienced once before, on the night he took her hand and led her to his hotel room.

'You don't think very highly of me, do you, *cara*?'

He spoke softly, serving only to irritate her further. She wasn't a sullen child to be appeased.

'Your reputation isn't exactly squeaky clean, Dante. What am I supposed to think?'

She wasn't about to stand there and discuss this tonight, least of all admit how much she liked him—and more. She was tired—which, together with the pregnancy, must be the reason for her emotions being all over the place. It couldn't be Dante. She didn't want it to be Dante—didn't want him to affect her.

'I never go back on a deal, Piper. *Ever.*' A firm and sharp edge speared into his words, and if they'd been discussing anything else she might just have fallen for it. 'I needed to know about your father's illness. It's the sort of detail a loving fiancé *would* know.'

'Very well.' She flounced away from him, desperate to reinstate the distance between them. She couldn't deal with the scent of his aftershave invading her senses, the heat of his body so very close to hers, and definitely not his dark penetrating gaze, watching her so intently. 'What do you need to know?'

'When did he die?'

Piper closed her eyes briefly and took a deep breath, not sure she could do this now, but acutely aware that what he said made sense. If they were to look like a newly engaged couple he had to know at least *something* about her.

'The night I met you in London was the first anniversary of his death.' She lifted her chin and looked into his eyes, unwittingly sending him a challenge to ask more. A challenge he took.

'So you used the attraction between us as a way to escape?' He visibly stiffened before her, his whole body becoming rigid and his dark eyes almost fusing her to the spot.

'Yes,' she stated boldly, still ashamed at the way she'd needed to rebel against everything she'd stood for, every moral she'd been brought up to believe in. The only problem now was that she could see why her mother had insisted they both move to London. To keep what little of her family she had left together. Wasn't she herself about to throw her life into this man's hands for the sake of her unborn child?

'Why me? Had you planned this outcome all along? This unexpected pregnancy?'

He flung his hands up in a gesture of frustration and turned away from her, giving her time to recover. But any recovery was short-lived. The next time he looked at her angry sparks glittered in his eyes.

'Was that why you didn't insist on contraception?'

'No!' she gasped, and stepped back away from his anger. 'I thought you were telling me it was taken care of.'

He moved towards her and she took another step back until she met the coolness of the wall behind her, finding strength in it.

'Did you perhaps know who I was that night?'

'I had no idea who you were, and if I had I would never, ever have left the party with you.' Angered by her silly notions of fate having brought them together, on that night of all nights, she met his fury head-on. 'I can't do this any more.'

He moved menacingly closer. 'What can't you do?'

His voice had deepened, his accent heightened, and the look in his dark eyes of anger blending with veiled passion made her heart thump so hard it almost hurt.

'This pretence,' she flung at him, unable to unlock her gaze from his or stop the pounding of her heart.

'And what pretence would that be, *cara*?'

'The…the engagement.' She stammered the words out as he moved a little closer, those sexy eyes looking deep into her soul, as if finding the answer she couldn't even give herself.

'I think you mean the cold indifference you have adopted since you arrived in Rome.'

'It is the only way to get through this charade.' She hated it that her voice gave her away and turned into a whisper, that his close proximity was starving her of the last remnants of stamina and strength she had left after the last few hours.

'But it is *not* all a charade—is it, *mia cara*?'

He touched her face, the contact of his fingers on her skin so soft, but she couldn't stop the deep breath being dragged from her. And she hated the satisfaction which played on his lips and sparked in his eyes. She hated him and yet she wanted him. Badly.

'Of course it is.' Her breathing was impossible to control and she drew it in deep and hard as he looked down to her neck, where he must surely see her pulse beating wildly, and then to her breasts, which rose and fell with each deep breath. 'You mean nothing to me.'

'Don't lie.'

The intensity in his eyes sent a spiral of hot need flooding down through her, right to the very heart of her femininity.

'Or I may have to prove you wrong...prove how untrue that is.'

'Don't you dare!' she gasped in shock, while inside a traitorous voice called, *I dare you to.*

The glint in his eyes fired with desire and she knew exactly what he was going to do. He was going to kiss her—and she wanted him to. She wanted to feel his lips on hers, to taste him and so much more. But that wasn't the deal they'd made. The deal they'd made had been on paper only, was one that meant they would have nothing physical to do with each other and certainly nothing emotional.

'Never challenge me, Piper. I always accept—and I always win.'

'Not this time.' She glared up at him, more angry

at her own reaction to him than at his boast of always winning.

'So...' His brows rose suggestively and he placed the palm of one hand on the wall, leaning over her so that his face was so close she only needed to lift her chin and her lips would find his. 'The challenge still stands, no?'

'No...' She dragged the hoarse whisper out, hoping for resolve but knowing she sounded more as if she'd dissolved.

'And if I kiss you will it do nothing to you?'

'Of course it won't. There is nothing between us.' Thankfully that declaration had sounded more convincing.

'Are you quite sure, *cara*?'

His palm spread across her face, the pad of his thumb caressing the line of her lips, and she hated the way her eyes closed and the sound of her breath was ragged and uneven before a soft sigh slipped from her.

Why should she fight it? Whatever it was that had exploded between them in London was still there. She wanted to experience it again, to lose herself in the moment of oblivion. She wanted him—and didn't having what you shouldn't want get things out of your system?

Dante braced his arm against the wall as he looked down at Piper. His thumb tingled from sliding it over the lips he ached to kiss. He hadn't slept with a woman since that night in London, telling himself he was too busy, but now he knew it was because he'd still wanted Piper. Somehow she'd crossed over the usually impenetrable barriers around his emotions and now, after spending a week with her, he had to accept the truth. He still yearned for her and there was only one way to deal with such needs. Sate them.

He looked down at her. Expectancy was in those luscious green eyes. She wanted him as much as he wanted her. The hot, sultry passion which swirled in her eyes matched that which spiralled deep within him. Pure carnal lust. Just as it had been the night they'd come together so explosively in London. A night which had changed his life in more ways than he'd anticipated since she'd dropped her bombshell news that morning in his office.

'You are so beautiful.' His thoughts became words— not out of a need to charm, as was his usual seduction routine, but because he wanted her to know what he truly felt. 'And all I want to do right now is kiss you.'

She wrapped her arms around his neck and he pushed his body against her, pinning her to the wall, delving his fingers in the mass of soft red curls which framed her face. His eyes met hers briefly as their faces almost touched, and it satisfied him to see insatiable desire spark higher than ever, setting off a wild reaction within him.

She was his. This woman was his. And tonight he would reclaim her in the most basic way. He lowered his head, intending to brush his lips over hers and tease her into wanting him, but drew in a sharp breath as her lips met his, the need in them undeniable as she took control of the kiss, demanding almost too much from him.

He cursed in Italian against her mouth, tasting her as he did so, tasting her hunger and the desire which matched his, spark for spark. He pressed her harder against the wall, feeling her breasts against his chest and her hips moving wantonly, making him harder than he'd ever been.

He pulled back, briefly stunned by the ferocity of the desire which had leapt like flames around them. The fire of lust threatened to claim them, and right now it was all he wanted.

Piper plunged her fingers into his hair, pulling him back to her. 'Kiss me,' she demanded, and he smiled as he recognised the woman he'd made love to in London.

The hot temptress who'd pushed him further than any woman had ever done was back, and this time she wouldn't be slipping away. Not until he was ready to let her go.

'I intend to do more than kiss you.' The guttural growl which left him sounded positively feral, and his whole body pulsed with desire, demanding immediate satisfaction.

Before he could say anything else she pressed her lips against his once more, the kiss demanding and erotic. She gasped into his mouth as his tongue met hers, sending his heart rate soaring. Only once before had he experienced such wild passion, such fierce desire, and that had been with this woman. The one who'd given her virginity to him and now carried his child. She was truly his. No matter what happened that would never change.

He slid his palm down her throat, pausing as her kiss deepened, became more demanding. Then he moved his hand over her breast, her nipple a tight bud beneath the fabric of her dress, and he had an uncontrollable urge to rip the fabric from her, to expose the delicious breasts so he could taste them and nip at them with his teeth until she cried out with pleasure as she had done that last time.

'Dante…' She groaned his name softly against his lips and pressed her hips tighter against him.

An explosion of hot need was rushing through him.

There wouldn't be any stopping now. This fiery desire had to meet its conclusion, and fast.

While he kissed her, teasing her tongue with his, he slid his hand down to her waist then on to her hips, grasping the fabric of the dress and rucking it up until he could move his hand inside it and feel the soft, warm skin of her thigh. She stopped kissing him and he looked at her as desire throbbed relentlessly in every part of him, demanding satisfaction.

The look in those green eyes still dared him, still goaded him to take her. Her breath was fast and hard, her lips bruised, but still it wasn't enough. He began to stroke her gently with his fingers, and watched as she held her breath when he touched her through her panties. She was as hot for him as he was for her.

'Do you still dare me?' he said hoarsely as he ceased his exploration, moving instead back to her hips and the thin strip of lace which was all that stopped him from claiming her as his once more.

Anger sparked in her eyes, making fireworks of passion and fury explode in them.

'Yes,' she whispered raggedly as her fingers entwined in the hair at the nape of his neck, sending shivers of pleasure he'd never known before down his back. 'I still dare you.'

He held her gaze as he hitched his fingers around the lace and gently pulled. She continued to glare at him, and that mix of anger and fiery passion was almost his undoing. She raised her brow, its slender arch lifting higher in the most alluring way.

'Are you sure, *cara*?'

'I dare you,' she whispered fiercely, in a sexy and husky way, doing untold things to him.

In one swift tug he'd pulled her tiny lace panties apart at the seam.

'Dante!' She gasped in surprise, but made no move to prevent anything else he might do.

'And do you still insist there is nothing between us?'

'Yes.' Her green eyes widened as he moved his hand, trailing his fingers through the curls which shielded her hot, feminine warmth. 'Nothing at all.'

'Yet you want my touch, don't you, *cara*?'

She closed her eyes as he slid his fingers between her thighs. Hot need pulsed through him as he felt how much she wanted him, but he *had* to remain in control. He had to be the one to lead this frenzied and unexpected dance of desire.

'Dante, we can't… Please don't…' She gasped as his touch teased her, pushing her closer and closer to the brink.

'We can and we will.'

He continued to touch and explore her, increasing his need to thrust deep into her—but first he wanted to push her to a climax, to prove how much she wanted him. She writhed against him and clung to him as that climax shook over her body. She was so responsive, so hot. He wanted her right there, against the wall. He couldn't stop now.

Piper opened her eyes, hardly able to believe what had just happened. She felt weak, but still wanted more, and that heady need drove any last remnants of sense from her mind as her shaking hands moved downward to unfasten his trousers. She had to feel him. She had to touch him in the same mind-blowing way he'd touched her. And more importantly she had to take back the control he'd stolen from her with such alarming ease.

He bowed his head almost to her shoulder as with one hand he intervened and freed the hard length of his erection. She felt its heated hardness as he nipped at her neck, the sensation so wild, so new and exciting, she thought she might lose her mind. A deep growl came from him as she wrapped her fingers around him.

Before she could act on any of the new and strange needs filling her body Dante lifted her up. Instinctively she wrapped her legs around him, using the wall behind her to keep her where she wanted to be—intimately against him.

He looked at her, his eyes so black with desire, so intense, they sent a shower of need all over her. Emboldened by the power she now seemed to possess over him, she moved her hips until she could feel the heat of him touch her.

Something wild and unknown was whipping around them like a storm, and it spiralled ever higher. All she could do was look down into the blackness of his eyes as he held her and then the storm stilled. The air around them was heavy with expectancy. She'd heard of the eye of the storm, but had never expected it be like this—with a man like Dante Mancini.

'Dante?' she said expectantly, wanting more and yet suddenly wondering if she'd gone too far.

His answer was a demanding and bruising kiss, and she closed her eyes as his tongue forced itself into her mouth, starting up the wild and erotic dance once more. She moved her hips as he held her against the wall, positioning herself so that she could feel him, tease him, punish him.

A fluid Italian curse left his lips as he broke the kiss to pull back slightly and look at her. Again that expectancy filled the air. His eyes turned sinfully black and he moved with her. In that moment she realised she hadn't been in control at all—she hadn't even been the one teasing or punishing him. But she didn't care about any of that any more. All she wanted was Dante deep inside her. *Now.*

As if he'd read her thoughts he thrust into her, pushing her hard against the wall as his fingers gripped her naked thighs, keeping her just where he wanted her. Just where she wanted to be. She clung to him as if her life depended on it. Maybe it did.

Passion engulfed her as he pulled back, then thrust into her again. An explosion of pulsing need erupted inside her as each thrust took him deeper into her. She moved with him, as if her body had been born to do this with him. He'd awoken the woman in her that night in London, and now all she wanted was to be totally possessed by him.

As she moved his lips sought hers in a kiss so wild and passionate her head spun with dizziness and she closed her eyes, giving herself up to the sensation of being Dante's. With each passing second their breaths became harder and faster. Erratically he kissed down her throat as she let her head fall back against the wall, unable to do anything other than follow the moment.

'Dante!' she cried out as he pushed her higher and faster towards yet another climax. Each frenzied move he made was taking him deeper inside her, exactly where she wanted him to be.

His reply, savage and foreign, only heightened her need for him and she moved with him in a wild dance where all sense or reason was lost.

'You are mine, Piper—*mine.*'

As the world around her exploded his hoarsely whispered words didn't mean anything and she cried out again, aware of Dante's harsh cries as he too found his release.

She clung to him as her body began to shake but didn't dare say anything. Her pulse slowed and she knew she'd played a dangerous game—and lost. The last words he'd said before they'd both exploded with desire had been triumphant, proving that whatever had sparked between them in London was still there and that she wanted him as much as ever.

He looked at her, his dark eyes still wild and full of desire. Slowly he released her, and when her feet touched the floor she was glad of the wall for support. Without a word he took her hand and led her to the stairs.

This wasn't finished yet—and neither did she want it to be.

CHAPTER EIGHT

PIPER LAY CONTENTED in Dante's arms, her back pressed against him as he held her. She studied the gold signet ring on his right hand as he slept. The elaborate 'A' clearly meant something. Was it the initial of a woman who had broken his heart, making it impossible for him to love again? Was that why he was always so cold and calculated?

Dante stirred and she turned round in his embrace to look at him. With his hair tousled from lovemaking and then sleep he looked irresistible, but she would have to resist him. Now was not the time to risk falling for him and she suspected she was perilously close to doing just that. Right now there were practical issues to discuss.

'*Buongiorno, mia cara.*'

His husky voice was as sexy as he looked, and she wondered if she hadn't left him in that hotel in London whether she would have woken to such a warm greeting. Would he have been as pleased to see her in his bed as he was now? Probably not. She wouldn't have had anything to offer him then—nothing to barter with as she did now. No, she was right to have left that night. But she was glad she knew what it was like to wake within the warm embrace of this man's arms.

'Morning.' Shyness crept over her.

'You didn't run out on me this time, *cara*.'

His eyes darkened, and she knew she would have to leave the bed before he convinced her otherwise.

'No, but that's exactly what I am about to do now.' She threw back the covers and tried hard to pretend that she didn't care at all that she was naked and that he was watching her every move.

'And why would that be?'

A shiver of pleasure slithered down her spine. His voice was tantalisingly sexy but she ignored it and grabbed her robe and headed for the shower.

'We have things to discuss about our deal and where we go from here.'

She spoke over her shoulder, and without waiting for his response went into the en-suite shower room and turned on the shower, trying not to think too hard about the fact that their engagement would not only help him get the deal he wanted so badly, and salvage his reputation with the charity, it would also involve their families. Neither of them had a father in their lives, but their mothers deserved to know about the baby, be a part of its life.

She discarded her robe and stepped under the warm jets, closing her eyes as the water cascaded over her. She could still hear her mother's voice when they'd spoken after her arrival in Rome. It had only been then that she'd been brave enough to tell her about Dante, knowing that it might very easily appear in the press, and she still needed to tell her about the baby.

Lost in thought, she didn't hear Dante as he stepped into the shower, and she gave a startled cry as he pulled her against him. Through the warmth of the water pounding down on her she was in no doubt of his intentions.

'What are you doing?' She laughed, never having expected this. It was something lovers would do, wasn't it? And she and Dante were as far from being lovers as they had ever been.

'Making the most of this gorgeous body whilst it's still naked.' He kissed her—a long, lingering kiss—and her senses became heightened by the water as it spilled over them and she willingly kissed him back, wanting this last moment of passion with him before she broached the subject of their engagement and what it would mean to everyone.

'Come back to bed,' he said in a husky voice.

The fire of desire was burning bright in his eyes, fuelling her own even more. He turned off the shower and took her hand and led her out, pausing to wrap her in a large towel. She cuddled into it, sneaking a glance at him as he took a smaller towel and dried his body before wrapping it around his hips. That didn't quell the throb of desire just being this close to him ignited, and the slow burn of desire rose inside her once more.

Before she could say anything he led her back to the bedroom, back to the large bed and the rumpled cream sheets, tossing aside the distinctly masculine bronze covers.

'I intend to make love to you again before we discuss anything.'

'But we should talk.'

'No talking.'

He pushed her gently back onto the bed, the towel she clutched around her falling open, exposing her to his gaze. But he didn't take advantage of that for too long. He dropped the towel he'd slung around his hips to the floor and joined her on the bed, kissing down her body.

As he reached her still flat stomach he pressed light

feathery kisses to it, and in her lust-drugged stupor she imagined him kissing his child. His hands caressed her waist in the most loving of gestures and she had to squeeze her eyes shut against a tear that threatened to fall.

Piper clutched at the sheets when he moved lower, hardly able to believe the sensations rushing around her. Love and lust were becoming entwined and she knew it was dangerous. This wouldn't sort things out, but it was certainly a distraction she was prepared to endure. He made her feel alive. He made her feel beautiful. And after years of thinking she didn't deserve love it was almost too much—because this wasn't love. It could never be love.

He kissed his way back up, over her stomach to her breasts, teasing each hardened nipple in turn before moving over her, the hardness of his erection encouraging her to become his once more. It was a temptation too much and she welcomed him into her, relished the fizz of desire with each move he made and abandoned herself to the moment once more.

Dante's body still hummed from the amazing sex he'd enjoyed with Piper since they'd returned to his villa last night. He'd never intended to take her so roughly, and especially not against the wall in his living room, but she did something to him no other woman had done. Just as she had done that night in his hotel room in London. She made him lose control, made him forget everything. She drove him wild.

Now he watched her cross the living room to join him as he sat in front of a newly lit fire. It might not be winter yet but he wanted the comfort of it and the way it made him relax, and he wanted to share this special time with Piper. For the first time ever he wanted to allow a woman close—for a while at least.

'Oh, an open fire. Now, *that's* something I'm not used to.' She smiled at him and sat in a large chair, curling her jean-clad legs under her.

'It's much better from over here.' He surprised himself by inviting her to come closer to him. It might be down to the way he always felt relaxed here, or the intimacy they'd shared since arriving, but he wanted her close. He'd never wanted *anyone* close. What was happening to him?

'I guess so.' Shyness entered her voice and a blush spread over her cheeks as she went to sit on the sofa next to him, concentrating intently on the fire as if she couldn't look at him. 'It's quite romantic, really.'

Romantic? Had he been trying for 'romantic' when he'd lit it, envisaging them curled up together enjoying each other's company? He'd wanted to escape everything, just for today, but romance was the last thing he wanted to make her think of. He didn't believe in romance and definitely didn't want it in his life. Such things led to more complicated emotions like love, and that was something he didn't want to tango with—for any price.

'I find a fire relaxing,' he said guardedly. 'It's one of my winter pleasures when I'm here at the villa.'

'We do need to talk.' She spoke with caution and glanced across at him. 'About last night.'

'Do you mean the amazing success you made of coaxing Bettino D'Antonio round with your talk of art, or what happened when we returned?' He also spoke with caution, anxious that she didn't make too much of the hours they'd spent in bed, the amount of times they'd had sex. He never thought of it as making love. That would give it an entirely different meaning.

'The dinner.' Indignation cracked in her voice. 'Do you really think Bettino was impressed?'

Dante moved across the sofa towards her, took her hand and pressed her fingers to his lips. '*Mia cara*, you positively charmed him, and I am certain that it will be not one but two contracts which will be coming our way.'

He had a good feeling about the deal now, and he knew he had Piper to thank for that. Her talk of art, of wanting to run her own curating business, had been so spontaneous, so full of enthusiasm, D'Antonio had been unable to resist her—and if truth be told neither had he. He'd sat and watched as her eyes had sparkled with genuine joy and shone with pleasure whilst she was talking about art. He'd also been just a little put out that he hadn't known exactly how important the subject was to her. She'd told him she liked to visit art galleries, but it was obvious it was far more than that.

'But I'm not qualified. I didn't finish my course and I don't have a business.' She paled as the implications hit her. 'I can't take a contract—not when there are good companies out there already. And there's the baby...'

'A business can be started right now if you want. Your knowledge of the subject is more than enough.'

'You don't know that.'

'I'm sure it's sufficient, at least. How far into your degree were you?'

'I'd nearly finished. I was in my last year when my father got sick. I only had my final exams to do, really. I meant to go back, but...'

'That's more than enough to start with. And a commission from D'Antonio would set you up—if that's what you want.'

'I'll think about it.'

The reservation in her voice made him want to hold her and tell her he'd help her. Why did he want to do that? Why did he feel the need to tangle himself up emotionally with this woman more than he already was?

He shrugged, letting her hand go, and sat back, studying her pensive expression. There was more—much more to her reservation. He could feel it.

'I have other things to do first.'

She looked up at him and he held her gaze, challenging her to speak her mind, say what was bothering her—because something was.

'What is so important, Piper?'

She looked uncertainly at him and apprehension settled over him, suffocating the relaxed peace he'd found.

'I'd like us both to go to London.' After holding his gaze for the briefest of moments she looked down, her long lashes shutting him out.

'Is there something in particular you wish to do there? Somewhere you want to be seen to validate our engagement?' He kept his voice light, but inside the fingers of dread were closing in, threatening to choke him. This woman, who'd claimed to want nothing from him, now seemed to want much more than he could ever give.

'Yes.' She nodded. 'I'd like us to see my mother.'

The thump to his chest as the reality of his fears hit him was hard. 'No. This engagement is to secure a business deal and to legitimise our child. There is no need to bring family members into it.'

Unease shrouded him. What would *his* mother think when she read in the papers or the glossy magazines that he was to be married? Worse still, that he was to be a father?

'Surely *your* mother will want to know? Even if you can't tell her the sordid truth.'

The spike of hurt in her voice should have made him feel guilty, but already he could feel his emotions closing off, feel himself withdrawing. They'd shared a night of passion and it should have changed nothing, but somehow it had changed everything.

'My mother will know only what she has to, and I suggest you do the same with your mother. This is not a real engagement and there isn't any need to complicate it further.' Anger surged through him as he fought back the fear of what his mother would think of his latest deal, of the false hope he might give her that he'd finally left the past behind.

'Haven't we already done that with last night?'

She hurled the accusation at him, her green eyes wide and full of hurt. Already he was upsetting her, causing her pain. As soon as he became close to anyone he did something to hurt them or turn them away, until ultimately they left his life.

'*You* complicated things in London, leading me to believe protection wasn't required.' Immediately he took his usual stance of self-defence, angry that she'd made him feel and, worse, that he cared how *she* felt.

'No wonder your brother left home as soon as he could!'

Dante saw a mist of red descend at the mention of Alessio. As if he didn't already have enough to worry about, she'd opened that wound too. '*Never* bring my brother into this. He and my mother are the reason I fought to make a living, the reason I had to make something of myself. Everything I did, I did for them. I wanted to give them a better life, but it was too late for my brother.'

She looked up at him, her earlier prickly demeanour evaporating. 'Too late? Why?'

The questions filled the void which had opened up between them, connecting them once more in a way he wasn't sure he could handle.

'My brother kept the wrong company, and after he became a teenager he was always in trouble.' Dante felt the pull of the connection between him and Piper just as surely as he felt her sympathetic gaze on him. He sensed the danger in opening himself up, exposing emotions he'd buried many years ago.

'What happened?'

She looked as beautiful as he'd ever seen her. But something inside him had changed. She'd opened a door he'd closed and forgotten about. A door that couldn't be closed again now.

Mentally he shook himself. It wouldn't do either of them any good to be weighed down with emotions. 'He resented my authority over him and rebelled against anything I said.'

'But isn't that what all teenagers do?'

Her smile was warm as she leaned closer. He inhaled her perfume, the same scent which had tormented him in the elevator at his office the morning after his meeting with Xander, Zayn and Benjamin. His life was unrecognisable now.

'Not all teenagers run away, leaving behind a distraught mother.' He gritted his teeth together as the sound of his mother's sobs filled his mind. Piper had opened up the memory and now he couldn't stop it coming back.

'Did you find him? I mean…he *did* come back, didn't he?' She stumbled over her words, probably due to the anger that must be clearly etched on his face. Damn it, he had no wish to talk about this with anyone—least of all this woman.

The pain of those first days after Alessio had gone still haunted him. Every time he'd looked at his mother he'd known she blamed *him*, known it was his fault. He'd driven Alessio away. He'd tried to be a father figure before he had really become a man himself, taking on the role of disciplining his wild brother when he had been only seventeen. For three years a battle of wills had raged between him and Alessio—until his sixteenth birthday. The day he'd walked out of the small house where his mother had struggled to bring them up. It had been the last time they'd seen him alive.

'We had no idea where he was for four years.'

'So you *did* find him?'

Dante recalled the horror of the day he'd found out the truth of Alessio's disappearance. The fact that his brother had died alone years before was something he could never forgive himself for.

'I found out that he'd died alone at the age of eighteen.'

The gasp of shock which came from Piper told him what he already knew. It was shocking, and it was *his* fault. He stared into the flames of the fire which had cooled to a gentle orange glow, wrapping around the logs. He couldn't look at Piper. He didn't want to see the shock or the blame on her face. It would only confirm what he'd believed ever since that day.

'That is so sad,' she said in a whisper, but still he couldn't look at her.

'He died at the hands of a rival street gang. It was my fault. I should have made him come home when he first left. It was my job to keep him safe.'

She touched his arm and he looked at her. The compassion in her eyes was too much. 'It's *not* your fault, Dante.'

'I failed him, Piper. I failed him *and* my mother. I didn't do what I was supposed to do. I didn't protect and care for them.'

When Piper had told him she was carrying his child he'd appeared to give more importance to the deal and salvaging his reputation, but it was the need to look after her and his baby which had driven him to such drastic action. He'd never thought it would be possible for him to care, to want to put himself in a vulnerable position again, but as soon as he'd known why she'd come to Rome it had been the only thing he wanted to do.

Piper looked at Dante. The pain in his eyes was too much to bear and she wanted to hold him, tell him it wasn't his fault and try and ease his pain—just as he had done for her when she'd finally confessed to the blindness which had affected her left eye since birth. That hadn't mattered to him and this didn't matter to her. She wanted him to see he *wasn't* to blame—not when he'd been so young himself.

'You mustn't blame yourself,' she said, and gently squeezed his arm, wanting to offer some kind of comfort.

'You don't know anything about it.' He pulled his arm free of her touch, and the rejection stung her far more than any icy words.

'I want to know.' She watched as he pressed his thumb and finger against his signet ring, just as he'd done whilst she'd read over the contract he'd drawn up. He'd stood over her then and tension had crackled in the air, just as it did now. 'What if I meet your mother? Shouldn't I at least know something?'

He swore harshly in Italian, but she resisted the urge to step back and drop the subject. She needed to

know about his past. Not only because she might meet
someone who knew, but because she wanted to—for her
child. His mother was her child's grandmother. Could
he deny her that?

'There will be no meeting between you and my
mother. I will explain the true situation to her, and I
suggest you tell yours. That way neither of us will give
false hope to anyone.'

'False hope of what? Love and happiness?' She tried
to keep the hurt from sounding in her voice, but his
rejection of her cut deep. Even so, what he said made
sense. Maybe telling her mother the truth, instead of
dressing it up as a fairytale romance, would be best.
At least that way she wouldn't have to explain when
he walked away from her, leaving her a single mother,
alone in the world except for her own mother.

'Love and happiness are for fools,' he said, and
scowled at her, reminding her of that morning in his
office when she had been positively the last person he'd
wanted to find waiting for him. He touched his ring
again, drawing her attention back to his brother.

'Whatever happened to your brother, it's *not* your
fault.' She moved towards him again, desperate to know
more and understand.

'I wanted to make a better life for my mother. She
had a tough time bringing up two boys alone and in
poverty, and Alessio was wilful and rebellious even
as a child.'

Piper recalled the article she'd read in *Celebrity Spy!*
Whilst going to great lengths to expose his playboy
lifestyle, it had credited him with having made his own
fortune. Had he really been motivated by the need to
provide for his brother Alessio?

She looked at him, then at his hand. 'Was the ring his?'

The question was out before she could think, before she could stop it, and for a second the air around her froze as he looked at her. She bit her bottom lip and watched as he looked down at his right hand, at the gold signet ring she'd studied as he'd slept beside her that morning.

'I bought it for his sixteenth birthday and planned to give it to him that evening, after a family meal, but Alessio had other ideas and he'd long since gone. I spent the night consoling my mother and being angry with him, wanting only to banish the selfish youngster from my mind and my life.'

She put her hand to her mouth to stifle a gasp of shock, but it still slipped out. 'That must have been terrible for your mother.'

'I have never forgiven myself for doing that to her.'

'You?'

'If I hadn't ruled Alessio so hard, trying to shape him into the man I wanted him to be instead of allowing him to find out who he was, this conversation wouldn't be happening.'

'I still don't see how it's your fault,' she said, exasperation getting the better of her.

'That, *cara*, is because you do not know me. Nothing good will come of you being entangled in my life.'

'Our child will come of it, and to me that is good.' She flung the words at him, angry that he wouldn't let her close, wouldn't let her past the invisible barrier he had around him.

Slowly he moved towards her and reached out, touching her face. Her anger melted away and she yearned for more than a caress to her face.

'You have a very generous nature. Never let anyone change that. Least of all me.'

Before she could say anything else he brushed his lips over hers and her eyelashes fluttered down. As he moved back, away from her, it was as if he was going behind a barrier of ice. She could still see him, but the coldness in his eyes, the frozen set of his shoulders, warned her that what they'd shared during the weekend was finished.

'What happened between us here is over. We made our deal and stated our terms and now it is time to bring it all to a conclusion.'

CHAPTER NINE

THEIR FIRST MORNING back in Rome, Piper awoke alone in the bed—just as Dante had warned her. After an exquisite weekend entwined around his lean body she knew that what they'd shared in Tuscany was over. He had a deal to secure and she had a role to play.

She'd sensed his withdrawal as he'd driven them back to Rome. Each passing hour had distanced him from the man he'd been in Tuscany. He'd returned to being the man she'd seen arriving at his office that morning, the aloof man who trusted nobody and kept everyone at a distance. The ruthless businessman was back.

She slipped from the bed, her limbs still aching from the hours of wonderful sex with Dante. How could she, an innocent woman who'd had no experience of men before she'd met Dante, have become such a different woman? One who matched his expertise and skill as a lover? Without even touching her he'd had her yearning for him. And she'd responded with eagerness, wanting to give him as much pleasure as he gave her.

Even though her body belonged to him she couldn't give him her heart, couldn't allow herself to fall for him. Whatever it was between them, it had to stay as lust—although if she was brave enough to admit it she'd acknowledge that her emotions had long since passed that point. Something she had to conceal from him. The deal they'd struck was just that. A deal.

She pushed back a wave of nausea and strengthened her resolve to put aside her emotions as she made her way to the doors leading onto the terrace. She'd quickly realised he favoured the outdoors in the mornings, even though winter had brought a chill to the air.

'Good morning,' she said.

'I had not expected you to be up yet.'

He strode over from where he'd been standing, looking out over the city, moving back inside, and as he passed she caught his freshly showered scent and aftershave. He poured coffee and she tried hard to regain her assaulted senses from the strong aroma. For a moment, as dizziness and nausea took charge and she clung to the doorframe, she wasn't aware that he was talking to her.

'Are you well?'

'I…' Her head spun and words refused to form. She reached for the back of a chair in a desperate attempt to remain standing as her stomach turned over and blackness threatened to claim her.

She heard Dante's angry words as she closed her eyes. She wanted to fight it, but couldn't, and she let herself slip into the calm oblivion of darkness. Then she felt his arms around her, her body pressed against the safety and strength of his, and forced her eyes open, forced her head to stop spinning.

He looked down at her as he lifted her into his arms. 'You are going back to bed to wait for the doctor.'

She wanted to fight him, wanted to tell him that most women felt faint and suffered sickness in pregnancy, but she was scared. She'd never felt so ill in her life, so weak and defeated. Surely this wasn't right? But she had nobody to ask for reassurance—nobody but Dante. She was completely at his mercy.

She closed her eyes as another wave of dizziness hurtled over her.

'The fact that you are unable to argue with me is worrying,' he said, and she opened her eyes again, allowing the deep tones of his voice to drag her back from the dark oblivion her body so desperately sought.

She fought the hurt which spiked through her at the angry tone of his words. Where was the tender and gentle man she'd made love with yesterday morning as the sun had risen over the Tuscan hills? What had happened to the man who'd opened up to her, pulling down his barriers to let her into his world?

He'd shared things with her she suspected he hadn't shared for a long time. If he'd kept those barriers lowered for long enough would she have found a warm and loving man who was hurting and blaming himself for something which wasn't his fault? A man who needed love? Could she love the man she'd seen that day in Tuscany?

Yes, she could.

The realisation hit her as his hold on her tightened, but she couldn't allow herself to love this man. He looked down at her, fierce hardness etched on his handsome face as he negotiated the furniture and took her back to the bedroom she'd just left.

He laid her on the bed, his arms lingering around her, keeping her close and reminding her of the passion they'd shared over the weekend. Her gaze met his and the caramel-brown of his eyes darkened, the emotion within them unreadable. She drew in a breath which sounded as ragged as if he'd just kissed her and he pulled himself away, pressing his palm briefly against her forehead before standing tall at the bedside. For a moment she thought she saw genuine concern in his eyes, but quickly it was chased away by hard anger.

'I wanted to talk about our need to do more to create a love affair real enough to silence the gossips of the world, But not now. You need to rest.'

A tremor of sickness and disappointment washed over Piper. The only thing he was concerned about was his stupid deal. 'Very well,' she said as he looked down at her, feeling the warmth of his touch still on her forehead. 'Our charade will continue until there isn't a shred of doubt that you are a reformed man.'

She couldn't keep the spike of anger from her voice as panic rushed over her. What if he backed out of the deal now? What if he refused to have anything to do with their child?

'Not until you are well. Think of the baby, Piper, and do as I say. Just for once.' Exasperation entwined with anger, making each word short and sharp.

So he cared about the baby, did he? Suddenly she felt very scared—for herself and for the baby. She turned away from him as tears began to slip down her cheeks. This wasn't what she'd come to Rome for. A fake engagement to further his business was not worth risking her baby over, and that was what she was doing now. Risking her baby.

Tears cascaded down her face, but she kept her face hidden from him, not wanting to see the anger in those eyes or the harsh lines of annoyance on his face. Finally she heard him leave, and his fluid Italian curse could not be mistaken as his footsteps receded.

Guilt hung over Dante as he waited for the doctor to come out of Piper's room. He'd done it again. Let down someone who was relying on him. He hadn't cared for Piper as he should have, had thought of nothing but himself, and now she was ill. Worse than that, his selfish need to get the deal of a lifetime had put his baby at risk.

He closed his eyes against such dark thoughts, against the past mingling menacingly with the present. What if she lost the baby—*his* baby? It would be his fault. Just as Alessio leaving home had been.

With alarming clarity he realised he wanted this child, his son or daughter, but that didn't alter the fact that the woman who carried his child had agreed to his suggested deal, creating her own terms. Neither did it change the fact that after the way he'd handled things with Alessio he wasn't fit to be a father.

The click of the door as the doctor came out jolted him from that dark and painful thought. He wanted to ask if she was going to be okay, if the baby was well, but his mouth had become dry and words refused to form.

'Your fiancée and your baby need rest, Signor Mancini, and love and care.' The old man's smile was in total contrast to the warning tone of his voice. Or was that guilt, making him imagine the doctor's disapproval?

'Then rest is what she will have,' he said, firmly putting aside the option of love and care. He couldn't do either. Piper would be better without him in her life, but what of his child—his flesh and blood? Could he allow the past to chase him away from his own child? Even if it was a child he'd never intended to have... never wanted?

'I will call again tomorrow.'

'*Grazie.*'

He couldn't say anything else and for a moment stood looking at the door of the bedroom, terrified of the future that lay within. Already he'd hurt Piper, pushed her too hard in creating their fake love affair, insisting on changing her and parading her around Rome. Once they'd arrived in Tuscany their time at the villa had been so different, so unexpected. He'd gone back on his self-made promise and had lost control. As if he'd wanted to see what he could have if only he opened himself up to feeling emotion. Had *he* caused this? Had his selfish desire for her made her ill?

He walked slowly into the bedroom, the accusations of the past walking alongside him like dark shadows. He wanted to protect and care for Piper, but how could he when his heart was stone-cold? How could he when he'd already proved he wasn't fit to be a father?

'I'm sorry to be a nuisance,' she said as she propped herself up against the pillows, tears still shining in her eyes. Tears *he* was responsible for.

Something clutched at his heart, squeezing it hard, but all he could feel was guilt. 'It is me who should apologise,' he said crisply, averting his gaze from her still pale face to look out through the window over the rooftops of Rome. 'I expected too much.'

'But what about the party this evening? How can we convince everyone if I am not with you?'

A tremor of panic wobbled in her voice, ratcheting up his guilt.

'There will be other parties. You must rest for the baby's sake.' He turned to look at her and the worried frown on her face cut deep into his heart, proving he wasn't as cold and detached as he'd thought.

'I just want all this over, Dante.'

She swallowed hard and took a deep breath, and he looked into her eyes, where beneath the tiredness he saw fierce determination.

'There is nothing we can do about the deal but wait.'

Compelled to go to her, he sat down on the edge of the bed and took her hand in his. What was it about this woman that made rational and sensible thought almost impossible? She'd changed him, made him yearn for things that were impossible. Was it that hint of what might have been if his past hadn't blocked the way what made her so alluring, so very tempting and irresistible?

'Is that all that's important to you, Dante? The deal?'

Piper couldn't keep the disappointment from her voice. After everything they'd shared at the weekend, all the barriers which had been broken down, he still only wanted the deal.

She held her breath as Dante moved back towards the bed and sat down on the edge, taking her hand in his. She looked at her pale skin against his tanned hands and as his fingers tightened around hers couldn't ignore how safe it made her feel. His hand was warm and large and very comforting.

'All I want is for you to get well.'

Dante's voice, soft and alarmingly sexy, drew her gaze up and to his face. Something new and unreadable was in his eyes, making her breath catch audibly in her throat.

'You wouldn't have become ill if things had been different, had gone as planned.'

Piper watched as his free hand closed over the top of hers, making pulling her hand away impossible—just as pulling back her emotions was becoming so difficult. The only thing which hadn't gone according to the terms of the deal they'd agreed was their time in Tuscany. Their weekend of being lovers. Did he regret it?

'What things?' she asked, needing to know what was going on. She was falling deeper and harder for him and she had to know how he felt. He was such a closed-off man, this might be her only chance.

'We agreed that not being intimate was part of the deal. "A marriage on paper" was, I think, the term you used.'

His fingers were caressing her hand, distracting her from thinking too deeply about what she'd said and what she'd allowed to happen. She was about to tell him that when he spoke again.

'I should have had more control.'

'Dante, you mustn't blame yourself all the time.' Her voice was a whisper as he looked directly into her eyes as if searching for the truth. For a brief moment she thought he might lean forward and kiss her. Instead he spoke firmly, and the moment of reflection was over.

'We are both responsible for what happened in Tuscany.'

How could she tell him she'd been so desperate for his touch, his kiss, that she would have sold her soul to the devil if it had meant she could be his once more? What would he think of her if she did?

'It won't happen again. You have my word.'

He withdrew his hands, leaving hers feeling cold. She pulled away, clutching both hands against her to deflect the pain those words had caused. She didn't want his word. She wanted it to happen again. She wanted to be loved by him. Truly loved.

'Then we still have a deal.' The words shot from her before she had time to consider their meaning.

He stood up, a hardened glint in his eyes, the softness of moments ago gone. '*Va bene.* As soon as you are rested we shall resume our act of lovers. There are many more events in coming days where our appearance together will set the tongues of gossip wagging.'

Inside, the weakness which had washed over her that morning slipped away and a steely determination to finish this once and for all replaced it. Reassured by the doctor that she'd just been doing too much, and the baby wasn't in any danger, she was now determined to achieve her part of the deal. All she had to keep telling herself was that this was for her baby, to keep its father in their lives.

'As I said, I just want to get this over with. So please make whatever arrangements you want for tomorrow night.' Her voice was hard, but it didn't appear to affect him at all.

'There is an opera tomorrow night I'd like us to attend. If the doctor assures me everything is as it should be we shall attend.' Any hint of concern had left his face and his voice. The mercenary man who'd put the deal to her was back—and firmly in control.

'Everything is fine, Dante. It is normal for a woman to feel unwell early in her pregnancy.' She tried to keep her voice light, but couldn't look at him.

'That may be so, but I will not take any risks.'

Piper's heart thumped ever harder. Was he trying to say he cared about her—or more? Did this mean what they'd shared in Tuscany had been real and not just a moment of lust?

Before she could say anything, or allow those thoughts to grow, his firm words cut down any hope. 'The baby is vital to this deal.'

With those cruel words lingering in the air, he left, unaware of just how much emotional pain she was in after stupidly believing there was the hope of something more between them—something they could build on for their child's future happiness.

CHAPTER TEN

THE FOLLOWING EVENING Dante waited on the terrace as the lights of Rome sparkled around him. He felt free out here, free to think—or at least that was how it had been until he'd let Piper into his life. Now she filled his every thought, sneaking in where no woman had ever been, making everything complicated. On top of that, his mother had heard of their engagement and despite his denial that he'd fallen in love, despite his telling her that it was purely for business, she was pushing to meet his fiancée. Guilt had sliced into him at the obvious hope in her voice that it was really something more.

'I wasn't sure what an evening at the opera required.'

Piper's now familiar accent cut him off from his thoughts and he turned to see her standing in front of the open doors which led back into his apartment. The light from within filtered around her, showcasing her curves and making him want things he had no right to want. He'd never seen her look so beautiful—or desirable. The red dress she wore was moulded to her body, and the way the fabric crossed over her breasts to form straps caught his attention, infusing him with the kind of need he'd been valiantly denying since their time in Tuscany.

'Red is perfect,' he snapped ungraciously as he

fought down memories of their time together over the weekend—time that could not be repeated.

He'd thought that by giving in to the lust he'd still had for her since London the desire would go. That was all it usually took for his interest in a woman to wane. But then he'd never met a woman like Piper—a woman who made him feel different, made him long for things the likes of which he had no right to want. Not when he'd messed up his brother's and his mother's life. The reality of it was that he wasn't any better than his father, and that was something he'd promised himself as a young man that he would be.

'In that case I'm ready to leave.'

She clutched a silver purse and as she turned, lifting the skirt of her dress to step back into the apartment, he noticed silver sandals, the straps around her ankles suddenly the sexiest thing he'd ever seen.

Did they *have* to go out this evening? The thought of staying in filled his mind, stoking the embers of passion which had burned bright in Tuscany. The thought of relaxing in Piper's company before taking her to bed—*his* bed, not the damned spare room.

He cursed under his breath. No. The charade of their engagement had to be played out. He had to remember why he'd even agreed to it in the first place.

Benjamin Carter's words came unbidden from the back of his mind where he'd relegated them. *'We need to find women who are happy to marry quickly and conveniently. Women we can trust, who will be discreet. Loyal.'*

Piper turned as he entered the apartment. 'Sorry, did you say something?'

'It's time we left. The idea of going to the opera is not

for enjoyment but to make our engagement known—alert the press and offset that article.'

'Yes, I'm aware of that.' Her green eyes speared him with their sudden frostiness.

'Va bene.' He opened the door to his apartment and waited for her to walk through. 'If we get noticed this evening only one or two more dates will be needed, and then hopefully the deal with D'Antonio will be concluded in my favour.'

'Then let's give everyone something to talk about.'

She flounced out and stood in stony silence as the elevator took them down to his waiting car. The silence settled between them as they sat in the back of his car for the short drive to the opera house.

As they entered the grand building he was pleased to see Piper taking her role in his life seriously. She smiled, posing for photographs with him as if she'd been born to a life of high celebrity. She wore the designer clothes with effortless ease, and was so far removed from the redhead who'd sat in his office wearing jeans and a jumper it was unbelievable that it had been little over a week ago.

Even after they'd entered the building and the press had moved their attention to other rich and famous faces Piper kept up the show. He watched her as she spoke with an older couple and knew he should be pleased she'd settled into this new role, but he found it unsettling just how easily she had. She'd moved from being an ordinary girl to one with wealth at her disposal. Playing the role of his fiancée was one she enjoyed, and she seemed determined to sample as much of the lifestyle as she could.

As Piper returned to his side, a genuine smile on her lips, he saw Capricia Conetta bearing down on them and winced inwardly. This would be a true test of Piper's new confident self. Capricia was *not* a woman to hide behind pleasantries.

'*Ciao*, Dante.' The tall, willowy brunette embraced him, kissing him on both cheeks before turning her attention to Piper. 'And *you* are the woman who has managed to persuade the notorious Dante Mancini to put a ring on her finger. Bravo, you. You are obviously a better woman than I am.'

'It was more a case of him persuading *me* to wear it.'

The haughty reply Piper flung at her unknown adversary was unexpected, and Dante resisted the urge to laugh at Capricia's expression.

'Just don't assume you can ever tame him. He is a ruthless man—in the boardroom as well as in the bedroom.' With those spite-laden words hanging in the air, Capricia turned and waltzed off with great drama.

'An ex-lover, by any chance?' Piper turned her attention to him and he nodded, not at all proud to have been associated with such a woman, but before he could respond she quickly added, 'Can we take our seats yet?'

He sensed that the bravado she was hiding behind was in danger of slipping. She wasn't as unaffected by her confrontation with Capricia as she wanted him to think, and she'd gone pale. 'Are you sure you're well enough to go?'

'Of course. The show must go on and all that.'

The bitter snap in her voice told him otherwise, but he guided her to their seats.

'A box?' she queried, a hint of nerves in her voice.

'We are here to be seen. A lovers' date.'

'Of course—how silly of me.'

* * *

For most of the performance Dante had sat on her left and watched Piper, who had been enthralled by all that had happened on the stage. She'd seemed totally oblivious to his presence. He knew it was because he'd been on her blind side, but the fact that she could dismiss him so easily from her mind when he could barely stop thinking about *her* irritated him more than he cared to admit. Not once had she turned to him, shown any display of affection that would have proved to the watching people that they were in love.

Now he sat round a table with four other guests, all of whom were trying to draw as much information as possible from Piper about their engagement. She smiled politely at them, but whenever *he* looked at her she glanced away shyly. The blush that crept over her face should have irritated him, but for some strange reason it didn't. It highlighted how different Piper was from the likes of Capricia, and served only to intensify what he was feeling for her. Even though he wanted to feel nothing at all—for anyone.

'I never thought you'd succumb to marriage,' one man said, and raised his glass at him, irritating Dante further.

But he raised his glass in acknowledgement and recalled his recent conversation with his mother, and her assumption that finally he'd made peace with himself and could settle down and raise a family. If only she knew the truth... But she never would.

'Have you set a date?' an older woman asked Piper, who now turned her attention to him, a smile fixed on her pretty face. But he recognised the message asking for help in her eyes.

'Next summer,' he supplied, and didn't miss the rise of Piper's brows. 'In Tuscany.'

Piper's stomach flipped over at the thought of where she'd be next summer—not only a new mother, but married to the father of her child. How had everything happened so fast when all she'd wanted to do was tell Dante he was to be a father? She'd thought fate had given her a helping hand after she'd seen the article, allowing her to discover the name of the man whose child she carried.

'A summer wedding! You will, of course, have a feature in a magazine?' demanded the woman, before turning her attention to Dante. 'Just make sure it's better than the last one you were named in.'

Piper glanced quickly at Dante, saw his jaw clench against the less than veiled sarcasm and couldn't help herself from reaching out and touching his hand, which was held in a tight fist on the table. He looked abruptly at her and she smiled.

'It will naturally be very different. It will be about what I am certain will be the happiest day of my life.'

Piper's breath caught audibly as he looked at her. The undisguised passion burning in his eyes would leave the older couple in no doubt that he was in love with her. Then, to her surprise, he lifted her fingertips to his lips and kissed them, his gaze firmly fixed on hers.

'Of that I have no doubt,' the older woman said, before launching into an avid discussion in Italian with her husband. And, even though she didn't understand a word, Piper could tell that *she* was the topic of that conversation.

The remainder of the evening went well and Dante's attention to her never once slipped. He'd played his part to perfection, and she too had done the same. She knew he was hoping their engagement would become the talk of Rome society, and that photos of them at the opera would grace the pages of the very magazine which had instigated this whole deal.

All night Piper had tried so hard to keep the smile on her face, but now she ached from the effort and was pleased to be able to shut the door on Rome and the people she'd been mixing with all night. Her nausea hadn't completely abated, and the effort of being an adoring fiancée had become too much. She was exhausted.

She couldn't believe the lifestyle she was now living. It wasn't only the luxury of nice clothes, fabulous places to go or staff on hand to cater to her every need that left her cold—it was the veiled and icy superiority of the people who lived such a life. Whilst Dante appeared comfortable in that world she wasn't entirely convinced he belonged there, or that he wanted to be a part of it. He had seemed more relaxed and happy in Tuscany.

'I'm not sure I enjoy all this attention,' she said as she watched him pour himself a drink.

She should just go straight to bed, but she wouldn't sleep—she was sure of that. Since they'd left the restaurant he'd cooled towards her. His display of affection had been entirely that.

'It takes time to get used to it,' he replied as he put the top back on a crystal decanter, unwittingly giving an answer to her unspoken question.

'How long did it take *you*?'

She wanted to talk, wanted to feel closer to him, to know more of him. Just being physically close wasn't enough—not for her, the girl who'd always dreamt of being whisked away to a happy-ever-after by a knight in shining armour. And even though he was far from that he'd made her feel like a princess this evening.

'I don't recall.' He skilfully evaded her question. 'You look tired. Should you rest? For the sake of the baby?'

So he was concerned—not about her, but the baby. The child he didn't really want…the one that came as part of the deal he'd struck with her to salvage his reputation. Didn't that make him as shallow as all the men and women she'd mixed with tonight?

'Yes, I am.' A hint of concern crossed his handsome face as she spoke a little too sharply. 'I will say goodnight.'

'I will be leaving early tomorrow morning,' he said, and took a sip of his brandy, preferring to look at the amber liquid as he swirled it around the glass and not at her. 'But I suggest you have a restful day. We have a party tomorrow evening.'

'What time do you want me ready to perform my duty as your fiancée?' She surprised herself with the fierceness of her question, and if the rise of his brows was anything to go by he too was shocked.

'We shall leave at seven.'

'Very well,' she said as she walked towards the room that should be his. Despite their time in Tuscany, and the passion which had leapt to life, he showed no intention of sharing it with her. She should be glad—it was, after all, what she'd wanted—but the sting of his rejection of her as a woman cut far deeper than she'd thought possible.

She would have to toughen up, otherwise she would never see this wretched deal through. All she needed to do was remember why she was doing it—for her baby.

CHAPTER ELEVEN

PIPER'S ENERGY AND enthusiasm for her role of Dante Mancini's fiancée had all but gone. Dante had become more distant each evening—at least in private. Publically he'd become ever more charming and attentive, which only highlighted his withdrawal.

She glanced out of the window as the car moved through the busy traffic of Rome, trying to quell the now ever-present nausea. At Dante's insistence his doctor had called again today, but had reassured them that it was all part of pregnancy and would pass.

Dante's voice dragged her from her thoughts. 'We will be arriving in just a few minutes. This party is one of the highlights of Rome's social scene and the press will be in full attendance.'

'I understand,' she said, and looked across the car, lit by the lights of Rome. 'Tonight will be no different to the other nights. I intend to keep my side of our deal.'

'Just as I will keep mine.' He looked at her, and for a moment the car zinged with the attraction that still drew her to him.

Did he really mean that?

'I hope so, Dante. *You* are doing this for a deal, but I'm doing it for our child.'

'Also a deal.' The clipped reply not only dried the

conversation, but confirmed to her that he was as mercenary as ever. Those memories of closeness when she'd been ill must have been imagined. *They* were just a deal.

When the car pulled up at one of Rome's top hotels and she saw the throng of photographers lingering around the red carpet it made her wish she didn't have to go out there and face them all. The photographers were the least of her worries. It was the women who lived the life she was supposed to be fitting in to. Women like Capricia Conetta, who were not only past lovers of Dante's but practised in the art of snobbery. Not once had Piper felt she truly fitted in.

Dante got out of the car first, and then held her hand as she stepped onto the red carpet. The emerald-green dress showed much more of her legs than she was happy with through the long slit at the front, and she tried hard to ignore the sinfully sexy look in Dante's eyes as they filled with unconcealed desire.

It was all part of the act, she reminded herself. He was acting the role of doting fiancé. In public, nobody could question his attraction to her—nobody could doubt he wanted her—but once they were alone that act was abandoned. It was something she had to learn to do too, if she was going to survive this charade.

'Smile,' he whispered as he leant close to her—so close that when she looked up at him his lips were only a breath away from hers.

Her eyes locked with his, the rest of the world was forgotten, and all she wanted was to be kissed. All she needed was to feel his lips on hers, taste him as he pressed his body against her.

She felt her lips lift into a smile, but still she couldn't break the spell which had snared them. She heard him say something but had no idea what, or even in what language. All she could focus on was his eyes, so dark, so sexy. As his lips touched hers she closed her own eyes, unable to bear the feel of his kiss but wanting it so badly.

He didn't pull back, didn't move away, and the kiss remained light, so teasing it was pure torture. She sighed against his lips, and when he did pull back her eyes flew open. It was then she realised that the night was lit up with flashes and that all around them photographers were calling. The crowd, gathered to watch the arrival of the rich and famous, called and cheered. She blushed and swallowed hard, not knowing what to say.

'That was very convincing, *cara*.'

The mischief which sparkled in his eyes made her tingle, and excitement washed over her. She'd almost given herself away, almost let him see and feel her growing feelings for him. And that would have been the biggest mistake of all.

Finally she regained her senses. 'I thought that was what you wanted.'

Before he had a chance to respond she turned and faced the photographers, leaving him no choice but to hold her at his side. She smiled. It wasn't for her, or even for Dante. It was for her child, and for the deal she'd made with this man she'd first spent the night with because she'd wanted to prove she was alive, to prove she could feel, and most importantly could do what she wanted. How wrong it had all gone.

Moments later he led her along the red carpet and into the hotel, and momentarily she felt lost and drained of emotion. That kiss, as light as it had been, had sapped all the strength from her.

He touched the small of her back as he guided her through the already thronging party guests. Their entrance had gained the interest of some of the guests, and Piper's heart sank when she saw Capricia weaving her way through the other guests, her gaze firmly fixed on Dante.

Capricia was the last person she needed to see when she felt so fragile, so out of place in the world she'd slipped into. All day she'd fought the growing need to walk away, to forget the deal and forget Dante, but she wasn't sure she could do that. She had to think of her baby.

'*Ciao*, Dante.' Capricia all but hung on to Dante as they kissed on each cheek. 'I see you haven't tired of the protégée yet?'

Piper bit back a retort at the insult, spoken in English and clearly meant for her to understand. She didn't want to be like this woman. She remembered her childhood, standing alone at school because nobody wanted to be friends with the girl who was blind in one eye. Even then she'd had no stomach for joining in and being one of the crowd. With sinking resignation she knew she didn't belong in this world—and never would.

'Like *you* would have done?' Dante said, his voice holding a hint of flirtation. But the steely glint in his eyes gave away his true mood.

Capricia seemed oblivious to it, focusing only on the light-hearted flirtation.

'Now, if you'll excuse me, I'd like to spend time with my fiancée.'

Dante had seen the colour drain from Piper's face even before Capricia had arrived, full of gusto as usual. Dante smiled at the shock on Piper's face now, as he all but sidestepped the woman he'd had a brief affair with and took her hand, leading her through the guests.

Guilt nudged at him. He'd noticed Piper looking paler and more uncomfortable today, and had insisted on her seeing the doctor for reassurance that both mother and child were well. He didn't want to take any chances.

He felt guilty enough about pushing her into appearing with him night after night, but it had been necessary. The need to convince the world as well as Bettino D'Antonio that he had turned his back on his playboy ways and was settling down was paramount. He'd also decided to offer *Celebrity Spy!* an engagement exclusive. It would be the surest way to show as many people as possible that he was committed to his new lifestyle.

'Sorry about Capricia,' he said softly as he handed Piper a glass of water. 'That little scene is not the sort of thing that needs to be witnessed by anyone if we are to pull this deal off.'

Damn it. That wasn't what he'd meant to say. He'd wanted to tell her that she shouldn't have to listen to that—not in her condition. He'd wanted to show he cared, show he was on her side. How had it come out sounding so mercenary? So like the Dante Mancini the world thought he was?

'It just goes to prove how unbelievable it is that you have become engaged.' She didn't meet his gaze, but sipped at the water and looked around her, as if she were interested in those who had turned out for the party.

She confused him. In one moment he thought she liked all the attention, the glamorous new clothes and being part of the limelight, and then she'd say something that didn't fit in with that kind of woman.

'It's not been as easy as I had thought.' He'd spoken his mind before he'd had a chance to think again—something he never usually did...or at least he hadn't until this woman had come into his life.

'Have you heard anything from Bettino?' She glanced up at him and he couldn't miss the fierce gleam in her green eyes, making them blaze like gemstones.

He looked into the champagne which bubbled in its flute and tried to suppress the unease he felt at not having heard anything from D'Antonio yet. He'd been sure that Piper's talk of art had been enough to bring the old man round. Not yet, it appeared.

'No.' He drank down the champagne and knew he was glowering at her. He could see the uncertainty on her face. She thought he blamed *her*. Despite that thought, he couldn't temper his words. He was totally unaccustomed to not getting what he wanted in business. 'I don't understand what is taking him so long.'

'It hasn't even been a week yet since we had dinner at his villa.'

She was trying to appease him, but he could feel his temper rising.

'Too long,' he snapped, and then looked at her, trying to assess what she was going to say. Did she too think their engagement deal hadn't helped him get D'Antonio on-side?

'You could come home with me and meet my mother. If we arrived together in London that might help.'

'No.' Inwardly he cursed. Why was she so hung up on including her mother in their so-called deal? He'd explained what was what to *his* mother, who hadn't understood at all, so why did Piper need to give *her* mother a false impression of their relationship? 'I did suggest that you explain the true situation to your mother.'

He spoke quietly, but with a steely glint in his voice as he tried to keep the topic of their conversation from the other party guests. There was still a chance that his deal might come off, and just as importantly that the charity he supported would continue to want him as a patron. Helping underprivileged children realise they *did* have a value in life was something he had to do—especially after he'd been shown that one single act of kindness which had started him on his own journey of self-discovery, ultimately making him the wealthy man he now was.

'I'm only trying to help convince the media that what we have is real.'

'But it isn't, is it, *cara*?' He looked down at her, silently acknowledging that the only real thing they had was the spark of sexual attraction which had got them into this predicament in the first place and then compounded it, changing everything.

All he wanted to do now was return things to the way they'd been the morning she'd signed that contract. And if he had to push her away to make her see how unsustainable their situation was then that was what he'd do. And there was a guaranteed way to do that.

'I'd like to offer *Celebrity Spy!* an engagement exclusive.'

'What?'

Piper blinked in shock. Had she heard right? Had he actually said he'd invited the very magazine responsible for their current situation into their lives—and their lies?

'It will be the best way to show everyone we mean business.'

His dark eyes bored into hers, daring her to object, but there was no way she could do this. He'd asked too much this time, taken his need to win a business deal too far.

'*You* mean business—not me.' Disappointment

flooded her. If that didn't prove she was nothing but a business deal, even after their weekend in Tuscany, nothing would.

'You agreed to sign the contract. You even added your own terms, Piper. You can't back out now. We *will* do this interview. At least then you won't have to tire yourself by attending parties each and every night.'

Around them the hum of the party continued and Piper glanced away, looking at the women, dripping in sparkling stones and dressed in designer gowns that would probably never be worn again. She didn't belong here—at least not on this side of things. She belonged behind the scenes, in the frenzied preparations for such events.

'This isn't my world, Dante.' She could hear the resigned tone to her voice, knew that she had to find her strength if she was going to do what had to be done.

'Do you not enjoy the attention, the new clothes and the glamorous places?'

'It's not what I'm used to.'

'I find that hard to believe, *cara*.'

His voice became deep and sexy as he leant closer to her, and she knew it wasn't because he wanted to do that but because it was part of the act.

'Very well, we will leave as soon as possible.'

For the rest of the party Piper tried to ignore the icy tone of Dante's voice and his determination that their deal was as normal as any other. It wasn't for her. She'd made a deal for her child's future happiness—not a stupid business deal. And even if he did want to look better for the charity he supported it did very little to soothe the pain of his rejection. Neither did it justify appearing in a magazine posing as his fiancée.

As she stood there at the party, watching the vain and

false women, she knew that no matter what her original intentions had been she didn't want her child to grow up as a part of this life. It was a life she didn't belong to, but it was one she would have fitted into, learned to be part of, if only Dante had genuinely cared about her. He'd never love her, and their marriage would never be the fairytale she'd always dreamed of, but it could be a happy one in which to raise their child if he put aside the business deal part of their relationship.

As the hour ticked passed midnight and her energy levels dipped to an all-time low she knew it was over. She'd tried to make a go of it, tried to give Dante what he wanted, but she knew now that nothing she could do would ever be enough for him.

She wanted to leave, but the image of the contract she'd signed burned in her mind. She'd agreed to be his fiancée and then his wife for two years. Could she really endure all his world threw at her and trust that he'd keep his side of the deal?

The stark answer came back at her.

No, she couldn't.

CHAPTER TWELVE

PIPER HAD TRIED to be rational, tried to keep emotion out of her decision, but after the loneliest night of her life she finally accepted that being with Dante couldn't work. If he didn't want to commit fully to the deal they'd struck that morning in his office how would he ever be there for his child?

She'd couldn't bear the thought of her child being distraught when its father didn't show up one day, as planned, and she knew now that was exactly the kind of father Dante would be. Nothing would ever be as important as chasing the next deal. And, whilst she could never deny Dante access to his son or daughter, she wanted more for her baby. She wanted her child to have what she'd had from her father—unconditional love and a father who was there for them, no matter what.

Dante had already shown that was not how he envisaged fatherhood. The fact that he had no intention of involving his mother in their child's life left her in no doubt as to just how small a part he was prepared to play once the baby was born.

She packed the few belongings she'd arrived in Rome with into her bag and dressed in the jeans and jumper she'd worn the day she'd waited for him in his office. After a quick glance round the bedroom, which after their time in Tuscany she'd hoped he would join her in, she left, and went in search of the man she was supposed to be engaged to. Calmness had settled over her. It was over. Whatever *it* was.

'*Buongiorno.*'

He didn't even look up from the paperwork he was reading and her heart sank a little further. He had no interest in her. She was merely a pawn in his game-plan for success. He'd used her—used the fact that she'd wanted to do the right thing by him and tell him personally that their night together had resulted in a baby.

'Working so early?' She kept her voice light as she poured a glass of water and stood watching him, committing everything about the man she loved to memory.

The man she loved.

That thought stopped her, and she stood looking at him, wondering when that had happened. When had she given her heart to a man who didn't even know what emotions were, let alone love?

'I have a meeting this afternoon, and I won't be home until late this evening. So tonight you may rest. We have a dinner engagement tomorrow evening, and I will then arrange the exclusive engagement interview.'

His words, spoken so coldly, as if he was talking to an employee, broke through her startling thoughts and she looked at him. She loved this man, and she was having his baby, but it meant nothing to him.

'This isn't what I wanted, Dante.'

She said the words before she'd had a chance to think, but once they were out there, settling between them, relief filled her. She had to be true to herself and the baby. It didn't matter what she felt for Dante. Her love counted for nothing. He was unreachable, and it would break her heart to stay and try to find the man he could be— the man she wanted.

She recalled all he'd told her about Alessio. He'd had emotion then. Had the loss of his brother changed him that much?

'What isn't?' He looked at her and frowned, and the sharpness of his voice drew her thoughts back from the avenue they'd been wandering down.

He had no idea. Did he really think she wanted this lifestyle? This materialistic life where emotions were masked? Where everyone seemed to have a hidden agenda?

'The—the deal we made.' She stumbled over her words before finding an inner strength. 'It's never going to work.'

He put down the papers and came towards her, suspicion in his eyes. 'What are you suggesting?'

He was so close that if she closed her eyes and took in a deep breath she'd be able to inhale his aftershave, that fresh from the shower scent she adored so much. It reminded her of their weekend in Tuscany.

She shut her senses down, refusing to allow them to drag sentiment into her decision. Now was not the time. She had to be strong and firm—for her baby, if not herself.

She stood taller and looked into his eyes, seeing the mistrust deep within them where once she'd seen desire and passion. If they could have remained locked away in Tuscany maybe she could have got through the barriers he had around him, the impenetrable wall he used to keep people out. But as soon as he'd returned to Rome, to his sophisticated world, any genuine warmth and understanding between them had gone.

Along with his latest suggestion of an engagement

exclusive, it just added to the feeling that he'd used her—and that hurt more than anything.

'I can't be what you want.'

Those dark eyes which had once been filled with desire for her had become granite-hard, but she forced herself to say what had to be said.

'And you, Dante, can't be what I want. It won't work.'

'We made a deal.'

His eyes narrowed, but she refused to be intimidated even as he stepped closer, threatening the strength she had to hold onto.

'Yes,' she snapped, and moved back from him, needing to escape the intensity of those eyes. 'And I have tried to keep *my* side of that deal. It's not my fault Bettino hasn't gone with your company, and it certainly isn't my fault that the social circle you keep hasn't done anything more than speculate about our engagement.'

'They will speculate in an entirely different way if you revert to your usual style.'

The distaste in his eyes wasn't lost on her. He'd looked at her the same way as she'd stood before him in his office. Hurt spiked through her, reminding her of her childhood, of standing alone whilst friends whispered about her. She knew exactly why he didn't want her any more, and it had very little to do with what she chose to wear. She'd told him the truth. That she wasn't perfect. And now, because of that, she didn't fit into his world—or his plans.

'I can't be what I'm not, Dante.'

Strength she hadn't felt in days finally came to her, driving her on to do what she knew was right—even though it hurt, even though it meant turning her back on the man who'd stolen her heart. She didn't want to be that lonely child any more. Her father's love had given her the courage to accept who she was and be that person, and she needed a man like him—not one like Dante.

'Just as you can't be what I need.'

'What are you trying to say?'

The hardness in his voice almost shattered her resolve to carry through the decision she'd come to last night as she'd tossed and turned.

'I can't stay—not like this.' She spread out her palms in a gesture of hopelessness.

'What *would* you stay for? More clothes and jewels? Money?'

The ferocity of the accusation in his voice sliced at her already unbalanced emotions. He thought she was as materialistic as women like Capricia, that a shopping spree and a party would make everything right.

She gasped in shock. 'If you really think I would stay for any of that then you don't know me at all.'

Shock and disappointment were in danger of showing, so she turned from him and crossed the room, heading for the sanctuary of the bedroom. She had nothing more to say to him. She might have fallen in love with him, but if she'd had any doubts about leaving what he'd just said had confirmed it was exactly the right thing to do.

She turned and gave him one last look, and the anger in his handsome face was almost too much. 'Goodbye, Dante.'

Dante's mind reeled with shock. She was going to walk away—not only from him, but from their deal. He should be pleased. After all he had no wish to become a married man, much less a father. The thought of being responsible for someone again still filled him with pure fear. He couldn't be anyone someone needed—not when the guilt of Alessio's death still raged within him.

When Piper had told him why she'd come to Rome that guilt had deepened. She'd torn him apart, along with his life, when she'd told him she wanted something from him he just couldn't give. He wasn't capable of loving a child, of being there to see it through the trials of life, not when he'd failed his own brother so spectacularly. He couldn't do that to someone again.

'We made a deal, Piper. You signed the papers, agreed to become my wife, and that deal does not end until two years after we are married.' He forced his mind from the implications of insisting the marriage went ahead.

'What kind of marriage would it be if we continue on this disastrous course? What kind of parents will we be if this baby can't even know its grandmothers?' Piper's voice resounded with frustration.

She placed her hand over her stomach, which as yet showed no sign of the child she spoke of, but his doctor had at least confirmed she was pregnant. Should he have demanded she take the test she'd mentioned? Confirmed he was the baby's father?

Questions raced through his mind. He'd been so distracted by Piper's reappearance into his life he hadn't thought it through. Not a problem he was used to admitting. He was usually completely in control.

The last time he hadn't been in control, when he'd played the wrong cards in life, his brother had slipped away in the early-evening darkness. He'd been angry with Alessio, but even angrier with himself. Once again he'd pushed someone away by caring. He'd loved his father and he'd left them without even a goodbye. He'd loved Alessio, tried to be a father and a brother to him. All he'd wanted to do was give his brother and mother the best. But the night Alessio had left he'd closed off his heart, shut down his emotions and become the hardened man he now was. It was safer that way.

'I will not have my mother dragged into our sordid little deal.'

He knew exactly what she was doing and he wouldn't allow it. His mother had experienced enough heartache. She already blamed him for all the pain in her life, and he was damn sure Piper would not be allowed to add to her worries. All she'd ever wanted was for him to forgive himself and settle down, have children. How ironic that she would now get her wish—but he hadn't forgiven himself. That was impossible.

'You can't pretend our marriage is real—not to your mother.' The shock in her voice was clear as she stood in front of the door to his bedroom. A room he hadn't used since she'd arrived. Yet he'd slept with her in Tuscany, enjoyed the sensation of sleeping with her in his arms—something he'd never done before with any woman. Deep down he knew it had been much more than just being relaxed in the villa, that it had to do with the woman he'd held after making love to her. And it scared the hell out of him.

'I have already emailed her to explain the situation. That our engagement and subsequent marriage are for the sake of The Hope Foundation.'

He saw the pain and shock in her gorgeous eyes, saw the sparkle slip from their gemlike green, but it was the best way. It was as if he was on the brink of a crater, filled with bubbling emotion, and if he made one wrong move he'd fall in and be consumed by those emotions.

'And for your deal with Bettino.' The hurt in her

voice was plain. 'I don't believe that you can forget your deal. But what I *can* believe is that you are so cold and unfeeling you emailed your own mother with that news. How could I have ever thought that I...?'

Her words trailed off, but he didn't want to know what she'd been about to say. From the expression on her face, the worry in her eyes, he knew. How could she ever have thought she could marry him? He didn't want to hear the truth. All he wanted to do was push her further away.

Instead of thinking about the only woman who'd ever remained in his mind after a night of passion— the only woman he might have loved if things were different—instead of dwelling on that revelation, he turned his attention to his mother, and the impending meeting he had planned with her later that day.

He had been summoned to his mother's home after sending the email, but he wasn't going to admit that to Piper. He had no wish to give her such ammunition, and he certainly didn't want his mother calling at the apartment to meet Piper. He knew instinctively that if the two of them met he would lose control of everything, and control was what he sought to have at all times.

Tonight he would meet his mother and paint Piper as a woman who was as calculated and mercenary as he was. Under no circumstances would he tell her that Piper carried his child. That would give his mother too much hope, and he'd already done that to her when he'd assured her that he would find Alessio after he'd ran away. Several years later, when he *had* found him, he'd never seen such pain on his mother's face. He'd given her false hope and he wouldn't allow that to happen again.

* * *

Piper couldn't believe what she was hearing. Where had the loving man she'd spent the weekend in Tuscany with gone? This cold and mercenary man was far worse than *Celebrity Spy!* had painted him. He was everything she didn't want in a husband—or as a father for her baby.

She had no choice. She had to go. She had to leave behind her foolish dreams of happiness and return to London. She had no one else in the world but her mother, but still she didn't need such a cold-hearted man as Dante.

'How long did it take you to decide that getting engaged to me would win you your damn deal?' She hurled the words at him, icy hatred in her eyes as she watched him pick up his briefcase, put in the papers he'd been reading and click it shut.

He was going to walk out on her, leave her to fester with his rejection while he went about his day and worked into the night. He looked at her, his dark eyes assessing, and an icy chill slid over her—one that filled her with courage and determination to do what was right.

'We will talk again this evening.'

'I won't be here this evening.' She tossed the words into the charged atmosphere.

He came towards her and she stood her ground. 'You *will* be here. You signed a contract. But, more to the point, I can give you the kind of lifestyle you want.'

She walked slowly towards him, her gaze locked with his, disbelief that he could be so cold, so accusing, churning in her stomach, making her more nauseous than she'd ever been. Angrily she pushed that aside. 'I signed a contract to play the role of your fiancée in order for you to win a deal. *You* are the one who wanted to change me, turn me into someone I wasn't, someone I could never be.'

'I have not yet secured that deal.'

'You don't own me, Dante.'

Her voice quivered with passion mixed with frustration and he knew she was right.

'And I won't let you change me.'

The floodgates of emotion had opened and she couldn't hold back any longer. All the hurt and humiliation she'd bottled up rushed out before Dante could say anything.

'I can't be what you want, Dante. I'm not a puppet you can shape to fit your circumstances—and, more to the point, neither is our baby.'

'Are you trying to say you have nothing to gain from our agreed deal? What about all the clothes and jewels you have?'

'None of them matter.' Her stomach turned over again and she thought for one minute she would have to rush away to the bathroom. Would he even care?

'So what does matter, *mia cara*? What is it you really want to gain?'

There was an undertone of controlled annoyance in his tone, and she just didn't feel well enough to deal with it right now.

'If we are going to be married for the sake of the baby then I want my baby to know its grandmothers—especially as he or she won't have any grandfathers.' She stood boldly, pushing home her point, and for a moment she thought he was going to disagree, to give her a justifiable reason for not involving his or her mother in the baby's life.

'I can't have this conversation—not now, not ever.'

He put on his jacket and picked up his briefcase. 'We made a deal. Let's just stick to it, no?'

'No,' she said firmly, and saw his eyes widen in surprise. Had nobody ever said no to the all-powerful Dante Mancini?

He marched to the door, yanked it open and turned to face her. 'We made a deal, Piper, and nothing changes—not a thing. But right now I'm late.'

'Just go, Dante. I never want to see you again. I made a big mistake coming here—one I intend to rectify.'

CHAPTER THIRTEEN

DANTE LOOKED BRIEFLY at his phone as Bettino D'Antonio disconnected the call. He should be punching the air for joy. He'd got the contract, but somehow with Piper gone he didn't care. None of it mattered if he didn't have her to share it with. His elation at having secured his most lucrative deal yet was swamped by misgivings.

He cursed under his breath and slid his phone back into his jacket pocket.

'Problems?' His mother's question couldn't quite drag him from the low he'd been in since he'd arrived back at his apartment two days ago to find Piper had actually gone against their contract and left. Just as she'd told him she would.

She'd taken nothing other than what she'd arrived with— not even the engagement ring she'd selected. She'd left it on his desk, next to her copy of the contract, making it clear what she thought of both. He'd never felt more adrift in life as he did now.

'No.' He tried for an enthusiastic approach, but fell way short of it if the expression on his mother's face was anything to go by. 'That was about the deal I've been chasing. I've got it. I now own one of the biggest solar energy companies.'

His mother frowned and for a moment he saw Alessio in the reproach that filled her eyes. He'd always thought Alessio took after their mother. They had the same nutmeg eyes, and she would often look at him the way his younger brother had. It was another constant reminder of his guilt, as if Alessio was still there, reprimanding him for not looking after him.

'Was the deal worth it?'

'Of course.' He tried not to think about the deal he'd made with Piper, the deal for his child, just to secure a contract to make his renewable energies company one of the biggest in the world.

'Are you certain about that?'

What was his mother trying to do? Make him feel even worse than he already did?

Stifled by emotions he just couldn't analyse now, he grabbed his car keys. 'I need to get back to Rome—put things in motion with D'Antonio.'

'You need to go to London first.'

His mother's voice was gentle, as always, but beneath that softness he heard steely determination.

'You have things to sort out there, Dante.'

It was as if he'd slammed into a wall, and exactly the reason he'd wanted to keep Piper and his mother apart. His mother had never met her, didn't know about the baby, but already she was on Piper's side. Even though he'd explained about the cold and calculated deal Piper had agreed to—leaving out one important detail—his mother was looking for more. What *was* it with women wanting happy-ever-afters that could never exist?

'I will not be chasing after *that* particular contract. It has fallen through, but at least it appears to have achieved what I wanted.' As he finished speaking he gritted his teeth against his anger that Piper had walked out on him—again. Anger that was mixed with hurt. He missed her. He wanted her. In a way he'd never thought possible. And she'd walked away.

'Is a contract for a solar energy company worth more than your happiness?' his mother asked quietly, but the firmness of the question let him know just what she thought of that. She'd always told him he worked too hard.

He was proud of his company, but he never stopped working—never stopped making it bigger and better, as if he was still searching for something to make things right. Because so far nothing was right. Why should now be any different from when his father had left or Alessio had gone missing? He was getting what he deserved once more. He'd messed up again. He'd driven Piper away, and with her his child.

'Business is my happiness. Now I have to go.'

He couldn't discuss this now. Not when he knew his mother spoke the truth. A truth he wasn't yet ready to admit.

Dante turned to go.

'You have to stop punishing yourself, Dante. Alessio's death wasn't your fault.'

His mother's words made another step too difficult. His mind raced back in time to the day he'd last seen his father and the words he'd said before he left. *'Look after them.'*

It might have been just something to say for a man so selfish he had walked out on his young family but Dante, at almost eight, had assumed the role of protector and, even before he'd finished school, provider. His need to succeed had come from that moment.

'You were a child when your father left…'

His mother's words snagged his attention and he

turned to look at her, unaware that he was clenching his fists so tightly the car keys dug into his palm.

'I never wanted you to take his place. I wanted you to be a child, to grow up in your own time.'

'I couldn't watch you struggle.' He growled the words as pain engulfed him. 'He left me in charge. He made me the man of the house when I was still a boy.'

'And I blame myself for what it's done to you.'

The raw emotion in his mother's voice only intensified the anger he felt towards his father and his guilt at letting Alessio down.

'You shouldn't shut love out of your life, Dante. Live for yourself—not your father.'

As the words sluiced round in his mind images of Piper—of her smile as they'd enjoyed their time in Tuscany, of the passion in her eyes as he'd made her his once more and the pain in her voice as she'd told him she couldn't do it any more—collided with the past. Had love played any part in that for her?

'I don't need love.'

He'd spoken more to himself than his mother, but as the harsh words left him he knew it was a lie. With Piper he'd seen what love and happiness could be like, had glimpsed a life he had no right to want.

'I've seen the photos, Dante, and the television coverage. That woman loves you.'

'No,' he snapped quickly. 'It's all part of the deal to make the world think we are in love.'

'Just as you love her.' She walked towards him, her eyes pleading with him. 'Go to her, Dante, and make this right—for you and for her, but most of all for the baby.'

The air around him snapped, and shock snatched his ability to speak. How did his mother know what he'd tried so hard to keep from her? *Maledizione*. He'd only told Elizabeth Young out of necessity.

'I'm right, aren't I? A woman knows these things.'

He knew then it was pointless denying anything.

'About the baby? Yes.' Resignation filled him. The one thing he hadn't wanted to do was give his mother hope of being a grandmother, hope that he'd settle down and have a family. He'd never wanted that—until he'd met Piper. Now he would have to break his mother's heart too.

'No, I'm right that you love her.'

The insistent tone wrenched him from his despondent thoughts. 'You've got it wrong.' He flung the words at his mother as he left her villa, needing the solitude of his car and the drive back to Rome.

He needed to think, to process everything, to sort his emotions out—emotions he'd banished from his life years ago. Emotions he shouldn't want, but did. So why did he want them back now?

He was in love with Piper.

Piper's morning sickness had become much worse since her arrival back in London. She had spilled the whole story to her mother, who'd held her as she'd cried. As the tears had dried Piper had felt guilty, sure her mother would blame herself for dragging her away from Sydney and all she'd grown up with.

Her friends, Katie and Jo, had rallied round with emails and calls, giving her support, but there wasn't much else they could do so far away in Sydney, and Piper had never felt so alone. She wished her father was there to tell her it would be all right in the end. She could almost hear him now. *'There's a happy-ever-after out there for you, Piper, don't ever forget that.'*

He'd said it many times to her as she'd grown up, and she'd always teased him about it, but right now a happy-ever-after with Dante was all she wanted. But that was a futile wish, and leaving Rome—leaving the man she loved—certainly hadn't felt right.

For the first few days in London Piper had been angry with Dante, but now she had reached a stage of acceptance. The man she loved didn't and couldn't love her. It had been four days since she'd left Rome and she'd heard nothing from him. She didn't even know if he'd got his deal with Bettino D'Antonio. All she knew was that her heart was breaking and she didn't know how to mend it.

A firm knock on the front door of the house her mother rented startled her from her misery and a little light of hope sparked in her heart. Had he come for her? Then it faded as quickly as it had flared. Dante wouldn't come after her—not when he was incapable of any kind of emotion. He wouldn't let it into his life. He was completely closed off to it. He'd probably already moved on to the next woman in his life, while she would remain in love with him for ever, with their child a legacy and constant reminder of him.

With a heavy heart she opened the door, the blast of cold from England's winter weather momentarily taking her breath away. Then she saw Dante, and her knees weakened and her stomach somersaulted.

He looked devastatingly handsome. The warm coat he wore over his suit gave him an air of distinction, and she remembered how she'd thought the same that night of the party. The night he'd kissed her, right there in front of everyone, as they'd stood on the red carpet, cameras flashing, recording the moment. That kiss had been so full of passion and desire, as if he'd really meant it, had really wanted to kiss her. It had given her hope—but false hope, and she'd had to accept it was all part of the act.

'Piper?'

The question in his voice as he said her name unsettled her nerves, and the firm and determined expression on his face warned her not to expect things she knew he couldn't give. Not when she'd run out on their deal.

She'd had to leave. For her sanity. Each day her love had grown, and the pain of knowing he'd never love her had increased until it had become unbearable.

'What do you want, Dante? I thought we'd said all we needed to say.' She folded her arms and stood on the doorstep, the partially open door behind her. All she wanted to do was protect herself, hide her love, her elation at seeing him, but the embers of something dark smouldered in his eyes, increasing her nerves tenfold.

'We have things to settle—about the baby.'

He took a step towards her and instinctively she held her ground. She couldn't let him over the threshold of her new life. It was still such a painful choice, and she was scared he'd make her fragile strength evaporate, make her change her mind.

'I suggest we leave all that to the legal experts.'

She wasn't going to force him to be a father, to be part of her baby's life, and she certainly wasn't going to sort out the final details with him now. She'd taken her mother's advice and arranged to seek legal help, determined to find a way out of their contract.

'Is that what you want?'

His voice was icy-cold, his eyes so dark she couldn't decipher what emotion was in them.

'I didn't want *any* of this.'

The pain of it all—of holding back her emotions—made those words a strangled cry and she turned, fleeing into the house. She heard the front door close behind her, heard the noise of the street subside, and knew there was no getting away from him. She stood in the living room of the small terraced house, looking at her reflection in the mirror above the fireplace, wondering how her life had become so wildly complicated.

Because you love him.

The words rushed around her mind. When had it happened? *How* had she fallen in love with a man such as Dante? She didn't really need to ask those silent questions. She already knew. She'd fallen in love with him the night they'd first met—the night he'd made her his for evermore.

As she looked into the mirror Dante entered the small room, his gaze meeting hers, and the intensity of it sent a shiver of awareness all over her. For a moment she wished he loved her too, that he was here because he couldn't imagine life without her in it.

'What was it you came to Rome for?'

Dante's question was fired at her, but she held his gaze in the mirror, trying to read those dark eyes which hid every hint of emotion.

Finally she turned to face him, but the firm set of his jaw, shadowed with stubble as it had been that first morning in Rome, made her nerves desert her.

'We've gone over this, Dante. All I wanted to do was let you know you were going to be a father. Nothing more. You were the one who turned it all into something else. You made it into a deal—something sordid and soul-destroying—just to win a business deal.'

'Then why did you sign the contract?'

His accent had become more pronounced and that

shiver of awareness notched up a level. How could he affect her so much after all he'd done?

'I wanted my baby to have what *I* had—a father who cared, one who would spend time with it, and most importantly one who would be there, no matter what. But you can't be that—can you, Dante?'

She knew she was pushing him, forcing him to face all he'd hidden from since Alessio's death. But what else did she have to lose? *Nothing.*

A flicker of pain crossed his face, showing itself in the darkness of his eyes so very briefly she wondered if she'd imagined it.

'No, I can't be that man.'

His abrupt admission sliced at her heart and she closed her eyes against the raw emotion in his voice.

'That man isn't inside me, Piper. I can't be what you need.'

Her eyes flew open and she saw he stood closer to her now...so close that if she chose to she could step into his embrace. But would that make things right?

'Just as I can't be the woman you need, Dante. But I *could* live in your world, be all the things you need, if only...'

Her words faltered and she lowered her gaze, unable to look into those eyes any longer. How had she been so stupid? She'd nearly admitted that his love was all she needed to make everything right. That if she could love him too then nothing else would matter.

'If only what, Piper?'

He stepped closer and reached out, pushed her hair from her face so gently she was sure he had been anxious about startling her. She looked up at him, shyness engulfing her at the sight of the desire which burned in his eyes. But she wouldn't be swayed by lust—not again.

'It doesn't matter,' she said slowly, and stepped away from him, not able to bear being so close without being in his arms. 'I guess if you'd got the deal it would have been worth it.'

'I did get the deal.'

Dante had to clench his hands in an attempt not to reach for her again, not to touch the softness of her flame hair, or feel the warmth of her skin. Everything she'd said suggested their deal had been all about mutually beneficial arrangements, that every moment they'd shared in Tuscany had been just part of the deal.

He was shocked at how much it mattered, but it did. As he'd sat on the flight to London he'd played his mother's words over and over in his mind. Each word had confirmed what he'd known all along, what he'd been running from since he'd seen her again in his office. He wanted Piper. He loved her. And that terrified him.

'So everything you set out to achieve has happened?'

She prickled with indignation and injustice, and he'd done that to her.

'*Sì*, it has—but I still have my part of our deal to keep.' He watched her pretty face frown in disbelief at his words, and knew if he'd been on the receiving end of the way he'd treated her he wouldn't trust a word he said.

'I don't expect anything from you, Dante. In fact I don't want anything except for you to go back to your life and let me live mine. Go, Dante—just go.'

How could he go back to his life and leave her here? 'No, that's not possible.'

She glared at him, the angry sparkle in her eyes, reminding him of fireworks. For the second time in his life he was far from in control of a situation. The fear that had swamped him when Alessio had left was nothing compared to the way he felt right now.

'No, I'm not going back—not until I've made things right with you.'

'Right? Nothing can ever be right now.'

Her eyes glittered with unshed tears. He was hurting her, but he had to say what he needed to—no matter how hard it was going to be.

'I want us to be married, as planned.'

'Are you *insane*?' Her voice rose as she spoke, her eyes wide in shock. 'I can't live a lie like that.'

'Just as I can't.'

'Your whole life is a lie, Dante, so why have you developed a conscience suddenly?'

'Because I was wrong.' Nerves made the admission almost stick in his throat, but he forced himself on. 'Because I love you.'

Silence fell over the room. Like a sheer veil, it doused all the angry tension. Piper stood in the middle of the room, so very close he could reach out and touch her, but she felt further away than she'd ever done.

'You don't mean that.' The whispered words slipped from her as she searched his face, looking for evidence of lies or truth.

Finally he moved towards her. He had to tell her now exactly how he felt or lose her for ever. 'What we have—'

'Is just lust.'

She cut across his words, savaging his attempt to tell her he couldn't live without her. But he hadn't got where he was in life by admitting defeat, so easily.

'At first it was,' he admitted, lifting his hands quickly in frustration and walking away from her to stand at the large bay window which looked out onto the street.

He turned back to her. 'But that has changed. I don't know when it happened, or how, but I love you, Piper.'

He reached into his pocket and retrieved the engagement ring he'd bought her in Rome.

'I don't believe you.'

His heart sank. She didn't want him—didn't want to listen to him, to hear how much he loved her. 'Then there is nothing more to say, except that you are the woman who changed me, who made me see life again as it should be and taught me that I can love someone—and that someone is you.'

'What about the deal?' she asked cautiously. 'Is that why you still want us to marry?'

'The only deal I want from you is one secured by two words at the altar.' He held the ring up between his thumb and finger. 'I want you to wear my ring—for real.'

She moved towards him and he waited, hoping, needing her to come freely to him so he could hold her and kiss her, knowing she was his.

'Is that a proposal?'

She smiled, and her teasing words brought relief and a smile to his own lips. There was hope.

'Sì, mia cara. Vuoi sparsami?'

She frowned at him, then whispered, 'Say it again in English.'

'My darling, will you marry me?'

To his relief she flung her arms around his neck and as she kissed his face, his lips, gave him her reply. 'Yes—yes, of course I will. I love you, Dante.'

He took her face between his hands and looked into those green eyes. 'And I love *you*—for ever.'

EPILOGUE

PIPER STOOD OUTSIDE the church as the hot sun of summer beat down. Her best friends, Katie and Jo from Sydney, were taking their roles as bridesmaids very seriously and fussed around her, straightening the long cream lace gown she and Elizabeth had selected as a wedding dress soon after Mia had been born.

'You look gorgeous. You are positively glowing,' Katie said as she stood back, and Piper knew it was love that shone from her.

'Not as gorgeous as this little one,' Jo added as she handed Piper the most precious addition to her bridal outfit.

Baby Mia was wearing a pale pink dress, the same shade as Katie and Jo's, with an amazingly intricate and delicate mini-bouquet of wild flowers trailing from her.

'Here she is. Your little flower girl.'

'I'm so happy,' Piper said as she looked at her friends.

Mia gave a little moan of protest at being moved, but quickly settled into her arms. Piper still couldn't believe the perfect little bundle was hers, or that life could be so good.

After she'd returned to Rome with Dante her life had changed, becoming the loving fairytale she'd always longed for. Even fitting in with Rome's social circle had been easier with Dante's love. Now she was about to top it all and become his wife.

'So what are you waiting for? Go in there and marry the man of your dreams.'

Katie grinned at her and Piper's heart fluttered along with the butterflies in her stomach.

As she left the sunshine for the cool and dark interior of the old church she saw Dante standing with his back to her and her heart went out to him. She knew even after all his admissions that this would be hard for him without Alessio, just as it was hard for her without her father, but together they'd heal each other.

She walked towards Dante, admiring him as he turned to look at her, his handsome face full of a happiness which matched hers. His dark suit fitted him perfectly, showcasing the toned and delicious body she knew so well.

With each step she moved nearer to him, nearer to being his wife, she passed their friends, flown in to the small Tuscan village from all over the world, and then their mothers, and she smiled, pleased they had found a new friendship in each other, and that her mother had made the move to Italy to be close to her new granddaughter. Each mother had known hard times, but each of them had recognised the love between her and Dante long before they themselves had.

Piper had worried that walking up the aisle alone would be hard, but as her father's words played again in her mind, she knew he'd been right all along. Dante was the happy-ever-after which had been out there for her, and she'd found him because of her father. If she hadn't been so upset that night she would never have left the dinner party with Dante.

Just before the flower-decorated altar Bettino

D'Antonio waited for her, ready to step into his role of giving her away.

Then Dante turned to her and his smile was full of love, his eyes full of warmth, and it felt like coming home. 'You look beautiful.'

A warm glow filled her at his words, and then he touched his daughter's face and took her hand.

'Let's get married.'

As words of Italian and English flowed around them, binding them together in marriage, she could hardly take her eyes from this man she loved with all her heart.

'I love you, Piper Mancini,' Dante said as he brushed his lips lightly over hers.

'And I love *you*, my darling husband.' Piper smiled at him, then looked down at her baby daughter—the most perfect wedding gift.

'I'm so very happy,' he whispered as he looked into her eyes. 'And so in love with my beautiful wife and gorgeous daughter.'

Before she could say anything he kissed her again, so very gently, yet so wickedly full of desire she thought she might dissolve right there.

'Come. It is time to start our new life,' he said as he put his arm around her and led her back down the aisle and towards the sunshine, passing friends, family and—more significantly—other soon-to-be reformed bachelors.

* * * * *

THE LAST HEIR
OF MONTERRATO

ANDIE BROCK

For my mum.
Who would have been very proud.

CHAPTER ONE

IT WAS THE scar that halted Lottie in the doorway. A thin, livid wound, it sliced down from his brow, skipping over the eye socket before continuing an inch along his cheekbone. The sight of it clutched at her stomach, weighted her feet to the floor.

'Rafael?'

Silence stretched tightly between them as they stared at each other across the dark panelled office.

'Charlotte.'

'How…how are you?'

'Still alive.' As he eased himself to stand against the edge of the desk his voice was cold, flat. 'As you can see.'

'Yes. Indeed.' Lottie swallowed. Upright now, he stood with his hands splayed on either side of him, fingertips anchoring him to the desk. 'I was very sorry—to hear about the accident, I mean.'

'Thank you.' His clipped reply snipped at her words, clearly designed to stop any outpourings of sentiment.

Not that she intended to show him any, of course. She knew she wasn't here to display any sort of concern, express any sympathy. Rafael wasn't the kind of man to tolerate such emotions. Especially from her.

She watched as he moved out from behind the desk and walked stiffly towards her, tall and rigid in a sober grey suit, his height towering over her as they came together. For a second they stood there, like repelling magnets, until Rafael bent forward to brush her cheek once, twice, three times. Lottie closed her eyes as she felt the whisper of his breath, the touch of his skin; *him*.

He pulled away immediately, leaving her staring up at his injuries.

Scratches of various lengths and depths crisscrossed his face and a purple bruise spread colourfully down one side. The scar, Lottie now realised, resembled the lash of a whip. That didn't help at all.

'So…um…your face…?' She knew she shouldn't go on about it, that he would hate her even mentioning it, but she needed reassurance, needed to stop looking at him as if she was witnessing a pig having its throat cut. 'I assume the injuries are quite superficial?'

'You assume correctly.'

'And the rest of your body?' His unnerving stare stupidly made her blush. So much for trying to appear detached. She gave a small cough. 'I mean, what other injuries do you have?'

'All fairly consistent with someone who has plummeted twelve thousand feet from the sky.'

'I'm sure.' Lottie pulled a face at the idiocy of her question. How many people had fallen twelve thousand feet and lived to tell the tale? Anyway, she already knew the extent of his injuries; it had all been there in the newspaper article: punctured lung, dislocated shoulder, three cracked ribs. 'Did you ever find out…what went wrong? Why your parachute didn't open?'

'Misfortune, fate—call it what you like.' Rafael shrugged his shoulders as if already bored with the subject. 'It's of no consequence now.'

'No, I suppose not.' But despite his casual dismissal

Lottie didn't doubt that the accident had been thoroughly investigated. And if someone had been found responsible it would be their own life they should be worrying about now. 'But you were very lucky, as it turned out.'

'Lucky?' His tone suggested otherwise.

'I mean lucky that a tree broke your fall. It could have been so much worse.'

'True.' His reply was deadpan. 'I could have been dead.'

'Ha!' Why was she laughing? Nothing about this was the least bit funny.

It was pure, unmitigated torture.

She had prepared herself, of course, endlessly rehearsed how she would behave, what she would say when faced with Rafael again. She'd still been running through her calm and measured responses on the aeroplane over here, her twitching lips attracting the attention of her nosy nine-year-old neighbour. She had bullied herself into believing that she was ready. That she could cope—survive this one last meeting.

But as she looked at him now, past the recently inflicted injuries to the man beneath, the man she had fallen so madly in love with, all her confident convictions seemed to slide away. She remembered every tiny detail of his face. The thick, untidy brows that arrowed above almond-shaped deep brown eyes. The harsh sweep of his jawline, the square chin where a small cleft nestled, dark with stubble.

Yep, she remembered everything. She wished she didn't.

'Well, thank goodness for that tree, eh?' Shifting her position, she crossed one leg in front of the other, the balletic pose spoiled by the hand that was shoved deep into the pocket of her jeans. Her voice sounded hideously chirpy but it did at least mask her desire to ask where this tree was, so she could throw herself on its dirty roots and thank it for saving Rafael's life. 'I'm so glad it was in the right place.'

A curl of disdain twitched Rafael's perfectly formed lip. 'How nice that you should care.'

It didn't sound nice—not at all. Everything about his cold, sarcastic manner, the harsh light in his eyes, the formal, brittle posture, was telling her one thing. He hated her.

If Lottie had hoped that time had washed over their past, smoothed the jagged edges of her actions, time had seriously let her down. It had been two years since she had left, wrenched herself away from the wreckage of their marriage and fled back to England. But being back at Palazzo Monterrato, staring at Rafael now, she knew that those two years were as nothing. The atmosphere between them was almost as horrendous, as harrowingly painful, as the day she had left.

'Of course I care.' Something about the absurdity of his comment made her want at least to attempt to put the record straight. Make him see that, despite her all too convincing performance, she wasn't all bad. 'That will never change.'

'Very touching, I'm sure.' Rafael's words sliced through her tentative confession. 'But your misplaced sympathy is of no interest to me.' He moved back to his side of the desk. 'You are here because there is an important matter I need to discuss with you. Please, sit down.'

Lottie took a seat opposite him, her rapped knuckles clasped in her lap, her back very straight. She knew what was coming; she had been waiting for this ever since she had received his email.

It had been just another afternoon at work when she had opened her inbox and there it had been: a message from Rafael Revaldi. To see his name like that, out of the blue, had sent a hot flush of panic through her body. She had had to count to three before she'd even dared open it, darting a look at the only other people in the exclusive London art gallery—a whispering gay couple, admiring a vast canvas they were never going to buy—in case they had noticed her alarm.

The curt, dictatorial message had stated that it was necessary for them to meet; two different dates for the following week had been marked for her consideration and flight tickets would be emailed on receipt of her confirmation. As her mind had whizzed with the flurry of possibilities it had quickly settled on the cold blanket of truth behind the message. He wanted a divorce.

Tipping her chin, Lottie forced herself to meet his gaze, affecting as much detachment as she could muster, determined to be strong now. 'I know why I'm here. Let me assure you that I am as keen to get this over and done with as you are. I have no intention of being difficult, of trying to prolong the situation.'

There was a dangerous flash in Rafael's eyes before they narrowed to conceal anything further. He said nothing.

'If you have already had the papers drawn up...' she was babbling now, in her hurry to get this over with '...and it's just a matter of signature I can sign straight away and—'

'Let me stop you there, Charlotte.' Raising a hand, he silenced her, a gold cufflink glinting in the low afternoon light. 'I have no idea what you are talking about.'

'The divorce, of course.' Lottie felt heat rising to her cheeks at the very use of the dreaded d word. 'I know I am here because you want a divorce.'

Rafael leant forward, the fine fabric of his jacket pulling taut against his broad shoulders as his elbows rested on the desk in front of him, his hands linked.

'And what makes you think I want a divorce?'

Lottie looked down, picking at the skin around her fingernails. 'Because it's been two years.' She could feel his eyes boring into the crown of her bent head and forced herself to look up and confront him. 'And two years is the legal time necessary to apply for a consensual divorce.'

'And you think *that* is why I have brought you here?' His words were mocking, biting.

'Well, isn't it?'

'Believe me, Charlotte, if and when I want a divorce it will happen. The vagaries of English law are of no interest to me.'

Of course, Lottie corrected herself, how foolish of her. She should have known that as far as Rafael was concerned laws were something other people abided by. He had the power and the cunning to circumnavigate them, adapt them to his own needs.

Quickly she scanned the face of the man opposite her, afraid to let her eyes linger in any one spot for fear of being unable to drag them away again. He presented a cold, harsh picture, with the damaged skin pulled tight across the sculpted planes of his cheeks and jawline.

Why was he denying it? Did he get some perverse pleasure from watching her squirm? If so, that pleasure had to be locked deep inside him, for she had never seen him look more severe, more forbidding. She *knew* he wanted to divorce her; receiving that email had only confirmed the bleak realisation that had been silently gnawing away at her for nearly three weeks now. Ever since she had innocently stumbled across that online newspaper article.

Rafael Revaldi, Conte di Monterrato, cheats death in terrifying skydiving accident.

The words of the headline had made the cappuccino shake in her hand, the bite of sandwich turn into a ball of concrete in her mouth. Gripping the computer mouse, she

had frantically read on, desperate to find as much information as she could, as fast as she could, her hitherto steadfast
vow not to type Rafael's name anywhere near the search
engine box vanishing like vapour in the air.

But there had been way too much information. The Italian celebrity magazines were positively bursting with sen-
sational details about the daredevil Conte who had plunged
twelve thousand feet to earth and miraculously lived to tell
the tale. Any legitimate concern had soon morphed into
a gluttonous feeding frenzy to find out every little bit of
gossip about him that she could. And what she'd discovered—apart from the predictable images of him scaling
mountains or kayaking over waterfalls—were women.
Beautiful, eligible women. Glued to his side as they smiled
at charity galas, shook hands with dignitaries, walked beside him on the red carpet. And all of them had one thing
in common: a vice-tight grip on his arm and a look in
their eye that said, *Tonight he's mine and I intend to keep
it that way.*

Any fanciful ideas Lottie might have had about jumping on a plane to be with him, to make sure for herself
that he was really okay, had been wrenched away from her
there and then as she'd stared at the frozen smiles of those
women. They were all the proof she needed that Rafael
had moved on. That she had no place in his life any more.

Which was fine. Even if being here with him now, talking about severing all ties with him, sliced through her
like a cold blade. She just needed to remind herself how
far she had come. Yes, her life was finally back on track,
and that realisation stiffened her resolve.

Pushing back her shoulders, she attempted a haughty
glare to match his sullen one. She needed an explanation.

'So if, as you seem to be implying, I'm *not* here because

you want a divorce, perhaps you would do me the courtesy of telling me exactly why I *am* here?'

A heavy silence hung between them, marked out by the weary ticking of a long-case clock somewhere in the shadows.

'You are here because I have something to ask of you.' He paused, a muscle twitching beneath the hard, tight mask of authority.

Lottie watched as he uncharacteristically twiddled a gold pen between strong, tapered fingers so that it tapped—first one end, then the other—lightly on the desk before him. She found she was holding her breath at the absurd realisation that Rafael was nervous.

'I think we should try again.'

Shock ricocheted through Lottie's body. And despite herself—despite everything—the see-saw carrying her heart flew into the air.

'Try again?' Her mouth was so dry the words sounded shrivelled.

'Yes. I think we should try again. For a baby.'

The see-saw crashed down to the ground with a shuddering thump.

'A *baby*?' She hadn't meant it to sound so sneery, so nasty, but incredulity had taken her words and twisted them with bitterness.

'Yes, a *baby*, Charlotte. I see no reason why we shouldn't at least consider the idea.'

No reason at all, Lottie reasoned numbly, other than the fact that their marriage had been a disaster, he hadn't spoken to her for two years and he obviously still hated her guts. 'Why would you even think…?'

'I have found a new IVF specialist—someone in Iran,' Rafael continued with baffling logic. 'He knows the situation—that we still have one frozen embryo. He is very confident that this time it will work, that this time we will succeed.'

An Iranian IVF specialist? What on earth was going on here? Despite the controlled voice, the even tone, the powerful sense of conviction running through him was clearly, disturbingly unmistakable.

She had seen it before, of course. Rafael's determination to get her pregnant. But that had been in a previous life, before they had split up. After Seraphina had died.

Born at just twenty-five weeks, their daughter had only lived for a few precious hours. The trauma of the accident, followed by premature labour and a complicated birth was now little more than a foggy blur—almost as if it had happened to somebody else. But the pain of watching their tiny daughter's vain struggle for life would stay with Lottie for ever.

When Seraphina had finally died, and the clips and wires had been removed from her perfect, breathless body, Lottie had gazed at the still warm bundle in her arms, brushed an oversized finger against the soft down of her cheeks, convinced that nothing could be worse than this, that this was the bottom of the blackest pit. But fate had had one more arrow in its quiver. It seemed that the accident meant she would never be able to conceive naturally again—that IVF was their only hope of ever having another child.

Rafael had set about making it happen with a tenacious stubbornness that had bordered on obsession. They had embarked upon a series of IVF treatments, none of which had worked, and after each crushing disappointment it had seemed he was more obstinate, more insistent that they would not fail, that nothing was going to prevent him from achieving his goal. It had taken over their lives and eventually destroyed their marriage.

Lottie pushed the blonde hair away from her face with a hand that shook slightly in the way that the memory of Seraphina always weakened her limbs. She needed to put a stop to this madness now.

She drew in a sharp breath. 'Well, you have wasted this man's time. The idea of us having a baby is totally ridiculous. Why would we even consider it now? After all this time? When our marriage is obviously over?'

Rafael stared across at the wide violet-blue eyes that were searching his face for an explanation. *Certamente*, their marriage was over, all right. It had ended the day Lottie had walked out on him. The day she had told him that she didn't love him. That she had never loved him.

He cursed silently, struggling to keep his frustration inside, rein in the storm of his feelings. He had to remain calm. Not let himself be riled by her fake show of concern or her harsh dismissal of their shared past. He was already a hair's breadth from totally screwing this up, and he knew it.

But what he *hadn't* known was the way his heart would start pounding in his chest the second she walked into the room, as if jolted from a dormant slumber or poked into life by the jab of a stick. What was that? Anger? Betrayal? Lust? Whatever it was, it was damned annoying.

He'd been so sure that the two years they had been apart would have killed any desire he might have had for her. Now he knew that was not the case and he cursed her for it. She had no right to look like that—all heart-shaped face and soft pink lips, her slender body clad in skinny jeans and a plain white shirt, demurely buttoned almost to the top but still failing to conceal the unconscious jut of her breasts as she squared up to him.

Scowling, he raked a hand through his hair.

'Because an accident like this makes you think, Charlotte—that's why. Makes you realise that you are not invincible, that you need to plan for the future—a future when you are no longer around. Ten days in a hospital bed focusses the mind, believe me, and it gives you plenty of time to work out what's important.'

'Go on…'

The gentle probing of her voice was threatening to undo him, unleash a side of him that had nothing to do with the purpose of this meeting.

'What is important is this place.'

Roughly gesturing around him, he was rewarded with a sharp stab of pain that shot through his shoulder, mocking him with its power. He would not let it show. Whatever else, Lottie must not see his weakness. He knew she was watching every movement of his lips, analysing every syllable of his words. Grimly he carried on.

'The principality is my number one priority. Generations of Revaldis have held the title of Conte di Monterrato. Now it is my turn and I will do everything within my power to ensure its protection and prosperity.' He paused, conviction pushing back his shoulders, swelling his chest. 'As you well know, Charlotte, I am the last in line…' he shot her a piercing stare '…and as such it is my duty to provide an heir.'

Monterrato. An heir.

Lottie felt the cold fingers of the past reach out to grasp her. So nothing had changed. It was still all about Monterrato, about providing for its future, continuing the line. The place was like an obsession with Rafael—everything to him; his life, his blood. *She* was also the last in line, as it happened—the sole daughter of John Lamb, deceased, and Greta Lamb, now Lawrence, remarried and living in South America. But you didn't hear *her* banging on about it.

'Well, if you are so keen to have a child I suggest you

find someone else to have one with.' Twisting her bottom on the seat, she sniped back at him, chin high, chest forward. She knew she sounded like a bitter old crow but she couldn't help herself. 'Judging by the number of women that seem to constantly surround you, I'm sure you could have the pick of party socialites only too happy to produce endless beautiful Monterrato heirs for you.'

Thunder rolled across Rafael's face.

'For God's sake, Charlotte.' His fist banged down on the desk, rattling the ormolu inkstand on its lion's paws feet. His eyes were glaring wildly with some unseen force as they locked with Lottie's, now saucer-shaped with alarm. 'Why can't I make you understand? It is *our* baby I want.'

Lottie's mouth fell open, soft with astonishment. This was not the calm, composed Rafael that she knew. The man who was so totally in control of his emotions that she had never seen him break down—not even when their baby had died. He was certainly not the kind of man to lose his temper. At least he never had been.

A thought suddenly occurred to her. He had been in a terrible accident—an accident that had resulted in injuries to his head. Was it possible that he was suffering from some sort of post-traumatic mood disorder? Would that explain the jumpy, volatile, almost out of control man before her?

'You are right, Rafe, I don't understand.' She lowered her voice to try and coax the truth out of him. 'Is it something to do with the accident? Has it affected you in some way?'

The scrape of his chair across the polished parquet floor made Lottie start as he lunged to his feet, leaning forward across the desk with the stillness of a viper about to strike.

'Why would you say that?'

'I don't know. I just wondered…' And, judging by his

attitude, she had hit the nail squarely on the head. 'Do you want to talk about it? You never know—it might help.'

Turning his back Rafael strode towards the windows, the floor creaking beneath his forceful steps. 'There is nothing to talk about. It happened. That's all there is to it.' He all but growled the words over his shoulder.

Maledizione. Talking about it was the very last thing he wanted to do. He felt his breath heaving in his chest with the wretched frustration of it all, felt the unfamiliar sense of powerlessness fuelling his temper.

But what had he expected? That Lottie would agree, with no further explanation, to bear him a child just like that?

He could have lied, of course. Wooed her back until he'd achieved his goal, then told her it was all a sham. Just the thought of the challenge heated the blood in his veins. He could feel her eyes scanning his rear view, sense her biting the inside of her cheek as she waited, the rise and fall of her breasts with each shallow breath, the way she slid her hands between tightly pressed thighs as she perched on the edge of her seat. All of which sent hot waves of desire through his body that would make taking her to his bed—hell, taking her across the desk there and then, for that matter—the easiest thing in the world. And who would blame him, after the way she had treated him, if he used her for his own pleasure? But, no, sex wasn't the answer—no matter how tempting it was.

Outside the light was starting to fade, and with the lamps still not lit the room had taken on a grey, almost smoky hue. Lottie feasted her eyes on the proud silhouette, tall, muscular, brooding against the dying light, committing the image to memory before wrenching her gaze away again.

'Well, in that case there is nothing more to be said.'

Her breath juddered and she rose to her feet. 'There is no point in my being here.'

'No! Stop!' Despite his injuries he was beside her in a couple of long strides, grabbing hold of her arm as she reached down to pick up her handbag.

There was a frozen second of astonishment as they stared at each other, then Lottie's eyes moved from the hand that gripped her forearm to the darkening face of the man it belonged to. Instantly dropping her arm, Rafael stepped back, pushing the ruffled hair away from his forehead.

'I'm sorry. Forgive me.'

'Rafe? Whatever is it?'

Throwing back his shoulders, he fixed her with a penetrating stare.

'Okay, Lottie, if you must know I will spell it out for you.'

His voice was harsh, but the anguish and pain held deep in his eyes sent a shiver of alarm through Lottie.

'The fact is that, as of four weeks ago, I am no longer able to father a child. You and our frozen embryo are my only chance of ever producing an heir.'

CHAPTER TWO

'You can't ever have children?' Lottie stared at him, her face a picture of horror.

'Correct.' Rafael remained where he was, his feet firmly planted, his arms behind his back.

'You are...infertile?'

'I think we've established that.' He glowered at her. 'And, before you let your imagination run away with you, that's *all* it means. Everything else is working quite normally, thank you.'

Lottie flushed. He had, of course, read her mind perfectly.

'But why? How?'

'I'll spare you the details, but basically the tree that saved my life prevented me from being able to produce another. A bizarre twist of fate, I think you'll agree.'

The flush turned into an exaggerated wince. Lottie simply didn't know what to say. She could only imagine the devastating effect this must have had on Rafael. Not to mention the physical pain at the time.

'But is it permanent? I mean, won't it heal? Or isn't there some medical procedure that can make it right?'

'It would seem not.' Rafael shifted his position, alerting Lottie to the fact that she was staring at his groin. 'Believe me, I have explored every avenue.'

'Oh, Rafe.' Suddenly Lottie was rushing over to him, flinging her arms around his neck and hugging his unyielding body. 'I'm so sorry.'

Picking her arms from around his rigid neck with a look of distaste, Rafael let them drop by her sides and took a step back. 'It's not your sympathy I am looking for. It is an arrangement of a much more practical kind.'

Lottie gazed up at him, eyes wide with concern.

'I'm *so* sorry,' she repeated, her mind still struggling to take in this shocking disclosure. 'This must be very difficult for you to come to terms with.'

She put a hand out to touch him but he moved out of her reach, crossing his arms in front of him to form a barrier.

'Have you talked this through with anyone? Had any counselling? You mustn't keep it all bottled up inside.'

'Pah!' Rafael gave a derisive snort. 'I do not need counselling, thank you, what I need is a solution to the problem.'

No change there, then; Lottie didn't know why she had even asked the question. She stared at the proud, haughty man who stood stubbornly a few feet away from her. Here was someone who would rather die than give in to his emotions, whose approach to any problem was to get it fixed and move on, rather than take time to grieve or heal.

'Sometimes there is no solution, Rafe. You just have to accept it.'

'Of *course* there is a solution,' he bit back, 'and it lies with you.'

So this was it, then. The reason she was here. Not to sign divorce papers, to end their marriage, but as part of a last desperate attempt by Rafael to provide a Revaldi heir. Lottie bent her head, covering her eyes with her hand as she tried to order her thoughts, formulate some sort of response, explain to him that, no matter how deeply she felt for his predicament, she simply couldn't do it.

'I realise that you hold all the power,' Rafael cut in quickly, hurrying to fill the empty silence before Lottie could say anything negative, 'and that puts me at a disadvantage.'

Power? Disadvantage? Why was he talking like this? As if it were some sort of business merger instead of the birth of a baby, the creation of a new life that should be born of love and commitment and caring. That explained the suit, she thought suddenly. Rafael was simply trying to broker a deal.

'I will agree to your terms, Lottie. Anything. Just say the word and it will be yours.'

'No, Rafe.' She had to stop him now, before this got any worse.

'If it's a question of money...'

Too late. Lottie felt heat rising up her neck, sweeping across her face, as the hideousness of his suggestion took hold.

'Stop it!'

She was starting to shake with a mixture of outrage and sadness—sadness that he could get her so wrong, that he had never understood her at all.

'Do you seriously believe that you can *buy* me? Buy our baby?'

'There's no need to be so melodramatic.' Pushing back his shoulders, he regarded her coldly over the jut of his chin. 'I'm merely trying to find a mutually satisfactory arrangement. Don't tell me you *enjoy* working in that...' he paused, distaste written all over his face '...so-called *art* gallery in London.'

'It's called earning a living.' Lottie glared at him. 'It's what normal people do. And, anyway, how do you know where I work?'

'I made it my business to know.'

'What do you mean by that?' Even as she asked the question the answer hit her like a snowball in the face. 'You have been spying on me?'

'You might call it spying. I call it research. Obviously I had to make sure I had all the available facts at my disposal before I contacted you.'

His calm, rational voice was stoking the fire that was already roaring away inside Lottie.

'There were certain things I needed to ascertain: your career, for example, the state of your finances, whether there was a man in your life.' He shot her a cold, penetrating stare.

Lottie gasped. How *dared* he? And, worse still, how dare he look at her now as if this was perfectly acceptable behaviour? She felt violated, exposed, as if he had stripped away the thin layer of her composure and left her standing naked and shivering in front of him.

'You are telling me that you have hired some private investigator to follow me, lurk in the shadows, pick through my rubbish bins, train his grubby little binoculars on my windows?' The words were tangling around themselves in their hurry to get out and strangle him.

Rafael gave a short laugh. 'Charming though your old-fashioned image is, things have moved on a bit since long macs and trilby hats. The wonders of the internet have taken over.'

'Well, however you did it, it's despicable.' Lottie swept back the hair from her heated face, lifting its weight from the nape of her neck in an attempt to cool herself down. 'You had absolutely no right to go poking about in my life.'

Scowling, Rafael lowered his brows to an aggressive V. 'Needs must, Lottie. Exceptional circumstances call for exceptional measures. Believe me, I wouldn't be doing any of this if there was any other way.'

And that little statement was supposed to make her feel better, was it? If so, then time had clearly not improved Rafael's understanding of the female mind.

Lottie held her glare in place, fearing that, despite her very real anger, her face might easily crumple with the intense sadness of it all. Because of course Rafael wasn't trying to make her feel better, was he? He was just being his usual brutally honest self. Even at a time like this he wasn't able to dress up the situation for his own gain. His nature was to say it as it was and achieve his aim through the sheer power of his conviction.

Quietly she turned away from him, knowing what she had to say but not trusting herself to look into his eyes as she said it. 'I'm sorry, Rafe, but my answer has to be no. We both know that it would never work.'

Instantly Rafael came towards her, repelling her words with a dismissive arm gesture and an expression to match.

'You don't know that.' His voice was hard, uncompromising, as his eyes bore down on her. 'There have been major advances in IVF procedures even in the past couple of years. I'm sure we have every chance...'

'I'm not talking about IVF procedures.' Throwing back her head, Lottie confronted the full force of his gaze. 'I'm talking about us—me and you as a couple. I'm saying that *we* would never work.' The hostility in her voice was there to mask the knot of pain of their failed marriage that sat deep in her stomach, refusing ever to go away.

'Perhaps I am not making myself clear.' Rafael gave her a look of pure disgust, turning his back on her, then swinging round again with eyes that pierced the gloom. 'I'm not asking for any sort of reconciliation. I am asking you solely to be the mother of my child. Nothing more.'

Nothing more? Despite the darkly oppressive atmosphere it was almost laughable, the way he described it—as if he were asking her to redesign his kitchen or landscape his garden. Except that it didn't make her feel like laughing. More like crying.

'What I am trying to say is that I will expect nothing else of you.' Relentlessly, Rafael pushed on. 'I know that that side of our marriage is over. Rest assured I will not be making any...' he paused, firing a look of icy contempt at Lottie '...any *demands* of you.' Distaste soured his mouth, contorted his handsome features. 'You have my word on that.'

Lottie felt something die inside her. She knew it was true, of course, that sexually she was of no interest to him any more. That side of their relationship had floundered after Seraphina had died, bashed against the rocks of invasive fertility treatments and crushing disappointment. But still, hearing him say the words stretched the sadness inside her until she thought she might snap in two, fold over with misery.

But she had to accept it. Rafael had coachloads of women only too happy to cater to his needs now. Flashes of those internet pictures rose, unbidden, in her mind— the dazzling white teeth and pertly sculptured breasts.

She looked down at herself, at the faded skinny jeans she had worn to travel in and her favourite well-worn ankle boots, then switched her gaze to Rafael. There he stood, ramrod-straight before her, that aura of intense concentration almost shimmering around his dark form. The sombre suit was so beautifully cut that you weren't really aware of it—just of the way his body looked in it: powerful, immaculate, sexy. He epitomised everything that she wasn't, and being back at the Palazzo Monterrato only emphasised that fact.

Gathering together the last shreds of her composure, she raised her chin defiantly. 'Thank you for explaining that, Rafael.' Her voice sounded shrill, uneven, like an incompetent schoolteacher trying to keep control of a class. 'Though you really didn't need to point it out. When I said it would never work between us I meant in terms of the practicalities of our relationship.' On firmer ground now, she pressed on determinedly. 'Even supposing I ever did manage to get pregnant, how could we possibly raise a child together? We don't even...' She paused. There were so many *don't evens* that she didn't know which one to pick. 'We don't even live in the same country.'

With the silent step of a panther stalking its prey Rafael closed the space between them, and Lottie suddenly found herself staring at the broad sweep of his chest.

'Practicalities can always be sorted out.'

As he spoke over the top of her head Lottie realised too late that she had chosen a foolish argument. Rafael was the supreme master of being practical, sorting things out. As Conte di Monterrato that was what he did on a daily basis—oversaw the running of the principality, planned for its future, solved the problems. And that was exactly what he was doing now.

So close to him now, Lottie breathed in his familiar scent—the faint tang of cologne mixed with soap and something else, something indefinably, yearningly Rafael. She could almost feel the intensity that emanated from him, rolling her way, threatening to engulf her.

'I don't want you to think for one minute that I am underestimating the enormity of what I am asking of you.' His voice was very low, earnest. 'But at the same time...' his eyes ruthlessly scanned her face '...I don't believe it is an entirely selfish request. I know what being a mother would mean to you.'

Lottie gulped back the lump in her throat, her eyes widening at his startling assumption. 'Why do you say that?'

'Because I saw you, Lottie.' His pause shimmered with raw emotion. 'I saw the look of euphoria on your face when we found out that you were pregnant—saw the way your maternal instinct kicked in, stronger than any other bond. And then...' He carried on, even though he looked as if he was hurting inside. 'I saw the way you held our daughter in your arms.'

'No. Stop!' This was more than Lottie could bear and her hands flew to cover her ears.

'Admit it, Lottie. It was never me that you wanted, was it?' Relentlessly he surged on. 'It was the baby. The baby was the only thing that mattered. The only reason you ever agreed to marry me. And our marriage was nothing more than a sham. Your final brutal declaration—everything about your behaviour, in fact—points to that one undeniable truth.'

'I won't listen to this any more!' Turning away, Lottie stumbled towards the door, but he was still there—following her, beside her.

'You can still have that dream, Lottie. Even though our marriage may be over in all but name we can still be parents—you can still be that mother.'

'I have no idea why you are saying this.' Blinking back the emotion that was stinging her eyes, Lottie rounded on him, drawing on every last bit of strength she possessed. 'I can only assume you are confusing this with what *you* want, not me.'

'Maybe I thought that too at first.' Rafael positioned himself in front of the door, his towering shape blocking Lottie's exit. 'Until I saw the look on your face just now. I'm right, aren't I? You want a baby every bit as much as I do.'

'No, you are *not* right.' Futilely trying to move him out

of the way, Lottie grabbed hold of the door handle and tugged at it forcefully.

The door opened two inches before it slammed against Rafael.

'Be careful what you decide, Lottie.' He looked down at her calmly, totally ignoring the door battering against his heels as she continued to tug at it. 'Whatever you do, don't let your contempt for me influence your decision—get in the way of your own happiness.'

Finally he moved to one side and the door flew open, sending Lottie teetering off balance.

'That would never do.'

Kicking off her boots, Lottie threw herself down on to the four-poster bed and stared at the tapestry drapes above her, her breath heaving unsteadily in her chest, tears now threatening to spill. How could he do this to her? Taunt her with her failed attempt at motherhood using the preciously painful memories of Seraphina. It was simply cruel.

But that was Rafael. She knew he would stop at nothing to achieve his goal—use anything at his disposal to get what he wanted. Even if it meant tearing open her heart in the process.

Like a double-edged sword, the pain cut both ways, and one slash undoubtedly revealed the truth. She *had* always wanted to be a mother. Not in the vague, one day it would be nice, mentally picking out cute names way that her girlfriends seemed to view motherhood, but with a deep, unfathomable yearning that was intrinsically a part of who she was.

Maybe her own dysfunctional upbringing had made her realise that being a mother was the most important job of all and, rather than putting her off having children, had instilled in her a longing do it right. There was no doubt that when she had discovered she was pregnant with Rafael's baby it had flooded her with euphoric exhilaration. This was her chance to be the sort of mother she had always wanted, rather than the one she had had.

As the only child of a woman who, frankly, had had better things to do than pander to the whims of an annoyingly childlike child, Lottie had been largely raised by au pairs or home helps or whatever neighbour happened to be around. This had left Greta free to indulge in her real passion: travelling. Or, more specifically, cruising the world on luxury liners while Lottie had lived in a perpetual state of terror that one day there would be nobody to meet her at the school gates at all.

Funded by Lottie's much older father, who had thoughtfully taken out a comprehensive life insurance policy before he'd dropped dead when Lottie was still only seven, Greta had become addicted to the glamour of the cruising lifestyle: the handsome stewards in their crisp white uniforms, the perma-tanned dance hosts, the dashing captains. Eventually she had ended up in dry dock with one of the latter, when she had remarried and made a new life in Argentina.

But the other slash of Rafael's sword… Lottie screwed up her eyes against its searing pain, at the realisation that he'd got it so wrong. *'It was never me that you wanted… The baby was the only thing that mattered.'* Was it possible that he actually believed that? That she had really done such a good job of fooling him? And, if so, why did it make her feel so hollowed out with sadness?

Taking a deep breath, she pushed herself up against the feather pillows and gazed at the room around her. It was the same bedroom she had shared with Rafael—well, half of it, at any rate. The huge double doors across the middle of the room were now firmly closed, like a metaphor for their marriage.

How different would things have been if they hadn't lost Seraphina? If there had been no accident? If everything hadn't gone so disastrously wrong? Their daughter would have been three now, running around this crusty old mausoleum, breathing fresh life into it, maybe even joined by a little brother or sister.

But it had happened, and the sequence of events afterwards had happened, leading to her going back to England, starting a new life in London and putting the past behind her. Even if that new life *had* meant studiously avoiding babies of all descriptions—babies in buggies, baby adverts on the television—and even turning away from babies smiling gummily at her over their mothers' shoulders on the bus.

But she had never lost her yearning to have a baby, Rafael's baby. And she had never forgotten their last remaining embryo. The tiny blob of shared cells stored in a tank of liquid nitrogen represented the last vestiges of their relationship and it was always there, locked away deep in her subconscious. Occasionally she would find herself fantasising about the sort of child it might grow into, before hurriedly pushing the thought back in its box and turning the key once more.

And now...now the embryo was being offered its chance of life. Never in her wildest dreams had she imagined that circumstances would bring about a possibility like this. It was a mad, crazy, ridiculous idea.

Wasn't it?

Rafael paced up and down the length of the grand formal dining room, pausing only to check his watch once again. Where the hell *was* she? She knew that dinner was to be served at eight-thirty and she was now an hour late. Was she deliberately taunting him?

It was half an hour since he had gone up to find her, when the sudden, irrational fear had gripped him. He'd pounded his feet along the corridor to her room, convinced that she had gone—run away as she had before. He'd rapped sharply on the door, and the thirty seconds of silence before he had heard her moving about had seemed like an eternity.

But then the door had opened and there she'd been—all sleepy eyes and tousled hair, straight from a rumpled bed still warm from her body. And the sight of her, and that bed, had twisted a coil of lust deep inside of him.

Now that she still hadn't appeared he could feel the same fear spreading through him again. Ten minutes, she had said—just enough time for a quick shower. Pacing back towards the head of the table, he told himself to calm down, get a grip. Stop behaving like an idiot.

He was glaring at the heavy panelled door when it finally opened and Lottie hurried in, all breathless apologies and pointed lack of eye contact. Reaching behind him for the bell that rang down in the kitchens, he waited in cold silence as she walked the interminable length of the table to join him. He watched from beneath the sweep of lowered lashes as she carefully sat down, sliding long legs under the table, shaking open her napkin to cover her lap.

Tearing his eyes away, he seated himself beside her at the head of thc table, steadfastly refusing to acknowledge just how adorable she looked. Her hastily washed and dried hair had resulted in a cloud of tumbling blonde curls that she had loosely twisted into a knot on top of her head, and already escaping tendrils were framing her delicate features. A short jersey dress, its colour a darkest purple, hugged her slender curves in a way that already had the blood racing around his veins.

Lifting a heavy crystal decanter, he started to fill Lottie's glass, watching as her slender fingers curled nervously around the stem. Then, raising his own glass between them, he saw Lottie automatically doing the same. What exactly were they toasting? With her meltingly clear blue eyes mercilessly trained on him he felt for the bedrock of bitterness to help him counter their effect and found it in the pit of his stomach, where it had sat ever since she had left him.

'Your good health.'

It was hardly the warmest of toasts. Lottie looked at his darkly glowering face over the rim of her wine glass. She knew he was angry that she was late for dinner; he had already been in a bad mood when he had woken her up from her unexpected nap, banging on her bedroom door, demanding to know what was keeping her. But her promise of ten minutes had proved impossible to achieve and, torn between nervousness at keeping him waiting and a desire to make herself look at least half decent, the latter had won.

Though now she wondered why she had bothered. It would appear that her hastily applied makeover had simply darkened Rafael's already coal-black mood.

'Yes—*salute.*' After taking a small sip, Lottie put down her glass and concentrated on straightening the already straight silver cutlery, wondering just how she was going to get through this ordeal.

Almost immediately two waiting staff appeared, and in the flurry of dishes being revealed from under domed silver lids and food being expertly served onto their plates Lottie was able to ignore, at least for the moment, the ill-tempered man at her side.

When the staff finally left he pointedly waited for her to pick up her knife and fork before doing the same.

'I suggest we eat this now, before it is completely ruined.'

He really was determined to be relentlessly bad-

tempered, wasn't he? This evening was going to be horrendous.

But the meal was delicious and, seated beside Rafael
in this magnificent cavernous room, drinking mellow red
wine from the ancient, vaulted cellars beneath them, Lottie could feel herself being transported back to the life of
wealth and privilege that she had torn herself away from
so violently two long years ago. Rafael's world. And even
though he was casually dressed now, in jeans and a soft
cotton shirt open at the collar, he still looked every inch
the master—every inch the Conte di Monterrato.

The conversation was limited, with Lottie's attempt at
small talk falling on stony ground and Rafael seemingly
too intent on eating his meal to discuss the weightier subject, though it hovered between them like an uninvited
guest at the meal.

Instead Lottie found herself surreptitiously watching
him, drawn to the shape of his mouth as it moved, the
sweeping line of his jaw, now shadowed with a stubble that
covered some of the bruising, the way dark curls fell over
his forehead when he lowered his head, only to be pushed
back with an impatient hand. In the flickering light of the
candelabra set on the table between them his injuries were
much less visible, and he looked alarmingly like the old,
impossibly handsome Rafael.

The meal finally over, Rafael suggested that they go
into the salon and, reluctantly relinquishing her hold on
a crumpled linen napkin, Lottie followed him across the
marble hallway into the warmth of the relatively modest
room. Coffee and cognac were waiting for them on a low
table in front of the fire and they seated themselves side
by side on the antique sofa. Rafael started to pour her a
balloon glass of brandy but Lottie shook her head. She
had had enough alcohol; she could feel it seeping into her

bones, threatening to muddle her senses. Coffee was a much more sensible idea.

Wrestling with the heavy silver pot, she poured coffee into two china cups and passed one to Rafael. Then crossing her legs, she tried to settle herself beside him, one hand holding a rattling cup, the other one tugging her dress down over her thighs.

'So, have you thought any more about my suggestion?'

The truce was obviously over, and the air was immediately filled with the magnitude of his question.

'Of course I have.' She turned to face him, the sofa springs twanging beneath her. 'And I must say that I don't appreciate the emotional blackmail.'

Rafael spanned the fingers of one hand across his temples, shielding his eyes as if it pained him even to look at her. 'I was merely pointing out that you have a strong maternal instinct. There is no need to be ashamed about that.'

'I'm not ashamed!'

'So you are not denying, then, that in theory you would like to have a baby?' Suddenly he was giving her the full force of his gaze again.

'Yes...no. That is not the point.'

'Because if you would, Lottie, now is your chance to do something about it. I'm sure I don't need to tell you that with the fertility problems you have suffered your chances of having a child with someone else might well prove...challenging.'

'And yours would be non-existent.'

It was a cruel jibe and Lottie could feel the heat of it slash across her cheeks. But she wasn't going to take it back; he deserved it.

'Touché.'

He owned the few dark seconds of silence and Lottie felt increasingly bad with each one that passed.

'So we are both in the same situation. And that has to be all the more reason to make the right decision now.'

Lottie placed her cup back down on the table. He had an answer for everything, didn't he? Except Seraphina. He never wanted to talk about their baby daughter. Well, now she was going to make him.

She sucked in a deep, empowering breath. 'Do you ever think about Seraphina?' The out-breath of words whistled between them like a bullet. And she knew her aim had been sure by the immediate clench of Rafael's jaw.

'Of course I do.' His voice was sharp but he still couldn't hide the emotion behind it. Neither could the shuttered look in his eyes that were fixed on her face. 'How can you even ask such a question? Seraphina was my baby too, in case you've forgotten.'

The vulnerability had gone, immediately replaced with the more familiar animosity, but she had caught a glimpse of it—heard him say her name. *Seraphina.* Spoken with that beautiful Italian intonation. It was all she could do not to ask him to repeat it, over and over again, until she was full to the brim with it.

She looked down from his injured face to the hand that was resting on his muscular thigh, the back of it criss-crossed with the scars and scratches from his accident, reminding her yet again just what he had been through.

Impulse made her reach towards it, tentatively rest her own pale hand over the top of it. 'Maybe I have. I'm sorry.'

The connection between them was immediate, tingling with the sharp pinpricks of recalled intimacy, until Rafael quickly pulled away, running the same hand through his hair as if to cleanse himself of her. He moved slightly in his seat as he took control again.

'I know we can never replace Seraphina, nor would we

want to, but there is nothing to stop us having a healthy child, Lottie. I want you to understand that.'

'Rafe...'

'Just imagine, Lottie...a year from now we could be parents. We can make this happen—I know we can.'

'You don't know that.' Trying to hang on to the last vestiges of sanity, Lottie challenged him. 'Even if I agreed to the embryo transplantation there is nothing to say that it will work.'

'But there is one certainty.' His commanding voice was very low. 'If we don't try we will never know.'

Suddenly the room was stiflingly hot, its silence only broken by the hiss and rustle of the logs settling down on the fire. With the intensity of Rafael's dark eyes boring into her Lottie felt the heat sweep through her body, softening her bones, melting away the layers of resolve that had settled comfortably over her like a blanket of snow.

Could she say yes? Rafael somehow made the decision sound so straightforward. He made everything seem possible. But then he had no thought or care for the life she had made for herself in England. Built up so painstakingly, brick by brick, from the demolition rubble of their marriage. She had finally reached the stage where she felt financially stable and emotionally settled. Most of the time anyway.

Could she really take this enormous gamble and throw caution, common sense and self-preservation to the wind? Hurl them up into the blue sky and watch to see where they fell? The same blue sky that Rafael had fallen from, that had brought her here in the first place.

It was so tempting.

Rafael waited, as if sensing that words were no longer needed. So close now she could feel the soft whisper of his breath against her face, feel herself weakening beneath the unbearable scrutiny of his gaze and the lethal, sensual intoxication of his nearness.

Sitting up very straight, she pushed back her shoulders and mirrored his penetrating stare. This was her decision and she was going to make it.

'Right, I have made up my mind.'

The answering flash in Rafael's eyes was so intense that she had to blink against it, her mouth suddenly dry with the cotton wool words.

'My answer is yes. I will do it.'

CHAPTER THREE

THERE WAS A long second of astonishment. Then, jerking back to life, Rafael clasped Lottie's hands in his, squeezing them tightly in his strong grasp.

'You mean it?' He angled his head to see her face better, to make sure he had understood correctly.

'Yes.'

'You agree to using our frozen embryo?'

'Yes. That *is* what we are talking about here, isn't it?' She attempted a short laugh but it came out as more of a squawk, the panic of what she had just agreed to throttling her vocal cords.

'Then I thank you.' Deeply serious now, Rafael let go of her hands and, tipping her chin with his fingers, captured her gaze with his own. '*Vi ringrazio dal profondo del mio cuore*. Thank you from the bottom of my heart.'

'That's okay.'

Lottie cringed at her vapid reply. *Okay* was hardly a fitting response to Rafael's heartfelt gratitude. Or to the magnitude of what she had agreed to, come to that. But she couldn't think straight—not when he was so close, not when he was looking at her like that, with the soft touch of his fingertips searing against her skin. She needed to get away—away from Rafael and the way he was making her feel. If she had just made the most crazy decision of her life she wanted to be alone now, so that she could scream at herself in peace.

'Well, I think I'll go to bed.' She wobbled to standing. 'I am rather tired.'

'Of course.' Rafael was immediately beside her, holding her elbow. 'We can discuss all the arrangements tomorrow.'

That little statement did nothing to calm her nerves. She went to move away but Rafael held on to her, drawing her closer, his strong arms encircling her body, pressing her against his chest. Lottie froze beneath his embrace.

'You won't regret this decision, Lottie.'

She could feel his breath fanning the top of her head, lightly moving her hair.

'I will make sure of that. This time it will work—I know it will.'

'I hope so.' Her words were muffled against the soft cotton of his shirt.

She had no idea whether it would or not, but right now she had a more pressing concern—literally. The shocking way her body was reacting to his. The initial forbidden twitch of desire had spread through her body, stopping somewhere low in her abdomen, where it now sat, throbbing inside her, waiting for something to happen.

'I know so.'

He pulled her even closer and Lottie felt any resolve fade away as the heat between them intensified. It felt so good, yet so wrong, encased in his muscular arms, with the hard planes of his chest crushing her breasts against him with alarming effect, the lengths of their bodies touching, meeting all the way down.

Ignoring every screaming warning, she found herself arching her body very slightly, to push her pelvis closer to him, to feel more. And she wasn't disappointed. The rock-hard length of his arousal was instantly evident, making its presence felt against her, and her own body immediately went into clenching spasms of desire in response. A thrill of triumph rushed through her that she could still do this to him—that he wasn't as impervious to her as his icy façade would suggest. Up on tiptoes now, she tentatively moved her arms around his neck, wanting more, for *him* to want more.

She heard the guttural growl, followed by a soft Italian curse, then felt her arms being wrenched from his neck, left to fall by her sides as he jerked himself away from her.

'No!'

The word was like a lash-stroke across the exposed flesh of Lottie's desire.

'That is *not* what this is about.'

Standing alone, rejected and exposed, Lottie could only stare at him, watching with wide-eyed confusion as he strode over to the fireplace, kicking a stray log back into the hearth with a shower of sparks.

'I think we need to lay down some ground rules.' He barked the words over his shoulder at her. 'I don't want you getting the wrong idea.'

The wrong idea.

Lottie pulled her gaze from the rigid tension of his back to the empty space where he had stood. Her body was still twitching with desire, her legs trembling beneath her. But his words had shrivelled her heart. We wouldn't want Lottie getting *the wrong idea*, would we? As if he might actually have any *feelings* for her.

Pushing the hair away from her face, she straightened her dress and cleared her throat. She needed to take control now—convince him that she wasn't bothered, that he was overreacting.

'That's okay.' She attempted a throwaway laugh. 'It was nothing. There's no need to get all heavy about it.'

Rafael spun round and gave her a look that bordered on hatred. Swallowing back the bile, he planted his feet firmly apart, glaring at her. '*Si, certo*. Nothing.'

Lottie bit down on her trembling lip. Well, what did he *want* her to say, for God's sake? She was trying to make this better. The shameless way she had wanted him, the humiliation of being abandoned, the look of pure disgust on Rafael's face now—all conspired to make her feel suitably wretched. Now she had to put up some form of defence.

'What I mean is I am fully aware of the situation.' Her voice was surprisingly cold, clear. 'I have agreed to try for this baby with you, Rafael, not to resurrect our marriage.'

Rafael swung round to face her, thunder in his eyes. 'As long as we both know where we stand.'

'I'm sure we do. You have made your feelings towards me perfectly clear.'

'And yours towards me.'

'Yes.'

Lottie flinched. Her big black lie. Impossible to remove now. It was stitched into the fabric of Rafael's being. It was there in every twitch of his muscles, every hitch of his shoulders, every coal-black stare of his eyes.

With a couple of strides he was before her again, glowering down on her defensive body. Lottie faced the wall of his hostility, watching him struggle to control his breathing, his temper, his dislike of her. Struggling with all the things he would not say.

Finally he stepped back, his eyes refusing to leave her face.

'Then I am glad there is no confusion.'

Rafael drained his brandy glass and banged it down on the coffee table in front of him, the emotional roller coaster ride of the evening still wreaking havoc on his body. He ran a hand over his forehead, the ridge of his scar a timely reminder of the accident that had started all this.

He should have been feeling elated. If nothing else he had managed to persuade Lottie to agree to using their frozen embryo. Now he needed to get things moving before she changed her mind—or, worse still, went back to England, met someone else, forgot all about him. He had been fortunate, he had to concede, that that hadn't already happened. That she hadn't already taken up with some uncomplicated young man and started living a happily-ever-after that certainly didn't include him. But his investigations had revealed nothing apart from that slimeball of a boss at the gallery where she worked.

He flexed his fingers. *There* was a guy asking for a punch on the nose if ever there was one. But even if she was unattached now he had had no way of telling for how long. He'd had to act fast.

But not in the way he just had. *Dio...* His hand came down over his eyes. What the hell had he been thinking of, pressing himself up against her like a horny teenager? Displaying, oh, so physically, just how easily she could still turn him on? Because she did, didn't she? Every little *maledetto* thing about her sent his logical brain into a tailspin south. And to the trouble that was waiting for him there.

Though it hadn't just been him. The memory of the way Lottie had responded still pulsed through his veins. Had that been deliberate? A test to see what it would take to make him react? If so, he had shown himself to be the weakest of creatures. She had eventually swept from the room, seemingly not able to get away from him fast enough, presumably gloating with the satisfaction that she could turn him on just like that, just the way she always had.

Well, *enough*. Getting up from the sofa, he stretched

back his shoulders, circling them up and around to ease the
stiffness, almost enjoying the physical pain that shot down
one side of his body. He had to resist, be strong. Moving
over to the fireplace, he caught sight of his battered reflection in the enormous gilt mirror, demonstrating yet again
the mess he had made of his life. He looked away quickly,
only to be confronted by the carved marble cherubs on either side of him, mocking him with their adoring faces.

Sometimes it felt as if the whole world had it in for him.

The next morning dawned bright and clear and Lottie witnessed every stage of it. After a few fitful hours of sleep
she had given up and spent what was left of the night
huddled on the window seat, her duvet pulled around her.
There she had watched the starlit night giving way to the
first flush of pink, the curved sliver of the sun making its
miraculous appearance, rising with surprising speed until
it hung above its unmade bed, ready for the day.

Those silent hours had given her plenty of time to go
over everything—over and over, until she had thought her
head would burst with it. But now, up and dressed, warmed
by the coffee from her otherwise untouched breakfast tray,
she found her mind was surprisingly clear and she knew
what she had to do.

Pulling her phone out of her bag, she first texted her
friend and flatmate Alex, spelling out that she planned to
stay at Monterrato 'for a few weeks more'. There was no
way Alex would be up yet, so at least she was excused having to speak to her and face the barrage of questions that
this breezily worded statement would no doubt produce.

Pressing *'send'*, she couldn't help but smile at the
thought of Alex's reaction, already envisaging her colourfully worded reply.

The next one was more difficult. Informing Ibrahim,

her boss at the gallery, that the 'three or four days' she had taken off work to come here might actually now be more like three or four weeks was not going to go down well. He was prone to bouts of hysteria at the best of times and this was undoubtedly going to ramp up his rage levels. Still, it had to be done. So, punching his number into the phone, Lottie tucked her hair behind her ear, cleared her throat and waited for the soothing buzzing of the connection tone to be shattered by his familiar bark.

The *palazzo* was quiet and still when Lottie finally stepped out onto the landing, the air smelling of polish and freshly cut flowers. Descending the stairs, she looked cautiously around her, feeling the smooth mahogany banister run beneath her hand. She crossed the hall and, pulling open the heavy studded front door, took in a deep, restorative breath.

The Monterrato estate spread out in all directions, as far as the eye could see, sparkling with early-morning dew. In front of her stretched two rows of towering poplar trees, casting strong diagonal shadows across the long driveway that cut through the manicured lawns on either side.

Lottie descended one of the twin flights of stairs and crunched along the gravel path that followed the side of the *palazzo*. The crisp, cold air felt good against her cheeks and she breathed it in greedily, feeling it scour the insides of her body.

With her hands pushed deep inside her coat pockets she strode purposefully on, knowing exactly where she was going—past the kitchen gardens and the outbuildings, the deserted stables and the swimming pool, to a winding path that threaded through a wooded area.

The first signs of spring were starting to appear: snowdrops and crocus were defiantly poking their heads through the cold soil, scattered around the feet of the trees. The path gradually ascended until the trees stopped and there, perched on the top of a hill, was the Monterrato chapel, its burnt umber walls stark against the pearly blue morning sky.

A shallow flight of stone steps, overgrown with moss and weeds, led up to the chapel and the graves that were spread out around it, their headstones tipping drunkenly in the cold sunshine. This was the final resting place for generations of Revaldis, at peace in these beautiful surroundings.

Lottie moved respectfully between them, picking a pathway towards one particular very small grave. The sight of it clutched at her heart. There was the carved angel, still faithfully guarding the slab of painfully clean white marble, one cheek resting on her hands, her wings spread out behind her.

Squatting down, Lottie took a moment to steady herself as the memories came flooding back: the sight of the tiny white coffin being lowered into the ground, the sound of the first handful of soil as it had landed on the lid. Reaching forward, she touched the headstone, her cold fingers tracing the inscription, the words carved into her heart.

Someone had placed a posy of fresh flowers in a small urn and as she absently rearranged them a robin perched on the angel's head, watching her with its beady eyes. All was peaceful and still. Savouring the precious moment, Lottie uttered a small, silent prayer to her daughter and watched as the robin took off, carrying her blessings up into the sky.

'Lottie?'

Lottie swung round with a start. Rafael was standing a few yards away, tall and dark in a long black overcoat, the raised collar skimming his bruised jawline, like some dashing Victorian villain.

'I thought I might find you here.'

Stumbling to her feet, Lottie pulled her coat closer to her. 'I…I just needed to think—to be with Seraphina.'

'Of course. You don't need to explain. I will go…leave you in peace.' He was already turning away.

'No.' Suddenly she knew she didn't want him to go. She wanted him to stand with her, beside their daughter's grave, together. Not to distance himself in the way he always had. 'Why don't you join us?'

If the words sounded flippant they both knew the very real intent that they held. Lottie watched as Rafael hesitated, wariness, uncertainty and pride crossing his face before he quietly moved between the overgrown graves to join her, standing sentry-tall beside the towering angel.

There was a short moment of painfully poignant silence, abruptly ended when Rafael shifted his position and gave a small cough.

'You look cold, Lottie. We should go back to the *palazzo* There are things we need to discuss.'

'I'm fine.' A shiver so violent that it shook her shoulders said otherwise.

Registering the challenge in her voice, he increased the authority of his own. 'Then come into the chapel. It will be warmer in there.'

There was no point in arguing. Lottie followed him to the arched doorway of the chapel and watched as he turned the heavy iron ring on the door.

The small space welcomed them in with its domed sky-blue ceiling, sprinkled with hundreds of gold stars and the gilded altar at the back watched over by the Madonna and child. There was that particular, evocative smell—a mixture of wood and damp and incense.

Walking between the rows of ancient pews, Rafael went to light a candle at the altar, then joined Lottie on the front pew, his long legs stretched before him. They were quiet for a moment, neither wanting to break the spell.

'So…' Eventually Rafael spoke, his voice low and respectful of their environment. 'Your decision last night…'

He turned guardedly to face her, and Lottie noticed that the cold had puckered his scar to a white slash.

'…it still stands?'

'Yes, of course.' She returned his look defiantly.

'Good.' He let out a breath that lowered his shoulders. 'Then I thank you again. I'm sure I don't need to tell you how much this means to me.'

'No, you don't Rafael.' Lottie clasped her cold hands together. 'And, despite the novelty, please don't think that you have to keep thanking me either.'

'As you wish.' He looked at her curiously, trying to gauge her mood. 'Perhaps you would prefer me to move on to the practicalities?'

Lottie wouldn't prefer it, as it happened, but she knew that she had no choice. She scuffed her feet against the ancient tiles.

'Dr Oveisi will be arriving at two-thirty tomorrow.'

'What?' That stopped the breath in her throat.

'Yes. We were fortunate. He had a free day.'

Of course he had. World-renowned IVF specialists were bound to have plenty of time on their hands—empty diaries just waiting for a call. At least that was how it always seemed to work in Rafael's world.

'Tomorrow.' She repeated the word slowly, trying to get it to sink in.

She didn't know why she was surprised. Rafael was a man who, once a decision had been made, acted on it there and then. He was hardly going to suggest a cooling off period—thirty days in which she could change her mind, cancel her contract.

And, despite the shot of panic she had to concede that there was no point in delaying things. She wasn't going to change her mind. The sooner they did this, the sooner they would know if it had worked. And if it did…? Just the thought of that sent a giddy thrill of excitement all the way down to her wriggling toes.

Yesterday, when she had made her decision, it had almost felt as if someone else had taken over her body. Some reckless, feckless madam who had elbowed her sensible self to one side, gagged her with a frivolously decadent undergarment and said, *Yes, Rafael, of course I will agree to this preposterous idea.*

She had strongly suspected that the morning would see her deeply regretting the idea. But her sleepless night had produced more than the dark circles under her eyes. Those chilly hours of darkness had focussed her mind, made her see things more clearly than ever before. She had realised that Rafael was right; she *did* want to be a mother and, even though she hated to admit it even to herself, more than anything in the world she wanted to be the mother of Rafael's child.

This was her one opportunity to make it happen—the embryo's one chance of life. To say no now would be closing the door on that dream for ever, effectively agreeing that their embryo should be destroyed. Something she knew she could never, ever do. Today she was surprised to find that she felt strong—empowered, even, by her decision. This was a huge, massive risk she was taking, but what was it that people said? That life's biggest regrets came not from the things you had done but the things you hadn't? Well, she wasn't going to be accused of that—not this time. No way.

Gazing around the chapel, she felt a flutter of anticipation go through her. If their future chance of parenthood was now in the lap of the gods this felt like the right place to be: seated next to Rafael in this timeless capsule of calm, with the Madonna and child before them. She took strength from that.

'Tomorrow is all right with you?'

Rafael's question cut through Lottie's thoughts and she realised he was waiting for her reply.

'I thought we might as well move this on as fast as we can.'

'Tomorrow is fine.' She turned to face him full-on, even risking a bright-eyed smile. 'The sooner we can do this the better.'

Dr Oveisi turned out to be a rather dapper, middle-aged man with blue-black slicked-back hair and a fondness for gold jewellery. As Lottie nervously shook his outstretched hand she could feel the chunky rings against her sweaty palm.

They were seated in the grand salon—Lottie and Rafael side by side on the sofa, Dr Oveisi on a high-backed chair opposite. It soon became apparent that he was both highly intelligent and not a man to mess around. Rafael's kind of man. After the briefest of introductions he launched straight into questions about Lottie's fertility history, the failed IVF attempts and her current ovulation cycle.

All the while his fountain pen scratched over the notepad he held on his lap, making indecipherable black marks. But for all his lack of social skills Lottie quickly found herself trusting him. There was no schmoozing, no small talk—here was a man in the business of making babies, and everything about him said that was exactly what he intended to do for them.

Beside her Rafael sat quietly, listening intently. Lottie could sense his concentration, the significance of the conversation only really evident in the stiff posture of his body.

Moving on from Lottie's fertility deficiencies, Dr Oveisi turned his attention to the precious embryo. More notes were taken as Rafael confirmed that, yes, it had been frozen at five days old, and gave the name of the fertility clinic where it was stored.

'And there is only *one* blastocyst?' Looking up briefly, Dr Oveisi directed the question at Rafael.

They both knew the term blastocyst: an embryo that had been cultured for five days. Three gruelling rounds of IVF had left them horribly familiar with all the medical terminology.

'Yes.' The lack of emotion in Rafael's clipped reply was telling. 'Just the one.'

'Right.' Screwing the top back on his fountain pen and stowing it in his inside pocket, Dr Oveisi stood up. 'I think that is everything. I will arrange a visit from one of our fertility nurses to discuss Contessa Revaldi's hormone injections. Once we have a date for the transfer I will see you at the clinic.'

Allowing himself the smallest of smiles, he held out his hand to shake Lottie's, bowing slightly before leaving the room with Rafael.

Lottie found herself gazing at his vacated seat. This was all happening so fast. Dr Oveisi, for all his brusque impersonality, had made it seem real, tangible. Was it really possible that a few weeks from now she could be pregnant? Pregnant with Rafael's child?

As promised, the fertility nurse turned up the next day, carrying her bag full of potions. Lottie immediately liked her—a young Eastern European called Gina, obviously very bright, and attractive with it. Her crisp white uniform set off her slender figure nicely, her hair was scraped back into a bouncy ponytail and her intelligent blue eyes held a steady gaze.

Until she saw Rafael, of course. Lottie could almost see her trying to control the *phwoar!* response, fighting to remain professional in the face of this alarmingly handsome man.

Rafael treated her to a polite smile before announcing that he would leave them to it. Alone together, the two women exchanged a glance, and the flush on Gina's face took its time to recede as she turned away to open her bag, fumbling inside for her equipment.

Gina had intended to come and administer the hormone injections every day, until Lottie told her that she could do it for herself. It wasn't as if she hadn't done it before. She watched as Lottie pushed her first injection into her thigh and, obviously satisfied that she knew what she was doing, left her with instructions on the strict routine she had to follow until her next visit.

'And I don't need to tell you about the possible side effects either?' Gina gave Lottie a sympathetic smile.

'Headaches, stomach cramps, mood swings, hot flushes… Looking forward to it already.' Lottie grinned back. 'Been there—got the tee shirt.'

'Well, I hope it's a baggy one,' Gina replied. 'You'll need it to cover the baby bump!'

'Let's hope so.'

The two women looked at each other.

'This *is* Dr Oveisi we are talking about here,' said Gina. 'He takes hope and turns it into reality.'

Gina's faith was touching, even if it did sound a little like a line from a fertility clinic brochure.

Gazing at the array of medication spread out on the table

in front of her forcefully brought home to Lottie what she had to go through—what she had agreed to do. But there was no going back now.

'Yes, I promise I will tell you all about it when I get back. Yes… No… I'm fine. Honestly, Alex, there's nothing for you to worry about. Now, you get back to your Pinot Grigio and let me get some sleep. It's gone midnight here, I'll have you know.'

Lottie ended the call and twisted round to put her phone down on the bedside table. She loved Alex, she really did, but she was becoming increasingly difficult to fob off—especially after a glass or two of wine fuelled her slightly slurred determination to find out, *'Just what is going on over there, Lots?'*

Lottie had lived the past few days in a bubble of unreality—the situation being so crazy that she could hardly come to terms with it herself, let alone try to explain it to someone as excitable as Alex.

She had arrived at Monterrato convinced that she would be signing divorce papers, severing all ties with Rafael, and yet now here she was, trying to get pregnant with his baby and wanting it more desperately than she dared admit even to herself.

Turning out the light, she curled up under the duvet. Her life back in England seemed very far away right now, even though she knew she was going to have to face up to it again at some point—especially the small matter of her job at the Ibrahim Gallery. Ibrahim himself had made it quite clear that he would not authorise any extended leave and that if she wasn't back at her desk within the week there would be no desk for her to come back to. Bearing in mind that threat, she was now left wondering whether she actually had a job at all.

Meanwhile her time at the *palazzo* had settled into a bizarre pattern. Business took Rafael away a lot, and even when he was there Lottie saw very little of him. If he wasn't buried in his office he was chairing meetings in the boardroom, or out and about somewhere in the principality, dealing with the many and complex issues that being the Conte di Monterrato involved.

When their paths did cross he would politely enquire after her well-being. It felt genuine enough, even if he was just checking up on her—checking that she was following Dr Oveisi's instructions to the letter. But something about the way he'd glance at his wristwatch or feel in his pocket for his phone made it quite clear that he had no intention of prolonging their conversations.

It felt almost as if Lottie was just another of the many projects he was dealing with, but even though it still hurt his cool disregard didn't fool her for one moment. She knew this was typical Rafael Revaldi behaviour. That the more something meant to him the less he would let it show.

It was the nights that were the worst—especially when she knew Rafael was around. The thought of him so close, asleep in his bed just the other side of those dividing doors but so far removed from her emotionally, filled her with a yearning sadness. She realised that she had never felt more alone.

Now, as she lay very still, she could hear sounds from next door. Straining her ears, she listened to the creak of Rafael's footsteps on the wooden flooring, the faint hum of the shower. With her imagination intent on torturing her she pictured the low-slung towel around his hips, the damp-slicked hair on his chest and forearms, his biceps bunching as he roughly dried his hair...

Hearing the creak of the bed, she knew that the towel

had now been dropped to the floor and he was sliding, muscular and naked, between the cool linen sheets...

Finally the day of the embryo transfer arrived. It had been arranged that Lottie would drive herself to the clinic and Rafael, who had been in Paris for the past few days, would meet her there.

It was about a two-hour journey, but Lottie knew the way well enough. It was the same clinic where she had undergone the treatments before—where their last remaining precious embryo was stored. But somehow this time, with Dr Oveisi in charge, everything felt different.

As the countryside flew by Lottie settled into the journey. She loved driving this car—one of the fleet of vehicles that Rafael owned. It was a sleek black beast that ate up the miles with silent ease. And it was a relief to finally get away from the *palazzo*—away from the inquisitive eyes of the staff.

She knew they had to be curious about what was going on between the Conte and his bolter of a wife. She would have been, in their shoes. If it was a reconciliation it was a most peculiar one. Half the time Rafael wasn't around, and the other half he kept her at a distance so respectful it bordered on frigid. Hardly the behaviour of a reunited pair of lovebirds.

But with each advancing mile Lottie felt her nerves increasing. The radio was no distraction either. The jangly love songs seemed deliberately to highlight the absurdity of her situation. Slowing down a little, she felt for a bottle of water and gulped down several mouthfuls.

What she was about to do still seemed crazy—unbelievable. Even though she had thought of little else these past few weeks.

It was difficult not to when faced with a daily cocktail

of drugs and injections, but she had never allowed herself to get past this stage—past the actual implantation of the embryo. She couldn't put it off much longer. At some point she was going to have to confront the reality of what she was doing. Whether she was pregnant or not pregnant there were going to be life-changing consequences. And at the moment all of them seemed equally scary.

Rafael was waiting for Lottie on the steps of the clinic and kissed her formally on the cheek. They walked in through the sliding glass doors together.

He looked tall and handsome, wearing a dark grey suit and white shirt, open at the collar, a grey silk tie pulled loose. Lottie was struck afresh by the sheer force of his beauty, his charismatic presence and style. Even in the few days since she had seen him his injuries had healed more rapidly—the bruises faded to a pale yellow beneath his olive skin, the whiplash scar a pale pink line.

They exchanged a silent glance as they stood in the reception area, Rafael's armour plating of control firmly in place, Lottie's mouth too dry to say anything even if she had wanted to.

Dr Oveisi arrived, and as the three of them got into a lift to go up to the third floor he wasted no time in informing them that the assisted hatching of the frozen embryo had been successfully completed and everything was good to go. The expression of relief on Rafael's face was reflected in the mirrored walls around them.

And so it was that, less than half an hour later, the whole procedure had been completed.

Lottie hadn't wanted Rafael to be there—had tried to persuade him that he might prefer to stay in the waiting room, suddenly feeling ridiculously shy in front of him. But, fastening the green scrubs behind his back, he had merely given her a contemptuous look that had needed no words to clarify it. And she had to admit his presence had helped; like a towering wall of determination, it had felt as if his will alone was enough to make this work.

And when he had reached for her hand she had found herself gripping it as if her life depended on it. Or at least their baby's life.

Now he stood behind her as they stared at a computer screen and the doctor ran the scanner over Lottie's stomach, pointing out the tiny bubble of air showing where the embryo had been placed. Lottie stared at it, sending out all the positive vibes she could, willing it to do what it had to do.

'Now…' Dr Oveisi turned to look at the prospective parents. 'There are a few rules you will need to abide by for the next couple of weeks.'

From her prone position, Lottie nodded.

Rafael waited, sharp and alert.

'I am a firm believer that stress is the body's worst enemy when it comes to successful embryo implantation, and as such it should be avoided at all costs. Research is only just beginning to discover how important the right mental state of the recipient is. By that I don't mean that the Contessa should take to her bed and do nothing—far from it.' He looked directly at Lottie. 'I want you to use the next couple of weeks to do the things that give you pleasure—activities that will take your mind off the outcome of the procedure. So moderate exercise, mental stimulation and full marital relations are all advisable.'

Marital relations? The very air in the room seemed to gasp at the thought of it. That was the one thing Lottie could guarantee wasn't going to happen.

The sad absurdity of the situation forcefully struck her once again.

Finally Rafael and Dr Oveisi left the room, leaving Lottie to stay in bed for the requisite fifteen minutes. Gazing into space, she felt a myriad of conflicting and confusing thoughts crowd her mind. Had that really just happened? Was she really lying here with their embryo implanted inside her?

Up and dressed, and feeling a bit more in control, she went down to the reception area. The twin stares of the two receptionists alerted her to where Rafael stood, leaning against the wall, one long leg crossed over the other, talking into his mobile phone.

Seeing Lottie he gestured her towards him.

'Oui, oui, d'accord, deux semaines.' He raised his eyebrows at her before returning to his call, speaking in rapid French.

Lottie had always been confounded by the way he could do that—switch from one language to another with seamless ease. Fluent in English, French and German, as well as his native Italian, it seemed to be as natural to him as breathing.

As she waited for him to finish she suddenly had a vivid flashback. The two of them snuggled up together in the ridiculously narrow bed of the tiny student flat she had been renting when they'd first met, with the diffused afternoon sun filtering through the cheap cotton curtains. Rafael had been teasing her about her schoolgirl French, making her repeat words after him as he trailed his fingers down her naked skin, following them with a line of feather-light kisses. As each word had become more erotic than the last he'd finally claimed her pouting lips with his own, and the lesson had ended with something that was certainly never taught in school.

'Bene—everything is sorted.' Slipping the phone into his trouser pocket he turned, frowning slightly as he no-

ticed the flush on Lottie's cheeks. 'I've arranged a little trip away for us.'

Lottie readjusted her face. 'What do you mean?'

'We are going to Villa Varenna. I thought you might like that.'

'Well, yes...maybe.'

Now it was Lottie's turn to frown. The Revaldis had property all over the place, but this was her favourite— a beautiful villa, perched on the side of a stunning Italian lake.

'When were you thinking of going?' It seemed a strange time to be considering a holiday, when their lives were on hold until they knew if she was pregnant.

'Now.' Rafael's beautiful dark eyes regarded her calmly.

'Now?' Lottie repeated incredulously. 'How could we possibly go now?'

'Easy. I've already got the helicopter here. We can be there in a couple of hours.'

'But we can't. I mean—not now. I don't have any things...clothes, toiletries.'

'You're not seriously telling me you can't go because you don't have a toothbrush?'

Lottie gave him her best imperious stare. Just because he had come over all Mr Spontaneous, it didn't give him the right to mock her.

'I am just trying to be practical. What about the car— the one I drove here in?'

'All sorted.' He dismissed her concerns with a wave of his hand. 'There is really nothing to get worked up about.'

'I am not worked up.' She modulated her voice accordingly. 'How long would we go for?'

'Until we know for sure that you are pregnant.'

'Two weeks!' The voice soared again. 'Surely you can't just drop everything and go away for two weeks?'

'There are such things as computers, Lottie, and phones and modern technology. I'm not suggesting we paddle up the Amazon and live in a mud hut. I can work quite well from the villa. Neither am I suggesting that we drop everything, come to that. Let me put your mind at rest on that score.'

Well. That was her firmly put in her place.

'There is one thing, though. The villa is unstaffed, with this being a spur-of-the-moment decision. There is no one around. I could arrange it, of course, but I've decided not to bother. I thought we might enjoy having the place all to ourselves.'

CHAPTER FOUR

SITTING ON THE terrace of Villa Varenna was like having been transported to a different world. Only a few hours ago she had been lying on a hospital bed, staring at the central heating ducts. Now dusk was turning into night over Lake Varenna and the colourful lights of the properties scattered along the shoreline were glittering like a necklace of jewels. As the sky turned a milky blue against the jagged black shapes of the mountains the water was transformed to a luminous purple.

Lottie had never been able to get used to this—the sheer wealth and privilege of the Revaldi family. It was so far removed from her own upbringing she had never felt comfortable with it; growing up in a suburban semi had hardly prepared her for *this*. Her life had been all Neighbourhood Watch and twitching curtains—her own mother having given them plenty to twitch about when she had arrived back from yet another *little holiday* with a suntanned gentleman and a giftwrapped memento of some exotic place she had no doubt viewed from the deck of a cruise ship.

It was different for Rafael, of course; he had been born into this lifestyle—it was a part of him, who he was. And along with the wealth and privilege came an enormous amount of commitment and hard work. Lottie had seen for herself the weight of responsibility that came with the title of Conte di Monterrato—a title that had passed to Rafael on the death of his father.

Lottie had never met her father-in-law, Georgio Revaldi. He had died suddenly when she and Rafael were still living in Oxford, effectively ending their fairytale life there and then. Because that was what it had been, Lottie now realised. A Rafe and Lottie fairytale—a glorious, passionate, heady love affair that had been far too perfect to make it in the real world. It had been inevitable that the story would come to an end, that the book would eventually slam shut.

They had met one drizzly afternoon in Oxford when Rafael had appeared through the steam of the espresso machine in the coffee bar where Lottie had worked. Two hours, several cups of coffee and an impatient queue of customers had seen them briefly sketch in their lives to each other. Rafael had been finishing his business doctorate at the university; Lottie had ben in her third year at art school. It had seemed the most natural thing in the world that he would wait for her to finish her shift, that they would then run together through the full-on rain to Rafael's favourite English pub and arrive, laughing and dripping over the towelling bar mats, already totally and recklessly in love.

Because it *had* been reckless—especially Lottie getting pregnant so quickly. Even though they had been thrilled—speechless with joy, in fact—it had meant a hastily arranged wedding in an Oxford register office, and in retrospect Lottie could see that was hardly what Rafael's father would have wanted for his only son and heir. That in all probability she was not what he would have wanted for his only son and heir.

But she'd never had the chance to find out because

Georgio had died shortly after their wedding and that was when everything had changed. Rafael had hastened back to Monterrato, taking with him his pregnant bride, throwing Lottie into the totally unfamiliar role of wife of the Conte. And with the principality seeming to take up all of Rafael's time cracks had started to appear in their relationship even before the tragedy of Seraphina's death.

Lottie had been lonely, resentful of this wretched place Monterrato which had stolen the husband she had fallen in love with in England and replaced him with a workaholic businessman.

And nothing had changed now. The principality of Monterrato still came first. The only reason she was here was to protect its future, provide an heir. But even with that realisation gnawing away at her she couldn't hold back her excitement as she spread her hands across her stomach. That heir might…just might…be starting life inside her now.

Hearing a sound behind her, she turned to see Rafael coming towards her, carrying a blanket over his arm.

'I thought you might need this.' Shaking it out, he went to spread it over her knees, but Lottie edged further along the bench to stop him.

'I'm not an invalid, you know.'

'I know. I just thought you might be cold.'

'Well, I'm not.'

'Okay. Just bad-tempered then.' Whipping back the blanket, he threw it over one shoulder and looked down at her. 'What would you like to do tonight?'

Lottie darted a look at him, his shadowed figure tall and imposing as he stood there, matador-like, waiting for her answer. Surely he wasn't expecting them to do anything *else* today, was he? Wasn't an embryo transplantation followed by a helicopter ride to this place enough for one day?

'Do?'

'I mean about food.' His eyes glowed in the dark. 'Do you want to go out for a meal?'

'No, thank you. I'm actually quite tired. Not invalid tired—just...well, tired.'

'Yes, of course. I should have thought. In that case I will cook something for us.'

'You really *are* determined to make me an invalid, aren't you?'

The barb hit its target and Rafael pursed his lips against a spreading smile. 'That was uncalled for, young lady.' He regarded Lottie in the dying light. 'And, besides, I hardly think you are in a position to make accusations. Unless you have recently acquired some skills that were hitherto sadly lacking?'

'I may have done.' Lottie raised her chin in challenge. She hadn't, in fact—she was still as useless as ever in the kitchen. But he didn't have to know that.

'Well, in that case I will look forward to some gourmet meals during our fortnight here.'

Lottie's heart lurched inside her. However was she going to survive two weeks here, alone with Rafael? Looking at him standing there, feeling the watchful gleam of his dark eyes, food was the least of her worries.

'Shall we go in now?'

'In a minute. I just want to sit here a little longer.'

Indicating that she should budge up, Rafael sat down beside her.

Actually she had meant sit here *alone*. Suddenly the bench seemed ridiculously small for two people—especially when one of them was six feet four, with the musculature of someone who was no stranger to the gym.

'It *is* beautiful, isn't it?'

Edging a little further away from him, Lottie pointedly commented on the view, watching the way the colours of the water had changed to an inky blue. The sky was still several shades lighter, the first stars starting to pierce its skin. The fact that she was sharing it with someone who was making every nerve-ending in her body stand to attention was neither here nor there.

'*Si, molto bella.*'

Lottie held her breath as his arm slid along the back of the bench behind her.

'I thought perhaps you could do some painting while you are here.'

'Maybe.' Her breath came out with a huff. The arm behind her suddenly felt controlling, domineering, even if the idea of painting again did excite her. It had been so long since she had done any of her own work. And this would be the perfect place to paint.

'You mustn't give up, you know.' Misinterpreting her coolness Rafael held the back of the bench and swivelled round to face her, his knee touching her thigh. 'You have a considerable talent. It would be such a waste not to use it.'

'I'll bear that in mind.' Her acerbic reply was in no small part a response to the intimacy of his closeness in the dark, to the way she could feel the heat coming off his body, hear his breath as it met the cold air.

'Come on.' Standing upright, he gestured to her to do the same. 'We need to go inside and get you some food. Perhaps that will improve your temper.'

The kitchen was sleek and modern, all polished concrete and brushed steel. At first sight it appeared devoid of anything edible, but opening the fridge revealed that it was fully stocked with eggs, milk, cold meats and cheese, and the larder contained an impressive array of packets and tins, all neatly lined up for their inspection.

'I arranged to have a few supplies brought in.' Rafael's voice came from inside the fridge. 'What do you fancy?'

'I don't know.' Momentarily sidetracked by his rear view, Lottie looked away. 'Omelettes?'

'Good idea.' Coming out with the eggs, he proceeded to open every drawer and cupboard in the room before coming up with a bowl, a frying pan and a whisk.

Lottie perched herself on a stool at the island unit as Rafael moved around the kitchen gathering his ingredients. She was secretly enjoying this—not just the novelty of having him cook for her but being able to watch him do it, to let her eyes follow him around when he was too distracted to return her stare, match it with his own.

'Anything I can do to help?'

He was chopping peppers now, the knife coming down hard and fast on the wooden board. This was the point when Lottie had to look away—she'd never liked the sight of blood.

'You can open the wine if you like.'

'I think I might stick to water.'

Suddenly the knife paused, the blade glinting in midair. As Rafael pushed the hair back from his marked forehead Lottie could see the enormity of the day's events reflected in his eyes.

She gulped back a sudden lump in her throat. 'But I will pour a glass for you.'

One smoke alarm, a medley of half-cooked vegetables and a burnt omelette later, their meal was finally finished.

Laying down her knife and fork, Lottie looked across at the man on the stool beside her, trying to figure out what was going on in his head. Dark, complicated, charming, ruthless, passionate, controlling—he was all of those things and more. He hadn't changed, and no matter how much she tried to ignore it, Lottie knew that neither had her desire for him. He looked so handsome when he was relaxed like this, one leg bent, a scruffy leather boot resting on the bar of the stool, his faded jeans pulled taut against his powerful thigh. He was like a deadly potion, begging to be drunk.

'Well, thank you. That was….interesting.' Eyebrows raised innocently, she blinked at him.

'It was terrible, wasn't it?' Tearing at a hunk of dry bread, Rafael, obviously still hungry, put a piece in his mouth and chewed, his strong jawline moving rhythmically. 'But before you mock don't forget it's your turn tomorrow. Your chance to show me these new-found skills.'

'I never said they were *culinary* skills.' Letting her guard slip for a moment, Lottie batted back what was meant to be a light-hearted quip, but Rafael instantly stiffened, twisting round on the stool to face her.

'So what other skills might we be talking about?' His voice was suddenly hard, probing, the whole mood having changed in an instant.

'None —nothing.' Lottie frowned at him. 'I was just messing about.'

'*Have* you been messing about, Lottie?' Rafael's eyes bored into her, scanning her face for answers. 'That's what I want to know.'

'Rafe, stop this. That's not what I meant and you know it.'

'But there have been other men?'

Suddenly angry, Lottie reared up. 'I think you will find that is none of your damned business.' She could feel the heat sweeping across her cheeks, temper mixed with indignation and defiance shooting violet sparks into her icy blue eyes as she held her body taut. 'And besides, why do you even need to ask? Haven't your nasty little private investigators already given you all the information you need? In fact, why don't you tell *me* what I've been up to? You probably know more than I do.'

'Now you are being ridiculous.'

'So nothing, eh? Your grubby little spies could uncover nothing?' She glared at him. 'But it's still left you
wondering, hasn't it? Whether maybe they missed something—maybe I do have a lover tucked away that you know
nothing about?'

'And do you?' His voice was lethally low, his eyes warning her that she was entering very dangerous territory
with this taunt.

'No. I don't, as it happens. But what if I did? What right
do you have to poke your nose into my love-life when
no doubt *you* have had a string of women in your bed?'
She paused, her pent-up breath swelling her breasts as she
dared him, *willed* him to deny it.

But he just continued to glower at her, his egotism, his
gall, the downright sexual arrogance of him fuelling her
outrage and jealousy, bringing bile to the surface.

'Any women I might have had are none of *your* damned
business.' The weight of his words broke the cruel silence.

Slipping off her stool, Lottie knew she had to get away
from him. She was *not* going to fling herself into that bear-
pit of torture. Not today, at any rate.

'I'm going to bed.'

Suddenly he was beside her, pulling her towards him,
locking his arms around her unyielding body in the steel
ring of his embrace.

'Get off me.'

She struggled to free herself from his arms but then
stopped when the contact between them threatened to take
a different, much more worrying turn. As he loosened his
grip slightly, just enough to pull back and look into her
face, Rafael's blazing stare told her that he had felt it too.

Dropping his arms, he turned his back, walked away
from her. 'I think you need to remember what Dr Oveisi
said.' He spoke coldly over his shoulder. 'You really

shouldn't get yourself all worked up, you know. It's not good for you...' He paused, hesitating over his choice of words. 'Or for the chances of the pregnancy working.'

Could he be more arrogantly, impossibly infuriating? Lottie didn't know what enraged her the most. His audacity in cross-examining her about her love-life or the patronising way he thought he could control her.

'Don't you dare start telling me how to behave.' She fired off the words at the broad expanse of his back. 'You started this fight—twisting my words, cross-examining me about my love-life. You are the one that needs to think about their behaviour.'

'I suggest you try and get a good night's sleep.' Turning round, Rafael levelled cold dark eyes in her direction. 'I'm sure you will feel better in the morning.'

Wandering out on to the terrace, Rafael followed the pathway down towards the ornate iron gates that opened directly onto the lake. Turning the heavy old key in the lock, he let the gates swing open and descended the steep flight of steps down to the water, his footsteps hollow against the worn stone. A row of striped mooring poles stood to attention in front of him, the furthest one having a sleek speedboat tethered to it, the water gently slapping at its sides.

Seating himself on the boardwalk, Rafael let his legs hang over the water, absently staring down into the rippling blackness.

Today had seen the first stage of his mission accomplished. His only hope of fatherhood had finally been given its chance of life. Whether it worked or not was now down to the tiny blob of cells, five days' worth of shared genes, set free from its frozen prison, free to make its own decision about the future.

He should have been feeling elated—jubilant. This had

been his goal ever since he had been delivered the devastating news that the accident had rendered him sterile. But there was no elation, just anger—with himself and with the situation.

What had he been thinking, getting into an argument with Lottie on the very first evening? Wasn't he supposed to be making this a stress-free fortnight? It had come out of nowhere, that primal jealousy—fury, even—that she might have been with another man. He couldn't think about it, couldn't bear to go there. His investigations had revealed nothing, and she had said there was no one. He had to leave it at that.

But still the thought of her in the arms of another man tortured him as viciously now as it had when she had first left him. The idea that some bastard might have taken her to his bed, touched her, made love to her, poured a river of molten lava through his veins.

It wasn't as if *he* had remained celibate. Lottie was right. There *had* been other women—probably not as many as she imagined, but women who had shared his bed, satisfied his needs. But none of them had meant anything. Since the day Lottie had left him, the day she had told him she had never loved him, it was as if that part of him had died—the part that was capable of really feeling, the part that was capable of love.

But now that Lottie was back in his life he realised that the feelings he had thought were dead—had been *sure* were dead, in fact—were just buried, deep down inside him. Seeing her again, spending time with her, had brought them all back up to the surface, leaving them exposed to the elements like blind earthworms, ready to be pecked at by a circling crow.

Well, that was *not* going to happen. No matter how alluring she might be, how the turn of her head or the tilt of her chin might take him straight back to the lovely young woman he had fallen in love with, how unconsciously sexy, how damned infuriatingly, *grabbably* gorgeous she was… he was *not* going to open his heart to her again. After all, hadn't she spelled out her feelings clearly enough to him? Or lack of them, at any rate. What sort of fool would go back for a second helping of *that*?

Upstairs in the cream and white-painted bedroom, Lottie, wearing the sensible cotton nightie that had been mysteriously laid out for her, slipped into the freshly made bed, propping the pillows up behind her. Her head felt as if it might explode with everything that had happened that day. Pulling the duvet under her chin, she drew her knees up to her chest and hugged them tightly, trying to find some rational logic, something to justify the crazy madness of it all.

Except, of course, there was none. Rational logic would have screamed at her not to do this, to get straight back on a plane to England and flee the deadly cocktail of longing and torment that was Rafael Revaldi. Rational logic would have saved her from the way she felt now, her whole body churning with impotent resentment and powerlessness.

How dared he come over all caveman like that? What right did he have to challenge her about her love-life when she knew for a fact that he had scores of beautiful and eligible women throwing themselves at his finest leather handmade shoes? She had had to accept it, even if it did still hurt like a knife stabbing her in the gut.

It wasn't as if she had actually been seeing anyone—not seriously. There had been dates—nice young men who'd wanted to take things further, with earnest declarations of love, even, but none of them had come close to affecting her. She simply couldn't relate to them. Not after a real man. Not after Rafael. She was quite resigned to the fact that he had been the one and only man for her. She had always known it.

It was what had made leaving him the hardest thing she had ever done in her life.

But she had had to find the strength to walk away. Their future together had died along with Seraphina—despite or maybe because of Rafael's obsession with getting her pregnant again. It had been as if a baby would be the only thing to validate their marriage, that without a child he would have to face up to the reality of the situation. That he should never have married her. That she was a mistake.

Her bed was positioned opposite the window, with views over the lake and the mountains beyond. Lottie had left the shutters open, and now she slipped out of bed and padded over to the window to look out. She could just make out a dark figure locking the iron gates down by the water, then moving purposefully up the terrace pathway towards the villa.

Retreating into the shadows of the room, Lottie watched as Rafael's imposing shape came closer until he stopped abruptly and looked up at her window. Gripping the window frame, Lottie stared back at him. Their eyes locked for a moment. Then with a curt nod of his head he started walking again, until the villa hid him from view.

CHAPTER FIVE

FOR A SECOND when Lottie opened her eyes the next morning she couldn't remember where she was. Light was streaming into the room, and the picture-perfect view of the mountains and sky was like a painting, hanging on the wall before her.

But mad reality soon flooded back, nudging aside the blissful ignorance of sleep and replacing it with a checklist of worries. The embryo transfer, being here at Villa Varenna, two whole weeks closeted with Rafael, not to mention his boorish behaviour last night... They had almost come to blows within hours of being here, for heaven's sake. That hardly boded well for the rest of their stay.

Slipping out of bed, she went into the bathroom, stopping as she caught sight of herself in the full-length mirror. Her long blonde hair fell about her shoulders in sleep-ruffled chaos and her eyes, still drowsy with sleep, squinted back at her. Stepping back, she surveyed herself from the side, smoothing down the fabric of her nightie over her very flat stomach.

What was going on in there? Could she be pregnant? Was it really possible?

The realisation of how much she wanted this baby was shocking, dizzying. An outsider might have assumed she was doing this for Rafael—her final gift to him, a last attempt to atone for the brutal way she had walked out on him. Why else would she consider condemning herself to a loveless marriage solely for the sake of bearing him a child? But the outsider would be wrong. She wanted this baby—wanted it with every fibre of her being. Not to help Rafael out of his predicament, not out of guilt or selflessness, and certainly not because she cared about providing an heir for Monterrato. She wanted this baby for herself. It was her chance of motherhood. To be the mother she had always wanted to be.

Uttering a few silent words of encouragement to her tummy, she stepped into the shower and let the powerful jets of water pummel all thoughts from her head.

'Buongiorno.' Rafael looked up from his laptop as Lottie entered the kitchen, registering the cloud of freshly washed curls, the floral scent of shower gel. She was wearing a flimsy cotton dressing gown belted so tightly around her waist it was in danger of cutting her in two. 'Your things have arrived. I'd have brought them up, but I thought maybe you needed a lie-in.'

'How considerate.' She winced at her own acerbity. Today was supposed to be a new day, with the bitterness of yesterday put behind her.

'I hope you slept well?' Ignoring her ill temper, he pulled out a stool for her. He was wearing a white shirt, the sleeves rolled up above the elbow to reveal muscular olive-skinned forearms, liberally dusted with dark hair.

'Yes—fine, thank you.'

'Are you hungry?' He gestured to the plate of pastries beside him.

'Umm…'

He slid the plate towards her and watched as she seated

herself next to him, carefully arranging the dressing gown to cover her legs.

'They do look nice.'

'*Cornetti*, fresh from the *panificio*. I took the boat out early this morning.'

Slicing open one of the pastries, she spread it thickly with butter and took a bite.

'So, how are you feeling?' Closing his laptop, Rafael turned to give her his full attention, distracted by the grease-slicked swell of her pink lips as she chewed hungrily.

'If you mean by that do I feel pregnant, then, no—I feel just the same as yesterday.' She concentrated on her eating.

'Actually, I meant has your mood improved?' Every now and then he could glimpse the tip of her tongue, disappearing into the dark moistness of her mouth. 'But I guess you have answered that.'

'My mood is perfectly all right, thank you.' Wiping her fingers on a piece of paper towel, she tipped her chin to look at him.

'Good…good.'

He leant forward, watching her eyes widen as he did so, and removed a flake of pastry stuck to her lower lip, then sucked it off his finger. The intimacy of the gesture shocked him. What did he think he was doing? Lottie looked equally startled, immediately pulling back.

'You don't have to be like this, you know,' she said. Holding the collar of her dressing gown, she pulled it more tightly across her chest.

'Like what?'

'I don't know… Like, well…falsely polite.'

'Meaning…?' He stared at her.

'What I'm saying is, don't feel that you have to pussyfoot around me for the whole two weeks. It wouldn't feel right—and anyway the strain will kill you.'

'Pussyfoot?' He watched the blush spread across her cheeks as she looked down, moving pastry crumbs around on the plate with her finger. The word seemed to have taken on a far more carnal meaning. 'I had no idea that was what I was doing.'

'I just mean that we need to try and be normal.' She turned to look at him again, still fighting to control the colour of her skin. 'We both know the situation; it's not as if we need to pretend to each other. Playing the part of dutiful husband is not going to make me any more pregnant and it would just feel like a sham.'

'Well, thank you for pointing that out.'

As her sharp words hit home Rafael narrowed his eyes at her. It was obvious what she was doing: setting the ground rules, constructing a safety barrier between them to keep his unwanted attentions away. Just the idea that she thought she had to do that curdled his stomach.

'Fine.' His voice was harsh, cutting. 'I agree that we don't want there to be any misunderstandings between us. Like we might enjoy each other's company, or anything like that.'

Now it was Lottie's turn to feel the chill. Why was she being made to feel bad for pointing out the truth? The hostility he had shown her when she had first arrived back at the *palazzo* had demonstrated clearly enough what he thought of her.

'I think it's important that we are honest with each other, that's all. I know what Dr Oveisi said, and everything, but that doesn't mean we should be trying to fool each other.'

'Whatever you say.' Bored with the subject, Rafael stood up, fixing Lottie with a steely stare. 'Have you finished your breakfast?'

Well, *that* awkward conversation was obviously over. 'Yes, thank you. I'll go and get dressed now.'

'Wait.' He watched an immediate flicker of wariness cross her blue eyes. 'I have something to show you first.'

'You do? What's that?'

'Come with me and you will find out.'

There was a beat of hesitation before Lottie slipped down from the stool, a flash of leg emerging from the unflattering dressing gown.

'I hope you will accept one thing I have planned as a result of Dr Oveisi's advice without feeling the need to argue about it.'

Lottie followed him out of the kitchen and up the stairs, her heart thumping more wildly with every step. What exactly had he planned? Despite telling herself not to be stupid, only one piece of Dr Oveisi's advice clanged loudly in her head. *Full marital relations.* They appeared to be heading for a bedroom. She could feel her traitorous body already bounding ahead of her brain. Surely there was no way he could be thinking…? Could he?

Crossing the landing, Rafael flung open a door and gestured to her to go in before him. Cautiously, Lottie entered.

'What do you think?'

Beside her now, he watched her survey the contents of the room. An artist's easel had been set up in the middle, and a large number of stretched canvases of various sizes were propped against the wall. A palette, a pot of brushes, and a dizzying array of tubes of paint were laid out on a table next to the easel.

'I thought this room might be the best—with the light, I mean. It faces north.'

Lottie stared at it.

'Is something wrong?'

'No—no, of course not.'

'What, then?'

Desperately trying to compose her features in order to

banish any sign of disappointment, Lottie paced around the room. 'It's just that it's a bit over the top.' She attempted a small laugh as she gesticulated around her. 'I mean, we are only here for a fortnight—even Van Gogh couldn't paint this many canvases in two weeks!'

'Who said anything about two weeks? We can leave the room like this and you can come whenever you want—stay as long as you like when you are pregnant. It's beautiful here in the springtime.' Catching the look on Lottie's face, he narrowed his eyes. 'All pregnancy-friendly paints and solvents—I've checked.'

If only it was just the paint that was troubling her. Far more worrying was the way he was insidiously starting to control her life, beginning to manipulate her, make decisions about her future without even consulting her.

And more worrying still was the way her body had soared with excitement at the ridiculously misguided idea that he might be taking her to bed.

'We don't know if I am pregnant yet, Rafael.' Cross with herself, and determined to exert some control of her own, she knew the words sounded harsher than she felt. Moving in front of the window, she planted her bare feet firmly on the floor, yanked the belt of her dressing gown tighter. 'And even if I am, I'd like to remind you that nothing has been decided yet. I have no idea why you are assuming I will be living *here*.'

'Well, not necessarily here...'

'I mean here as in Monterrato. I *do* have a life of my own, you know—a flat, friends, a job.'

That last bit wasn't strictly true, of course. In fact it wasn't true at all. One final phone call from Ibrahim had seen to that. He had been predictably furious that she hadn't obeyed his instructions and been back at work within the week, and somewhere in amongst the shouted tirade she gathered she had been fired.

But funnily enough all she had felt was relief. Her twelve months at the Ibrahim Gallery had become increasingly strained as Ibrahim, a well-known and respected art dealer, had pushed the boundaries of their working relationship further and further. 'Meeting clients' had increasingly involved briefing sessions in a wine bar first, followed by dark taxi rides with him leeringly spreading himself across the leather seat towards her, the sour smell of whisky on his breath. She had made it very clear on more than one occasion that she would certainly *not* be going back to his place for any *debriefing*.

In retrospect, telling him exactly where he could stick his installations might not have been the wisest of moves—especially as his parting shot had been that she would never work in the art world again. Which was probably true. He was vindictive enough to see to that. But she would find something else somehow. She knew that much. She had started over before, and refused to be afraid of the prospect now.

The more pressing problem at the moment was the toweringly dark man staring at her from across the room. Staring at her with such intensity, such heart-racing, piercing concentration, that Lottie could feel it drilling through to her core, where it heated her from the inside with its seductive power.

'I'm sure there is nothing that can't be put on hold.'

The spell was broken and Rafael's bluntly dismissive words brought Lottie back to her senses, her heart-rate spiking with indignation. Why did he always assume that her life was unimportant?

'Once we know for sure that you are pregnant obviously the sensible thing will be for you to stay at Monterrato.'

'Well, your definition of "obvious" is *obviously* not the same as mine.' She stumbled over her tongue-tied sentence. 'What I am saying is, *if* I am pregnant there is no reason for me not to return to England at least until the baby is due.'

'No, Lottie.' His voice was calm and even, like water just before it cascaded over a hundred-metre drop. 'That is *not* how this is going to work. *When* we know for sure that you are pregnant you will be staying at Monterrato. For the whole of your pregnancy.'

The air between then hummed with tension.

'I think I need to point out one very important thing.' Pushing back her shoulders, Lottie placed her hands firmly on her hips. 'I have agreed to try for this baby, Rafael, not given you the right to control my life. You might do well to remember that.'

Dio! Rafael was having trouble remembering anything at the moment. She obviously had no idea, but standing in front of the window in that damned dressing gown Lottie was giving him a perfect silhouette of her body. He had tried not to notice, to look away, but the outline of her waist, the curve of her hips, her long, shapely legs, kept drawing him back. And now she had gone and thrust forward her breasts to taunt him still further.

'You need to get some clothes on.'

He saw Lottie frown at him. At the gruffness of his voice. At thc abrupt change of conversation. He knew he had to get away—away from the physical ache of sexual hunger that Lottie stirred in him.

Striding towards the door, he turned and gave her one last glance over his shoulder before marching back down the stairs.

He was heading for the study, but changed his mind. First he needed to do something physical—burn off some of the excess energy that was suddenly pumping through him. The next flight of stairs took him down to the basement, to the gymnasium and indoor pool. Flicking on the lights of the gym, he went over to the dumbbells, picked them up. The weight of them was comforting as he started to flex his muscles. A good workout—that was what he needed, to start getting his body back to the peak of fitness.

He stopped, one dumbbell suspended in the air. Fitness be damned. He snorted at his own deception. Who was he kidding? He needed a workout to rid himself of the image of Lottie and the immediate visceral effect that she had on him.

If he was going to have to put up with much of that temptation over the next two weeks he was going to be spending a *lot* of time in the gym.

Pressing down on the meat in the frying pan, Lottie watched as blood oozed out. She liked her steak charred to a cinder; Rafael liked his rare. Even trying to co-ordinate the food they ate seemed like a struggle.

These past few days at Villa Varenna had been awful, excruciating. Like actors in a play, she and Rafael had moved around this beautiful stage, moved around each other, oscillating between angry disagreement and unnatural politeness and restraint, their wariness of the situation, of the fragility of the arrangement, both painfully obvious and carefully concealed.

Three days in and counting. Lottie seriously wondered how they were going to survive two whole weeks. It wasn't just the pregnancy issue—though Lord knew that filled her mind every waking minute, seeped into her dreams at night. Mentally she veered erratically between exhilaration and desperation, depending on which imagined outcome had gripped her in its talons at the time.

The hardest part was simply being around Rafael, sharing the same space as him, realising the way he could still make her feel—the way she knew deep down that she had always felt. The two years of separation, the countless lectures she had given herself, were all washed away on a tide of longing when she was presented with him again in the flesh.

The beautiful, haughty, honed and hard-edged flesh that was Rafael.

Over the hiss of the pan she could hear him moving about in the next room, then music coming through the sound system above her head. Opera. *La Traviata*—sad and Italian. What was he trying to do to her?

'Ready yet?' Rafael strode restlessly into the room, wearing black jeans and a loose black shirt with the sleeves rolled up in his casual, infuriatingly handsome way.

'Nearly.' Lottie flipped over her steak. 'Can't we have something a bit more cheerful?' She indicted the music with a pained tilt of the head.

He disappeared again and there was a brief silence before Johnny Cash and his burning ring of fire started up.

'I thought this would go with your steak.' He was behind her now, looking over her shoulder. 'Or what's left of it. Is this one mine?' He indicated the plate beside the hob.

'Yes.' She shifted her position to block his view. 'It's resting.'

'Right.' Reaching over her to pick up the plate, he viewed it suspiciously.

The ensuing silence was enough to make Lottie spin round with the fish slice in her hand. 'Is there a problem?'

'*No, di certo*—absolutely not. Shall I take the salad through?'

They had taken to eating at the small table by the bay window of the sitting room. The views of the lake were a useful distraction from the inadequacies of the food, not to mention the inadequacies of their conversation. None of the big issues had been broached by either of them since their disagreement in the studio yesterday, and the practicalities of what would happen if Lottie was actually pregnant were being avoided like a minefield in a war zone.

For her part, Lottie had decided there was no point in getting into another argument with Rafael about something that might never happen. She had no intention of making this enforced captivity any more excruciating than it already was.

'How has the painting gone today?' Cutting into his steak, Rafael raised his fork to his mouth and his all-seeing gaze to her face.

'Good.' Lottie felt the familiar clench in her stomach at the sight of him. She struggled with an awkward mouthful of salad. 'I'm only doing small studies at the moment; I'm hoping I can scale them up to a bigger painting.' She paused as she caught the look in his eyes. 'That's if I'm here long enough, I mean.'

Rafael's jaw clenched but he said nothing.

'Trying to catch the light on the water is incredibly difficult.' She hurried on to avoid that particular quagmire. 'Just when I think I am getting somewhere I look up again and it's all changed.'

'A bit like life, really.' Rafael coldly turned his attention back to his meal.

Lottie looked down at hers.

'Had you been doing much painting since…since we last saw each other?'

Lottie noted his tactful turn of phrase, and his voice was even, but it was belied by the tautness of his body, as if he was holding back the desire to jump on his chair and scream *Since you walked out on me*.

'Um, no, not really. I've not had much time, what with

a full-time job and everything.' She chased a cherry tomato round her plate. 'I've kept up my drawing, though. In fact I've been doing a lot of sketches—you know, just for friends… portraits, treasured pets, that sort of thing.'

'I'm glad you have been using your talent. So, this job of yours…'

Laying his knife and fork down, Rafael steepled his fingers over his plate and fixed her with his most piercing gaze. Lottie braced herself for an interrogation, immediately on the defensive.

'Tell me how it is, working for a guy like Ibrahim?'

'It's okay.' She shrugged her shoulders. 'The job is well paid.' *Was well paid*, she thought silently.

'And what exactly does he expect for his money?'

'What are you suggesting, Rafael?' Her eyes flashed dangerously.

'I'm not suggesting anything.'

'Good, because if you were it would be deeply insulting.'

'I'm simply trying to understand why you would flatly refuse a settlement from me in favour of working for a jerk like him.' His lack of understanding was all too evident in the jut of his jaw. 'If you needed money you only had to ask.'

Lottie thought back to the obscene amount of money she had been offered by his solicitors a few months after she had left him. She'd rejected it without a second thought. It had felt as if he was buying her off: goodbye and good riddance.

'And *I* can't understand why *you* can't see that I want to be independent.'

'Of course. How foolish of me to keep forgetting that.' His voice was laced with sarcasm. 'So, tell me—how does this independence feel, being at the beck and call of that slimy bastard?'

'Better than being a kept woman.' Lottie glared back at him. 'And besides, I am not at his beck and call. I am perfectly capable of handling someone like Ibrahim. I can take care of myself.'

Rafael let his gaze rake over the feisty young woman before him and realised that she was probably right—she *could* take care of herself. She was no longer the innocent twenty-one-year-old he had fallen in love with but someone who, despite her delicate appearance, had the maturity to go with her fiery spirit, to cope with whatever life threw at her. Not that his protective instinct would ever go completely. He knew that despite everything he would still leap in front of a flying bullet for her without a second thought.

'I'm not worried.'

'Good.' Lottie chewed at her lip, very much hoping that was the end of that particular conversation.

'Especially as I know you no longer work for him.' The dark brows were raised infuriatingly.

'You *know*?' Lottie felt her blood pressure soar. 'How do you know?'

Rafael merely shrugged his shoulders in reply.

'Why do I even ask?' Lottie's voice soared to match the blood in her veins. 'I should have worked out by now that you have absolutely no scruples when it comes to prying into my life.'

'In actual fact Ibrahim contacted me.' Rafael's reply was maddeningly calm. 'He was inviting me to an exclusive preview—some conceptual artist that he seemed very excited about. Apparently he has enormous investment potential.'

Lottie glowered at him. 'And why would he contact you?'

'Because I am on his client list, of course. I'm surprised

you don't know that. But, then again, I guess it doesn't matter any more.'

'And presumably the only reason you were on his client list was because you were spying on me?'

Rafael gave a *well, you know...* sort of shrug. 'Anyway, I took the opportunity to mention your name and that's when I found out you were no longer in his employ.'

'And did he tell you why?'

'Funnily enough, he didn't seem to want to discuss you.'

'Then let me enlighten you. Ibrahim fired me because of *this*.' Using both hands, Lottie gestured around her, ending with two index fingers pointing at herself. 'He refused to give me any more time off. Sacked me on the spot.'

'Ah.'

'Yes—so basically I have no job to go back to. But *please* don't think that you have to feel guilty about it.'

'I don't.'

Everything about his easy reply told Lottie that her attempt at sarcasm was totally wasted.

'I was actually thinking that it is one minor complication out of the way.'

Typical! Rafael had managed to turn what was a real worry for her—she had bills to pay, after all, and the rent on her flat for starters—into something to his advantage.

But the more Lottie thought about it the more thankful she actually was that she no longer worked for Ibrahim. She knew she would be able to get another job. If leaving Rafael had done one thing it had taught her independence, made her stand on her own two feet.

Arriving back in England with nothing but a suitcase and an alarmingly small amount of cash, she had made the decision to move to London. She needed a fresh start, away from all the memories that would inevitably haunt her in Oxford. She didn't want Rafael to know where she was either—to track her down, demanding answers. Not that she'd needed to worry about that. Apart from that one email from his solicitors she had heard nothing from him at all. There had just been a big, fat hollow where that part of her life had been. The happiest and the saddest part.

Being alone in London had been horrendous to start with. It had seemed such a lonely place that first winter as she'd desperately tried to find a job and somewhere to live, eventually renting a depressing bedsit, feeding coins into a meter for the hissing gas fire, sleeping with her head under her pillow to try and block out the yelping screams and scary silences of her neighbours. She had thought that winter would never end.

But it had, and it had been followed by a particularly beautiful spring. Which had been even worse. Watching lovers in the park, lying on the grass kissing, parents proudly pushing buggies towards the swings, excited toddlers leading the way... It had felt as if the whole world was happy and in love, deliberately taunting her with its joyfulness.

But time had passed and she had made some friends and found a new job, which had meant she'd been able to afford a better apartment, and suddenly things had started looking up. Slowly, slowly, she'd realised that she was no longer waking to the sick feeling of dread any more. The job at the Ibrahim Gallery had provided her with a good salary, even if the boss had made her skin crawl, and suddenly she'd realised that she had moved on, grown up, was in control of her own life again.

Until she had received Rafael's email. Until her old life had reappeared and thrown up the extraordinary situation that they were in now.

She watched Rafael as he leant away from the table, rocking his chair on to its back legs, stretching his arms behind his head. He turned to look out of the window and she could see his reflection in the glass. Dark, shuttered, deep in thought, but as intensely attractive as ever. He wore his beauty casually, as if he didn't notice it even if everyone all around him did. He had no vanity, no interest in showing himself off to the world—just a confidence, an inner belief, an unconscious power that meant he had the ability to achieve whatever he wanted to achieve.

Until the accident.

Lottie was struck again by the enormity of how that must have affected him. She gazed at his chiselled profile, at the whiplash scar which, even though it could never disfigure his beautiful face, was a permanent reminder of what he had suffered.

Since that first day in the office at the *palazzo* he had never talked about the accident. Just as he never talked about anything that mattered. As Johnny Cash's last gravelly note faded to silence she decided to try to get him to open up.

'Tell me about the accident.'

She spoke softly and he swung round to look at her, his guarded expression melting her heart once again.

'What did it feel like, Rafe?'

'It is not an experience I would recommend.' He scraped his chair back sharply, and immediately began to gather up the things on the table. 'Shall I make some coffee?'

He was trying to get away from her, and from any sort of discussion about the accident. But Lottie stopped him.

'In a minute.' Reaching forward, she rested her hand on his forearm, feeling the warmth of his skin, the way his muscles flexed beneath her touch. 'There's no rush.'

As she increased the pressure on his arm she became acutely aware of their skin-on-skin contact, the feel of the dark hairs that were raised beneath her fingertips, before the arm was moved away and folded beneath his other, defensively in front of him.

'What did you feel when you realised that the parachute wasn't going to open?'

Rafael glowered at her. 'What do you *think* I felt?'

'I don't know—that's why I'm asking you.' Stubbornly, she refused to give up.

'Disbelief, horror, panic. Take your pick. There wasn't much time for the existential stuff.'

Still the sarcastic flippancy.

'Did you lose consciousness as soon as you hit the tree?'

'Yes.' He let out an exasperated sigh, seeing that she wasn't going to let this drop. 'I didn't know anything about it until I woke up in a hospital bed, thinking what a bloody fool I was.'

'A fool? I thought you would be feeling pretty darned lucky.'

'Well, that as well. But realising what I had done to myself—the permanent damage, I mean. It could have all been avoided.'

'But you weren't to know—about the parachute, I mean.'

'No. But if I hadn't been jumping from aeroplanes in the first place...' He stopped, as if realising he was giving too much away. 'Anyway, I'm done with all that stuff now.'

Lottie stared at him from beneath the sweep of her lowered lashes. 'You say that now. I bet once you have completely recovered you will be throwing yourself into the path of danger again, every chance you get.'

'Is that what you thought I did?' He looked at her with cold surprise.

Lottie felt herself weaken under his penetrating gaze. 'Kind of. Let's face it—you were always skiing down some

mountain or scaling up it or flinging yourself from it. Especially...' she paused '...especially after Seraphina died.'

'You make it sound like some sort of death wish.'

'That's a bit extreme. A diversion tactic, maybe, a form
of escapism.'

'Escaping from what?'

'I would have thought that was obvious. From me, from
our marriage, from Seraphina's death.'

'*Che assurdità!*' He turned away, muttering something
furious in Italian under his breath. 'As usual your ama-
teur psychology has brought you to completely the wrong
conclusion. Now, if you will excuse me, I've got some
work to do.'

Leaving the plates where they were, he gave her a curt
nod before striding from the room, his pride and dignity
hurrying to keep up with him.

Was she right? Of course she damned well was. Closing
the door to his study, he leant back against it, screwing
his eyes shut against the realisation. That was what riled
him more than anything—why he hated getting into any
so-called conversation with Lottie. The way she wheedled
things out of him, picked at subjects that he wanted left
alone, attempted to uncover truths that had to stay well
and truly buried. Why had he even got into that stuff about
giving up action sports?

Even if it was true.

He *had* spent more and more time doing extreme sports
over the past few years, turning it from an escapist hobby
into an obsession, a way of purging himself. He had told
himself he needed something to ease the pressures of running the principality, and there was some truth in that.
There had been plenty of times when the massive responsibility had weighed heavily on him and flinging himself

off a mountain, as Lottie had so charmingly put it, had given him some release. Pushing himself harder and harder had felt good—addictive, even,—and he'd consoled himself that it was done in the name of a good cause as he had raised huge sums of money for charity.

But there had, of course, been another reason. The one that Lottie had homed in on, jabbing at it like a dentist probing a bad tooth. He knew that the real reason he'd pushed himself harder, further, to take more and more extreme risks, had been because of the adrenalin rush it gave him. And the reason he'd needed that adrenalin was because it had been the only thing that had given him a temporary respite from his feeling of loss. The loss of his baby, his marriage, his wife.

But no more. He'd been given a second chance. A second chance at life and a second chance of producing a life. And he wasn't going to do anything to jeopardise that.

CHAPTER SIX

'COME IN.'

At the soft tap on the door Rafael looked up from his laptop and saw Lottie juggling with a sliding tray, pushing the door open with her hip.

'You mentioned coffee after dinner, so I thought I would bring you some—*us* some.' She indicated the two mugs beside the cafetière.

'Thanks.'

He made no move to clear a space amongst the paperwork strewn around his desk, so Lottie pointedly gave the tray an extra rattle until he got the message.

'There.' She sat herself opposite him and they both watched as Lottie lowered the plunger on the coffee and poured them both a cup. 'You're still working, then?' She held her mug in both hands, inhaling the steam.

'It would certainly appear that way.'

No one could do the arctic chill like Rafael.

'What are you working on?' She picked up a sheet of paper from the desk, feigning absorbed interest, but, sensing his scowl, silently replaced it.

'Nothing you would be remotely interested in. Now, I really don't have time for this, so if you would like to leave…'

'I might be interested if you told me what it was.'

'Why are you here, Lottie?' His sharp words cut through the air between them.

Lottie twisted a curl of hair around her finger. 'I thought maybe we could carry on the conversation we were having earlier. The one you abruptly ended when you walked away.'

'I hardly think you are in any position to criticise me for walking away.' The sharp words came out of nowhere. 'That was something *you* managed to do in a spectacular fashion.'

Ouch! Lottie hadn't seen that one coming. Now she deeply questioned the wisdom of seeking him out. Especially as he was closing his laptop, turning the full force of his dark eyes and even darker mood firmly in her direction.

'That's not what we were talking about.'

'Well, we are now. Since you seem so determined to rake over the past, why don't we examine your part in it?'

'No, Rafe—stop this.'

'How about we start with the night you walked out? Talk me through it, Lottie, the sequence of events, just so I have them clearly in my head.'

'I don't want to do this.'

'Well, too bad—because I do. You wanted to talk, so let's talk. How long had you been planning it, Lottie? Was it a sudden realisation? A spur-of-the-moment thing? Oh, no, it couldn't have been.'

His cruel laugh cut through Lottie like a knife.

'Not when I bear in mind that you had never loved me. You must have been desperate to get away from me— plotting your escape for months.'

He was wrong—so wrong about everything. But Lottie refused to go there, refused to face the coal-black intensity of his piercing eyes and rake over that dreadful night. Even though every single minute of it was seared on her soul for ever.

The hardest decision of her life had been made quickly. The negative result of their third IVF attempt had finally tipped her over the edge, driving the last nail into the coffin of their marriage.

A phone call to the airport had seen her stuffing a small suitcase with clothes and creeping down the steps to a waiting taxi. It had been dark, and even though she'd known Rafael wasn't in the *palazzo* she had winced at the noise of the idling engine, the slam of the doors before they'd finally driven off, Lottie wide-eyed and silent, hunched in the back of the car.

Completely numb with the enormity of her decision, she had been waiting for her flight, gazing at her reflection in the wall of windows overlooking the twinkling lights of the runway, when Rafael's dark shape had appeared behind her like an apparition of foreboding.

His mood had been angry, forceful, as he had demanded to know what the hell she thought she was doing. Would it have been different if he had asked her to stay? Shown some compassion, vulnerability, even? She didn't know. But his boorish attitude had only served to reinforce her decision that they were finished—she had to leave.

She'd had to make him see that she wasn't going to change her mind—that he had to go away, leave her alone with her misery. And there had been only one sure-fire way to do that.

She could still see the look on Rafael's face as she had said the words.

With the Tannoy above their heads announcing the final call for her flight, she had dragged up every ounce of bravado and acting ability she had and blurted out the words.

'I don't love you, Rafael, and I never have.' And they were words that had haunted her ever since.

'I'm still waiting, Lottie.'

'And I am going to bed.'

She went to move, but Rafael leant forward to grasp her wrist.

'Oh, no, you're not. Not until we have had this out. I am waiting for you to explain to me what the hell went wrong with our marriage.'

'Do I really need to explain?' Shaking her wrist free, Lottie hid behind her defiant glare.

'Yes, actually, you do. Because obviously I am lacking the power to be able to work it out for myself.'

'Fine.' If attack was the best form of defence she would face him, head-on. 'You were working all the time, and when you weren't you were off somewhere, doing some crazy activity by yourself, *for* yourself. After we lost Seraphina we never took the time to heal. Instead my life became a miserable round of IVF treatments and invasive procedures in your quest for a precious heir, and when they didn't work you just became more distant and more cold. You never paid me any attention and you never wanted to talk to me. I was lost and lonely and miserable.'

Swallowing down the racking sob that was building up inside her, she covered her face with her hands and felt it shudder through her body.

There was silence.

Through her parting fingers she saw Rafael's face, so twisted with disgust that she had to look away.

She sniff-sobbed loudly. 'Well, you *did* ask.'

'Indeed I did.' His voice was laced with ice. 'And you have certainly delivered. Have you finished now? Or is there more you would like to get off your chest?'

'Yes. Actually, there is.' His coldness and sarcasm only

served to push the floodgates open further. She wanted to hurt him now, the way he was hurting her. 'Our sex-life.'

Rafael's eyes narrowed dangerously. 'Go on.'

'Well…' Lottie gulped down another sniff. 'How can you pretend you thought everything was fine with our marriage when you hadn't even been near me for months?' She paused, aware that she was ripping open her chest to expose her heart, but unable to stop now. 'When you re-alised the IVF wasn't going to work, when you realised I would never give you your precious heir, we didn't even share the same bed any more. You never wanted to make love to me—in fact you never wanted to touch me at all. How do you think that made me feel?'

Rafael looked as if he had been punched in the stom-ach, but Lottie felt no sense of triumph. The intense pas-sion they had shared at the start of their relationship had been so completely overwhelming that Lottie could never have imagined Rafael turning away from her the way he had after Seraphina died. It had tortured her then and it still tortured her now. Especially as she knew, staring at him across the desk now, that those feelings for him were as strong as ever. That her body yearned for him to make love to her again.

Swearing under his breath in Italian, Rafael raked a hand through his hair, what little patience he'd had obvi-ously exhausted. 'You are unbelievable—you know that, Lottie? You have the audacity to come out with this non-sense, pretend that somehow I am at fault for the failure of our marriage, when we both know full well the real reason.'

They stared at one another. Lottie both waiting and dreading to hear what he was going to say next.

'The real reason is because you just didn't care enough. In fact, I don't think you ever cared at all.'

* * *

Lottie shut the door of the villa and walked out on to the terrace. It was a beautiful night, still, star-lit and crisp, but she didn't feel the chill against her skin. Her body was still burning from the heat of their clash, hurt and anguish pumping violently through her veins as she went over and over the things they had said. The ocean of misunderstanding and mistakes and mixed-up longing that lay between them.

Staring out unseeing at the lake, she could feel the anxiety churning around inside her. The consequences of what they had done, the way this could change their lives for ever, were still being ignored by both of them. They had done nothing to sort out their problems, try and find a way through the shared agony of their past, put it right for the future. Instead they avoided the subject or, worse, let it explode between them, just as it had back then, showering them with bitterness and confusion.

What sort of basis was that for bringing a child into the world?

'There you are.'

Rafael was jangling his car keys in his hand when Lottie finally came downstairs. He wore casual jeans and a white tee shirt with a beautifully cut grey linen jacket over the top, a grey cashmere scarf draped around his neck. That unmistakable Italian style he epitomised so well.

'I hope I haven't kept you waiting.'

She'd expected a growled reply but instead was startled to see that he was staring at her, his eyes moving over her in a most disconcerting way.

'What?' She shifted uncomfortably.

Still he didn't say anything, his mouth a tight line, his jaw firmly closed.

Lottie looked down at herself. Why was he staring at her like that?

When Rafael had announced at breakfast that he was taking them out for a meal that evening Lottie's heart had sunk. Was this going to be another torturous evening together, only worse because there would be no escape?

But, conceding that he was trying to make an effort, she'd decided she had to do the same. Maybe between them they could try and improve the brittle atmosphere that had pervaded the villa over the last few days. And, besides, it might be nice to get dressed up for once—swap her paint-splattered jeans for one of the dresses swinging in her wardrobe.

She had been shocked, that first day in the villa, to find along with her own small suitcase, sent over from the *palazzo*, another much larger case, containing several cocktail dresses: vestiges of her previous life with Rafael. The life she had been thrown into so suddenly on the death of Rafael's father and the role she had never been given time to adjust to: the role of Contessa di Monterrato.

Somehow she had assumed Rafael would have got rid of all these clothes—given them away or tossed them into a pile and set light to them. She wouldn't have blamed him. Pulling them out of the rustling tissue paper one by one, she had held them up against herself, remembering the woman she had been when she had worn those dresses, standing beside Rafael at tedious functions, watching the way he could work the room, knowing that every event, no matter what it was called, was simply another public relations exercise—a business meeting in all but name.

They weren't happy memories, and Lottie had quickly selected one garment before pushing the rest, along with the memories, to the back of the closet again.

The dress she had chosen was simple and elegant, made

of a deep blue silk that had an iridescent quality that caught the light as she turned. And, despite its past, it made her feel good. At least it had done until she had been subjected to the full force of Rafael's raking gaze.

Now might have been a time for Rafael to say something complimentary—tell her how nice she looked. Even an appreciative nod would have done.

'You'll be cold.'

So much for that. His deepening frown and the tight pull of his lips suggested nothing but irritation.

'Don't you have a stole or something?'

A *stole*? What century was he living in? They were travelling to a restaurant in his luxury sports car, not a horse and carriage.

'I'm fine.'

She inhaled sharply, suddenly cross with herself. Why had she spent hours trying to make herself attractive to him? Fiddling about with her hair until she perfected the loose bun at the nape of her neck, carefully applying subtle make-up, slithering this dress over her scrubbed and moisturised body. Why the hell had she bothered?

'Put this on, anyway' Stepping towards her, he took off his scarf and, carefully looping it over her hairstyle, arranged it, still warm from his body, around her shoulders.

'Thanks.' Lottie had to move back from him before she could breathe.

Something told her this evening was going to be awful.

But she was wrong. The local restaurant was small and informal, and after the usual amount of fussing and flapping from the staff that always accompanied Rafael wherever he went they were soon seated in a quiet corner, with a single candle flickering on the table between them.

The food was delicious—a selection of freshwater fish served with aromatic sauces and big bowls of fresh pasta.

They both ate hungrily and the conversation flowed surprisingly easily. Rafael started, as he always did, by asking about her day's painting, then actually answered her questions about his day, telling her about his plans for a new marina that was about to start construction, about the vineyards that had to be monitored closely at this time of year, the local elections that had just taken place.

He looked so composed, so handsome, so like the old Rafael she had fallen quite madly in love with.

Lottie tried to concentrate, to focus on the many and varied problems and opportunities obviously involved in being head of a principality like Monterrato. But mostly she found herself being drawn into the hypnotic spell of his deep voice, the way his Italian accent imbued the most mundane of English words with a mantle of sensuality. She watched the way his beautiful mouth moved as he spoke, the bottom lip just that bit fuller than the top one, both biteably, irresistibly kissable. The bruising on his face had faded to almost nothing now, and the scar on his forehead was hidden by a dark twist of hair but still visible where it sliced down the top of his cheekbone. A shadow of stubble darkened his jawline and upper lip; she remembered the feel of that stubble against her cheek, against other parts of her body too…

Enough! She needed to stop this before her internal organs stalled in homage to his beauty. Or, worse still, betrayed her in some hideously embarrassing way. She couldn't even blame it on the alcohol. Sticking firmly to water, she had had no more than a single sip when Rafael had offered her a taste of the local wine he had ordered. You could hardly get drunk on a sip of wine, now, could you? Other forces were obviously at play here—far more dangerous ones.

'Can I ask you something?' Putting his knife and fork

together, Rafael took the napkin from his lap and touched it to his lips. Suddenly his deep brown eyes were focussed intently on her face.

'Yes, of course.' Lottie laughed nervously under his close scrutiny. 'As long as it's not whether I think I might be pregnant.'

Her flippant remark was met with a derisively raised dark brow.

'Because I really have no idea…' She tailed off, registering that this was not a subject he was prepared to be light-hearted about. 'No more idea than you.'

'I realise that.' He rolled his shoulders back, his gaze never leaving Lottie's face. 'I know we have to wait for two weeks before we can do a pregnancy test. That prior to that there are unlikely to be any discernible manifestations. I know the form, Lottie. I haven't forgotten that we've been here before.'

'No, of course not.'

Discernible manifestations? How did he manage to make what they were doing sound so clinical, so detached? Because for him it was, Lottie reminded herself painfully.

'But my question *is* related to that.'

'Go on.'

'Why, Lottie—just to clarify things for me— did you agree to bear me a child?'

Lottie gulped. This was typical of Rafael. Just when things were going peaceably he would lob in a grenade of a question to ruin things. She looked down, the escaping twists of her hair falling forward as she did so, brushing against her cheeks. Even the fish head on her plate looked as if it was waiting for an answer.

'I don't know, exactly.' She raised her eyes again, immediately caught by the net of his gaze. 'I suppose it was a combination of things.'

Rafael ran his hand down his jaw to his chin, leaving it there as he tilted his head to look at her.

'Basically, I suppose you were right when you said you knew I had always wanted to be a mother. It's most probably the maternal instinct in me that made me say yes—as simple as that.'

'These things are never simple, Lottie.'

'Well, perhaps I need to prove that I can be a good mother. A better mother than I had, at any rate.' She smiled at him, not wanting this to get too heavy.

'Well, from what I've heard that won't be difficult. How *is* the lovely Greta?' He raised his eyebrows at her.

'She's very well.' Lottie gave a small laugh. 'As far as I know she and Captain Birdseye are perfectly happy living the high life in Argentina.'

Rafael had never even met her mother. Their early relationship had been such a whirlwind, with Lottie getting pregnant just weeks after she and Rafael had first met, then their hastily arranged wedding and the move to Monterrato—all happening before Greta had managed to find the time to come over. Subsequent invitations had been politely declined because of the *'considerable distance'* between them. Lottie could only agree with that—and she wasn't just thinking about the thousands of miles across the Atlantic.

'I think maybe she has finally found what she was looking for.'

'Let's hope so. And have *you* found what you were looking for?' His gaze swept over her. 'The baby, I mean?'

'We don't know there is a baby yet.' Lottie lowered her eyes, carefully folding her napkin as she tried to inject some realism into the conversation. 'But you falling out of the sky has certainly opened up the possibility, if nothing else. A faint smile touched his mouth.

'So you should be thanking me, really?'

Lottie felt her shoulders drop a little. Could she detect the teeniest sign of a thaw?

'If you like.' She risked another smile, then felt ridiculously hurt when, instead of returning it, he abruptly looked away. 'I suppose what I am saying is that I said yes to using our last embryo because I want this baby every bit as much as you do. Even if my reasons for wanting it are different.'

'What do you mean by that?'

'I mean that my motive is purely emotional—maternal, if you like. Whereas yours is sensible, practical. I know how important it is to you, to Monterrato, that you produce an heir. But that's not why I said yes. I said yes because I want a baby of my own. Nothing more complicated than that.'

Her little speech done, Lottie sat back, sure that Rafael would be relieved. After all, hadn't she just let him off the hook—given him a get-out so that he knew he didn't have to be grateful to her? But she was to be disappointed. Because instead of relief, his look was one of barely controlled temper.

Rafael heard his own pent-up breath hiss between his teeth as he stared across at Lottie. He had thought that going out for a meal would be a good idea—get away from the villa, eat some decent food for once. But he had been wrong. Sitting opposite her now, in the warm and intimate atmosphere of this candlelit restaurant, it no longer felt like a good idea at all.

The evening had started badly when she had first appeared in that flimsy dress. The way the fabric skimmed over her slender body, subtly highlighting the contours of her breasts and hips, then stopping short of her knees to reveal those long, shapely legs... Just the sight of her had all but winded him. And when he had held the door open for her and seen those skinny strap things crossing over her shoulderblades it had taken all his control, and more, not to thread his itchy fingers through them and tear them apart until the dress fell at her feet.

And right now he was still being taunted by her bare shoulders, the shadowed hollows of her collarbone, the elegant sweep of her neck—by everything that she unconsciously did to him. Fighting it was becoming more and more difficult, and he knew he had to use the only weapon in his armoury. Animosity.

'Just for the record—' he spat the words at her '—you are not the only one with emotions, Lottie. You are not the only one to feel things. Despite your cold, calculating opinion of me, I am flesh and blood beneath. Sensible and practical I may be, but that doesn't mean I don't feel things every bit as deeply as you. Perhaps you would do well to remember that.'

'Yes, of course.' Verbally slapped down again, Lottie felt the sting on her cheek as vividly as if he had struck her. 'I didn't mean to imply anything to the contrary. I was just trying to explain the differences between us.'

'That really isn't necessary,' Rafael growled back at her. 'I would have thought the differences were all too clear.'

'Yes.'

Biting down on her lip, Lottie fought to supress the pain of his angry words. The pain of knowing just how true it was that whilst Rafael still stirred up overwhelming longing and desire in her, she only evoked bitterness and resentment in him. She cast about for a suitably acerbic reply—something she could hurt him with as he had hurt her—but it was too late. Turning away, Rafael had already called for the bill.

CHAPTER SEVEN

RAFAEL WOKE WITH a start. He could hear something—a noise somewhere in the villa. As he slipped out of bed a glance at the clock showed it was two-forty-five a.m. Pulling on his jeans, he walked silently across the landing to Lottie's bedroom. The door was closed and he stood there for a moment, listening. Nothing. She was probably sound asleep; it had been several hours since she had flounced off to bed, refusing his offer of a hot drink, leaving him nursing a whisky and a bad mood.

The evening hadn't ended well—just like every other evening since they had been in this place. Every evening since Lottie had been back in his life, in fact. He knew he was failing miserably when it came to following Dr Oveisi's instructions to make these two weeks as stress-free as possible for Lottie. But there was only one bit of Dr Oveisi's advice that he knew for sure he could fulfil—and all too easily. He was wrestling to control it every second that he spent with Lottie. And each day at Villa Varenna was making it that bit more difficult.

The villa was quiet. Perhaps he had imagined it. After padding down the stairs he stood in the hallway, straining his ears. Yes, there it was again, coming from the basement.

A plan was immediately forming in his head. If he could

get into the gym he could grab one of the dumbbells and clobber whoever it was over the head before they had a chance to get away. He could feel the adenaline starting to surge through his body. Slowly he crept down. The noise was coming from the pool—he could hear the splashing quite clearly now.

Burglars didn't take a dip before they robbed a house.

Standing in the shadows behind the glass wall, he could make out the shape of Lottie's body moving leisurely through the water, swimming to one end, then pushing off and starting back again. The only illumination came from the submerged pool lights and she looked dark against the bright turquoise of the water, arms and legs elongated by the shadows.

He should go. As he turned away the metal button of his fly tapped against the glass and he froze, casting his eyes down as if to make himself invisible.

'Who's there?'

He could hear the squeak of alarm in her voice. What the hell was he doing, lurking in the gloom?

'It's me.' Clearing his throat, brusquely he moved along to the glass door, pushing it open authoritatively. 'I heard a noise. Came down to see what it was.'

'Oh.' She stared at him for a minute before swimming over to the edge of the pool and hanging on with fingertips that were level with his bare feet. 'You scared me.'

'Sorry.'

He looked down at her head and shoulders, streaming with water, her hair slicked back darkly over her forehead and then fanning out around her like seaweed. Closer inspection revealed that beneath the blue of the water she was naked. *Dio.*

He looked away with a jolt. 'What on earth are you doing here at this time of night anyway? You realise that it's nearly three a.m.?' Gruffness covered the growl of desire.

'I couldn't sleep.' She pushed off from the edge of the pool, took a couple of strokes, then stopped to look at him again, treading water. 'I decided to take a midnight swim. A three a.m. swim,' she corrected herself.

The idea had come to Lottie after several hours of fitful tossing and turning. Their evening out had ended on such a sour note, with a silent drive back to the villa and Rafael refusing even to look at her as he headed for the kitchen to fix himself a drink. Lying in bed, staring at the moonlit shadows on the ceiling, she had tried to work out just where it had gone wrong—why it always went wrong.

She had heard Rafael come upstairs, the soft click of his bedroom door. Wide awake, she'd thought back over their time together in the villa: the fraught atmosphere, the tension that had been building and building between them.

She knew that it was more than just the hurt of the past that had caused it, though that would never leave them. It was the raw, fresh assault of the present too. The insidious, sensual, sexual connection that their close confinement had revealed. *That* was what they were both fighting. *That* was what made their time together so unbearable.

Her night-time dip had been a good idea and had made Lottie feel strangely calm. Maybe it was the lack of sleep, but somehow the warm water caressing her naked body had not only washed away her stress but also heightened her sensuality, producing an almost carefree drunkenness. She was in a beautiful place, with a beautiful man, and there was a chance—maybe a good chance—that she was pregnant with his baby.

And now he was here, standing at the edge of the pool, staring at her, the muscular planes of his naked torso shadowed in the dim light. The sight of him stirred an impulsive recklessness in her.

'I'll leave you to it, then.' With one last piercing look Rafael was turning to go.

'Why don't you join me?' Her words had escaped before she knew it, echoing around them and halting Rafael's movement.

He glanced back at her as she bobbed up and down in the water. 'Why would I want to do that?'

'For fun, Rafe. We are supposed to be having fun, remember? It's doctor's orders.' Swimming a few strokes closer, she stopped again and looked at him earnestly, her eyes wide and daring.

Fun. Rafael realised that that was something Lottie had been full of—certainly when he had first met her. It had been one of the many things that had made him love her. She had been so different from anyone he had ever known before—different from the women he was forced to socialise with in Monterrato. Those women were like strategic pawns, carefully chosen because they were the daughters of heads of state or influential businessmen. Part of the reason he had insisted on going to England to do his business doctorate had been to get away from the whole hideous mating ritual.

But he had never expected to find Lottie—never expected to fall so blindly in love and for Lottie to get pregnant so quickly. That had led to the hurried wedding and what now felt like the happiest period of his life. His father had been livid, of course. Rafael still had that furious letter somewhere—their last exchange before Georgio had died of a massive heart attack. Which had to be a coincidence. He was *not* responsible for his father's death. He just wished Georgio had had the chance to meet Lottie. She would have softened his angry heart.

He could see Lottie, waiting, looking up at him, her arms and legs moving silently, tentacle-like, beneath the brightly lit water. She was goading him to join her, probably thinking there was no way in the world that he would. Because he wasn't fun, was he? And, worse than that, he had drained the fun out of Lottie, or at least had a damn good go at it. He could see that now.

Like some vampire of doom he had weakened her carefree spirit, her zest for life, first by throwing her, totally unprepared, into the role of Contessa di Monterrato and then with the death of their baby and his subsequent determination to get her pregnant again. It was a wonder she had any fun left in her at all.

Well, he would show her.

Walking round to the shadows at the far end of the pool, he stripped off his jeans, positioned himself on the edge and with one smooth dive plunged under the water, resurfacing several seconds later right in front of Lottie. And the look on her face was priceless.

Suddenly she was all arms and legs, swimming away from him, but still close enough that he could see her bare buttocks just under the surface of the water.

'Catch me if you can!' The words were sprayed over her shoulder.

She had to be joking. Watching her splash chaotically away, he counted to three before powering after her, beside her again in a couple of crawl strokes. He grabbed hold of her leg as it kicked to escape from him.

Her head went under the water then reappeared and she came up spluttering. 'That's cheating.'

'Don't issue a challenge you can't win, Lottie.' He was tall enough to stand in this part of the pool, but Lottie was still treading water to keep herself afloat, her arms paddling on either side of her. Reaching forward, Rafael placed his strong hands under her armpits to steady her. Suddenly the drag of the water moved them together and their naked bodies were only inches apart.

Rafael cursed silently. What the hell was he doing here? He knew he should move away—right now—before he did something…they both did something they would seriously regret. But Lottie was still looking at him, torturing him with her steady bold gaze. He felt his traitorous body immediately jerk into action beneath him, trying to rob him of any last self-control.

'Sometimes a challenge isn't there to be won or lost.' Serious now, Lottie's voice was seductively soft. Water was running in rivulets down her face as she tipped it up to meet his, her lips soft and full and maddeningly tempting.

Rafael lowered his head. 'Nevertheless, if this is a challenge I had better warn you it is a very dangerous one.'

'Let's call it something else, then.'

She was so close now, Rafael could see the clumps of dark wet lashes framing her wide eyes.

'More something that has to be confronted.'

Who made that final move? Rafael wasn't sure, but suddenly all resistance gave way to inevitability and their lips were touching. Tentative at first, but with their softness rapidly turning from firm to bruising, from cold damp to searing heat as they plundered each other's mouths without preamble, both taking and giving with equal lack of thought for anything except this one moment, caught up in the forbidden delirium of the kiss.

Their tongues tasted and tangled, their breath hot and gasping as the power of their desire overtook them, dousing all rational thought. With her hands threaded through Rafael's wet curls Lottie pulled him even closer to her, their faces sealed by the damp and by the kiss that was juddering down the length of their seemingly weightless joined bodies beneath them.

Pulling away, Rafael took a gasp of air, peeled their bodies fractionally apart and dragged words from the tiny part of his brain that still had some rational thought.

'Is this what you want, Lottie?' His heart was thumping dangerously fast, and the sight of Lottie's kiss-swollen lips was doing nothing to ease it. 'Because if not you need to say so now—before it's too late.'

Lottie gazed back at him, her eyes heavy with desire, her body aching with an all-consuming need. This *was* what she wanted—what she wanted so badly that she was physically trembling with the power of it, the realisation of it. It didn't make it right, but it made it impossible to resist.

Unable to voice the words, she simply closed the watery gap between them until their bodies met again, moulded against one another in a perfect fit of sexual intimacy.

Rafael let out a guttural growl of raw sexual need and paused for a split second—all it took for that last bit of reason to vanish. Then, sweeping Lottie up in a slippery embrace, he waded towards the end of the pool with her, the water swirling hurriedly out of their way. Splashing up the shallow steps and across the marble tiles, he pushed open the door through to the gym, then strode over to the rubber mat in the middle of the dark room. He half slipped, half fell down on to it with Lottie still in his arms. Locking his elbows, he dug his slippery damp toes down into the mat and straddled Lottie, above her in a press-up position, staring down into her eyes.

This was madness—total madness. But there was something inescapable about it. Since that first second she had walked into his office at the *palazzo* this was all he had wanted to do. To take her, to consume her, to try and fill the yearning chasm that had gripped him ever since she had left.

With the muscles in his biceps rippling, he started to bend his arms as he slowly lowered himself down over her wet and shivering body, his lips seeking hers again, needing the reassurance that this was what she wanted. And she did.

With her cold mouth opening, her lips formed a sexual cavity that longed to be plundered. Rafael gave out a rasping moan and claimed it, his tongue immediately diving into its depths. Then, peeling away, he bent his head, moving his mouth down to her breasts, kissing and licking the soft, wet, chlorine-tasting swell of each one before taking the cold-puckered nipple in his mouth to suck hard, then harder, as he felt Lottie squirm erotically beneath him.

This felt so good. She might not love him, but he could still turn her on—he could still make her body writhe and twitch for him. He gasped when he felt Lottie's hand move down to where he wanted it most, taking his erection in its cold grip, owning his rock-hard length as she moved the skin up and down with trembling fingers.

Her body contorted beneath them, sticking and sucking on the wet mat as she positioned herself for him, ready to be taken. Reluctantly grabbing her hand, he moved it back over his shoulder. He felt her nails dig into his shoulder-blades. If this wasn't to be over in a matter of seconds he needed to take control. He slid his own hand down between them, running it over her damply matted pubic hair, slid a finger inside her, parting the warm, soft folds, feeling the tight muscles clench around it as he touched her clitoris and started to rub it with soft but assured pressure.

Hearing her moan, he covered her mouth with his own again, wanting to absorb the energy of her pleasure into his own body, to feel it with her. As she arched her body against his finger he increased the speed until he knew she was almost there. But not quite. Shifting his hips, he replaced his finger with the tip of his penis, then stopped, savouring this second, before sinking his length into her—halfway at first and then, fractionally altering his position, pushing again, more forcefully, until his entire hot, throbbing length was inside her, being gripped mercilessly by her muscles.

With a small yelp Lottie dug her nails into him further as she clung to him feverishly.

'Lottie?' He just about managed to grate out her name as he raised himself up to look into her eyes.

'Don't stop.'

The deep tremble in her voice, together with the far-away look in her eyes that he remembered so well, was all the confirmation he needed.

As she pulled him back down on top of her he felt her muscles tensing and clenching around him, holding him tightly, urging him on. He had to move faster now, increase the rhythm. The want in him was growing and swelling all the time, demanding release. And Lottie matched him, driving him on to join her, to be right there with her when it happened, and he knew that neither of them could hang on much longer.

With no more than five or six deeply penetrating thrusts he felt her body shudder, heard the irregular gasping, panting of her breath and knew that she was there and that he couldn't hold back any longer. A shuddering, squeezing climax surged through his body, so powerful that it seemed to take Lottie with him, and he covered her lips with his own to silence his low, animal growl. As their wet-slicked bodies gripped and convulsed against each other it felt as if the world could end now and neither of them would notice.

CHAPTER EIGHT

BUT THE WORLD hadn't ended. And even before the last shuddering convulsions had left their bodies Rafael was pulling away, looking down at her, the hunger of desire in his eyes turning to a cold watchfulness.

'I'll find us some towels.'

He was up on his feet now, and Lottie watched his naked body as he padded silently across the room, returning with two towels.

'Here.' Handing one to her, he avoided her eyes as she crouched forward to take it and wrap it round her protectively hunched body. 'You mustn't let yourself get cold.'

'No.' He was tying a towel around his waist now. 'Rafe…' Lottie stopped, not sure what she wanted to say but desperate to ward off the chill that couldn't be warmed with a fluffy towel.

'You need to get to bed, Lottie.' He hurried to block any further conversation. 'We both do.'

Everything about his posture, the tone of his voice, the tight line of his mouth, made it quite clear that he was talking about separate beds.

'It's getting very late.'

If she didn't open her eyes it wouldn't be true. Lottie could feel the sunshine streaming in, insistent against her closed lids, making it plain that the next day had dawned whether she liked it or not. That time didn't stop just because of what they had done last night.

Colourful images flickered frame by frame behind her eyes, like an excruciating X-rated home movie. The pool, the gym, the mat...what they had done on the mat... And, worse still, the way Rafael had behaved afterwards.

She had no one to blame except herself. Unfortunately she could remember with bruising clarity the sequence of events, and if it hadn't exactly been totally one-sided she had definitely been the one who'd started it. Maybe she could blame it on her hormones. After what she had been through they had to be all over the place. Or the hypnotic effect of the pool, perhaps. But deep down she knew there was only one thing she could blame it on. The relentless, carnal, erotic effect that Rafael had on her.

And she was only human. There was only so much temptation a woman could take.

She thought back to the image of Rafael at the end of the pool, peeling off his jeans, gloriously naked in the shadows before diving into the water... Sensuous shivers ran through her again. But the temptation had been her undoing, as her screwed-up ball of a heart could testify now.

The sex had been amazing, of course. They had always had the most incredible connection—as if their two bodies had been specifically designed to fit together for the most explosive of results. But last night had felt like something else...as if the lid had been blown off the pressure cooker of their lives, right there and then, in that dark room, on that slippery gym mat. The pain of the past, the strain of the present, the hopes of the future—all detonating in a mushroom cloud of intensely powerful sexual intensity. She could still sense the aftershocks rippling through her.

But it wasn't those memories that were scratching their

nails down her skin now—not the image of his lean, honed body as he'd spread himself on top of her, not the excruciating pleasure when he had pushed inside her, and not even the realisation that no one else could ever, *ever* make love to her like that, make her feel like this.

No. This gash of pain came from what had happened afterwards: the look of distaste on Rafael's face when he had handed her that towel, the way he had almost herded her back up the stairs, watched while she had closed the door of her bedroom, almost as if she was not to be trusted, as if at any moment she might fling herself at him again, force him to make love to her. *That* was what was crucifying her now.

Snapping open her eyes, she pulled back the coverlet and got out of bed. She had to be strong now, not agonise over her mistakes. She would focus on the day ahead, on the reason she was here. The baby—if there was a baby— was the important thing. Wincing slightly, sore where Rafael had been, she took determined strides towards the bathroom.

Rafael was nowhere to be seen when she finally ventured downstairs. Which was a relief. She certainly didn't want to see him. Even if she *had* spent the last hour bracing herself for the awkward meeting, repeatedly going over in her mind how she would be with him: cheerful, light-hearted, casually flippant about what had happened the night before in a *Ho-ho, that was fun, but obviously it didn't mean anything and obviously it won't happen again* sort of way.

But in the event none of her acting skills were needed. Lunch came and went and still there was no sign of him. Several times Lottie passed his study door, pausing gingerly outside to see if she could hear anything. But all was quiet, and she certainly wasn't going to debase herself any further by tapping on his door to see if he was there, looking as if she cared or, worse still, as if she was going to make repugnant demands on him again.

By the evening, when there was still no sign of him, she had convinced herself that he had gone for ever, abandoned her alone in this beautiful place. And she didn't care if he had. In fact it would be for the best. It would save a lot of embarrassment all round.

As twilight started to turn into dusk Lottie decided she needed some fresh air and, pulling on a warm jumper, walked out on to the terrace. There was a full moon tonight, illuminating the garden with a ghostly light, sharpening the outline of the plants and trees so they appeared to be harder, more aggressive versions of their daytime counterparts.

Opening the iron gates, Lottie paused, gazing at the moon's searchlight across the rippled water. It was stunning. Slowly she started to descend the steps to the water, treading carefully through the shadows. The last thing she wanted was to fall now—now that she had been effectively deserted. Heaven knew when anyone would ever find her.

As she neared the bottom she became aware of the sound of an engine and, looking up, saw a speedboat coming towards her, Rafael at the helm. She watched as he came closer; he was standing up, the top half of his body visible above the windscreen, one hand on the wheel, confidently manoeuvring the sleek vessel towards its mooring.

Cutting the engine, he let the boat drift towards the mooring pole and jumped ashore with a rope in his hands.

'What are you doing here?'

It wasn't the warmest of greetings.

'I just was just admiring the view. Across the lake,' she added hurriedly, in case he might have thought *he* was the view.

'Have you eaten?' Pulling the boat towards him, he leant in to retrieve two carrier bags before turning to face her, one in each hand.

'Um, no—not yet.' Lottie stared back at him. Everything about his cold stance suggested that this was a purely practical question rather than a cordial invitation.

'Well, there's plenty of food here.' He shook the bags in his hands. 'I'm going to have to work this evening, so I'll just get a sandwich, but you should make yourself a proper meal.'

'Right.' His uncompromising tone left no room for negotiation, but still Lottie tried. 'If I'm cooking I might as well make something for you too.'

'No, thanks. Like I say, I will just grab a sandwich.'

'Fine.' If he was going to be like that then so be it.

For a moment the two of them faced each other, the moonlight illuminating their profiles, only the slapping sound of the water breaking the silence. Lottie had prepared herself for some awkwardness, but this was more like hostility. She realised that all her fears were founded. She hadn't been mistaken about that look on his face last night. He really did find her repugnant. Up until now she had thought that last night was just a mistake—something that should never have happened. Now she saw it for what it really was—a hideous betrayal, an abhorrent debacle that shamed her to the core.

And everything about the cold, arrogant temperament of the man standing before her now made it quite plain that he thought the same.

Turning away from him, she started to ascend the flight of steps back up to the terrace, furious with herself when hot tears of self-pity started to roll down cheeks already burning with shame and humiliation. She could hear him behind her, taking the steps two at a time, the carrier bags rustling in his hands.

'Lottie, wait.' Catching up, he dropped the bags, putting a hand on her shoulder in an attempt to stop her getting away. 'About last night…'

'Forget it, Rafael.' Shaking him off, she continued to march up the steps, determined that he wasn't going to see her tears. There was certainly no way she was going to talk about it, listen to him telling her that it had been a mistake or, worse still, that he was sorry. That was more than she could bear.

With each step her shame and despair was joined by temper and then anger, until by the time she reached the top she was seething—so much so that she stumbled, falling forward in an ungainly half-trip, half-run that made her heart hammer in her chest.

'Lottie!' A second after his call he was beside her. 'Are you all right?'

'I am fine.' Drawing herself upright, Lottie struggled to regain her balance before she marched off up the terrace path, her defiant words rippling in her wake. 'You really don't need to worry about me.'

Rafael was unpacking the groceries in the kitchen when he realised that Lottie was watching him from the doorway. He looked up quickly, registering the flush of her cheeks, the halo of hair, full of static from the woollen jumper she had just pulled over her head, the rise and fall of her breasts beneath the tight fabric of the tee shirt beneath. She looked both sexy and vulnerable. But, more than that, she looked as if she was fighting to hold in a lot of things she was desperate to say.

'I'll be out of your way in a minute.'

This produced nothing more than a shrug of her shoulders.

'I've bought some prosciutto and fresh pasta, and there are plenty of vegetables or salad if you would prefer.' He shut the fridge door and leant against it.

'Thanks.'

She had swept into the room now and brushed past him to fill the kettle. The air was full of the floral scent of hostility.

'Look, Lottie, if this is about last night...'

'Last night?' She flashed him a contemptuous stare. 'Did anything happen last night?'

'There is no point in being childish.'

His patience was wearing thin now. He was tired from lack of sleep and the long and tedious telephone conference that he had had to take away from the villa because of her. He was hungry, and he was furious with himself for letting last night happen.

'I think we have to acknowledge the foolishness of what we did and ensure that we don't find ourselves in that position again.'

The ice in Lottie's cold blue eyes almost froze the words in his throat.

'I'm sure we both regret it now.'

He certainly did. Even though he had been twitching to make love to Lottie for weeks now. Even though every little thing she said or did set him off, and even though there had been countless times when he had wanted to pull her to him, feel the luscious softness of her against him, rip off her clothes, claim her naked body for his own—any or all of the above. But he had been convinced he could handle his infatuation, he really had. A master of control, it was inconceivable that he would give in to his weakness.

When they had been at the *palazzo* it hadn't been quite

so difficult. With the pressure of work and meetings and business trips—not all of which had been strictly necessary—he had been able to keep out of her way, distract himself enough with the hundred and one things that needed his attention. Plus the place was big enough to hide in. Though the thought that *he*, the Conte di Monterrato, respected head of the principality, formidable businessman, someone who had never run away from anything in his life before, should be hiding himself away from this young woman—a woman he had vowed never to let get to him again—held an irony that wasn't lost on him.

But in the villa there was no escaping her. It shocked him, this visceral effect she had on him. It almost knocked the breath out of him and he needed all his powers of self-control to keep up the façade of indifference, to stop the mask from slipping and revealing the unadulterated lust beneath. Now he knew all his pretence had been for nothing and he had been shown to be the fool he really was—a fool for exposing himself again to the woman who had broken his heart and a fool for ever thinking he could resist her.

As if to drive home the point Lottie moved past him again, turning her back on him and bending down to take a saucepan out of the cupboard. He stared at the pale strip of skin above the low waistband of her jeans, at the way the denim stretched tautly over her pert behind. *Dio!*

'Well, that's nice to know.' Banging the saucepan down onto the hob, Lottie reached across for the kettle and recklessly sloshed in water. 'Thank you for enlightening me about how I feel. For telling me that I regret it every bit as much as you do. That makes me feel so much better.'

'Lottie…' Rafael reached for her arm but she backed away from him with the agility of a springbok.

'Don't touch me, Rafael. Don't come anywhere near me.

Last night was a mistake. You have made that perfectly clear. Now, if you would like to get out of the kitchen, I would like to prepare my meal in peace.'

Picking up a knife, she sliced at the plastic film of a container and shook pasta into the pan. 'The meal I will be eating alone, because you are *too busy* to join me.'

'I am just saying, Lottie, that after last night it is probably best if we give each other some space.' Rafael raked an exasperated hand through his tangle of dark curls.

'Well, what are you waiting for?' Lottie gestured towards the door with the knife. 'There is plenty of space out there.'

'If I have upset you then…'

'Don't you *dare*.' Lottie's blue eyes flashed from cold to fire with murderous intent. 'Don't you dare tell me that you are sorry.'

Watching the computer screen close down in front of him, Rafael leaned back in his chair. He should have had more than enough work to keep his mind occupied—apart from anything else he was hosting a charity dinner in a week's time, a fundraising event for the premature baby foundation he had set up in his daughter's name. But despite staring at spreadsheets and banging out emails for a couple of hours the tension of his confrontation with Lottie had still refused to lessen.

Using his foot, he pushed himself away from the desk and stood up, stretching the bunched muscles of his arms out before him.

What made this so unbearable—what made his mood black enough to block out the moon—was this feeling of loss of control. He had lost it last night—spectacularly so. Given in to his carnal instincts. No, more than that, he had given in to Lottie herself. And it pained him to recognise that that meant so much more than just sex.

Despite his best efforts to regain control this evening all he had done was make things worse. His bad-mannered behaviour had simply stirred up the simmering cauldron of unspoken tension and newly raw feelings.

All of which made him want to go out and kick something. *Hard.* Made him want to go out and do something that would put him in extreme danger. Because that was what he did when he felt like this. An adrenaline junkie, he needed his fix—it was the only thing that went half-way to easing his pain.

But not this time. Risking his life was not the answer—he could see that now. He had to face up to the reality of the situation and deal with it. From tomorrow there were six more days to get through here in the villa—surely he could do that? If playing happy families wasn't going to work he would have to come up with some other strategy.

Six more days until they could do the pregnancy test, find out what their future held.

Moving over to the window, he stared through his troubled reflection to the quiet dark of the night. If the test was positive…well, they would obviously have to work out how they were going to proceed. But the joy of knowing he was going to be a father would more than compensate for any difficult decisions. And if it was negative…

Pressing his forehead against the cool glass, Rafael felt the cruel fingers of doubt squeeze at his heart. If it was negative not only would he have lost his only chance of having a child, he would also have lost Lottie.

Turning away, he picked up a couple of files from the desk and, tucking them under his arm, headed for the door.

There was no doubt that if there was no baby then Lottie would disappear from his life for ever.

Cursing himself for even caring, Rafael slammed the door behind him.

CHAPTER NINE

LOTTIE FOUND THE note when she came downstairs, propped up against the coffee machine.

> *Urgent business in Milan. Back tomorrow. Contactable by mobile, any time.*

Holding the piece of paper in her hands, she stared at the familiar handwriting. She could almost feel the chill coming off the page, the frostbite in the words. So he had gone, then. They only had two nights left in the villa but he hadn't been able to stay, to put up with being around her any longer. She didn't believe for one moment that it was business, urgent or not, that had taken him away. It was *her* he wanted to get away from. Everything about his behaviour over the past few days had made that perfectly clear.

Cold didn't begin to describe it. A polar vortex was more like it—a chill factor of minus thirty whenever they came across one another…something that had happened less and less as the days had gone on. Rafael would be working in his study or punishing himself down in the gym while Lottie spent her time upstairs painting, all the time listening for the sound of Rafael's footsteps to make sure she wouldn't have to meet him on the stairs, or share the kitchen with him when they both hurried in to make some hastily prepared food before disappearing again to eat alone.

Lottie felt bad enough about what they had done—the Big Mistake. She was furious with herself for the way she had behaved, for inviting Rafael into the pool with her, for making it so obvious just how much she wanted him. The image of them on that mat simply refused to go away: the raw animal sex, the way she had clung to him like a half-starved waif, clawing at him, urging him on, desperate to bring him to orgasm with her, to share that ultimate sexual intensity. She had gone over it in her head a thousand times but she was still no closer to understanding how it had happened.

But it had, and now her fury wasn't just limited to herself. It had spread, like a bush fire, to encompass Rafael as well. Okay, so maybe she had started it, but she wasn't going to take responsibility for the whole debacle. If Rafael found her so distasteful—as his behaviour over the past few days clearly showed he did—why the hell had he succumbed to her, made love to her? No—correction—why had he had sex with her in that fiercely passionate way? Had the thought of sex just been too tempting? Even sex with someone as offensive as her? Because if that was the case that was *his* problem. It certainly didn't give him the right to treat her the way he had these past few days.

Filling the kettle, Lottie sat on a barstool, watching the water starting to bubble through the plastic panel.

Beneath the anger lurked another emotion: sadness. Sadness that she and Rafael couldn't even spend two weeks in each other's company without it descending into this. No matter what silly hopes she might have harboured that they would be able to get on, be normal together—be friends, even—that was exactly what those hopes had been: silly.

Or, to put it another way, downright ridiculously stupid. And as for them being parents…

Dropping a teabag into her mug, she doused it with water. She couldn't begin to face that problem yet. She might never have to, of course. And that, in itself, would bring an anguish all of its own that she refused to think about now. Squeezing the life out of the teabag, she dropped it into the metal bin with a clang.

For now she would concentrate on the positive. She had twenty-four hours to herself—twenty-four hours when she could breathe normally, without the constant shadow of Rafael being around to torment her. She decided she would make the most of the time—starting with a solid day's painting. Channelling her pent-up energies into something creative seemed like the best idea.

Picking up the note for one last look, Lottie screwed it into a ball and dropped it into the bin before heading upstairs with her tea.

The next day arrived, clear and blue. Day fourteen. The day that would alter the whole course of her life. Without Rafael around Lottie had slept surprisingly well and now, up and dressed, she was already on her third cup of decaffeinated coffee.

She had had a good look at her body in the shower that morning, sure that if she really was pregnant it would have to show somewhere. She knew that sore boobs were one of the first signs, so she had paid particular attention to soaping them under the pummelling of the water, desperately trying to convince herself that they were more tender than usual. By the time she had finished they had felt a little different—but then so would any part of her body that had been mercilessly scrubbed for five minutes. The fact was there were no signs; she had absolutely no idea if she was pregnant or not.

Now she fiddled with the mobile phone in her hand. There had been no messages from Rafael. But why would there be—even if she had been obsessively checking for the past hour? No doubt he had enjoyed his night of freedom as much as her. Why would he spoil the relief of not being around her by bothering to text her?

Not for the first time she found herself imagining what he had done last night, her tortured mind immediately flinging him into the arms of some exotically beautiful woman who would be only too happy to soothe his scarred brow, give him a night of pleasure to take his mind off his troubles. She forced herself to stop right there. This day was going to be momentous enough without chucking in any unnecessary masochism.

She realised that she had no idea what time Rafael would be back, and she certainly wasn't going to give him the satisfaction of asking. Absently feeling the weight of her phone, she considered what to do. He might well be on his way now, but she was damned if she was going to be sitting here waiting for him. No. Her decision was made— she was going to go out and buy a pregnancy testing kit.

The very thought of it made her shiver, every nerve-ending zinging with excitement and anticipation and fear. With a shaky hand she started to look up the number of a local taxi firm to take her into the nearest town. But then she stopped. She had a better idea.

The villa was deserted when Rafael arrived back later that day. He could sense the silence as soon as he strode in, even before he had checked the downstairs rooms and started pounding up the stairs, two at a time. Pushing open the first door, he could smell the oil paint and turpentine as he gazed about him, taking in the large canvas that was on an easel in the middle of the room, the vibrant colours of an evening sunset vividly portrayed by Lottie's unmistakable sweeping brushstrokes.

But no Lottie.

Turning, he felt his heart-rate increase as a terrible thought took hold. He marched across the landing to her bedroom, his eyes raking over the untidy room, searching for clues. Going over to her wardrobe, he flung open the doors; there were her clothes, swinging gently on their hangers, a small pile of shoes scattered beneath.

Breathing heavily, he went and sat down on the edge of her bed, relief pulsing through his veins. *Grazie a Dio*. She was still here, then. He glanced down at her bedside table. There was the book she was reading, opened facedown, its spine cracking, along with a jumble of bracelets, some make-up, a lipstick. Picking up the latter, Rafael felt it between his fingers, removing the top and twisting it to reveal the raspberry-red colour. She had been wearing this the night they had gone out for that meal. The same night they had ended up having passionate sex on a wet gym mat.

He ran his hand over his eyes at the memory of the appalling way he had behaved. But as he looked around at the unmade bed, the rumpled sheets, the indentation on the pillow where her head had been, he knew that Lottie was like a forbidden substance to him. She got to him in a way that no other woman ever could. He didn't know why, and much as he had tried to figure it out, tried to deny it to himself, he now realised it was just an irrefutable, indisputable fact.

But where the hell was she? Initial relief gave way to another wave of anxiety. Supposing she had already done a pregnancy test and it had proved negative. Had she taken herself off somewhere to lick her wounds? Was that why she had disappeared?

Rafael knew just how much Lottie wanted this baby. He thought back to when they had discussed it—when she had tried to explain about her deep-rooted desire to be a mother, about wanting to do right all the things her own mother had done wrong.

And how had he reacted? With compassion and understanding? Or even with relief that here was a young woman who knew her own mind, who was doing it for herself, not as some sort of twisted favour to him? No, he hadn't reacted in any of those ways. He had bitten her head off, snarled at her about how he had feelings too. He could still see the look of hurt in her eyes before he had turned away. What he didn't know was when he had turned into such a bastard.

Marching down the corridor, he checked his phone yet again, to see if she had answered his messages. He could feel anger surging through him now, pushing the anxiety to one side. It was an emotion he was far more comfortable with, if he was honest. Jabbing at her number, he cursed when, after a few rings, it went to voicemail. He heard himself bark, 'Where the hell are you?' before returning the phone to his pocket and thundering out onto the terrace.

Scanning the sun-rippled lake, he watched the traffic of assorted boats weaving about on the water. With no particular plan in mind, he started to descend the steps to the water's edge, stopping with a jolt and a thudding heart halfway down. The speedboat had gone. Fear gripped his heart and a hundred different scenarios ran through his mind, each one worse than the last.

What had happened here? Whatever had possessed him to leave her alone last night? How in the name of God could he have been so selfish?

With panic and fear wrestling in his chest, clawing at his throat, he ran down the remaining steps, pulling the phone out of his pocket, punching in the number for his security team, already visualising the ransom demands, the terrifying danger Lottie could be in.

A loud toot made him look up. A speedboat—*his* speedboat—was heading towards him, with Lottie at the wheel, waving casually. What the—? A new, but nonetheless urgent anxiety gripped Rafael; she was going far too fast, she was using only one hand, and she was heading straight for the moorings.

'Slow down!' Cupping his hands over his mouth, he screamed at her over the roar of the engine. 'Cut the engine!'

The boat did an erratic zig-zag as Lottie stood up to try and hear what he was saying.

'Cut the engine!'

Finally comprehending, Lottie gave him an okay sign and the throaty roar stopped. But the momentum of its speed was still carrying the boat far too fast as it cut through the water towards him.

'Sideways on!'

He could see Lottie clearly now, cheeks flushed with the fresh air, blonde hair streaming out behind her. At least she had both hands on the wheel now.

'Turn!' Indicating with wildly flailing arms, he tried to get her to understand what to do. 'Turn the wheel. Come in sideways!'

There was a crunch, followed by a long scraping sound, followed by a delicate, 'Oops…'

Unscrewing his eyes, he saw his speedboat now indignantly at rest against the far end of the dock. And Lottie, wobbling as she tried to stand, calmly getting ready to disembark.

'*Mio Dio!*' He was beside her in a flash, extending an arm to help her ashore. 'Are you hurt?'

'No, of course not.' Refusing to make eye contact, Lottie let go of his hand the second she was on dry land. 'I'm not quite so sure about the boat, though, I'm afraid there might be a bit of a scrape…'

As she turned back to look at it Rafe caught hold of her arm, spinning her round to face him.

'I don't give a damn about the boat.' He glared down at her, his voice harsh with immense relief. 'What the hell do you think you were doing? You don't have the first idea how to drive that thing. You could have killed yourself.'

'Well, I didn't.' Shaking her elbow free, Lottie defiantly glared back at him. 'And for your information I actually managed perfectly fine until you started interfering.'

'Right.' Rafael matched her stare. 'So it's *my* fault, is it? My fault that you were hurtling towards the shore at sixty knots per hour?'

'Yes—yes, it was.' Lottie wasn't going to back down. 'You made me lose my concentration.'

'Well, all I can say is it's a good job I did. Your "concentration" was going to end up taking you to the bottom of the lake—along with a pile of fibreglass that had once been my boat.'

'Don't exaggerate.' Tossing her head, Lottie turned to retrieve her bag from the seat of the damaged boat.

'Where have you been, anyway?'

'Just to do a little shopping.'

'Why didn't you answer my calls?'

Retrieving her phone from the bag, Lottie registered the seven missed calls. 'I was driving, remember? Surely you know you shouldn't use your phone when you are driving?'

She raised her eyebrows at him, all too aware, but not caring in the least, that she was seriously winding him up.

'So, where *is* this shopping?' Not that it mattered. But, needing the distraction, Rafael looked around and could see no evidence of it.

'Here.'

Their eyes met over the chemist's bag that Lottie slowly withdrew from her handbag and the world around them suddenly skidded to a halt.

'Ah. I see.'

Silence hung heavily between them.

'You are going to do it now?' His voice seemed to come from a long way away, his eyes remaining fixed on the unremarkable bag.

Lottie nodded. 'I guess so.' She gave a throwaway laugh. 'Now's as good a time as any.'

There was another brief silence.

'*Buono.*'

Brisk now, businesslike, Rafael took a step towards her and attempted to put an arm around her shoulder. But Lottie refused to respond and it ended up more like a manly pat on the back. Awkwardness pushed them apart again.

'Come on, then.' Clearing his throat, he tried again. 'Let's do this.'

Rafael was standing by the window, his back to her, when Lottie emerged from the bathroom. She was delicately holding the tester stick in front of her, as if it was made of plutonium, or something capable of destroying their lives.

'How long?' Turning, Rafael looked at her, then at it, the catch in his voice betraying his tension along with his shoulders, which were hitched unnaturally high.

'It says up to three minutes.'

Lottie could barely speak. Sinking down on the bed,

she tried to regulate her breathing—to breathe at all, in fact. She felt dizzy, her hands shaky and clammy as they gripped the plastic time bomb.

Crossing over to the bed, Rafael gently took the tester stick from her and placed it face-down on the table. He squatted beside her, taking her hands between his own, his warm strength pumping into her.

'I want to say something to you, Lottie.'

Lottie didn't want to hear it—not now, not ever, actually. She couldn't face any more emotional trauma. This waiting was threatening to kill her, *literally*. She realised she couldn't breathe any more and the room was starting to spin.

'Lottie.' Giving her hands a shake, Rafael halted her panic attack enough to make her suck in a breath and look at him. 'I want to say thank you for doing this.'

'There's no need…'

'Yes—yes, there is. Whatever the outcome, I truly appreciate that you were prepared to at least try to give me my last chance of being a father.'

Why was he talking like this? As if he already knew the result was going to be negative? He who had always been so convinced that this time it would work. Did he know something she didn't?

Lottie looked at him with fear in her eyes.

'I know this is the last thing you expected when I asked you to come to Palazzo Monterrato. That you actually thought you had come to sign divorce papers.' A tightness pulled at the corners of his mouth as he spoke. 'And if there is no baby you will, of course, have your wish. I will put divorce proceedings into place straight away and you will have your freedom. But either way I want you to know you have my heartfelt thanks.'

Well, thanks to that little speech Lottie now felt a whole

lot worse. As she looked into the shadowed depths of his eyes she wondered yet again how everything between them had managed to go so horribly wrong. How something that had started with such love and passion and hope and excitement had ended up with her sitting here, on the edge of a bed, waiting to find out if she was pregnant by a man who didn't love her, in the hope of having a child that they would never be able to parent together. Not in the true sense of the word, anyway.

The last thing she wanted was his *heartfelt thanks* or, worse still, her freedom. Suddenly she knew what she wanted him to say more than anything in the world. She wanted him to say that everything would be all right— that no matter whether she was pregnant or not he loved her and that was enough. That they could build a future together, be a couple, have a happy life, grow old together.

She forced out a slow, deliberate breath. The thought that that thing, just inches away from her, held not only her fate but also her heart in its little plastic window was almost more than she could bear.

Speech done, Rafael released her hands and stood up. Then, looking at his watch, he raised his eyebrows at her.

'No.' Lottie's hands were trembling so badly she couldn't have picked it up if she'd tried. Her stomach was heaving as if she was going to be sick. 'I can't do it.'

'You want me to?'

Lottie nodded, watching in horrified slow motion as his arm stretched across to pick up the tester stick, registering the rolled-up sleeve, the tanned forearm, the strong, purposeful hand raising it, turning it over. Then she screwed her eyes shut.

For a second there was nothing but blind silence.

'Well?' She heard her unrecognisable voice squeak the question.

Still nothing.

She opened her eyes. There was Rafael, still in front of her, still holding the tester stick in his hand. His expression was—what? Blank? Stunned? With a sickening plummet of dread, Lottie suddenly realised that his eyes were shining with the gleam of tears.

Oh, God. Oh, no.

'It's positive, Lottie.' His gaze swept from the stick in his hand to her incredulous face, his own face a picture of wonder and awe. 'We are going to have a baby.'

The restaurant was full, couples at every table, with candles and roses and love in the air. As they were shown to their table by a deferential waiter Lottie realised what day it was: San Valentino—Valentine's Day. And just for tonight Lottie was going to let herself join in, soak up the atmosphere, be part of it. She was with the most handsome man in the restaurant, probably on the planet, as several female glances following their entrance confirmed, she was in the most euphoric bubble of happiness, and she was pregnant.

Yes, sirree, definitely pregnant. Both the tester kits she had bought had proved positive, and one of them was still nestling unhygienically in her handbag—as if throwing it away might suddenly make her *un*pregnant again.

She had never seen Rafael looking like this before. An inner happiness was shining through him, radiating from him. At first glance a stranger might not have noticed the difference, just seen the same stunningly handsome man as before—it wasn't as if he was grinning from ear to ear or slapping people on the back and buying them drinks. But Lottie could see it, and that made it all the more special.

She hugged the realisation to her chest that *she* was responsible for this, *she* was the one who had brought about this change in him. She could have gazed at him all night—

he looked so totally, utterly beautiful. But obviously she wouldn't do that because that would be weird. And besides she was hungry—starving, in fact.

A bottle of pink champagne appeared at their table, and after pouring them both a glass Rafael raised his, waiting for Lottie to do the same.

'*Buon San Valentino.*'

'Thank you. And Happy Valentine's Day to you too.' They clinked glasses and Lottie looked into the happy bubbles. 'But perhaps I had better not.'

'I'm sure half a glass won't hurt. Besides, you have to drink pink champagne on Valentine's Day. It's the law.'

'Is that right?' Taking a couple of delicate sips, Lottie let the dry fizz slip down her throat.

This was what happiness was—this little capsule that they were in now...her, Rafael and the impending baby. Even though she knew that things were going to be difficult, that she and Rafael faced all sorts of challenges with the baby and with their relationship, she refused to think about that now. This evening she was going to allow herself to be unquestioningly, unreservedly happy.

Raising her head, she realised that Rafael was studying her, his head tilted to one side, the champagne glass still in his hand. She looked down again, for some reason feeling shy, worried that he might be able to read her mind, but he reached across the table for her hand, covering it with his own.

'What were you thinking?'

Phew. Obviously he was lacking that particular superpower.

'Nothing.' Nothing she was going to tell him. He was big-headed enough as it was.

'Happy?'

'Yes.' She looked at him solemnly. 'You?'

'More than you could ever believe. Thank you, Lottie.'

'That's okay. I didn't exactly get pregnant all on my own, you know.'

'True. I suppose I should be a bit proud of myself too.'

'I was talking about Dr Oveisi.' Her eyes flashed mischievously.

'That is cruel, young lady, and you know it.' He shot her a heart-melting glance. 'Now, start being nice to me or I will call that violinist over and make him play for you all night.'

'Don't you dare.' Rafael knew all too well that she found those things toe-curlingly embarrassing. 'From now on I promise to be sweetness and light.'

They ate artichokes and roasted sea bass, shared forks full of food and light-hearted chatter, and all the time the sensual sexual chemistry fizzed between them just as it always did whenever they were together. Only this time it went unchecked, insidiously binding them with its invisible threads, pulling them closer and closer together.

They smiled at each other, teased and flirted, pulled faces over the sharp coldness of the lemon *gelato*, drank tiny cups of bitter coffee, then finally left arm in arm to stroll back to the wounded speedboat for the short journey back to the villa.

'Warm enough?' As the boat hummed quietly through the water Rafael looked across at Lottie.

'Yes, fine.' The night air was prickly with cold but she was wearing Rafael's thick woollen coat, cosily tucked in, loving the scent of him that was coming off it. 'Look at all those stars.'

Throwing back her head, she watched as they passed overhead—thousands and thousands of them. They made her feel brave, somehow, as if what they were doing was right, part of the future, part of a wider scheme of things.

Returning her gaze to the front, she realised Rafael was looking at her.

'Oi—keep your eyes on the water, you.'

'I hardly think you are in a position to tell me how to drive this boat.' Grinning, Rafael faced forward again. 'The poor thing is still bearing the scars of your little outing. Very expensive scars too, I might add.'

'Yeah, sorry about that. I suppose I *was* going a bit fast.'

'Totally out of control, more like it. Allow me to show you how it should be done.' He pulled down the throttle to no more than a gentle hum and the boat slowed down immediately. Rafael guided it perfectly alongside the mooring pole.

'Show-off.'

Rafael shrugged his shoulders immodestly. Leaping out of the boat, he secured it to the mooring pole and then held out a hand to Lottie.

This evening had been so perfect she realised she didn't want it to end. As they climbed the steps, walked along the terrace pathway and into the villa, she felt as if she were in a fragile fairytale—one that might turn into pumpkins and rats at any moment if she wasn't careful.

Once inside, Rafe removed his coat from her shoulders. 'Drink?'

'A cup of tea would be nice.'

'It shall be yours.'

Lottie sat on the window seat, gazing out over the lake. *Pregnant.* She could hardly believe it. And although she knew she shouldn't jinx it, something inside her—some inner sense—told her that this time everything was going to be all right.

A rattling tray announced Rafael's return, and after carefully placing a cup of tea in front of Lottie he removed his own tumbler of whisky and came and sat beside her on the sofa. Lottie realised he had something in his other hand.

'I bought you this.' His voice was low, almost gruff, as he opened his hand to reveal the 'something'. It was a small blue velvet box.

Lottie looked from the box to Rafael, her eyes questioning.

'Thank you.' Surprised, she wasn't sure what to say. 'I'm afraid I don't have anything for you.'

Rafael frowned at her, puzzled. 'Why would you?'

'Well, I'm assuming this is a Valentine's Day gift?'

'Hardly!' He all but snorted. 'I just happened to see them and thought you might like them.' Handing her the closed box, he pulled back. 'Think of them as a token of my gratitude, if you like.'

'Right...' That had told her. Gratitude was as good as it was going to get.

Opening the box revealed a pair of gold and enamel earrings shaped like little violets, their perfect petals shaded to a deep purple in the centre, where a small, gold nugget nestled.

'They are beautiful!' With one in each hand Lottie held them before her.

'I'm glad you like them. I thought the colour was pretty, that they would go with your eyes...' His voice trailed off.

'I love them. Thank you.'

'Are you going to try them on?'

'Yes, of course.' But he was too close, watching her too intently, and in spite of fiddling with her earlobes Lottie couldn't get them to go in. 'I need a mirror, really.'

'Here—let me.' Squatting before her, Rafael took the earrings out of her hand and proceeded very delicately to fix first one, then the other to her ears. Feeling his breath blowing sweetly against her cheeks, Lottie found herself painfully holding in her own.

'There.' Job done, he sat back on his heels.

Touching her earlobes, Lottie looked into his face. 'Thank you.'

She leant forward, intending to give him a polite kiss on the cheek, but he intercepted her, catching her face in his hands. Their eyes clashed. Her heart thudded wildly.

For a second neither moved, each trying to gauge the other's reaction. Then Lottie, realising that she had no idea how to read the mind of the man who crouched before her, gave up.

To hell with it. This was her night to do what *she* wanted. And what she wanted more than anything else was Rafael. As she gazed into his beautiful face she had never felt more sure of anything in her whole life. The joy of knowing she was pregnant with his baby was almost overwhelming her body with happiness and pride. But there was one more thing that could make this day absolutely perfect. And it was right in front of her now.

Linking her hands behind Rafael's neck, she pulled him the few inches closer she needed to bring his lips to hers. Rafael let go of her face, but instead of mirroring her action his arms fell by his sides. Undeterred, Lottie pressed her mouth against his, her lips already pouting and swollen, her fingers threading through his hair, pulling him closer to increase the pressure.

Still Rafael resisted, but when she opened her mouth, slid her tongue between his lips, gently plundered inside, she could feel his stubbornness evaporate as he started to return the kiss in the way only he could—with fire and deep passion. It sent a shudder of pure craving through her body.

Coming off his haunches, he wrapped his arms around her, pulling her up with him as they wobbled to stand, each clinging unsteadily to the other, desperate to find each other's lips again. Pressed so tightly to him, Lottie revelled in the heat coming off his body, in the feel of his muscular arms imprisoning her against his granite chest, the thrilling evidence of his arousal, hard and insistent against her pelvis.

And tonight of all nights there was no way this could be resisted.

As if both were under the same crazy spell they started to tug at each other's clothes.

Lottie pulled roughly at the buttons of his shirt sliding her hands inside, across the muscular planes of his chest, the hair coarse beneath her fingertips, his nipples tightening under her touch. Slipping the shirt over his shoulders, she started on his suit trousers, pulling down the zipper and easing them over his hips. They pooled on the floor around his ankles, revealing the straining boxer shorts. *Oh, yes!* She ran her hand over the huge swell of his member, which was trying to force its way free, and felt him clench beneath her touch.

Rafael moved away fractionally, standing on one leg and then the other to rip off his socks and kick the pile of discarded clothes to one side. Then he turned his attention to Lottie, gripping her shoulders and spinning her around. With trembling hands he lowered the zipper of her dress, peeling it open to expose the satin-smooth sweep of her back, the neat curve of her waistline, the pert roundness of her bottom beneath skimpy white panties. He let the dress slither to the floor and turned Lottie to face him again.

She looked so damned hot, standing there, her chin raised in some sort of defiance, wearing nothing but a bra and panties, with a violet flash in her eyes that said not so much *Take me* as *I challenge you not to take me*—a challenge that Rafael already knew he had lost.

Stepping forward, he lowered his head to the level of her breasts, trailing light kisses over the softness of the flesh above her bra before homing in on the channel of cleavage, plundering it with his tongue.

Lottie gripped at his hair, pulling him closer, the touch of his lips on her breasts sending waves of exquisite pleasure through her body. She wanted more. *Now.*

Unfastening her bra, Rafe let it fall to the ground between them as he cupped her breasts, first one and then the other, pushing them upwards so he could take her nipples in his mouth, his hot breath shrinking them to shrivelled peaks of longing even before his lips had circled them, his teeth had grazed their hardness.

He let his tongue trail down her chest, feeling her stomach muscles clenching violently as he passed her tummy button and reached the top of her panties. Moving a hand to either side of her hips, he yanked them down with a single movement and cast them to one side. Then, putting his hands back on her hips, he shifted sideways until he was in the perfect position to slide his tongue inside her.

She was so wet. Her body was such a giveaway it was almost embarrassing. If she had wanted to play it cool, pretend in any way that she could take him or leave him, she'd have had no chance. Rafael only had to touch her, initiate the very first moment of lovemaking, and her body started screaming at him to take her. Now she was standing there so turned on she was literally trembling, arching her body to increase the pressure of his tongue against her, her head thrown back with indecent abandon, her fingers buried and tugging at his hair as his tongue increased in pressure, sending spasms of yearning pleasure shooting through her.

As the first shudders of orgasm started to roll through her she felt him stop, come up to a standing position, rip off his boxer shorts and press the steel rod of his erection hard against her stomach.

'No, *cara*...' Rafael's voice was a deep sexy whisper. 'Not yet.'

Scooping her off her feet, he crossed the few steps to the sofa, laying her down, ready to cover her body with his own. But, sliding across, Lottie made room for him beside her, before quickly wriggling on top of him. She wanted to do it *her* way this time. And as she looked down into his eyes she could see that he had no intention of stopping her.

Pure, unadulterated desire flashed between them. An unstoppable force.

Spreading her legs, she reached for his throbbing shaft, holding it against the tight, warm wetness of her need. With a low moan she felt Rafael shift beneath her and the tip of his penis enter her. She shivered erotically. She needed him inside her now—the whole of him, not just the swell of the tip but his entire length, thrust deep, deep inside her.

And that was what happened. With a gasp of pleasure she felt him plunge into her, her muscles clenching round him, intense pleasure shooting though her. Gripping on to her hips, his strong hands held her steady for a second, but she was desperate to feel him even more deeply and, leaning back, she ground her hips into his and started to move.

Matching her bucking thrusts with his own, he increased the pace all the time, along with the total ecstasy, until she was totally lost in it, only dimly aware of Rafael's hoarsely whispered words.

'Not yet, *cara,* keep it going…you can do this…a bit more, a bit more, a bit…'

Finally the words stopped as she fell down on top of him and felt the violent orgasm rack through his body, taking her with it in an amazing, overwhelming crescendo.

CHAPTER TEN

WHEN LOTTIE WOKE the next morning she was in Rafael's bed with Rafael beside her, propped on one elbow, looking down at her with those beautiful brown eyes.

'*Buongiorno.*'

'Good morning.' She snuggled towards him, tipping her profile up, the little violet earring digging into the skin behind her ear.

Sweeping a twisted strand of fair hair away from her eyes, Rafael bent to place a light, almost polite kiss on her lips. 'Did you sleep well'?

'Mmm…very well, thank you.'

Raising her arms, she pulled him back down under the covers, curling her naked body against his. Spending the night in the same bed as him had felt so right. Especially after what they had done together last night.

'How are you feeling this morning?' Despite the innocent question she could feel the temptation in him.

'Pregnant.' The word was muffled against the warm skin of his neck. She felt him nudge against her, trying to move her position so that he could see her face, but she resisted, smiling to herself in her dark, sensuous, happy place.

'Really?' He adjusted his position so that his chin was now resting on the top of her head. 'Do you actually feel any different?'

Different? The word was too bland to describe the total change of Lottie's state of mind. After the tension of being imprisoned in the villa with Rafael, the hurt and anger of the past few days, the terrible gripping anxiety of the pregnancy test, she now felt free, relaxed, euphoric—as if suddenly everything was going to be all right. The massive weight she had been carrying around, even if she had largely refused to acknowledge it, had been lifted, and now she could float with happiness. And judging by the feel of Rafael beside her now, the completely different mood they shared this morning, it was exactly the same for him

'No, not different in that way.' She tipped her head up to answer his question. 'I meant pregnant as in that was my first thought when I woke up.' She smiled at him. 'The realisation that it really is true.'

Rafael stared down at her, his deep brown eyes glowing softly. 'I know. It's amazing, isn't it? *Sorprendente*. But we do have nine months to get used to the idea.'

'Yes.' Lottie returned his gaze, her own eyes dancing indigo blue. 'Aren't we lucky?'

'Yes. We are.' His hand slid under the covers and found her flat tummy, running over it in a gentle smoothing motion. She knew he was thinking about the baby, but her thoughts were turning in a very different direction.

'I guess we should get up.'

'You're right.'

His hand slid lower, and lower still, until it found the place she'd so much hoped it would. Maybe he wasn't thinking about the baby after all.

'Do we really have to go back to the *palazzo*?' She arched her back, brushing her breasts against him. 'Can't we just stay here for ever?'

'Nice try.' He reciprocated by moving his finger lightly

against her. 'But I have a stack of business to attend to. Not to mention a charity dinner to oversee.' His voice was becoming increasingly guttural.

'Hmm, we'd better get going, then.' Taking her own hand down under the cover now, she watched as his eyes widened.

'I couldn't agree more, Contessa Revaldi.'

Holding her shoulders, Rafael slid underneath her, transferring his hands to her hips so that he positioned her perfectly on top of him.

'But first there is a little business here that I need to attend to.'

'I see what you mean.' Lottie squirmed on top of him. 'And not all that little…'

The helicopter ride back to Palazzo Monterrato seemed to take no time at all—which was just as well, given that their morning in bed had somehow turned to afternoon and dusk was already falling when Rafael expertly landed the noisy machine on the helipad.

Lottie watched as he flicked off the controls, removing his headset and seatbelt, then turned to wait for her to do the same. It was stupid, but she was reluctant to get out. She would have liked their journey to go on for ever, to be cocooned in the glass bubble of happiness that she'd shared with her handsome pilot. But end it had, and as they walked up the long driveway towards the *palazzo* Rafael cleared his throat, obviously building up to saying something.

'So, about this charity dinner…' He stared straight ahead as he strode beside her. 'Obviously I want everything to go perfectly.'

'Charity dinner?' Lottie turned to look at him. 'What charity dinner?'

'The one I told you about earlier.'

Lottie frowned, trying to recall. 'I don't remember. When is it?'

'Tomorrow.'

'Tomorrow? Here at the *palazzo*?'

'Of course.'

She waited, but no more information was forthcoming, the only sound coming from the gravel that crunched beneath their feet.

'So what are you saying? That you want me to make myself scarce?'

'Why would I want you to do that?' He glanced at her quickly before fixing his gaze straight ahead again.

'I don't know.' Suddenly unsure of herself, Lottie faltered.

'What I would like is for you to play the role of hostess.'

'Oh.' She hated these things, and the unfriendly way he was suggesting it didn't make it any more appealing. 'Are you sure? Won't people think it a bit odd— I don't know—get the wrong impression about us.'

'I don't give a damn about what people think.' Rafael's tone went from cold to harsh. 'And I said *play the role*, Lottie. It's not as if I am expecting you to actually believe in it. I merely feel it would be fitting to have you by my side for the evening.' He came to an abrupt halt outside the villa. 'Especially in view of the charity concerned.'

'So what is this charity?' Lottie stared up at him, her breath short as she matched his sudden hostility.

'The Seraphina Foundation.'

'The Seraphina Foundation?' Lottie's eyes widened, and her heart contracted with the pain of hearing their daughter's name. 'I didn't even know there was such a thing.'

'Well, you've hardly been here to know, have you?' He

shot her a withering look. 'It has actually raised a great deal of money for intensive neonatal care.'

'That's good…'

But it didn't make her feel good. The more she thought about it the more hurt and excluded and resentful she felt that this charity bearing her daughter's name existed and yet she had known nothing about it. It was as if Seraphina had been taken from her, stolen away by Rafael and his team of accountants.

She brushed past Rafael and started up the steps to the *palazzo*. She was being ridiculous—she knew that. How could she be resentful about something that was saving the lives of tiny premature babies? Giving them the chance of life that Seraphina had never had? How could she be so unutterably selfish?

Once inside, Rafael closed the door behind them. 'I imagine you must be tired after the journey.'

It was a statement—something not to be argued with—and certainly no attempt to appease the swing of her mood. His tone of voice made it quite clear that he had no intention of pandering to her obvious strop.

'I have work to do now but I'll let the kitchens know we will need something to eat. Where would you like yours?'

What was it about this place? Palazzo Monterrato? It seemed to Lottie that it refused to let her be happy, that something in the very bricks of the building made it sit up a bit straighter whenever she was around. Like the bored bully in the playground it stubbed out its fag, pushed itself off the wall and decided there was some sport to be had. And Lottie was its favourite target.

It had been raining when she'd woken that morning, splattering against the shuttered windows. And she had been back in 'her' half of their enormous bedroom, alone again in the bed. Only this time she'd felt more alone than ever.

Rafael had not emerged from his office for the rest of the night after their conversation, abandoning her with nothing but a cold supper and a sub-zero mood. She had tried not to be upset—had run herself a bath, taken her book to bed and propped herself up against the pillows, still thinking that he might tap on the door, creep into the room and slide his warm body in next to hers. But she had been deluding herself—as the grey light of this morning pointed out so heartlessly. The bed beside her was still empty, her book was on the floor, where it had slipped from her grasp, and she had nothing but a crick in her neck to show for her misplaced optimism.

And today she had this god-awful dinner to get through.

Pulling on her jeans, she stomped down the two flights of stairs to the kitchens with the idea of making herself a cup of tea. But the place was a hive of activity, the staff in the throes of preparations for this evening, and she was politely told that breakfast would be brought to her, wherever she would like it served.

An hour later her mood had still not improved. Bored with its company, she decided to find someone to share it with and, rapping on the door to Rafael's office, she strode in without waiting for a reply.

'Sì, verremo più tardi.' He looked up from his phone conversation, not best pleased at her interruption, judging by the dark scowl on his face. 'Sì—ciao.' Ending the call, he put down the phone and fixed her with a hooded stare. 'Lottie. Can I help you?'

'Yes, you can, actually.' She wanted to say that he could help her by telling her why he hadn't come to her bed, why she had had to sleep alone again. But there was no way she would give him that satisfaction. No way she would tell him how much she longed to feel his arms around her every single night. Instead she turned to a safer grudge.

'You can tell me what you mean by starting a foundation in Seraphina's name without even telling me.'

Rafael sighed heavily. 'Not this again. I really had no idea that I needed your permission.'

'Well, you did—well, not my permission, but you could have asked…at least told me what you were doing.'

'And would that have made any difference?'

'Yes—yes, it would. If I had known about it I would have felt a part of it. Maybe I could have done some fund-raising of my own, in England.'

This produced a derisive snort. 'Do you happen to know many wealthy benefactors?'

Lottie glared at him furiously. 'I do, as a matter of fact. The art world is full of people with more money than they know what to do with. I'm sure I would have been able to get some substantial donations—that's if you had had the courtesy to tell me about it.'

'And what would you have had to do to get these *substantial donations*, I wonder?'

His sneering insinuation made the blood pop in her ears. 'Certainly not what you're suggesting. I have no idea why you think the only way I can get on in the world is by sleeping with wealthy men.'

'Because I am a man, Lottie, and I know how their minds work.'

'Well, you don't know how mine works.'

'That, I'll grant you, is true.' Pressing his fingers to his temples, Rafael leant back in his chair, the bitter expression on his face clearly showing that he wasn't agreeing with her—he was simply acknowledging the disaster of their marriage.

Sitting upright again, he steepled his fingers, looking at

her over the top of them. 'If you are so keen to contribute to the Seraphina Foundation I suggest you make a start by being the perfect hostess tonight. I'm sure you can be charming enough when it's for a good cause. People have paid a lot of money for this event, and there is plenty more where that came from. It will be our job to persuade them to part with it.'

Lottie scowled at him. He might as well have told her to run along and make herself look pretty. Well, she wasn't going to be dismissed that easily. Pulling up a chair, she sat down opposite him, ignoring his dangerously narrowed eyes.

'So tell me about it— the Seraphina Foundation. How long has it been going?'

Rafael sighed heavily again. 'Two years or so.'

'So you started it shortly after I...' Lottie faltered, suddenly wishing she hadn't gone down this line of questioning. 'After I left.'

'Yes.' His look told her that he had no intention of doing anything to ease her discomfort.

'And how much money has it raised?'

'I don't have the exact figures at my fingertips.'

Her silence indicated that she wasn't going to be fobbed off with that.

'It is a considerable sum. People can be very generous with a little persuasion.'

'And where has the money gone? I mean to neonatal units across the principality, or just one particular hospital?

'Originally it was for Ospedale D'Aosta, but now that project has been completed we intend to carry on. There are many other hospitals whose neonatal units desperately need money to update their equipment and facilities and attract the best specialists in that field.'

He stopped abruptly, as if Lottie had tricked him into talking about this.

'Now, if you will forgive me, I have a lot of work to get on with.' Infuriatingly he looked down at his computer. 'I suggest if you need any more information you look at the website.'

Lottie was sorely tempted to tell him what to do with his suggestion. But there was something about the hitch of his shoulders, the very slight unsteadiness in his voice, that held her back. It made her realise that he wasn't purely dismissing her because she irritated the hell out of him— though that was undoubtedly true—but because this was a subject close to his heart…painfully close…and the last thing he wanted was for Lottie so sense his vulnerability.

Well, too bad.

'So Ospedale D'Aosta has all the latest equipment now?'

Just saying the name of the place hurt, and she wrapped her arms around herself for comfort. It was the hospital where Seraphina had been born—where she had died so shortly afterwards.

'That will be useful if I go into premature labour again.'

Rafael's head shot up, and there was a look of such outrage on his face that Lottie's hand flew to her mouth. She wished she could stuff the foolish words back in.

'You won't! You heard what Dr Oveisi said. That despite the accident—what happened—you are no more at risk of a premature birth than anyone else. There is no reason at all for you not to go full-term this time.'

'I know—I know all that, Rafe.'

Lottie watched as he fought back the impulse to say any more. She knew only too well that her default setting was to hide behind flippancy and come out with some stupid comment like that. But she had never expected such a reaction from Rafael. That emotional response had come straight from the heart, from a place buried so deep inside him that she had started to think it didn't exist.

'I'm sure this time everything is going to be fine.' Her throat felt tight with emotion and she swallowed noisily. 'It's not as if the same thing could happen again.'

'No.' Rafael glared savagely at her. 'We can both be sure of that.'

The catastrophic chain of events that had changed their lives so dramatically had started late one summer's day when Rafael had hurried out to the stables to greet a newly arrived horse. Lottie had gone with him, for no other reason than it had been a beautiful summer's evening.

There had been a time when there could be several feral horses pawing and snorting in the stables at Monterrato. Another of Rafael's adrenalin diversions. He had loved the challenge of training those spirited beasts, those wildly unpredictable animals that sometimes even experienced trainers had given up on. Uncharacteristically, he'd seemed to have endless patience with them, and respect too, relishing the thrill of gaining their trust, seeing their fears subside, eventually allowing him to handle them.

That particular evening had seen the arrival of a massive black stallion called Abraxas. Standing some distance away, Lottie had heard the furious clatter of hooves from inside the horsebox, thought she was obeying Rafael's instructions to 'stand the hell back', and had watched as the magnificent beast had bucked and reared down the wooden ramp.

What had happened after that was little more than a blur. With a violent toss of the head and a flash of black, sweaty muscle Abraxas had somehow shaken himself free from the reins held by Rafael and come careering wildly in her direction. The next thing she had known she was curled up on the ground, clutching her swollen stomach, aware that something bad…really bad…had just happened.

Now several long years had passed and the stables stood empty and neglected. But as Rafael and Lottie faced each other in the quiet of the room it was clear that the memory of that savage night still gripped them as brutally as ever.

The helicopter ride to the hospital…the panic and pain of the birth…Rafael striding up and down corridors, powerlessness fuelling his anger as he tried to do something—anything—to end Lottie's agony, to get the baby delivered safely, to save both their lives. And afterwards, when Lottie's life had been out of danger and their tiny, fragile daughter had been fighting for hers, his initial relief had turned to desperate frustration when he'd been told that they didn't have the specialist equipment to save his daughter—that her only hope of survival would be a transfer to another hospital.

He had been on the phone barking out orders, insisting he would take her in his helicopter—had had to be almost physically restrained from scooping up little Seraphina against his broad chest and dashing off with her into the night. But in the end she had proved to be just too small, too weak, and her featherlight grip on life had slipped away before even Rafael could do anything about it.

Getting up, Lottie moved around the desk towards him. She longed more than anything to feel his arms around her, for him to comfort her, to be able to comfort him. She longed for them finally to be able to share their grief instead of having it push them apart, the way it always had.

But, scraping back his chair, Rafael was up on his feet before she had reached him, his arms folded across his chest, his expression dark, forbidding. Everything about the granite set of his jaw, the tight line of his mouth, was telling her to back away, now.

'You need to go now. I have calls to make.'

'Why do you do this, Rafe?' Her voice was choked but she wasn't going to give up. She stood her ground, barring his way, her blue gaze fixed firmly on his face. 'Why do you push me away, lock me out, every time Seraphina is mentioned?'

'I don't know what you are talking about.'

'Yes, you do. You know exactly what I'm talking about. You are doing it right now—look at yourself!' She stood back, theatrically gesturing to him. 'You are virtually ordering me out of the room.'

'I really don't have time for this, Lottie.'

'That's just it, isn't it? You never have time when it comes to talking about Seraphina, about how her death affected us. How are we ever supposed to move on when you flatly refuse to discuss it?'

'There is nothing to discuss. It happened. That is a fact. And no amount of talking is going to change that.'

'And *not* talking about it doesn't make it go away.' She watched as his eyes darkened to black. 'Why don't you try, Rafe? Try to open up? It's got to be better than this...' she stumbled over the words '...this frozen chasm of silence.' Lowering her voice, she fought to control the burn of tears in her throat. 'Why can't you share your feelings with me?'

Taking several paces towards the window, Rafael stopped and turned on his heel to stare at her again, his face a mask of agony. 'Trust me—you wouldn't want to share my feelings.'

'What do you mean by that?'

'I mean that you really wouldn't want to be in my head where Seraphina is concerned.'

'How can you say that?' Lottie was aghast. 'Please Rafe, I'm begging you, just speak honestly with me. Stop shutting me out.'

'Right.' Marching back to the desk, he slammed down the palm of his hand, flashing Lottie a murderous look. 'You have asked, Lottie. You say you want to know my feelings—so here they are.' Sucking in a heavy breath, he jerked back his head, his fists balled by his sides. 'I feel her loss every single day of my life. I feel anger and sadness and bitterness and frustration. But most of all I feel guilt. A deep, abiding guilt that will be with me till the day I die.'

They faced one another in terrible silence.

'There—is that what you wanted to hear? Are you happy now?'

Lottie felt for the edge of the desk to steady herself against a wave of dizziness. 'But it was a tragic accident—you must accept that.' Her voice shook. 'No one was to blame.'

Raising his hand, Rafael silenced her. 'How could I possibly accept that when I was the one who brought the wretched horse to the *palazzo* in the first place? Who was supposed to be responsible for controlling him? I am the one who took you to the wrong damned hospital—who wasn't able to get Seraphina transferred quickly enough.' The pain of his words contorted his beautiful face. 'Need I go on?'

'Stop it, Rafe, you are being ridiculous. It wasn't your fault. It was nobody's fault. No one could have foreseen what would happen.' She reached out to touch him, desperately wanting to be able to ease his misery, but Rafael turned away and her arm was left lowering in mid-air.

'I *am* to blame, Lottie. I *am* responsible for Seraphina's death. And nothing you can say will change that.'

The grand ballroom glittered for the occasion, its enormous chandeliers twinkling above the heads of the noisily chattering guests seated around the dozens of tables.

Waiters moved expertly between them, pouring the finest Monterrato wines into crystal glasses, serving course after course of delicious food. In the background huge floral arrangements lined the walls and a pianist played soft classical music. And seated side by side at the top table were the host and hostess.

Lottie thought the evening was never going to end. She was struggling, really struggling to keep up the façade, when the whole time all she could think about was her earlier conversation with Rafael. His words were going round her head in a continuous loop, muffling the polite questions of the guests on their table, tripping up her hurried answers.

She had been totally amazed by Rafael's bitter confession that he felt responsible for Seraphina's death, was consumed with guilt for what had happened. Why had she never realised this before? But then why *would* she have done? He had always flatly refused to discuss anything to do with Seraphina. And, judging by the way he had sharply dismissed her from his office, he deeply regretted having discussed it now.

She had tried her hardest to play her part, to do her duty—standing beside Rafael with her beautiful oyster silk evening dress sweeping the ground as they greeted the guests, shaking endless hands, air-kissing expensively perfumed cheeks, smiling politely enough for a rictus grin to set in. More than once she had witnessed the raising of a finely shaped eyebrow, the pout of a recently sculpted lip, as the glamorous and good had politely filed past, no doubt itching to get out of earshot and start whispering amongst themselves about the surprise reappearance of the Contessa.

Well, who would have predicted that?

Lottie cast her eyes around the guests at their table

now: a well-known politician, an Italian ambassador, a hugely wealthy investment banker, and their immaculately groomed wives. She wished they would all go home. The wives had soon lost interest in her, turning their attention instead to the gorgeously handsome Conte, each one vying for his attention with decreasing subtlety as the alcohol flowed and the evening wore on.

The banker's wife, Eleanora, seemed particularly determined to flaunt her charms in his direction, leaning forward to touch his hand, purr into his ear, making sure he had the most advantageous view of her expensively acquired cleavage.

Lottie quietly loathed her for it—loathed all of them as she watched them flirting with her husband. But mostly she loathed herself for caring, for allowing her inner green-eyed monster to make an appearance and having it point out to her so eloquently that Rafael should have married one of these glamorous, rich, titled women. How could she ever have been expected to compete with them? Their marriage had been doomed from the start.

To make matters worse, a sideways glance confirmed that Rafael looked particularly stunning tonight, in a dinner suit and black bow tie. Nobody could wear clothes like Rafael, but it wasn't just that; it was his magnetism, the effortless unleashed sex appeal that lay beneath the starched white shirt that turned the eyes of every woman in the room in his direction.

He had been perfectly polite to her all evening—when the attentions of these parasitic women had allowed—but Lottie could sense the cool reserve, the hastily erected impenetrable barrier between them. She could see it as clearly as if it were made of steel.

Finally the evening was over and the last of the guests were escorted to the door to be whisked away in their chauffeur-driven limousines. Lottie was exhausted, but she didn't want to go to bed. She wanted to find Rafael, to talk to him some more, to go over what he had told her and make him see that none of it was his fault.

She found him back in the ballroom, striding tall and dark amongst the post-party debris, thanking the waiting staff individually by name and politely dismissing them. Lottie watched from the doorway as, alone now, he pulled out one of the gilded dining chairs and sat down heavily, stretching out his legs and placing his hands behind his head as he leaned back.

'Rafe?'

Instantly pulling himself upright, he turned to look at her, the chair creaking beneath him. 'Lottie. I thought you had gone to bed.'

'Not yet.' Weaving her way between the tables, Lottie selected a chair and sat down next to him. There was an awkward silence as she rearranged the skirt of her gown. 'I thought the evening went well.'

'Yes—yes, it did.' His undone bow tie lay blackly around his neck, where the top button of his shirt was open. 'Thank you for your part in it. I know you don't find these things easy.'

Lottie bristled. Why was he thanking her as if she was just another member of his staff? And what did he mean about her not finding it easy? Had she looked as awkward as she had felt?

Sitting very straight, she hid behind a mask of dignity. 'Well, I hope I conducted myself appropriately.'

Rafael's dark eyes turned in her direction at the frostiness of her voice.

'Obviously I want to do everything I can to help the Seraphina Foundation. Now that I know it exists, that is.'

'Yes, of course.' He ignored the barb. 'It was a worthy performance.'

Worthy performance?

Heat swept through her body at his derisive, arrogant comment. Taking a deep, controlling breath, she felt the bodice of her gown tighten around her, pushing her breasts upwards.

Rafael looked away.

'And how would you describe *your* performance, then?' she asked.

Rafael's eyes swung back, eyes dangerously dark beneath the sweep of his lashes. 'I did what I had to do.'

'Oh, you did that all right, Rafael. You were lapping up the attention of those fawning women, weren't you? Why don't you admit that you loved every minute of it?' She threw the acid words at him. 'That awful Eleanora woman was virtually climbing inside your trousers and you did nothing to stop her.'

His very Latin shrug of the shoulders had Lottie digging her nails down into her palms. Without using a single word he had managed to convey not only his disregard for her opinion but his contempt for her feelings. Her remarks had been so petty that they weren't even worthy of a reply.

Lottie was still struggling with silent, impotent rage, berating herself for letting this hideously jealous harpy escape, when she heard Rafael getting up from his chair, muttering something softly in Italian under his breath.

'Look, Lottie, why don't we just agree that we have both done our best, that the evening was a success, and leave it at that? Now it's late and you need to go to bed. It's important you don't get overtired.'

Lottie glared at him, fury stinging the backs of her eyes. It was important that she didn't get over-stressed, overwrought, over-bubblingly, seethingly angry too. But he didn't seem to care about *that*.

'And I take it I will be going to bed alone?'

The words escaped before she could stop them and her hand flew, too late, to her mouth. She already knew that Rafael wouldn't be coming to her bed that night. He had made that perfectly clear without the need for any words. Why on earth was she demeaning herself by asking him to say it out loud?

But the shock of her question was totally eclipsed by the devastation of his answer.

'Yes. I have been meaning to talk to you about that. Obviously you are going to need your own space in the *palazzo*. I have arranged for a suite of rooms in the south wing to be made available to you. Your things will be moved there tomorrow.'

Lottie felt her anger seep away, only to be replaced by an emotion a hundred times worse. Like a tidal wave of heartache it swamped her, leaving her feeling weak and breathless and alone—terribly alone. So this was how it was to be. This was Rafael's vision for their future. She was to be locked away for the duration of her pregnancy— exiled like a swelling Mrs Rochester—in the south wing. And after the baby was born...? Who knew what he had planned? Presumably something even more hideous. An island somewhere so remote that he would be able to pretend that she didn't exist at all?

She raised eyes so heavy with sadness that they could hardly bear to look at him, desperately trying to find something in the tight mask of his face, the cold blackness of his eyes, that she could take some comfort from. But there was nothing. Just the twitch of a muscle beneath the scarred cheekbone.

'The south wing, you say?' Her voice was barely more than a whisper in the cavernous quiet of the room.

'That's right. I thought that would be for the best.'

'The best for whom, exactly?'

'For you—for both of us. For all concerned. I think it's important we lay down the ground rules right from the start. So we both know where we stand.'

'Oh, I think you have done that, Rafael.' Lottie bit down hard on her lip to try and stop it trembling. 'Rest assured. I know exactly where I stand.'

Stumbling to her feet, she snatched up a handful of the oyster silk of her gown, turned and fled from the room.

CHAPTER ELEVEN

LOTTIE OPENED HER eyes to the cold reality of a new day. Going into the bathroom, she held her hair back with one hand as she splashed cold water onto her face, roughly rubbing it dry before returning to the bedroom and looking around her.

She had made her decision and she was strangely calm. She was leaving. Leaving Monterrato and leaving Rafael. And this time there would be no going back.

She had spent the night thinking everything through as clearly as she could. Staring at the tangled mess of their relationship, she had forced herself to try and unravel it, following the thread, carefully picking away at the knots, refusing to stop no matter how painful it had been.

And the more she had unravelled the more obvious it had been. Rafael wanted her solely for one thing. To bear him an heir. She had known that right from the start—he had been brutally honest about it. But somehow the truth had got lost along the way, obscured by the fanciful notions insidiously creeping in, fooling her into thinking that he might actually have some feelings for her, that there might even be a chance of them reuniting as a couple.

But last night all those notions had been cruelly dispelled. Rafael's vision for the future left no room for any silly ideas about happy families. And the truth hurt—more than hurt. It was an agony that would never, ever go away. Because when it came down to it that was all they had, she and Rafael, the one true constant that she could always rely on with their relationship. Pain. And hurt. And that was all Lottie could feel now.

But she knew she had to use that pain to give her the strength to leave now. Because strength was the only language Rafael understood—the only way to fight him. If she showed any weakness, let him see her true feelings, he would use them, twist them to his advantage, ensure that she would never be free of him. She had to be strong—for herself and the baby. He would always be its father—of course he would—but that didn't give him the right to blight the rest of her life. Because that was how it would be if she stayed here. Nothing more than a half-life, constantly tormented by the love she had for him—a love that he would never return.

Walking around the bedroom, she gathered up her belongings, stuffing them into her suitcase. She picked up the oyster silk dress, holding it at arm's length, watching the way the fabric shimmered down to the ground. Then, folding it over her arm, she took it over to the armoire and placed in on a hanger beside the other beautiful dresses that she would never wear again.

She caught sight of her reflection as she closed the mirrored door, shocked for a moment by what she saw: the dark circles under her eyes, the unnatural pallor of her skin. Yes, this was what Rafael Revaldi had done to her. Jutting out her chin, she attempted a defiant stance, balling her fists by her sides, practising the measured, authoritative way she would tell Rafael of her decision.

Just thinking about confronting him made her feel physically faint, but she knew it had to be done and it had to be done now. Whilst she still had the strength to go through with it.

Descending the staircase, Lottie strained to see if she could hear Rafael's voice anywhere in the *palazzo*, but the only sounds came from the ballroom, where the cleaning up operation was obviously in progress.

He wasn't in his office, or the dining room, nor in the grand salon or indeed the ballroom. Feeling increasingly sick, Lottie hurried outside. Standing at the top of the steps, she shielded her eyes from the low sun, scanning the calm vista with a thumping heart, as if Rafael might be about to jump out from behind a poplar tree at any moment.

She ran down the steps, round to the back of the *palazzo*, searching everywhere, anywhere she thought he might possibly be, getting increasingly frantic when there was still no sign of him. Where the hell *was* he? She could feel panic creeping over her, its icy fingers wrapping around her chest, restricting her breathing.

Finding herself at the edge of the woodland area, she stopped and took in a shuddering breath. A breeze had picked up and it whipped the hair across her face, catching it on her open lip, blurring her vision.

She would go to the graveyard. Go and see Seraphina—take a few minutes to calm herself down, gather her strength.

She shivered as she walked through the woods towards the chapel. The weak sunlight offered no heat as it filtered through the framework of bare trees. Finally reaching Seraphina's grave, she slumped against the devoted angel, feeling the cold of the marble seeping into her bones. She wasn't sure how long she'd leant there before a sudden noise had her heart thumping in her chest.

'Lottie!' Suddenly Rafael appeared from nowhere, crashing towards her. 'What the hell are you doing here?'

Lottie jerked herself upright, swamped by anger, dread, and most of all pain at the sight of him.

'I came to spend some time at our daughter's grave.' She threw back her head, the wind catching her hair again, lifting it from her shoulders. 'Not that it is any of your business.'

'Your irresponsible behaviour is making this my business.' He sounded black with temper. '*Per l'amor di Dio*, you haven't even got a coat on!' What are you trying to do? Make yourself ill?'

Before she could reply he was beside her, tugging off his jacket and flinging it over her shoulders.

'*Dio*, you are freezing—come here.' He pressed her against his chest, wrapping his strong arms around her, rubbing her back through the waxed cotton fabric of the jacket.

'Get off me.' Her voice was muffled against his shirt and she wriggled herself free from him, stumbling round to the other side of Seraphina's grave from where she glared aggressively at him. 'Leave me alone.'

Rafael glared back, mystified. 'What's the matter with you?' And then, as a terrible thought occurred to him, his voice dropped. 'Is everything all right?'

'Yes.' Lottie forced herself to hold his stare. 'If by that you mean the baby, everything is fine.'

Relief flooded Rafael's eyes, but seconds later they darkened again. 'So what, then? What are you doing here? What is going on?'

His questions shot at her like rapid gunfire.

'Why are you behaving like this?'

'I can behave however I want.'

'No, you can't. Not if it puts my child at risk.' His voice was raw, clear and cold. 'When it comes to protecting my baby's life, you will do exactly as I say.'

'Oh, you think so, do you?' Lottie matched his anger with her own. 'Well that is where you are wrong. As a matter of fact I have been looking for you.' The warning look in Rafael's eyes threatened to steal her courage but she blundered on. 'To tell you that I am going back home—to England.' She could feel her heart pounding frantically behind her ribs at the enormity of what she was saying. 'For good.'

There was a beat of silence between them, pierced by the single caw of a raven overhead.

'No. You are not.' Rafael's voice was dangerously quiet, his eyes burning with fire.

'Yes.' Lottie squared up to him as best she could, shivering violently beneath his jacket. 'I've made up my mind.'

'Well, you can just unmake it.' The lash of his words whistled across at her. 'I can assure you, Charlotte, you are doing no such thing.'

'You can't stop me, Rafael. I'm going to go back to England and have the baby there and—'

'Charlotte, if you think, for one tiny second, that I would let you leave the country, take our baby away, then you have seriously misjudged me.' His breath escaped in angry puffs of condensed air. 'What's all this about anyway?' The depth of his scowl all but closed his eyes. 'What is going on?'

'I've told you what is going on. I've made up my mind and I am returning to England.'

Rafael shook his head, fury slowing the movement. 'And I am saying you are doing no such thing. I have no idea what has brought this on, but I do know that you can stop this nonsense right now. My baby will be born here and will be raised here—by its father—at the Palazzo Monterrato.'

He hesitated, his scowl turning to a sneer.

'You have run away once and I'm sure you are capable of doing that again. Should you choose to leave after the baby is born, then so be it. But the baby will stay here. And for the time being you are going *nowhere*.'

The word resonated with ruthless force.

Lottie fought to control hot tears of fury and despair. His words were like a fish hook in her flesh. The more she struggled the worse the pain. If she had wanted proof of his feelings for her she had it right there. *Should you choose to leave after the baby is born, then so be it.* She meant nothing to him—nothing at all. Without the baby she might as well not exist.

Biting back the searing pain, she rounded on him, using anger to mask the agony, covering her misery with its red cloak.

'I'm sure you would *love* that, wouldn't you?' She spat the words at him. 'Once the baby has been born there is nothing you would like better than for me to disappear completely.'

Rafael stared at her. 'What are you talking about?'

'I'm talking about you—me—the whole ridiculous idea that we could ever live together, have any sort of meaningful relationship, baby or no baby.'

'Look…' Making a visible effort now, Rafael lowered his tone, inched towards her as if dealing with one of his feral horses. 'I don't know what this is all about, but maybe if you were to just calm down…'

He stretched out an arm towards her but she batted it away furiously, the jacket sliding off her shoulders.

'It's about the fact that I mean nothing to you— *nothing*! I am no more than a surrogate—worse than a surrogate. Because you can't just pay me off and forget about me. Instead you have to lock me away in some far-flung corner of the *palazzo*. But I am your last, your *only* chance of providing an heir for Monterrato and you hate me for it. Don't even try and deny it.'

Her voice was reaching a harridan screech as it picked up speed, denying Rafael any sort of reply.

'If it hadn't been for your accident you would have been rid of me for good. You would have carried on living your self-indulgent bachelor lifestyle for as long as you liked, eventually choosing a suitable mother for your precious children when the fancy took you from any number of painted, perfect, pouting women like the ones who were fawning all over you last night.'

A cold quiet descended as Lottie gulped in a shuddering, juddering breath that racked through her whole body.

Rafael just stared at her.

'So is that what this is about? This ridiculous behaviour?' Realisation coloured his words. 'Some petty rivalry with the women at the dinner last night? Perhaps you should be careful, Lottie.' His eyes glittered coldly, his voice suddenly terrifyingly soft. 'We wouldn't want to misinterpret this little outburst as a fit of *jealousy*, would we? Fool ourselves into thinking that you actually *care*. We both know better than that. Perhaps I need to remind you that who I see, who I take to my bed—'

'Stop!' With a piercing scream Lottie covered her ears. 'I don't want to hear any more.'

'Is none of your business.' His rapier tongue hadn't finished with her yet. 'You left me...remember?'

His words floated across the stillness of their daughter's grave. Across the great chasm of misunderstanding and pain that had blighted their lives.

'It's not something I am likely to forget.' Washed with grief, Lottie's words were barely audible.

That lie—that terrible lie. '*I don't love you Rafael, and*

I never have.' Delivered in a moment of tortured panic and accepted, just like that, as brutal, irrevocable fact.

'Well, that makes two of us.' He gave a derisive snort. 'You had me fooled, Lottie, I'll give you that. I had no idea—no idea at all—that that was coming. Idiot that I was, I thought we were for ever—imagine that? And all the time I meant nothing to you—you were desperate to be rid of me. When you finally came out with the fact that you had never loved me, well...' He stopped, his throat moving as if he had swallowed something sharp. 'If you want the truth, I will tell you. It crucified me, Lottie, totally crucified me.'

This was more than Lottie could bear. Her own pain she could cope with. She *had* to cope with. But seeing the suffering that twisted the muscles of Rafael's beautiful face made something snap inside her.

'I lied.'

'Chiedo scusa? I beg your pardon?'

'I lied, Rafe. When I said I didn't love you.' Her voice was very small.

'Sì, right—of course you did. I was there, Lottie, I heard you say the words, saw the look in your eyes as you spoke them.'

'I lied because I had to—because I knew it was the only way you would let me go.'

'Che diavolo?' Rafael snarled at her. 'If this is some misguided way of trying to make me feel better then don't bother.'

'You were talking about telling the truth—well, this is my truth. When I said what I said it was for your benefit, so you would be free of me.'

'How very kind.' The sarcasm in his voice was chilling. 'And why exactly would I want to be free of you?'

'Because our marriage was a mess—nothing but endless trips to fertility clinics and failed IVF attempts. Because I saw no reason for Seraphina's death to ruin both our lives.' Lottie gulped in a breath of cold air. 'I thought if I left I could take the pain of Seraphina's death away with me. That you would be better off without me.'

Fury contorted Rafael's face. 'Don't you *dare* bring Seraphina into this. You have never had the sole rights to that pain, no matter what you might think. She was *my* daughter, *my* little girl, every bit as much as she was yours, and I felt the pain of her loss—still feel the pain of her loss—every bit as deeply as you. More so, in fact, as I shoulder the guilt for her death.'

'Well, I didn't know that then. How could I have done when you refused to ever speak of her?' Her words were squeezed out between strangled sobs. 'I felt like I was grieving totally on my own.'

'How dare you say that?'

'I needed your support but you thought about nothing but producing another baby. It was like an obsession—as if without a baby there was no point to our marriage, no point in our staying together.'

'That's the most preposterous thing I have ever heard.'

'And when it didn't happen...when all the drugs and doctors and clinics failed...I knew that I had failed. I felt depressed and empty and useless.' Deflated now, she reached out to the angel beside her for support, to stop herself sliding to the ground.

'*Dio*, Lottie.' Rafael looked as if a part of his body had started to hurt. 'Don't you realise that I was trying to be strong? Watching you grieve broke my heart. The last thing I wanted was to make it worse by showing you my pain.'

Lottie sniffed loudly, trying hard to hang on, not to collapse in a pool of misery. 'Don't *you* realise that you made it a million times worse by not showing me your pain? If we had been a proper couple we would have grieved together and then thought about trying for another baby when the time was right. But that wasn't how it was. Getting me pregnant again was all that mattered to you.'

'No, Lottie, I won't have this. I won't have you rewriting the past. I was trying to rescue what was left of the disaster that I had caused. I was responsible for the death of our baby, for the fact that you could never conceive naturally again. I had to try and put things right as best I could. That is the truth of the matter.'

'Well, that may be your truth, but that was not how it felt to me.' The anguish twisting inside her like a corkscrew gave Lottie the strength to go on. 'To me it felt as if you'd only married me because I was pregnant. And when we lost Seraphina you realised it had all been a mistake, that you were stuck with me for no reason. That was why you were so determined to get me pregnant again—to justify our marriage to yourself.'

'Dio!' Rafael turned from her, stamping a couple of paces away before swinging round again. 'I don't believe I am hearing this. I can only assume you have concocted this ridiculous story to try and make yourself feel better. To ease your guilt you have somehow convinced yourself that it was all my fault—that I was the one to blame when you walked out on our marriage.'

'It's not a question of blame. I never said it was your fault. I'm trying to explain why I said what I did.'

'So by telling me that you had never loved me, by sneaking away in the night without even having the guts to tell me what you were doing, you were actually doing me a *favour?* You were freeing me from the chains of marital responsibility?' He shook his head with vitriolic disbelief.

'Yes.'

'Nothing to do with the fact that you wanted out of our relationship? That you had had enough of me?'

'No, nothing to do with that.'

'And you expect me to believe that?'

'Yes, because it's the truth. And I was right. You *have* led a better life without me. You have moved on…formed new relationships. If it hadn't been for your accident you would never have had to see me again.'

'Don't you *dare* tell me how I have led my life.' Rafael looked as if he was about to explode. 'You know nothing, Charlotte—*nothing*.'

'I know that you didn't come after me. Try to get me back.'

Incredulity raged in his eyes. 'After what you'd said to me?' He couldn't bear to look at her. 'There is such a thing as pride, you know. I was hardly going to beg. I can control most things in my life, but even I can't make someone love me.'

Suddenly the tears were streaming uncontrollably down Lottie's face. 'You didn't need to make me love you, Rafe. I have always loved you.' She covered her face with her hands, and her voice was muffled through her wet fingers. 'And I always will.'

CHAPTER TWELVE

RAFAEL STARED AT the forlorn figure shivering on the other side of Seraphina's grave. She looked so vulnerable, so fragile, standing there, her cold hands trembling in front of her face. Every fibre of his being wanted to go to her, to wrap his arms around her and hold her tight. To tell her that he could make everything better. But he couldn't.

Lottie's revelation that she had lied to him that night had knocked him sideways. It couldn't be true. The cruel way she had said those words, the look on her face when she'd delivered them, had left no room for doubt. She had meant them, all right. Now she had let time take her words and shape them into something more palatable, mould them into a convenient lie that would assuage her conscience.

Well, he wasn't falling for that—he wasn't going to let her hurt him again.

He could still feel the searing pain of her cruel statement, even after all this time, and that gave him strength. The strength he so badly needed to stop himself from reaching out to her, from holding her tearstained face in his hands, from raising her lips to meet his and kissing away the heartache of this whole wretched business.

'Aren't you going to say anything?'

Lottie's anguished voice cut through the silence and she gazed, petrified, across at him.

'What is there to say?'

Rafael turned his head away. He couldn't bear to look at her—knew that if he did he would weaken, that all the resolve he had built up over the last two years would be swept away in the tidal wave of emotion that the very sight of her beautiful tortured face threatened to unleash.

'You obviously think you know it all already. You have brutally choreographed my life without ever actually asking me if that was what *I* wanted.'

His livid gaze swept across the overgrown graves.

'Had you done so you would have known that you couldn't have been more wrong. I never viewed our marriage purely in terms of having children. However...' He allowed himself a quick glance in her direction, saw the tears that were silently rolling down her cheeks, dripping off her chin. He had to keep strong. 'If it makes you feel better to think that, if it eases some of the guilt you presumably felt, then go ahead—be my guest. It's not as if any of it matters any more. Just don't expect me to believe you.'

'Rafe!' Lottie uttered his name with a strangled cry. 'I am just trying to explain how I felt, that's all—explain why I left you.'

'Well, don't bother.' As he raised his hand to silence her his eyes were jet-black. 'It's way too late for that. I was taken in by you once, Charlotte. It's not going to happen again.'

Twisting away from her, he jammed his hands into his jeans pockets and kicked at the moss-covered path.

'I'm going back to the *palazzo* now. I suggest you do the same. Freezing to death out here is not going to solve anything.'

Lottie watched as his tall figure turned and marched its way between the ancient gravestones. At the top of the steps he paused, turning back to look at her, his anger channelled into uncompromising authority.

'And don't even think about running away again, Lottie.' His words cut through the cold air. 'I will be watching you.'

Back at the *palazzo* Rafael crashed into his office, kicking the door shut behind him. Away from the pitiful sight of Lottie, he felt the anger kicking in, slowly building and building until it threatened to engulf him completely. He had never felt like this before, so consumed with frustrated bile.

Turning on the computer, he realised his hands were shaking as they hovered over the keyboard. How could she talk about running away? *Again.* How dared she do this to him? And this time she was carrying his child, for God's sake. His chest heaved with the fury and injustice of it all.

He logged on to his email, desperately looking for a distraction to steady his heart-rate, regulate his breathing, stop him from marching out and doing something really stupid. Like finding Lottie again and demanding that she stayed here, with him. Not just for now, not until after the baby was born, not even for the next twenty years while they watched their child become an adult. He wanted to make her swear that she would stay with him for ever.

His mind flashed back to the dinner last night, the agony of sitting beside her all evening. She had looked so enchanting in that silk gown, the pale colour against her skin giving her an ethereal beauty, a tenderness that had made him want to both protect her and ravish her— not necessarily in that order. She had somehow twisted her hair into a plait over the top of her head, fastening it in a bun at the back. And with the violet earrings he had given her catching the light in her eyes he had never seen her look more beautiful.

He had known then, more forcefully than ever, that his decision to move her to the south wing was the right one. If he had any chance of holding on to his sanity he was going to have to keep away from her. Or keep her away from him.

He had woken this morning knowing that something was wrong, fear clutching at his heart, tightening its grip when, hours later, there had still been no sign of Lottie. Eventually he had given in to temptation and knocked on her door, but had expressly forbidden himself from looking in when there was no answer. Instead he had charged around the *palazzo* and its grounds looking for her, finally tracking her down at their daughter's grave. Only to hear the devastating revelation that she was leaving.

Like hell she was.

Rafael took in a heavy breath and, leaning forward, made himself concentrate on the growing string of emails. There was one from Dr Oveisi's office, asking for information regarding Contessa Revaldi's embryo transplant. Had she done a pregnancy test yet? Rafael quickly composed a brief affirmative message, saying that the Contessa was indeed pregnant.

Pregnant. Somehow now the news was leaking out it seemed more real. Lottie was pregnant and he was going to be a father. He should have been ecstatic, euphoric. When he had been lying in that hospital bed, adjusting to the devastating news that he was sterile, it had been all he could think about. The fact that he did have one last chance to be a father. He had plotted and schemed to achieve his goal and now it had worked just the way he had been determined it would.

So how had he ended up feeling like this? Why did his body hurt more now than it had when he had woken up from that damned accident, battered, bruised and broken?

Because of Lottie—that was why.

* * *

Lottie stood perfectly still, the clouds scudding across the sky above her. She couldn't move, frozen, numbed to the core, by her harrowing confrontation with Rafael.

She had known that telling him she was leaving would be the hardest thing she had ever had to do in her whole life. Last time she had taken the coward's way—*'sneaking away in the night'*, as Rafael's words had so painfully reminded her. This time she had had to do it face to face. She had foolishly tried to tell herself that she would be able to convince him, make Rafael see sense, that it was the only practical solution. That they could never live together, even in a place as huge as the *palazzo*, even if she was exiled to the south wing…

But nothing had prepared her for the onslaught of misery that had just happened. Never, in her most deranged of moments, had she ever envisaged admitting to him that she still loved him. Whatever could possibly have possessed her to do that? Had something deep in her subconscious persuaded her that he might say the same, say that he loved her too, that they could be together for ever? If so her subconscious deserved to die a long and painful death. Because now she no longer even had the one thing left she could call her own. Her pride. That lay in tatters at her feet, along with her shredded declaration of love for him and the gruesome mess that was her bleeding heart.

Lottie bent down and picked up Rafael's jacket, slipping her arms into the oversized sleeves, pulling it close around her, her body still shaking uncontrollably beneath it.

She had to leave. There was no doubt about that. Somehow she had to find the strength to explain to Rafael, coldly and clearly, why it was impossible for her to stay.

* * *

Pacing savagely round his office, Rafael stopped in front of the window. He had never felt like this before. So close to losing control. It was as if everything he thought he knew—everything about his character, his life—was being challenged. And found wanting.

He had been so protective of his own pride that he had refused to listen to Lottie, refused to let himself open up to her. Why had he not even considered that what she had just told him might be true? That maybe he *had* handled things badly after Seraphina died. That maybe he hadn't taken time to grieve. That maybe, just maybe, she *did* still love him.

And what the hell did he think he was doing now? Shutting himself away in his office when she was out there somewhere, hurting? Lottie—the woman who was pregnant with his baby, the woman who meant more to him than anything in the world. One thing was for sure: if he let her slip through his fingers again he would never forgive himself. He had to do something about it now. Before it was too late.

They collided in the hallway. Lottie, running in from outside, coming up against the steel wall of Rafael's chest. As his arms went out to steady her she pushed herself away and they stood there, facing each other, for several long, silent seconds.

'I was just coming to look for you.' Lottie brushed back the wild mess of curls from her face, from cold cheeks that were streaked with tears. She forced herself to meet his eyes, to squeeze the words past her closing throat. 'To tell you that I'm sorry, Rafael, so sorry…but I meant what I said about…'

'About having always loved me?'

She stopped dead.

'About…about…' she stammered, eyes wide with confusion, her heart swerving in her chest. 'About having to leave.'

His eyes were scanning her face with such intensity it felt as if he was searching her soul for the truth. But she mustn't falter now—not when she had got this far. She sucked in a breath, feeling it shudder down the length of her body. Somehow she had to find the strength to carry on, force the jagged words out of her mouth. Then it would be done.

'We both know I can't stay here, Rafael. I will return to Monterrato in time to have the baby, of course, and then we can work out the best way to proceed after that.'

There—it was said. She allowed her gaze to slide to the floor.

'Did you mean it, Lottie? When you said you had always loved me?'

The black and white squares of marble blurred beneath her feet. Why was he doing this to her? She was waiting for anger, denial, refusal, bracing herself for more of the blind rage that he had showed her earlier. She could cope with that. But this…? This was a far more excruciating form of torture.

'Yes.' Her voice was very small.

Tipping up her chin with his finger, Rafael locked his eyes on hers again. 'So when you walked out…when you said those words to me…?' He faltered, drinking in the violet-blue of her eyes, still searching for the answer, sure that it had to be held in there somewhere.

'It was a lie, Rafe. The biggest lie of my life.'

'And now? This is the truth?'

As he removed his finger from her chin Lottie realised that his hand was shaking.

'Yes—yes, Rafael, it is. This is the truth.'

'Then say it,' he growled from somewhere deep in his throat. 'Say the words, Lottie.'

Lottie gazed upwards, scanning his scarred, handsome face as if for the last time, before surrendering to the force in his eyes.

'I love you, Rafael.'

Lowering his head, Rafael brushed his mouth against hers, capturing her words with his lips, holding them, tasting them, letting the truth in all its naked glory pass from her body to his.

With aching tenderness the pressure of his kiss increased, until it flooded through Lottie's body like warm water, melting her against him, washing away everything else that had ever passed between them. Closing her eyes, she let herself float away. If this was their final parting kiss, then so be it—she would give herself up to it, surrender to the glorious feeling that obliterated every other thought. And remember it for ever.

Finally she felt Rafael's lips leave hers, felt him loosen his hold on her, and knew she was going to have to open her eyes to the cold reality of the future. She waited, looking up into his dark returning stare. There was an agonising pause before he lifted his hands, cupped them around her face and looked deep, deep into her eyes.

'*Anch'io ti amo.* I love you too, Lottie.'

Pulling apart at last, they moved into the salon. Rafael bent to put a match to the fire prepared in the hearth, then drew Lottie back beside him as they watched as the flames licked around the kindling, crackling it into life.

As he turned to look down at her his dark eyes were brimming with love in a way that Lottie had never, ever thought she would see again. Then he wrapped his arms around her and pulled her into the tightest hug.

'It will warm up in a minute.'

'I'm not cold.'

How could she be, locked in his arms, with his astonishing words still resonating in her head?

'Good.' He paused, running a hand over her tangled curls, tracing the shape of her skull with the flat of his palm. 'I'm so sorry, Lottie.'

'No.' Moving away just enough to look up at his face, Lottie stopped him. 'I should be saying sorry, not you. I'm the one who ran away, who didn't have the courage to tell you to your face how I felt.'

'I didn't give you the chance.' Drawing her back against his chest, he spoke the words softly over her head. 'I was so consumed with guilt…'

He resisted the pull of Lottie against him.

'No, let me say this—I have to say this. I was so consumed with guilt over Seraphina's death that it took over everything in my life. I refused to grieve, refused to even let myself witness your grief, because it twisted the knife in my heart still further. Every time I looked at you it was like a permanent reminder of what I had done—to our baby, to you. I thought I had taken away from you the only thing that mattered.'

'No, of course you hadn't, Rafe.' Forcibly loosening herself from the grip of his arms, Lottie tipped back her head to look at him. 'That wasn't how it was at all. You have to stop tormenting yourself.'

'So instead I made it my mission to try and change that terrible destiny. And when it didn't happen, when the IVF didn't work, instead of standing back and taking a long hard look at what I was doing, instead of devoting myself to trying to make you happy, I turned into some crazed adrenalin junkie, pushing myself further and further physically and further and further away from you.'

He stopped abruptly, the glitter of tears in his eyes. 'Can you ever forgive me, Lottie?'

'Rafael.' Shrugging off his arms, she raised her hands to his face, brushing away the dark curls from his forehead, grazing her fingers against the ridge of the scar. 'Listen to me.'

He had no option now but to meet her gaze, see that what she was saying was the truth. 'You were *not* responsible for Seraphina's death. Do you hear me?'

'But if I had taken you to the hospital in Milan... They had better equipment there—they might have saved her...'

'It was a much longer journey, Rafe. I might have given birth in the helicopter, and even if I hadn't Seraphina would almost certainly have died. She was just too premature, Rafe. Too tiny...too frail. You have to accept that. You did everything you could. But ultimately what happened was beyond your control.' She gazed at his beautiful agonised face, desperate to take away the pain, to make him see that he wasn't to blame. She lowered her voice gently. 'Even *you* can't control everything, you know, Rafe.'

'That I do know.' Rafael's huff of acceptance finally released some of the tension and a smile touched his lips. 'I can't control my feelings for you. I tried to stop loving you, Lottie—*Dio*, how I tried. But no matter what you did, no matter how much I reminded myself that you had walked out on me, that you had never loved me, I couldn't stop the love I had for you. And I hated myself for it.'

'I'm so sorry...'

Rafael brought his lips down on hers for another silencing kiss. 'No more sorries. No more regrets. We have made a mess of the past but now we have the whole of our future to put things right. And it starts here.'

He took hold of her hand and Lottie watched as he placed it on her abdomen, resting his own over the top.

Then their eyes met again with the miraculous realisation. They were a family already: Rafael, Lottie and the baby. Everything was going to be fine.

The fire crackled and popped in celebration.

EPILOGUE

Last night Contessa Charlotte Revaldi, wife of Conte Rafael Revaldi, gave birth to a son, Valentine Rafael John, at Ospedale D'Aosta.

As the Conte di Monterrato arrived to visit mother and baby this morning he announced that they were both doing extremely well and that he and his wife couldn't be more proud of their longed-for second child—a brother for Seraphina.

The couple's first child tragically died three years ago after a premature birth. A steady stream of friends and well-wishers have been visiting the hospital all day, with flowers and gifts for the happy family.

PUTTING THE NEWSPAPER down on the hospital bed, Lottie looked across at Rafael, who was cradling their baby in his arms, rocking slightly from side to side as he gazed into his son's sleeping face. They looked so right together, a perfect fit, with that small bundle of life snuggled against the powerfully muscled arms of his father. The present and the future. Lottie could already see the trouble they were going to cause her. And she couldn't wait.

'I meant to say, my mother rang this morning to congratulate us.'

'Greta? That was nice of her.'

'Yes, I was quite surprised, actually. I'd never really thought of her as granny material, but she seemed genuinely excited. She's even talking about paying us a visit.'

'I'll have to practise my best behaviour.' Rafael gave her a schoolboy grin over the top of the baby's head, leaving Lottie in no doubt that her mother would be totally charmed by him.

'And Alex, of course—she's been on the phone, demanding photos of Valentine and all the gruesome birth details. I think I've managed to put her off the idea of ever having a baby.'

'Some friend you are.' Rafael laughed. 'But, seriously, you were magnificent, Lottie. I can't tell you how proud I am of you.'

'That's because I had you there with me. And I would do it a thousand times over—because look what we got.' She tipped her head on one side.

'I can't stop looking.' Rafael returned his gaze to his son and there was a tender pause. 'I think he takes after you, you know—those beautiful wide eyes. And look at his tiny nose, and his lips, and his little ears.'

'So you approve, then?'

As he glanced up again Lottie saw that his eyes were shining with emotion, and when she saw his slight shake of the head and deep swallow she knew he was struggling to find the words.

'I can still hardly believe it. That he is really ours, Lottie, yours and mine.'

'Well, you'd better believe it. Especially when he is screaming his head off at three in the morning. And Valentine looks more like *you*, just for the record. That certainly isn't *my* hair!'

Rafael protectively smoothed his hand over his son's

shock of dark hair, then watched as it sprang back to up-right. 'Listen to your *mamma*, being rude about your hair. You and I both know you are perfect in every way.'

'He really is...' Lottie sighed with exhausted pleasure and laid her head back on the pillow. 'We did good, didn't we?'

'We did more than good.'

Sitting on the edge of the bed with the baby in his arms, he leant forward to kiss Lottie tenderly on the lips.

'We did *assolutamente magnifico*. And this is just the start, Lottie—the start of a wonderful life together: you, me and our son. A proper family at last. Now and for ever.

* * * * *

THE SURPRISE
CONTI CHILD

TARA PAMMI

PROLOGUE

LEANDRO CONTI.

The name floated, almost reverently, on the lips of the sweaty, gyrating crowd, bringing Alexis Sharpe to a sudden halt in the middle of the dance floor in an exclusive Milanese nightclub she'd only been allowed into because of her new friend, Valentina Conti.

Their friendship had been instantaneous when Alex, backpacking through Italy, had somehow found herself facing the attentions of an enamored but harmless Italian waiter. Tina had interfered and instantly decided that she liked Alex.

Valentina, vivacious, sophisticated and rich, was as different from Alex as Milan was from Brooklyn, but Alex hadn't been able to resist Tina's generous heart. The differences hadn't bothered her either until she had met Tina's older brother.

Leandro Conti... CEO of Conti Luxury Goods.
Gorgeous, sophisticated Italian magnate.

Brooding. Forbidding. Almost godlike in the way he surveyed the rest of them. As if he existed on a different sphere.

For a twenty-year-old from Brooklyn, and for one who blended into average and dull on a daily basis, that felt very true.

That he was at the nightclub in Milan was as rare as a UFO sighting. Suddenly, even the most raucous party girls pushed their hair back, adjusting dresses poured over hourglass figures.

They were hoping to catch his attention, Alexis realized, with a dawning sense of defeat.

Still, she chanced a glance.

The central glass dance floor suspended above water and the interplay of light created an illusion of a vast space. Yet the edgy elegance faded against the darkly stunning man.

That same hungry, fluttery feeling uncoiled in the pit of Alex's stomach.

Clad in a black dress shirt and dark blue jeans, the chiseled angles of his face tightly stark, he came to a standstill at the edge of the dance floor. That slate-gray gaze searched, and dismissed each face in turn.

How she longed to make sure he noticed that she, Alexis Sharpe, was a woman. That she couldn't be dismissed so easily...a compulsion she'd never felt before.

She faced every day that she lacked any special talent, that she'd been overlooked, even by her parents. This vacation to Milan had been a desperate escape she'd grabbed after being rejected at another high-flying Manhattan firm for a job. When she'd realized she wasn't equipped for a big career like some of her friends, that a menial job at her dad's health food store comprised her future.

A summer in Italy because you've been turned down at another job, her mom had said in that resigned tone of hers. *Rewarding failure, are we now?*

As if she hadn't expected anything different of Alex. The words had rankled but Alex needed this. A small rebellion in a life that had made her less than mediocre and thoroughly without merit.

And yet, when it came to Leandro Conti, she felt a reckless freedom, a vicious urge to stand out to him.

Like that time two weeks ago when he had arrived at

the dinner with Valentina, their brother, Luca, and their friends on the veranda overlooking the lake.

A soft breeze had rolled in from the lake and Valentina had whipped up a batch of margaritas. Alex had had just one sip and instantly put it down.

Leandro had dragged a chair out next to her, inquired over Valentina's twisted ankle, and then he'd turned that dark gray gaze on her.

"Other than chiding Tina that she is a big baby," he mimicked her tone, and Alex cursed herself for losing patience with Valentina that evening a few weeks ago, "how are you enjoying your trip, Ms. Sharpe?"

That accent of his had sent a shiver curling through her spine even as it stiffened at his condescending tone.

Shock that he'd sat down next to her had stolen speech from her. While his gaze had traversed over her messy, high ponytail, her forehead, her nose and, then briefly, her mouth.

A bare five seconds, maybe but Alex had felt the perusal like a caress.

Heat had clamped her cheeks and she gritted her teeth. "Alex, my name is Alex. Why do you refuse to say it?"

His greeting to her had always been unflinchingly polite, as if he was determined to deny her even that small satisfaction.

Valentina, both shrewd and kind, had warned Alex that her older brother wasn't someone to set her sights on.

Perversely, that warning had only intensified Alex's attraction to the man.

"Why do you shorten it to a man's name like that?" And then he had flitted that intractable gaze over the rest of her, her small breasts in her worn-out community college T-shirt, her midriff and her long legs in worn-out capris and her favorite sneakers. Moved up again. Four weeks amid Valentina and her friends dressed at the height of sophistication and it was the first time Alex wished she'd dressed up.

His thinly sculpted upper lip curled and Alex clenched tight inside. "Do you assume you are successful at hiding everything you are?" A taunt that no one else at the table could hear.

Shock buffeted her in waves as she looked inward.

Had she done that? Had she dressed to minimize herself, to willingly lay down in defeat before she could actually be rejected anyway by the world?

She met his gaze with a boldness she didn't know she had, this man who saw her so clearly. "I have no idea what you mean."

He sat at a perfectly respectable distance, yet fire uncoiled in every nerve. His warm breath feathered over the rim of her ear. "Little advice from your friend's brother, Ms. Sharpe. Stop looking at men like that." Then he looked at her again and those gray irises widened. "Unless you're fully aware of the weapon you wield."

He'd left then, without a backward glance.

Leaving Alex seething with humiliation and embarrassment and anger. Only then had she realized that he knew.

He knew that she was attracted to him.

And he had rejected her. Very thoroughly.

But she hadn't even retorted because it was as if her brain was incapable of higher functions when he was close. *Like now.*

The din of the nightclub, the slow jazzy tune that had men and women around her gyrating sensuously, the sweaty crush of the crowd and the heated scent of pheromones…everything faded as she studied him.

He stood about two feet from her, and yet, she was aware of every inch of that hard, lean body, could feel herself gravitate toward him.

As if he was a black hole and she was being sucked toward him.

Hasn't he made a fool of you enough already, some tiny self-preservation instinct asked.

Alex clutched it like a lifeline, forced her legs to turn away from him.

She didn't need an arrogant Italian to ruin her hard-won holiday this summer. To make her feel as if somehow she came up short.

She already lived with that feeling every day.

This trip to Italy, this whole summer was supposed to be about escaping, about being someone other than the Alexis who failed at everything, the Alexis who was nothing but a mere shadow of everything her genius brother Adrian had been. About living before she returned to being a disappointment to her parents.

Anxious to get away, she tripped in her four-inch stilettos. A leanly muscled forearm wrapped around her waist, steadying her.

Held tightly against a hard, male chest, her breath knocked out.

"*Grazie mille*," she managed one of the two phrases she knew, breathless against the press of the corded muscles just below her breasts.

"You can barely stand in those stilettos. Just because Valentina offers a free pair of Contis doesn't mean you should wear them."

Her head jerked up, the gravelly voice tugging at her nerves.

Leandro Conti stared down that aquiline bridge of his nose. Neon blue lighting from the strobes cast blue shadows on his narrow, angular face, teasing her with flashes of his thin-lipped mouth.

The scowl on his brow straightened her spine. "Are you

implying that I'm not good enough to wear your exalted designer shoes?"

"I do not imply."

"You're a jerk, Mr. Conti."

His gaze flitted down over her neck, and her body tightly encased in a sheath dress she'd borrowed from Valentina. Even the stretchy fabric couldn't make much of her nonexistent curves.

But under his stare, Alex felt scorched, marked.

"And you…are playing hard at being a grown-up. Unsuccessfully, I might say."

"Damned if I do, and if I don't, with you. At least three men wanted to take me home tonight," she taunted recklessly, even as hurt pierced her, "so I say take your unwanted, stuffy opinion—"

His fingers tightened over her waist, but never hurting. Though his expression remained coolly remote. Alex wondered if his grip told more truth about him than his words. "Ah… I didn't realize your goal was so low.

"Did my fashion-genius brother not advise you that those sturdy jeans and neon pink sneakers suit that innocent, American girl-next-door image of yours to perfection? It is the perfect lure."

His infuriating attitude scraped. But the thing that her juvenile mind focused on was that he remembered her neon pink sneakers.

"Of all the faults I attributed to you, being a snob wasn't one."

"What did you attribute to me then?"

"Arrogance. Cynicism. As much feeling as a rock."

He let her go then, almost shoving her away from him. As if she'd hurt him.

Alex tottered again on the heels. Her ankle throbbed.

His arm shot out again, accompanied by pithy Italian

she was glad she couldn't understand. Her body felt ragged, as if someone else controlled her limbs.

"Should you be drinking when you're among strangers in a foreign country?"

The sharp, almost caustic tone of his words, *fortunately*, canceled out the sensuous web she fell into.

Oh, he made her so mad. And bold. And hot. As if every inch of her skin was on fire, hungry, desperate to be quenched with his touch.

"I had one…*one* glass of wine." But since she'd barely eaten anything all day, it had gone straight to her head. "Not that I need to explain myself to you. Back off."

One eyebrow rose in that imperious face. Arrogance dripped from the man even when he didn't understand her. "Back off?"

His palm was a heated brand on her lower back while he was a fortress of wiry strength in front. Men she'd met at college were boys compared to Leandro Conti. Ergo, her utter lack of sophistication in handling him. "Leave me alone. You're not my keeper, something in that vein."

"So do you have a keeper, back home? I don't think they're doing a good job of looking after you."

"What is this? The sixteenth century?" she quipped.

He wasn't particularly amused but there was a gleam in those gray depths. An infinitesimal softening of that mouth. "You're not quite the lost little waif I thought, are you?"

She forced a laugh to cover up the tingling she felt all over. He smelled so good, like the most decadent dark chocolate with a bitter edge to it. The one that clung to the senses long after it was consumed. The one you glutted on knowing it was going to settle into your thighs and hips. "Is it impossible for you to speak without being insulting?"

"You will not get sweet words from me, Ms. Sharpe. Barely eighteen and roaming a foreign country, staying with strangers. You might as well hang a Take Me sign around your neck. I'd never let Valentina—"

The barb landing sharp, Alex spoke through gritted teeth. "I'm twenty and I'm not Valentina."

She'd die before she admitted that, since that first night that Valentina had brought her to the Conti Villa, all she had thought of was him. That it was his dismissive look that'd had her borrowing Valentina's dress.

That it was his attention, his gaze that she had sought from day one. That the thought of leaving, of going back to her dull existence without knowing his kiss, his touch, haunted her.

"And Valentina and Luca are my friends, even if—"

"If you consider my brother a friend, if you mistake his intent toward you," he said, as his nostrils flared, and she wondered if he was disgusted or angry or both, "you're more foolish than I assumed. I should have never let Valentina bring you to the villa."

"You find my presence so objectionable that you're avoiding the villa, aren't you?"

She hadn't meant to betray that she'd noticed his absence. But he didn't deny her claim either.

Hurt was a thorn nestled deep into her skin.

"Luca and I...we understand each other perfectly," she added defiantly.

Although he was right.

A day after she had arrived at their villa, Luca had cornered her twice, teased her, kissed her. Made it clear within an hour that he'd love to make it more. Alex had a feeling Luca would take any woman to bury whatever lingered under that easy charm. And just as easily discard her the next morning.

But she hadn't been tempted, *at all*. Alex felt nothing even as she admitted that Luca was sex on legs.

The man in front of her however...he made her feel

naked and languid and achy all over, with just one look from those gray depths. For all his grating politeness, he made her feel as if he saw her, the Alexis that wanted to pack a lifetime of adventure into one short summer.

Why, she'd no idea.

"Have you already slept with him then?"

If she'd been a violent person, if the amused glint in his eyes hadn't lulled her, Alex would've slapped him then. Instead, she slowly but firmly pushed his hand away and threw him a disgusted look. "Is this your job then? Follow around the women Luca tangles with and silence them with a dirty payoff—"

"I didn't intend to offend you," he offered roughly, and Alexis almost believed that he hadn't meant to. That it was curiosity rather than judgment in his tone.

She had it bad, if she was justifying his cheap remarks...

"Could there be a different intention?"

"You don't know Luca like I do. And you are..."

"I'm what, Mr. Conti? *The stereotypical American slut*? Easy? Weak enough for you to insult without knowing the first thing about me?"

Something almost like regret pinched his mouth. When his gaze flipped open again, a storm danced within it. As if some small part of him was uncoiling and awake. "Luca is a...*sucker*, as you call it, for your type."

She raised an eyebrow then. Maybe not so imperious like him but she was proud of herself. "And what type is that?"

He sighed. Satisfaction pounded in Alex's blood, the little sound of his capitulation a roaring defeat.

"You want your pound of flesh?"

"From the moment I arrived, you've looked at me like I was dirt beneath your handmade Italian shoes. I want every drop of blood that you owe me."

A hint of a smile caressed his lips, tilting one corner of his mouth up. The impact of it was like molten honey through her veins, turning her languorous and sluggish. "You're young and vivacious, a striking contrast of strength when compared to someone like Valentina. But your eyes, they betray your innocence and your vulnerability. You possess a distinct lack of artifice that is dangerously attractive. For a man like Luca with such jaded taste, you're like a fresh drink of water that might just sate his unquenchable thirst. It's enough to rouse a man's instincts, enough to make him assume, foolishly, that you need to be protected."

Heartbeat skittering all over the place, Alex stared, stunned. She had thought herself beneath his notice, inadequate to even catch his attention. "Why foolish?" she croaked.

"Because, as I'm realizing slowly, you might look innocent and vulnerable, but you're not weak."

"If that's an apology," she countered weakly, battling the fluttering feeling in her chest, "then it's the most convoluted one I've ever heard."

A couple of women, one dressed in black leather and the other a white cocktail dress, both so tight as if they were painted over their voluptuous bodies, passed them huddling Alexis toward him.

Their hushed whispers and awed mutterings were obvious enough for Alex.

Leandro Conti didn't usually hang around nightclubs. Or parade in public, she realized, in complete contrast to Luca who seemed to go out of his way to engage the media's attention.

Nor had he found her by accident. Valentina had already left.

Which meant he had come here looking... "Why are you here tonight?" When he frowned, she elaborated. "You barely seem to tolerate the normal pursuits and company like the rest of us."

"Have you studied me so thoroughly then?"

Alex blushed. How neatly he had trapped her into admitting that she'd been obsessed with him. But she'd never met anyone like him, didn't know how to hide her fascination.

His hand stayed on her elbow, separating her from the crowd. "My grandfather is convinced you're a gold digger out to get her claws into Luca. I've been ordered to make sure you don't succeed."

Her jaw fell open. Disbelief slowly cycled to righteous fury. And here she'd thought he'd come for her. "Go to hell," she whispered and took off.

Hot tears prickled behind her eyes and she resolutely locked them away. The arrogant jerk wasn't worth a single tear.

Somehow, she managed to only delve deeper into the mazelike nightclub, the sexy, almost hip-hop-like music chasing her. One minute, she was pushing through the throng, and next, she was looking at a lushly carpeted, quiet corridor with three unmarked doors.

Cursing, Alex turned around and banged into the one man she never wanted to see again.

Why was he following her?

"I told you to go—"

His fingers on her wrist viselike, he slid a card at the door and tugged her inside. "You're making a scene."

The door closed behind them with a finality that made Alex jump. But the stinging response that rose to her mouth died.

It was a VIP suite. Eyes wide, Alex studied it, a furious flush rising up through her neck.

Floor-to-ceiling glass paneling made up the far wall of

the plush suite, giving a perfect view into the dance floor and bar on the two levels.

Two lush couches stood against the far wall, adjacent to a small refrigerator. And on the other wall was a giant plasma screen that was currently turned off.

Gut swooping, she turned. "I don't think we should be here. This area…"

"I own this club, Ms. Sharpe."

Laughter, more sarcastic than warm, gurgled out of her. A villa in Lake Como, a nightclub in Milan, and a growing luxury goods collection that celebrities were crazy about—the Contis might as well be from a different planet. "Of course you do. Have you had men watching me all this time?"

The thick swath of his eyelashes shadowed his expression. "Valentina always has protection."

"And you told them to keep an eye on the American gold digger/slut, too."

"It was for your protection."

"And who protects me from you?"

The dim, somehow still classy purple lighting in the room didn't quite hide his flinch. But she was far too furious to wonder why.

"What do you intend? To lock me up here? To have me neatly packed away in one of your jets and have me dumped on the other side of Atlantic? To send me off silently into the night?" No, he wasn't allowed to dismiss her like this. Not when she felt so weak-kneed and aware of him. "You know your brother is a fast worker. What if I already have him in my *clutches*? Maybe Luca and I've already, *thoroughly*, f—"

"*Basta!*" he muttered, before his hand descended on her mouth while the other one locked her against the wall.

The rough, almost possessive grip he had on her hip branded her. But it was his gaze that held her rooted.

A flash of temper? A spark of emotion? Whatever it was, it lit his usually droll gaze.

He wasn't impervious to her.

Hot, reckless energy pounded through her, making her thrum with excitement. "You can think it, but I can't say it, Leandro?" She drawled her words, adding a lazy taunt. "At least, with Luca, I know I'll have a good time without insults."

Gray irises widened, bleeding into the dark black around.

The quiet room shrank around the two of them, an explosive current springing into life. The masculine scent of him was a whiplash against her senses, his fingertips pressing into her flesh.

Yet all Alex felt was charged up.

"Do you know what you so dangerously provoke? Are you prepared for it?"

A wealth of meaning reverberated in his statement and it lay between them, a grenade ticking away.

Drunk on the challenge in his molten gaze, Alex couldn't back down. "I don't care how wealthy you—"

His tapered fingers squeezed her palm gently. "I don't agree with my grandfather, *bella*."

"No?"

"*No.*"

"Then why did you come tonight?"

Tension filled the infinitesimal silence before he answered, "Luca told me he picked up a drunk Tina and couldn't locate you. I don't like the idea of you being out at night in Milan alone."

"You could've asked anyone else to do that. Your security team...you didn't have to come yourself. You could—"

"What you're hoping for, it will never happen, Alexis."

"You called me Alexis," she said simply, letting the warmth of his body float her away.

His head cocked to the side, and he rubbed her jaw.

Shock…he was shocked that he had said her name. The fingers that had been brushing her cheek pulled away. "Come, it is time for you to leave."

It was as if he'd slammed a door in her face.

He wasn't talking just about the nightclub or Milan, but Italy. He was telling her it was time for her to leave. Panic flared through her, but beneath it was a realization that sent her heart slamming against her rib cage. All these days…

"You want me," she accused. "You made me feel like I was the only one who felt it, as if I was gauche enough to read it all wrong—"

In a near-violent movement that sent her breath bursting through her, Leandro captured her wrists. Stilling her body from leaning into him. "This is a mistake."

Yanking her hands away from his grip, Alexis pressed her body against his.

A jagged sound wrenched out from his lips, throaty and low. Moving her hands up his chest, Alex tilted her head back. Every inch of his face was frozen in some kind of torturous agony. And she didn't intend to let him win.

She buried her mouth in the opening of his dress shirt. Velvet-smooth and hot, his skin burned against her lips. "Kiss me, just once. Show me what you feel, just once."

One hand snuck into her hair. Her scalp prickled as he tugged her up. Dark need pinched his features and Alex shivered, suddenly, finally, understanding the depth of the need he hid under that infuriatingly indifferent mask.

Anticipation roped with tension set her nerves on fire.

"You do not know who you're playing with."

She jerked back. "Am I so beneath you then?"

He shook his head. But the shadows didn't leave his eyes. "You're too young."

"I'm old enough to know what I want."

Flicking her tongue out, she tasted him. His hands vined

tight around her, flattening her nonexistent breasts against his chest, knocking the breath out of her. "You think I'll stop at one meager kiss?" Pure need punctured every word. "You think to play with my desire and walk away after a chaste embrace, to taunt me like you do these boys with your innocence?"

His warning only incensed her desire even more. "I'm not the one afraid, Leandro."

A volley of Italian fell from his mouth as she pressed her lower body to his. The ridge of his erection against her belly made her quiver.

His fingers descended on her hips, hurting her with their grip to keep her unmoving. "I will not touch my brother's seconds."

"We shared one kiss before I walked away. I'm not interested in Luca."

"You are the first woman in the world to claim that." Something flashed in his gaze even as his long fingers drew maddening circles over her wrists. "Which is why he likes you so much."

If her heart beat any faster, it would rip out of her chest. But still, she risked. And in this spine-tingling risk she took with Leandro, Alex felt more secure, more wanted than she'd ever felt in her life. "And you?"

It was as if all the walls he kept up fell down in dust and a primitive hunger filled his gaze. "I feel need, Alexis. When I look at you…all I feel is desire."

Even then, it was she that lifted her head, reached up and pressed her mouth to his. She, who had no experience with men, that wrapped her hands around his nape and refused to let go.

She that touched her mouth to his.

Soft and hot and hard at the same time, his mouth was a gateway to heaven and hell. Every nerve ending quivering, every instinct driving her forth, she ran the tip of her tongue tentatively, slowly, over that cruelly sculpted lower lip.

With a growl that made her belly tighten, finally he relented. Finally, he touched that hard, harsh mouth to hers.

Lights exploded behind Alex's eyes as if the world was a kaleidoscope of sensations and textures.

Masculine and demanding, he parted her lips and pushed in.

With his tongue and teeth, and with an expertise that made her sex shockingly wet, Leandro devoured her.

There was no playfulness, no seduction to his kiss, just as his words. It was a full-on sensual assault that left no doubt about where it was leading.

His hands skimmed everywhere—her breasts and the boldly taut nipples, her hips, the curves of her buttocks— before they crept under her dress and pulled it up.

Long fingers hitched her thigh around his hips until the heat of her was intimately pressed against the rigid length of him.

Every inch of her vibrated with excitement, desire, need, every inch of her thrummed at the sensation of power.

When he pushed her against the wall and covered her breasts with his hands, Alex whimpered.

When his fingers reached her wet core—alien and intrusive, her gaze flew to his, shocked and aroused and oh-so-willing. Her mouth dried at the stark need in those gray eyes.

Groaning, she came off the wall like a bow when he curled a finger inside her just so, driving a fork of heat through her pelvis.

When he flicked the rim of her ear with his tongue, and told her what he was going to do to her, Alex buried her mouth in his neck and gave herself over.

To the man, to the moment, to the incredible sensation of being wanted.

CHAPTER ONE

Seven years later

"DOES YOUR ARM still hurt, Mamma?"

Alex tucked the quilt around Isabella and kissed her forehead. "A little, baby," she said, opting for the truth.

She was only six but Izzie somehow always knew if Alex lied to her. Or maybe it was that penetrating, deep gray gaze that Alex had never learned to handle. "But the cast should be gone in a couple more weeks and Auntie Jessie said I was healing well."

Little chubby fingers traced the yet unhealed, inch-wide scar that ran from her left temple to her eye, bisecting her brow where a shard of glass had pierced the skin. This bruise, unlike the fracture to her ribs and arm, was only skin-deep yet looked much worse.

"It scares me, Mamma," Izzie whispered in a low voice.

Tears coated Alex's throat but she resolutely swallowed them back. "But you're such a brave little girl always, baby."

Her little chin wobbled. "I am but all the days you were in hospital and me here, alone. Grandmama didn't tell me when you'd come home."

Pushing herself completely onto the little bed, Alex gathered her bundle of joy closer. "It looks scarier than it hurts. See, I'm perfectly fine, okay?"

When Izzie nodded, Alex hugged her tight. Felt the tension unwind in her little girl's body.

But fear lingered, a bitter taste at the back of her throat, leeching warmth from her very veins.

The sixteen-wheeler that had crashed into her compact sedan from the side had wrecked it into a pulp of metal. It was a miracle she'd survived, the doctor had said, and without permanent damage, too.

But all Alex could think of was the alternate scenario...

She could've lost her life.

And Izzie would be...

Like a black cloud waiting to swallow her, she felt the loss of breath, the violent impact of the air bag, of the crunch of bone and the shaft of nightmarish pain in her left arm all the way to her fingers...

The acidic taste of fear in her mouth...

Her hands shook, her skin clammy with sweat.

She buried her face in Izzie's hair and took a deep breath.

As always, the sweet smell of her little girl's skin anchored her in the now. Pushed back the nightmarish fingers of that panic to the edges...but she knew it wasn't gone for long.

Anything could trigger it, she realized, remembering the almost episode at the store that very morning when the door had banged too hard.

She couldn't go on like this, debilitated by fear.

Control, she needed control of this fear for Izzie. She needed to do something that wouldn't paralyze her like this, something that would take care of her baby whatever the future brought...

And instantly her mind went to him.

The man with blue-black hair. The man who had given Izzie her shockingly clear gray eyes and her thick, straight black hair, unlike Alex's strawberry blond curls. The man who had refused to see her again. Or speak to her. Or answer a single phone call seven years ago.

Even in that second before she'd lost consciousness, she'd thought of him. Of the desperate yet muted violence of his passion as he'd kissed her that night, of the way he'd moved inside her, of the way he had driven her to the edge of such intense pleasure that she'd thought she'd fragment into a million pieces...

One memory brought another now...

The disgusted look in his eyes after when she'd hung on to him like a limp vine, as his lust-heavy gaze slowly focused on her, followed by utter shock and disgust, of the jagged, agonized howl that had fallen from his mouth...the way he'd withdrawn immediately, righted her clothes so coldly and clinically, the way he wouldn't meet her gaze as he drove them to the hotel Valentina and she'd been staying at in Milan...

The way he'd told her that he never wanted to see her again...

But now, now that she had faced almost certain death, Alex wasn't willing to slink away in silence anymore. Even if that meant facing his rejection and failing.

Failure had haunted her throughout her entire life. She'd lived through being a disappointment, first to her parents, and then to herself, again and again, but she wouldn't be one when it came to Izzie.

She deserved security, and she, Alexis, needed the peace of mind to live her life normally again. She needed to know Izzie would be taken care of if something happened to her.

The very thought of facing Leandro Conti again made her skin prickle alarmingly. But she'd do anything for her daughter.

"One of you will marry the Rossi girl."

Impossibile!

Leandro Conti's answer reverberated inside him to his

grandfather's ultimatum but walking deeper into the study, he stayed silent.

"Sophia Rossi?" his brother, Luca asked, shock etched into his face.

"*Si.*"

Leandro studied with interest the frail form of his grandfather, Antonio, behind the gleaming dark mahogany desk, still determined to intimidate his grandsons, while, next to him, leaning casually against the bookshelf, Luca adopted his usual devil-may-care attitude that infuriated Antonio so well.

Leandro sent his brother a warning glance. Antonio had not recovered completely from his heart attack a month ago.

Luca and his grandfather would have killed each other a long time ago, if it wasn't for him. And he was tiring of playing the referee among his family members.

He had begun when he was fourteen and at thirty-five, he was still doing it.

"We're too old for you to be arranging alliances for us, Nonno," Leandro finally said into the cutting silence. "I will not marry again. And—"

"Ordering me to," Luca interjected, "marry any woman is cursing the poor woman. Even one with steel balls like Sophia Rossi."

Something glinted in Antonio's eyes. "The only choice is which one of you will do it."

"Or what, Nonno?" Luca spat the words. "You will cut Leandro and me out of this…*venerable Conti empire*?"

Luca's tone made it clear it was anything but.

Because Luca's creative genius and Leandro's cutting-edge business practices over the past decade was what made Conti Luxury Goods a coveted designer label in Italy, and worldwide over the past three years.

That Antonio threatened them like this…it didn't bode well.

"I will inform," Antonio continued, "your sister that she's not a Conti, that she…is the product of your mother's shameful affair with her driver. I will disown Valentina publicly."

A filthy curse erupted from Luca's mouth, a fitting one while ice-cold fury filled Leandro's veins.

He had learned all through his life that Antonio would do anything for their family's business and knowing the kind of reckless, irresponsible, brutally selfish man his father had been, Leandro had even understood it.

But this was low, for a man Leandro respected, even liked sometimes.

Neither he nor Luca would let anything touch Valentina.

He swallowed the fury rising through him, and adopted an almost amenable expression. "Your heart attack has made you irascible, Nonno."

"You cannot persuade me away from my course, Leandro. I let you bring Valentina here…*your mother's shame*," he spat the words, "I even accepted her as my own, but do not think—"

"You love Valentina, I'm sure," Luca roared. "I thought you a better man than our father."

Antonio flinched. Apparently, even he couldn't stomach being compared to his son Enzo. "I accepted Valentina because that was Leandro's price to let me mold him for the Conti empire."

Luca turned to Leandro, disbelief in his eyes. "This is why you always let him rule your life?"

Leandro shrugged. "It was not a sacrifice, Luca. Snatching away the helm of the company from our father's hands, ousting him from the board of directors, marrying Rosa, they were all things I did because I wanted to. That I could protect Valentina's innocence was extra." He turned to Antonio, letting him see his anger for the first time. "Luca and I have put Conti on the global map, something even you hadn't dreamed about. What more could you want?"

"I want an heir to my dynasty." Understanding glinted in his eyes but Leandro refused it. "Enzo was an utter failure as a son, as a husband, as a father, but even he gave me heirs." Even the growl that fell from Luca's lips didn't detract Antonio. "This marriage to his daughter will silence that backstabbing Salvatore. Two birds with one rock."

Leandro shook his head. "This is not the way—"

"What choice do I have?" Antonio's voice loomed loud in the room. "You refuse to consider marriage and you…" Distaste robbed the old man of his words as he turned to Luca. "You change women like you change clothes.

"Death is not far for me, Leandro. I will not leave this world on the risk that Luca and you might be the last of the Contis."

His desk phone rang and Antonio picked it up.

Frustration raging in his veins, Leandro turned to Luca.

Both Luca and he had learned early enough in life that Antonio had a will of steel. He had built Leandro both into a weapon against his own son, their father, even as it broke his own heart. Whether he loved Valentina or not, he wouldn't back down from carrying out his threat.

"Luca—"

"Leandro, haven't you done—"

The loud click of the phone hitting its cradle punctured the silence and both of them turned to Antonio.

"It seems there is no choice."

Luca was the first to react. "What do you mean?"

"Salvatore Rossi's *daughter* has decided only one of you will do for marriage."

Thunder whooshed in Leandro's ears.

"She wants you, Leandro." His look toward Luca was

withering. "Apparently, she is smart enough to reject the Conti devil."

Luca's glittering black gaze, so much like their father's, turned to Leandro. A half smile played on his lips, and yet, Leandro had the sinking feeling that something else, something other than relief, hounded his brother. "Once again, the burden of this family falls to you, Leandro."

With that, he left the study.

In the ensuing silence, they could hear the noise from the veranda. Valentina's rapid words, along with laughter in between.

Valentina, who was all they had left of their mother...

"I begin to see the wisdom in the mode of life Luca has chosen. And the delirious freedom of hating you and this name and this...dynastic ego of yours..." With each word, his voice rose, fury pummeling him.

With shaking hands, he picked up the bottle of wine, the first that had been bottled at their Tuscan vineyard almost two decades ago, and thought of smashing it against the wall.

"Leandro..." Antonio's low entreaty only spiked his temper. Because of course, Antonio loved him. It hadn't been unconditional, true, but Antonio had been everything to the little boy who'd been shattered by his father's volatility.

But Leandro didn't throw it, didn't give in to the baser urge.

Leandro didn't believe in giving in to indulgent fits of temper, into foolish hopes that things were different, into thinking of his wants and needs before his duty or his family's well-being.

He didn't believe in being weak.

Only once in his life had he done that. Only once in his life had he lost control to the emotional turmoil that his father, and even Luca sometimes, seemed to feed on. In that moment, he had betrayed everything he stood for.

Even now, it wasn't Rosa's features he saw when he took himself in hand, when he had to appease his body's needs without seeking out dirty satisfaction in some strange woman's arms. He saw dark brown eyes, unflinchingly honest and hotly aroused, trembling pink lips, eager hands...

Shaking at the hold the memory had on him, *and his body,* Leandro put the bottle down.

"Another wife, Antonio? You have turned me into cattle."

Antonio looked tired. "To make the Conti name respectable again at all costs, to do everything that Enzo ruined, this was your choice, Leandro."

Leandro nodded. "Tell Salvatore that I will marry Sophia as soon as he pleases."

He had been alone far too long anyway. A marriage for the sake of children—he had nothing against that.

Memories of that long-ago summer crashed through Alexis as she stared at the majestic Villa de Conti, glittering against the night sky. The magnificent towering gates that they had just passed, the scent of jasmine that grew on the columns of the terrace porch, the breeze coming off Lake Como, and the glitterati of the Italian society dressed in designer wear and elegant diamonds, it was a sensory assault.

Fiercely intimidating, too.

Alex ran a hand over her white silk button-down blouse nervously, not that she could ever compete with this crowd. Dark blue jeans and white pumps finished her simple attire.

She was glad she had called Valentina. The lie had fallen so easily off her lips—that she was touring Italy again and would love to see her. Valentina had sounded delighted, pretending as if they had remained friends after that summer instead of Alex calling her out of the blue. Had even sent Alex a car to pick her up.

But she hadn't mentioned that Alex would be arriving at the villa the night of, what seemed like, a big party.

Thanking the driver, Alex exited from the car and looked up. Now that she stood there, anxiety made her empty stomach heave. Her mouth felt dry.

How was she supposed to locate *him* amid this crowd, much less tell him about Izzie?

Alex swayed, some primal instinct urging her to turn around and flee. But Izzie's welfare and her own peace of mind depended on this.

Shaking at the warring logic and instinct, she froze.

"Alex? Alexis Sharpe?"

Luca Conti stood at the top of the steps, looking dashing in a black tuxedo. The usual, ornamental blonde on his arm was such a familiar sight that Alex felt a burst of affection. She had a feeling he'd been on his way out.

While she tried to get her vocal chords to work, Luca dismissed the blonde and came down the steps.

Vitality radiated from him, an easy smile on his lips. As he came closer, the cast of those similar features left her reeling afresh.

Before she could blink, she was enfolded in a tight hug. Alex returned it slowly, her throat thick, her limbs shaking.

Why hadn't she tangled with this easy man, the desperate and shameful thought popped up.

Luca pulled back, studied her at leisure with those deceptively mocking black eyes. His grip around her waist tightened, in comfort, she realized as her shaking refused to cease.

"You've become stunning, *bella*. I knew I shouldn't have let you go that summer."

Alex smiled, grateful for his tease. "Thank you, Luca. Valentina knew I was coming. I…"

"But, of course, you are welcome, Alex." She could see the curiosity in his eyes, but he didn't press. Instead he offered her his arm. "Come, let us find something for you to drink and then we find Valentina, *si*?"

Alex shook her head. She had almost lost her nerve earlier, but not anymore. "I will see Valentina later, maybe. Luca…will you take me…can you please arrange for me to see your brother?"

"Leandro…" Shock reflected in his gaze as it met hers. "You came to see Leandro." It was not a question.

"Yes."

"It is not anything I could help with, *bella*?" he sounded sympathetic.

"No."

Something flickered in his gaze before he looked up at the villa, and then back at her but this time, his look was different, the playfulness gone. Alex was sure he'd deny her.

"Then let us go find my esteemed brother." Relief made her shiver. "I have to warn you, though, *cara*, that he is quite in demand, especially tonight. It will take us some time to reach him. Have patience, *si*?"

"Yes."

Her legs barely holding her up, Alex half leaned on Luca's arm. Her thudding pulse was a violent cacophony in her ears as they walked into the marble floored foyer and searched for that tall, lean frame that had haunted her dreams for seven years.

Alexis…

He'd thought he'd seen her an hour ago, her face paler than the simple, white silk blouse that clung to her curves.

Leandro had never been quite so shocked in his entire

life as he'd been the moment he spied that lithe figure on
Luca's arm.

For a few minutes, he had stood there, stock-still, wondering if he was hallucinating. Wondering if the eve of his
engagement to Sophia had unlocked the one face he had
tried to bury in the deepest recesses of his mind.

Wondering if his one sin was finally catching up to him.

Until Sophia had put a hand on his shoulder slightly
and called his name.

He'd turned to her, offered a quick smile and then
slowly, his very sanity up for question, searched that same
spot again.

There had been no Luca or her.

The long evening dragged on and on until Salvatore
Rossi had paraded him in front of all the guests, boasting
quite shamelessly that his daughter had snared a dynastic
connection like Conti.

And *Leandro Conti* of all.

Even Sophia had cringed at some point. Who, Leandro
admitted, he liked.

There was something self-sufficient and intelligent and
very contained about her. At least, he would have a comfortable marriage, he realized halfway through the evening, free of all the marital drama he'd seen between his
own parents.

Valentina's innocence or not, he couldn't take a marriage like that.

Within minutes of meeting her, Sophia had put his mind
at ease.

He'd danced with her as the band played a slow jazz,
then with his sister, who had chatted on and on about
some old friend.

It was past ten and Leandro found himself in the private sitting lounge on the first floor, away from the still
celebrating guests.

Salvatore Rossi and Sophia, Valentina, his grandfather,
two of his aunts and two of his dissolute cousins were present. Luca had acted strangely, even for him, ever since Antonio had announced this merger.

Leandro was about to go looking for him when he appeared at the entrance and behind him, walked in the one
woman Leandro never ever wanted to see again in his entire life.

The woman who'd known his one moment of weakness,
the loss of his control…

Valentina's cheerful greeting reverberated loud in the
silence of the room, the clatter of her heels on the parquet
floor as she went to the woman deafening.

It *was* Alexis he had seen earlier.

A neatly cut black jacket delineated slender shoulders.
A silk blouse clung to a lush figure that he didn't quite remember like that. She had been lithe, almost gaunt, break-
able in his large hands…and yet so violently passionate…
as if only Leandro could give her what she needed most.

Maledizione!

He was mad to be wondering about her body and yet his
gaze continued its perusal of her with a mind of its own.

Dark blue jeans hugged her long legs, legs she had
wrapped around him as he…his blood drifted south slowly,
a heady thrill filled his veins, a feeling he had never known
except that night…

Leandro gritted his teeth, willing his body under his
command. One look at her and he was ready to react like
an uncouth youth.

He lifted his gaze to her face, and stared in shock.

A jagged scar began somewhere beneath her hairline
and went through her left brow, the skin puckered. Yet
didn't minimize her appeal. If anything, it added even
more character to the strong lines of her face.

She was no dazzling beauty, then or now.

Hers was more insidious, seeping under one's skin before you realized, the kind that enthralled the more you looked.

It lay in that high forehead, the intelligence that shone in those tilted, light brown eyes, the irresistible combination of innocence and confidence in the way she greeted the world, the too-bold nose and the lush, wide, implausibly gorgeous mouth. In how sinuously she trapped one's attention, drawing in like a spider with her silky web.

She had been a roughly stunning sketch in black-and-white then. Now, now she was a hauntingly beautiful painting that had grown into its promise, that would bestow pleasure for years to come.

Her brown eyes, bold and direct, searched the room and settled on him.

A pure bolt of energy flew between them, locking them together as if they were the only people in the room, in the world.

Something inside him, something only she had known leaped and growled at the sight of her again.

Her skin paled under the brilliance of the crystal chandelier even as she held his gaze stubbornly. She held her left hand awkwardly against her body.

Cutting his gaze away from her, which took far too much effort, Leandro stifled the life out of that strange fever in his veins.

Why was she here now, after seven years? On the eve of my engagement of all nights?

Before he could voice a question, Antonio's stringent words shattered the choking quiet. "It is family here tonight, Luca. Your dirty playthings are not welcome."

Alexis flinched. When Luca would have interrupted, she stilled him with a hand on his arm. His usually volatile brother relented with a shrug.

Something ugly erupted in Leandro's gut. *Dio, she would make me jealous of his own brother?*

Leandro saw her falter, pull a deep breath and then face Antonio. "I'm not Luca's...*plaything*, Mr. Conti, nor *will I leave* before I say what I intend." Then she leveled that resolute gaze at him. "I need to speak to you alone."

Leandro hardened himself against the beseeching look in her eyes. After seven years, that she showed up tonight of all nights, there was only one thing she could be after—money. And that *perversely* made him angrier. "There is nothing you could say to me that you could not say here, Ms. Sharpe."

"Leandro..." his brother again.

Leandro held up his hand, more than furious now.

How long had Luca been in touch with her? How could there be such...a friendship between them if not so?

And why the hell did he care whatever was between them?

He skewered the woman with his gaze. "Whatever game you're up to, I'm not playing."

Anger burned in her eyes, her lithe body faintly trembled with it. "Fine, so be it." Her voice rang crystal clear in the rapt room, and still he could hear the tremble in it. "I came to tell you that you... *I* have a daughter." Her chin rose. "Her name is Isabella Adrian. She's six years old and she's beautiful and precious and she...*she's yours.*"

"No," fell from Leandro's lips, a snarling whisper in the quiet room. "That can't be."

His grandfather's and Salvatore Rossi's curses in Italian and Valentina's muffled gasp registered on the periphery of his consciousness.

Lips quivering, Alexis's chest rose and fell but she held his gaze over the distance. "A DNA test will prove I'm right," she said, as if she'd prepared the response. But it was the absolute purpose in her voice that held him mute.

A daughter...

His skin felt chilly as if all warmth had been leeched away from the world around him.

And yet, the crystal chandeliers in the room glowed bright, the fire cackled in the marble-wrought fireplace and the moon hung jewel bright in the sky outside.

The world continued spinning whereas all of the control he prided himself on deserted him, leaving him shaken to the core.

He shook his head, gasping for breath.

He looked at Luca. Who looked just as aghast as he did.

Only Alexis stood composed amid the curious and accusing glares aimed at her, her shoulders ramrod straight.

Alexis whose eyes gleamed with pride and love as she claimed that he was a father. Of her little girl.

His child...something Rosa had wanted so desperately for years.

Now, this woman, whom he'd tried to forget, claimed her daughter was his...*that his one moment of weakness had led to such a consequence?*

Everything inside him clenched tight, as if the merest breath could shatter him. Robbing him of speech even.

"Whatever your scheme, Ms. Sharpe, you have already made a misstep in your bait." Antonio finally spoke, his accented English falling like hard gravel over the marble floor. "If there were Conti bastards lying around for you to sully our name with, your claim would be believable if you said Luca fathered them.

"Not Leandro.

"Now before I call the *polizia—*"

CHAPTER TWO

"ENOUGH!" ALEX BIT OUT, her throat raw. Leandro's silence distressed her more than his grandfather's words. "I won't stand quietly while you call my little girl names."

She felt Luca's hand on her shoulder and drew strength from it.

Faking defiance she didn't feel, Alex held Leandro's gaze.

Disbelief? Disgust? Something finally flickered in his expression and she felt as if she was bucking, bending against the force of it.

Aquiline nose, thinly sculpted mouth and the sleek, sharp planes of his face...he was just as arrogantly beautiful as she remembered.

Seven years hadn't changed his feelings about that night then. She hadn't hoped differently, neither would she let him shame her.

She had done nothing to be shameful of. *Not then, not now.*

"You stay silent even as you know there's a chance that it's true? I was wrong to come here, wrong to think Izzie..." She took a bracing breath. "You and your family, you don't deserve to know her."

Alexis turned her back on them with her head held high.

Out into the corridor she went, her pumps clicking hard on the gleaming marble floor, ignoring the hollow ache in her gut.

It was the uncertainty caused by the accident, the uncertainty about Isabella's future, she told herself. Nothing to do with the man who stood there, unmoving like a rock while his family castigated her.

Having arrived at the end of the corridor, Alex stilled.

Approaching dusk hadn't dimmed the beauty of the villa one bit.

The corridor opened into a semicircular balcony, offering a view to the ground floor, the acreage surrounding the house lit up by solar lights and the dark waters of the lake beyond.

A tinkle of laughter from the guests below her brought her attention back. Pressing a hand to her throbbing temples, she faced her current problem.

She couldn't ask Valentina for a ride back. Would Luca help?

She turned and slammed headlong into a solidly male body. Threaded her fingers in that hard chest for purchase. "Luca, can you please…"

Crisply masculine and with a hint of aqua, the scent that filled her nostrils arrested the words on her lips. Her head jerked up so fast that she felt dizzy.

Penetrating gray eyes studied her.

"Why assume Luca?"

"Because he seems like the only decent person in your family."

She tugged at her arm but Leandro didn't relent. Her legs tangled with his, the hard, muscular length of his thighs against hers knocking the breath out of her.

Hard and hot, he made her head spin. "I have nothing more to say to you," she breathed into his shoulder.

"You think to announce what you did and walk away calmly? Probably into the media's mouthpiece? Make a mockery of the Contis?"

His grip viselike, he dragged her through a turn in the corridor that led to another sit-out area and then past a

40   THE SURPRISE CONTI CHILD

dark oak door. The hard thud of the door cut off the noise from the party, locking them away.

Breath rattling, Alex kept her back to him.

Her skin prickled at his nearness, her senses still jarred at the impact with his hard body. She rubbed fingers over her forehead, willing her heart to calm.

Slowly, she took in the sumptuous furnishings in the huge room, a dark mahogany study table to the side with papers strewn on it, the large four-poster king bed with dark blue sheets. That same cool aqua scent clung to the room. A small, framed picture sat on the nightstand on the opposite side, of a pretty woman with dark hair and delicate features.

Dear Lord, was this his room? Who was that woman then?

With her gut in a tight knot, Alex forced her gaze to the window. The view afforded here of Lake Como was even better. Spectacularly maintained gardens, acres of it, lit softly by moonlight and solar lights along the paths greeted her. Silence lingered in this part of the gardens.

Even his guests were not allowed to impinge on his private slice of heaven, she realized slowly.

This estate was not just beautiful but huge.

And this was only one of the many properties they owned.

The Contis were a dynastic family with an old-world wealth and Leandro…at the helm of it. And she had barged in on their illustrious party and told them that he had a daughter.

If her chest wasn't so tight, Alex would have laughed at the absurdity of it.

"You're afraid to face me now? After that performance in front of everyone."

Low and crisp, his tone was like fingertips sliding over

her bare skin. As if it was yesterday he had touched her and not seven long years ago.

Alex turned slowly, loathe to betray how unbalanced she felt in his presence.

He stood leaning against the closed door, minus the suit jacket, the gray of his dress shirt making his eyes gleam doubly. Leaner than she remembered, his features sharper. Even more settled into that powerful aura that had always clung to him.

The austere severity of his features from the sculpted jaw to that aquiline nose, the lean, wiry breadth of his chest tapering to a waist, the thinly sculpted curve of his lower lip, everything about Leandro Conti said leashed power.

Any moment now, she wouldn't find him attractive. Any moment now, she'd remember that the same mouth that could kiss so passionately and tenderly could also shred her to pieces as soon as he was done.

"I'm trying to overcome my shock that you cared enough to stop me." Instead, her insides thrummed with a thrill. "And if that was a performance, then you forced me to it."

Those eyes of his studied her relentlessly. Why didn't the infuriating man say anything? Demand a DNA test? Throw her out if he didn't believe her? Threaten her like his grandfather had done?

She had been prepared for all of that. Except his impenetrable silence, this unnerving composure.

It made her want to take a sledgehammer and smash it to pieces.

"You pulling me into a room like this, away from prying eyes should bring back memories for you," she threw recklessly. "Lucky for me, because it seems you erased that evening from your mind."

His chin jerked, and his eyes lost that inscrutable expression. "I was successful. Until this very evening."

Alex blinked at the hurt that pinged through her, as if her poisonous dart had found its way back to her. She didn't think he was saying it to get a rise out of her, like she'd done.

No, he merely stated fact.

"What would you have dared to remind me, Alexis?"

Her name on his lips was a possessive caress that threatened her paper-thin composure.

Suppressing the dangerous urge to take up the challenge in his tone, she said, "Your assumption that I'm dying to... *renew* our acquaintance smacks of arrogance. I'm here only for Isabella."

Whether he believed her or not, Alex didn't know. But then, from what little she knew of Leandro, he thrived on self-control. That he hadn't instantly called her a liar like his grandfather had done, his utter silence in the face of her declaration, said something else entirely, she realized with a little panic.

He circled the room, moving a thing here and there and finally, leaned against the bed. "How are you here, today?"

"I don't understand."

"How did you come to be here at the villa, tonight of all nights? Did you know—?"

"About the party? Of course not. You think I wanted to make a spectacle of myself in front of your exalted family? Valentina must have decided tonight was best."

One haughty brow rose on his face. "For what?"

"I hinted, pretty heavily, that I wanted to say hello to you and Luca. She assumed that I was eager to renew my friendship with Luca."

"And Luca?" The two words rang with his displeasure. Frustration made her voice sharp. "What about Luca?"

Something flashed in his gaze, the first sign that maybe he wasn't so composed. "How did you arrive on his arm?"

Of all the things he had said and unsaid today, this annoyed her most. "He was kind enough to escort me to you when I insisted on seeing you."

"You told me that night that you were protected."

The sudden shift in the conversation caught her off guard. "I was. I began the pill a few weeks before I left for Italy."

"In preparation for your fling abroad?"

His barb pricked her, but she'd rather he believe that he'd been the convenient choice. The one man she'd picked out of a lineup to have her supposed holiday fling with. "I was in over my head from the minute I saw you, yes." Resentment she'd swallowed for years flared. "What's your excuse then?"

"You think I blame you for that night." The idea seemed to shock him.

What else was she supposed to think, she wanted to throw back at him. Even now, he looked at her as if she was his worst nightmare. There was no point in scraping old wounds however. "Even the pill is not one-hundred-percent foolproof." He remained silent again and it began to scrape Alex raw. "If you don't believe me, then—"

"Since I'm still feeling the consequences of that...*very activity* seven years ago, I believe I will refrain from it."

"That's not an invitation. This trip isn't a ploy to renew that...madness. You probably find this hard to believe but not every woman wants a piece of your esteemed Conti pie." She was so angry she wanted to thump the man.

"Really?"

He made it so easy to despise him with his insufferable attitude.

To pretend that her skin hadn't prickled, her heart hadn't raced, that even the thought of Izzie had disappeared in that moment when she had spied him again in that lounge. To act as though, for seven years, she hadn't relived every moment with him a thousand times.

"Yes. I have too much self-respect to be attracted to a man who thinks I'm a liar and worse. To want a man who dismissed me like garbage back in my life."

Faint lines appeared around his mouth before he looked away.

Bloodthirsty enough after that scene in the lounge, Alex felt feral satisfaction that she'd landed another one.

"Why did you wait seven years to...make this claim?"

"Calling it a claim will not make it less of a truth." The taunt was instant and yet...she had a feeling it had taken him this long to work toward the subject of Isabella, to acknowledge the ticking bomb between them.

He pushed off the bed and Alex needed all her will power to not step back. "Did you think I would have no questions for you at all?" She remained silent and he continued. "Why didn't you let me know immediately?"

"By the time I realized I was...pregnant, I was almost ten weeks along."

"Is that why you kept...the baby?" He raised a hand to cut her off. "You were twenty. I...cannot imagine Valentina mature enough to manage herself, much less a child at that age."

Alex swallowed, the utter strength of her conviction that day amazing her even now. Her parents, her only close friend, everyone had advised her to give up the baby for adoption. "I just..." She shied her gaze away, her throat thick with emotion.

"Tell me why."

Jerked by his sharp tone, she lifted her gaze. "That feeling...it's inexplicable."

Something so raw and visceral flashed in his gaze that her skin prickled. Arrogant, heartless, cynical...she'd made her decision to come here based on the fact that Leandro was all those things. What if she was wrong?

Fear pulsed down her spine. "I called your office a week

after I found out. I... I was on hold for an hour. Finally, when your secretary came on, she cut me off, said you weren't interested.

"That I shouldn't call back." Alex tried to keep any complaint out of her voice now however anxious she'd been then. "I called you a few more times. Got the same answer again."

"You could have called your friend, Luca." He spoke softly, yet it cracked through the room like a gale of wind. "You could have come back to Italy. You could have told Valentina. You could have emailed me—"

"And what? Capitalized the subject line—*I'M PREG-NANT, IT'S YOURS*—like some spammer!" She colored furiously. "You wanted nothing to do with me. But... I still tried.

"I bought another ticket. I...thought you should know. The day before I was supposed to leave, my parents and I argued and my dad threw out his back at the store. I... I couldn't go off in search of you then, especially when you were determined to forget me.

"With taking care of the store and him, when Isabella came... I barely had the energy to go through each day."

"And later?"

How dare he sound as if it was her fault? "Later," she said, feeling suddenly tired, "it was easier to believe that Izzie was better off without your rejection." Easier to protect herself from the hurt he had wreaked on her.

The one time she had taken a chance to reach for something she'd wanted, she'd been rejected. Firmly pushed back into the forgettable category again.

There had been nothing special or memorable about her or that night for him. As if she was a mere blip in the life of another person yet again.

A disappointment, an inconvenience, a thing with no value or feelings whatsoever.

"Why did you change your mind now?" he bit out harshly. He ran his fingers through his hair while he paced the small room like a caged animal. "Or was that your plan all along?"

"Wouldn't that be perfect for you if I had some ultimate agenda? If I proved your worst assumptions about me right? That way you won't have to take any responsibility in all this…"

"*Dio,* why now, Alexis?"

It was his hoarse voice that halted Alex's self-indulgent tirade. This was not about her feelings. This was about her baby.

"I just… I was in an accident three months ago, a bad one." Automatically, her fingers went to the scar down her forehead and his gaze moved there. Throat raw, she continued, "It made me realize…if something happened to me, Isabella would be alone in the world. My parents…" She swallowed the fact that they had never approved of her having Isabella. "They're growing old. I can't sleep wondering about her future."

Once again, silence descended, his stare unnerving her on a whole new level.

"I brought her birth certificate," she said, busying herself with the handbag. "Just tell me where and when to bring her for the DNA test, although it'll be a huge help if it's in New York because I can't—"

"There's no situation that fazes you, is there? You set your course and you blaze through it, come what may."

Alex blanched. Softly delivered but his innuendo pierced just the same.

He thought this was easy for her? To see him after all these years, to realize that he still viewed her with that loathing? To know that she'd never been anything more than a quick indulgence?

But she swallowed her own feelings and focused on

what she needed to do. "I'm prepared to do anything to prove that she's yours, yes."

"And, in return?"

"Are you so afraid of what I would demand, Leandro?" The challenge escaped her before she could catch it, her femininity rearing its head.

An almost imperceptible widening of those stormy eyes. Something she wouldn't have even noticed if she wasn't so greedy about every nuance on his face.

"Do you have many to make then, Alexis? These demands?"

Why was she taunting him? Why this reckless, dangerous urge to provoke him? She pulled out the envelope she'd stuffed into her handbag. "Here's some pictures. Maybe you could visit us and meet Izzie a couple of times over the next couple of years so that you aren't a complete stranger? I could bring her here for holiday, to meet Luca and Valentina, if they're interested.

"All I want is a promise that if anything were to happen to me, you'd…"

Her words trailed away as Leandro became still. The muscles in his face pulled taut over his features, a white pallor to his olive skin.

Her outstretched hand lay between them. And his gaze on the envelope, frozen.

"Leandro?"

The swath of his eyelashes flickered. His rough breath rattled loud in the room.

With gut-wrenching clarity, Alex realized that he'd rather she was lying.

From the moment she'd spoken Isabella's name, it wasn't the veracity of her claim he'd doubted. What had kept him silent, even as his grandfather had shredded her, was that Leandro *needed* her to be lying.

"You wish Isabella didn't exist." Horror filled her, turning her voice into a whiplash. "Do you despise me that much?"

He jerked around, pain streaking through his eyes. "What I feel about her has nothing to do with you."

That's good, she told herself. She couldn't bear it if he despised Isabella like he did her. She wouldn't allow it.

How much do you know of that man? Her mom's question came back to her now.

She didn't know that much, really.

Her intense attraction to him seven years ago, her fascination with him, the connection she'd felt with him, had been inexplicable. She stole another greedy glance at him, unable to stop herself. Lean and tall, he wore his power effortlessly and she wondered if that had been the draw for her.

Hands shaking, she stuffed the envelope back into her handbag. She needed to leave. Before she made this about her. Before she asked any more of those stupid questions...

Before she forgot that this man had crushed her tender heart in such a way that it hadn't mended again.

"Show me the pictures," Leandro finally forced himself to say.

Alexis stilled with her back to him, her slender shoulders a tense line.

His voice sounded as if he hadn't used it in years, as if forming such simple words was beyond his capability. Told himself again and again that he was composed.

If he acted like it, he hoped his rioting emotions would catch on that he was composed, that he would survive through this new development in his life like he always did.

Giving in to the shame that he had behaved in a way he detested was only self-indulgent. Giving in to the guilt that clawed at him that he had abandoned his child...would only render him useless.

His head jerked up, the realization that he believed Alexis stunning him anew.

He believed that she was telling the truth, that her daughter was his?

Antonio would call him a fool, their lawyers would tell him to demand a DNA test. The rational, sensible part of him, which had been born out of necessity at a young age, warned that he was being reckless. That Alexis's poise, her self-sufficiency, her declaration that she wanted nothing from him, that they all could be lies.

She could have waited all these years just so she could make a bigger splash, demand a bigger payoff.

He wasn't unaware of his draw for women. If they fell like flies for Luca's charm, they went rabid because of how sacrosanct his privacy was to him, because the media, frequently and fervently, painted him as the perfect man, still mourning his wife.

Yet that same instinct that had drawn him to her drowned out everything else. "Show me the pictures."

Knuckles turning white, her fingers tightened over the straps of her bag. Her reluctance now would have been comical, if not for the fierce churning in his gut. "I didn't come to force you to be a father."

He moved closer, uncaring of the tremble in her lips, the slight widening of her eyes. Crowded her lithe body against the door, his self-discipline in tatters now. "You are afraid now? After you came all this way?"

Something in his tone must have finally registered because she pulled out the envelope.

He moved back toward the bed and spread them out on the dark cover.

There were ten, different sizes and in different poses.

His heart thundering, he picked up one eight-by-ten, a close-up. With jet-black hair that framed her face and serious gray eyes, and the cast of her features, drawn in chubbiness instead of sharp planes, the little girl was his mirror image.

The girl, *no, Isabella*...was his daughter. His own flesh and blood.

"There is nothing of me in her," came Alexis's reply behind him. Tentative and reverberating with a quiet joy. "Every morning, I look at her and I'm amazed that she's mine."

Inhaling roughly, he turned.

Raw emotion glittered in her eyes. Walking closer, unaware of her own actions, he was sure, she studied him avidly. He knew she was seeing her daughter, *no, their daughter* in his face.

Still, her gaze was like a physical caress. Possessive and hungry and intent. And deeply disconcerting for the instant ache it evoked in him.

He looked at the picture and then at Alex. "That determined chin, that's you."

A smile curved her mouth, transforming her into a stunning beauty. "Really?"

"Where is she now?" he asked, more to distract himself from the scent of her fluttering toward him. Subtle yet lingering. Like the woman herself.

"With my parents. Isabella and I live with them. A friend of mine has a boy of Izzie's age and she takes her during the day. You can keep the pictures." She looked through her bag and extracted visiting cards and extended them to him. Like a salesgirl pushing a product. "These have all my numbers and email address. Just call me in advance, because after the accident and this trip, I can't take off more—"

"In advance for what?" he repeated.

She shrugged but hurt shadowed her eyes. "Y'know... if you decide to see her."

He emerged from the emotional knockout, her intention in all the things she had told him tonight shaping into coherence. His gut tightened.

When he made no move to take the cards, she put them on the small study table. "I'll be in Milan for two more days if you have any questions." She worried her bottom lip between her teeth. "If you can arrange a car for me, I'll be off."

A growl he couldn't control emerged low in Leandro's throat.

She thought she would show him pictures of his daughter and then bid him goodbye? That he would call her and make an appointment like some distant relative?

Did she think he had no honor, no sense of duty?

Have you treated her like you have any?

"Stay tonight," he finally said, somehow managing to keep his tone smooth. A herculean feat seeing that his head was in a whirl, his world precariously tilted on its axis. And this woman, whom he'd tried to forget at all costs, suddenly was at the center of it. "You look like you'll faint any minute."

"I don't want to cause trouble—"

"Little late for that, yes?" He slid the pictures back into the cover. "Someone from the staff will show you to a bedroom. *Buenonotte*, Alexis."

Leandro paced inside his bedroom, the scent of a woman lingering inside the walls after so many years as disconcerting as the one who had left it behind. A million thoughts crowded him.

He remembered his secretary telling him that Ms. Sharpe had called. *Again and again.* He remembered the self-disgust at the mere thought of that night, the poisonous thoughts that Alexis was making a nuisance of herself.

Because he had had enough with his father's mistresses and one-night stands making a spectacle of them.

And the intervening years, if he focused too much on that, he would take it out on her.

Despite everything, she had finally come to tell him of his daughter's existence. The *what if she hadn't* scenario didn't bear thinking about…not if he wanted to remain sane.

With control he had learned in his teens, because someone had had to be strong for his mother and Luca, he bottled away the anger.

The Rossis would be waiting for an explanation, as would Antonio. His engagement to Sophia had been the biggest event of the summer among society and Salvatore wouldn't react to this new development lightly.

Leandro would have to make sure Salvatore didn't poison anyone on the Conti board against him because of any decision he took now.

He'd have to make sure Antonio didn't interfere with Leandro's intentions.

He'd have to tread carefully so that his sheer arrogance in dismissing Alexis seven years ago didn't ripple over anyone now. Like Valentina and Sophia. *And now Isabella.*

She was his to protect, to cherish, to love. A shock or not, he could never neglect his duty as a father. A child needed both parents, he knew that better than anyone.

He vowed in that minute that the next generation of Contis would be different, beginning with Isabella. Much as he'd tried, he'd failed Luca.

He wouldn't fail Isabella. He wouldn't let his daughter spend a day without knowing that she was loved and wanted.

If Alexis had other ideas, he would convince her otherwise.

The weight of the world seemed to lie on his shoulders and yet, Leandro felt energized for the first time in years.

CHAPTER THREE

JUNE SUN SHONE bright when Alex stepped out of her room and reached the curving balcony. A vague sense of premonition hovered in her gut, intensified by her sleepless night.

Something she had spied in Leandro's eyes, she realized.

"Alex, come have breakfast," came Valentina's voice from below.

Bracing herself, Alex looked down. It was only Valentina.

She went down the steps and walked across the courtyard to the perfectly landscaped gardens. Lushly scented air filled her nostrils, the sheer beauty of the surroundings relaxing her tautly stretched nerves.

Dressed in chic jeans and a ruffled top in pink, her hair *fashionably* messy, Valentina was the epitome of a fashionista. Alex was suddenly glad she wasn't wearing yesterday's clothes.

Plain cotton T-shirts, of the soft and screamingly expensive kind, and capri-style pants in various sizes and colors, even brand-new underwear had been left on the bed by the time she had returned from the shower.

Knowing who she had to thank for it, she ran a self-conscious hand over her midriff and settled down.

A bite of the rich, jam-filled *cornetto* the staff brought her righted her world, even if for a moment. The frothy cappuccino made her sigh.

Feeling Valentina's gaze on her, she lifted hers. "If I apologize for using you, it'll be false."

Valentina nodded, a thoughtful look in her eyes. "I did not see Leandro again last night. Luca says he believes you."

Comforted by Luca's easy acceptance, Alex clicked her cell on.

Valentina looked at Izzie's pic and let out a soft sigh. "I'm sorry for what my grandfather said," she offered, and Alex waved her away. The apology she wanted wasn't Valentina's. Not even Antonio's, as insulting as he'd been.

"Alex, you cannot…*imagine* how shocking this is for us—"

"I do—"

"*No!* That Leandro…was with you, and so soon after… That's not like him."

"What, he doesn't have sex like normal people?" Alex retorted, her skin prickling.

Valentina made a face. "Gross…but *si.* You know what the media calls Leandro and Luca?"

"What?"

"The Conti Saint and the Conti Devil."

"Callously dismissing the woman you just slept with makes for a saint in your country?"

"You do not understand—"

"I don't need to," Alex cut her off bluntly and the curiosity within.

She didn't want to know about Leandro's love life. Or why he had behaved so ruthlessly with her. Or that he was, apparently, the embodiment of the perfect man to the rest of the freaking world.

"Your timing…sucks," Valentina sounded sympathetic. "Seven years ago and last night."

How are you here, tonight of all nights…?

"Wait, what was last night?"

"Leandro's engagement party."

Engagement…it landed like an invisible punch, jostling

her insides. He could have married in the past seven years, could've had a string of lovers like her...

Thoughts tripped one over the other.

Was it that woman standing next to him? The woman on whose shoulder his hand had rested? Did he treat her better than he had Alex? Was it because Alex lacked...

No!

Nothing ever came out of berating herself that she wasn't good enough or memorable enough to hold the attention of a man like Leandro Conti.

Why would a stranger she'd built a fantasy around see anything special in her when her own parents didn't?

A besotted, naive novelty, that's what she'd been.

"It doesn't matter if he's engaged or has a string of playthings and mistresses spread out over the Italian coast, Valentina," her words came out harsh. "I don't care about Leandro."

"That heartens me," a crisply smooth voice interfered from behind her, "so much. It's almost *saintly* how uninterested you're in the life of the man you share a daughter with."

Sarcasm dripped from Leandro's every word. Sweet pastry instantly turned to ash in Alex's mouth. "Maybe it's time someone told you that you're not the great prize every woman falls over for."

"You assume this is what I think of myself? Why?"

"Your sheer disbelief that I'm not throwing myself at you, again," she snapped back.

With a wide-eyed grin, Valentina neatly slipped away.

Clasping her quivering fingers in her lap, Alex looked up. The sun directly behind him delineated the broad shoulders and the tapering waist while the breeze drenched her in his crisp, masculine scent.

The dark jeans and black shirt molded his lean frame.

The impact of such sheer masculinity was nerve-racking after another sleepless night.

Seven years hadn't dimmed his appeal even a bit. If anything...

Don't go there, Alex!

"Congratulations on your engagement." Steady and serene, she almost believed it herself.

He took her offered hand after a moment and clasped it.

Rough and abrasive and large, his palm stroked a dart of heat through her.

Alex jerked it back, like a frightened rabbit, heart pumping hard.

"*Grazie*, Alexis." Mockery laced with politeness. "Hope you'll forgive me if I don't introduce my fiancée to you. It might prove a little tacky after the shock she received on the eve of her engagement."

Her cup rattled on the saucer loudly in the peaceful courtyard, his sickly sweet tone jarring her. "I didn't know or I would've never—"

"I know."

His instant accord took the sails away from under her. "Neither did I come here hoping for some fat payoff."

"So you will refuse if I set up a trust fund for Isabella then?"

She quickly swallowed her shock. And the oily, uncomfortable feeling in her throat. "No. I...manage okay but I won't refuse something that'll surely help Izzie's future." It galled her to admit defeat in so many words, to recount her failure to a man who made everything he touched into gold. But for Izzie, she had to. "The accident, on top of some bad business decisions I made last year... everything's been tight. College tuition when she's ready is going to be astronomical."

His protracted look stung as she realized how he must view her ready answer. Defensive on top of feeling like a failure made her spine rigid and her tone caustic. "I have a six-year-old, a health store that's afloat for now and aging parents. I'm practical, not a piranha."

"Did I imply otherwise?"

"Whatever you decide, you can lock it up. I won't touch it."

Their gazes held, his inscrutable and hers confused.

If he believed that she hadn't known about his engagement, *and* that she wasn't looking for a retirement package in the name of Izzie, then why was there was a storm of fury beneath his smooth tone?

Why such a distant, adversarial glint in his eyes when he looked at her?

But asking meant getting personal. Asking meant allowing herself to examine why the news of his engagement sat like a jagged boulder on her chest. Asking meant learning how little of an impression she had left that night.

For as long as she could remember, her mom and her own failures at everything remotely related to academia and a career had made Alex clearly aware of all her shortcomings. She'd been measured, again and again, first against Adrian and then against his ghost and had come up short every time.

She didn't want to hear it from the man who had been an escape and a gift she'd given herself, too.

"I should be leaving," she said into the silence.

He flicked her a quick glance and nodded. "We'll leave in ten minutes."

Alex whirled toward him so fast that she lost her balance. A corded forearm pressed into her belly holding her up.

She closed her eyes, the heat of him stroking every suppressed desire.

Heart rapping a staccato beat, muscles quivering, she struggled to remember what had sent her into panic.

"*We*…you said *we*."

His arm rigid around her, his warm breath brushing her cheek, he studied her with an infuriating calm. "*Si.*"

Panic fluttered in her belly. "Why?"

"I'm coming with you."

"To Milan?"

"To New York."

Her gut flopped to her feet, leaving her hollow.

But his gaze remained serious.

Alex shook her head as if the action could bring her teetering world back to balance. "I don't understand."

Tapered fingers tightened over her slender wrist. Even in the sensual fog her senses waded through, Alex wondered if that was the true marker of his mood. "I wish to avoid the bother of calling you later, making an appointment, intruding on your busy life, dragging us all through the whole process again. With my forthcoming wedding and an irate fiancée to appease, it is better to get this out of the way."

"Get what out of the way?" she whispered.

Hardness edged in with the casual amusement in the narrow line of his mouth. "Meeting my daughter."

He'd shocked her.

A feral kind of thrill fizzed through Leandro's veins. Childish and uncharacteristic of him, he knew, but then, Alexis always brought out a side of him that he didn't know existed.

The longer she stared at him with that resolute light in her eyes, the sharper his awareness of his own desires became.

Elemental heat arose in him, his fingers tingling at the soft musculature of her belly, drenching him in remembered pleasure.

Last night, he'd been in shock. With a clear view of his plan this morning, the effect of Alexis's lush, understated beauty was stringent.

Her clean lemon soap scent lingered in his nostrils, more evocative than the most intrinsic perfume, provoking an overwhelming urge to bury his nose in the crook of her neck.

The neat braid she'd weaved her hair into made the scar stand out starkly against her pale brow.

Slender shoulders still held that battle-ready rigidity even though the way she had folded her arms and created distance between them, betrayed her.

Betrayed what though, Leandro had no idea. And that, he didn't like.

Her fierce stubbornness, her unerring resolve fascinated and frustrated him in equal measure.

Any other woman of his acquaintance would have shredded him in front of the curious guests, or lost a bit of that composure at being told that the man she'd dallied with long ago, the man who was the father of her child was engaged to be married.

Not Alexis.

The only time she'd lost her control had been at Antonio's disgusting words.

She was not the girl he had kissed so violently that night. On the cusp of womanhood, that Alexis had been an open canvas, her unflinching attraction to him utterly arousing, her languid, interested glances without artifice.

A temptation he'd failed to resist.

Now, this woman who faced him so calmly, so unwavering in her plans for *his role in their daughter's life*, without betraying the merest thought, even the merest hint of reaction at seeing him after all these years...she was a mystery.

Which meant he couldn't betray his hand either.

Only now, at the thought of him accompanying her, at his changing his plans, did she show a reaction.

"You look very pale, Alexis. Is something wrong?" he probed softly.

"It's not necessary that you come immediately," she said sharply. The T-shirt that he'd had the staff deliver hugged her round breasts as her chest fell and rose. "I mean, it's not a quick drive away and I can only imagine how…" she cast a glance behind her, as she continued, "occupied you must be with everything."

"Let me understand this. Are you discouraging me now?"

"No, I just…" Her unease was written in her pinched mouth.

Dark shadows cradled her brown eyes, and tenderness he didn't want to feel pierced Leandro.

He hadn't noticed it last night, but today he saw it clearly.

She was a wreck physically. That same instinct that had driven him to hold his brother and sister through the knocks they'd received, rode him now to hold her.

Fisting his hands, he waited for the urge to pass.

She wasn't his to care for.

"Is this not why you came? So that I could acknowledge Isabella and give you security about her future and then we continue in our merry ways?" Somehow, he managed to sound disinterested and unemotional at the whole prospect.

The pinched look instantly faded from her face. And Leandro had the answer to the question hadn't quite known to ask.

She wasn't going to fall in with his plans easily.

"Of course it is," she managed with a polite smile and walked away.

"This sneaky subterfuge is unlike you," Luca said at his side. Contempt sharpened his brother's usually laid-back tone. "Anyone who knows you can guess your intentions."

"Alexis does not." Trust his reckless brother to make him defensive.

"I would argue that she probably knows the true you,"

Luca smoothly interjected. "The man beneath the saint's skin."

Leandro flinched. The specter of his behavior toward Alexis seven years ago loomed large and loud in his mind. Demanding explanation and insight that he didn't want to give it. "If you expect elaboration on the event of seven years ago, no."

Scowling, Luca faced him. "*Event of seven years ago…* can you hear yourself? You seduced an innocent, and apparently, kicked her out the moment you zipped up. That is expected of me, not you."

Leandro cursed violently, Luca's crude words piercing him. Despite knowing that that's what Luca intended.

Innocent—that's what Alexis had been. And without meaning to, she had wielded it so well.

"Knowing the state you were in," Luca was relentless, saying, "you shouldn't have touched her."

"I know that."

"You used her, plain and simple."

Just like our father, his unsaid accusation hung heavy in the air. For Luca loathed even mentioning their father's name.

"*No*," his hoarse refusal rang in the silence. He saw Alexis tense at the balcony and gritted his teeth. "I never made any false promises to her. *Cristo*, I didn't even…"

He couldn't put into words how alive he had felt every time Alexis had looked at him with those innocent brown eyes. How acute and agonizing the thrill had been when he touched her.

How much he'd needed to be needed, wanted like that after Rosa's death. Only when he had seen the look in her eyes had he realized how much he craved to lose himself.

How vulnerable he'd been in the face of such honest attraction as hers.

Not her, him.

He'd been the vulnerable one, he'd been the one who'd been seduced so easily and she hadn't even been trying.

No, even if he found the words, he couldn't tell Luca.

It was much too private, much too raw. Just remembering that night—the out-of-control, desperate desire, the stingingly sharp awareness made his muscles curl in memory. "It was not as dirty as you make it out to be, Luca."

"It seems so from where I stand. And from where she does, more importantly. She's the mother of your child, Leandro. At least now, treat her with respect. Aren't you the one always carping about the Conti legacy?

"Do not continue what he started, do not let this become our legacy."

Last night had been shock. Today, shame pounded through him. His whole life, he'd never treated another person, man or woman, the way he had Alexis.

All because first he'd weakened and then walked away from the consequences.

The very same traits that he'd despised in the man who'd fathered Luca and him.

"Whatever poison Antonio might spout, tell me you don't distrust her motives?"

"I trust every word she said last night." The thing that had kept him up all night was how telling what Alexis *hadn't* said was.

Last night and this morning...

If only she'd betrayed a spark of jealousy, or insecurity, if only she was like any other woman he'd known who would have thrown a reckless tantrum in the situation he'd put her in...*but no!*

Even then, he'd known she was different. Even then, he'd known the core of steel she possessed beneath that innocence.

And what an enticing contrast it made...

Which was also why he'd been so violently attracted to

her, a voice whispered. Why he had reached out to her in a way he hadn't done even with Rosa.

"Then you deceive her on purpose. You have Salvatore dangling on the line like a dog, Antonio threatening to hurt Valentina—"

"Will you marry Sophia Rossi then, Luca? Will you take her off my hands so that I don't worry about Valentina and can focus on my daughter instead?"

Luca's stinging silence was answer enough.

"Trust me," Leandro gritted through his teeth. "I'm ensuring that I do right by everyone involved."

"And her, Leandro? What about Alexis?"

Leandro ran a hand over his nape. What was right and what he wanted instead had always diverged when it came to this woman. And that he couldn't immediately seize control of the whole situation, that he couldn't make it right by any means available to him had kept him pacing to the first light of dawn.

He'd always thrived on being in control—of himself and his emotions and his situations, to beat circumstances into creating peace.

He and Luca and later, Valentina, wouldn't have found peace or even the merest happiness if he hadn't been able to count on his emotional invulnerability.

But Alexis, *then and now*, made him flounder like an impulsive, hormone-driven teenager.

"She has nothing to fear from me."

His brother's silence sent the most irrational surge of unease through him. Luca had the wickedest sense of humor Leandro had ever known. Not to mention carefree charm and the knack of making everyone feel at ease with him. Everything Leandro lacked and had never coveted.

Dio, he was thirty-five. Too late to acquire new qualities or affect a personality change. Not to mention he wouldn't be of use to his family if he did.

"Stay away from her, Luca. Your *particular brand* of friendship will only make it harder for me to—"

A roaring laugh fell from his brother's lips. "You know better than to wave a warning in my face. Also how I like to even the scales."

"This is far too important to me." He wanted to growl at his brother like an animal, he wanted to banish Luca to some Neverland until he had it all sorted with Alexis.

The thought of losing a daughter now that he'd found her was unacceptable.

"Then why not tell her that? Why not put your cards on the table?" Luca countered.

"You think she'll meekly agree to what I want after my behavior in the past?" Leandro said softly as Alexis came down the stairs and waited at a distance for Luca and him to finish talking. "Or would you instead advise me to take the small place she offers in my own daughter's life?

"Alexis is unlike any woman you or I have ever known."

For the first time since the blasted conversation began, Luca smiled that trademark devilish smile of his. Wide and reckless, his gaze took in Leandro leisurely, right down to his fisted hands.

Leandro had never, in his thirty-five years, felt the urge to punch the smile off his brother's face as he did then.

"Your saintly nature could stand to be tested now and then, Leandro."

While Leandro fumed in silence, and awash in an increasingly frequent stinging bitterness in his throat, his reckless brother reached her and enfolded Alexis in his arms, kissed her cheeks, made excited sounds over the picture of Isabella on her phone and whispered God knew what with that easy camaraderie Leandro would never achieve with her.

Nor did he need to, he assured himself.

CHAPTER FOUR

IT TOOK ALEX almost half the duration of the long flight to New York to get her head screwed on normally again. Between the flight, her headache and the effect Leandro had on her, she was going to have a nervous breakdown soon.

On top of the shock that he was coming with her had been the private airstrip the tinted-windowed Mascrati had dropped them off at.

No uncomfortable economy seating purchased on Cheap-O-Fare for Leandro Conti or painfully long stopovers. The sleek Lear jet with its beige-and-black interior and wide, reclining-like-a-bed seats, the barely discernible hum as they took off had numbed her senses for a long while.

In lieu of this spectacular reminder of his wealth, all she'd been able to think of was what it said about him that he'd readily believed that she wasn't after his money.

He'd claimed to believe her seven years ago, too. Then why dismiss her so cruelly? Why hadn't he returned a single phone call?

I have to work, he'd told her once they had taken off, his mind clearly on other matters. He'd been on several calls since then, his attention on his laptop, Alex easily dismissed.

As always, a small resentful voice whispered. But then, there had never been anything remarkable about her, had there?

But once she'd settled in for the long flight, unease fluttered down her spine like a line of ants. It was clear that he'd postponed or canceled several meetings for this trip. Not to mention leaving his new fiancée behind, whose name she'd heard him mention more than once on his phone calls.

His actions didn't speak of a man who wanted to get an unwanted, distasteful complication out of the way so that he could go back to his pleasant life. Even as he'd claimed that was exactly why.

The continual, round-and-round, inconclusive thoughts all focused on the one man who'd always remained hurtfully elusive to her understanding on the heels of another sleepless night and the stress of the past few weeks made Alex's head pound in earnest.

Leaning her head back, she pressed her fingers onto her temples.

"Alexis, are you unwell?"

"I'm fine." Prickly, defensive and far too revealing than she wanted.

"Are we at war, *bella*? Because if so, I would like some notice."

The crisp scent of the ocean filled her nostrils and her eyes flicked open. He stood behind her seat, tall and broad, filling her vision. The stark, intensely masculine lines of his face were a sensual feast.

Before she could say no, his long fingers descended on her temples. "Here?"

His touch was cold.

Or was her skin unbearably hot?

With feathery lightness, he traced the width and length of the scar and the rucked tissue, again and again.

"Did they say if this would heal completely?"

"Years for the scar to disappear. I could have a skin graft, they said." She closed her eyes. "But I decided against it."

"You would rather bear the scar to remind you what you almost lost?"

Heart thudding at his perceptiveness, Alexis nodded weakly.

Her parents, even her friend Emma thought she should have the graft done. Put the accident behind her and move on. Count her blessings, they'd said.

She did count her blessings, but she wasn't the same person anymore. Whether in a good way or not, she didn't know.

Yet Leandro understood her so easily. "My mom thought it ruined my face," she said, hating herself for the insecurity she couldn't seem to squash.

Fingers resting on her chin, he tilted her up to face him. Amusement glittered in his eyes. Yet Alex didn't think he was laughing at her. "I didn't think you were the type to angle for a compliment."

"I'm not angling. I'm asking," she said, cursing the stubborn man.

Fingers tracing her cheekbones up and down, he tilted her face up so that she looked right into his eyes. His gaze touched her forehead, her brows, eyes, nose, mouth, chin, and swept upward again. "The scar detracts nothing from what beauty you possess, Alexis."

A curse flew from her mouth then. God, the man couldn't even hand out a pity compliment, could he?

"I hope you don't speak like that in front of Isabella."

"Did anyone tell you you're an arrogant jackass, Leandro?"

Amusement sharpened those cheeks of his. "Luca does, quite frequently. Although I have to say it feels especially satisfactory to hear it from your mouth, Alexis."

She was still struggling with that when his fingers moved over her forehead again, quick and firm, exerting just the right amount of pressure.

She groaned at the sweet relief, the sound wrenching from the depths of her. It was no different from the nurse or doctors who had checked her relentlessly those first few weeks after the accident, she tried to convince herself.

"Thanks." She held his wrists, intending to push him away. And felt muscled sinew, the hair rasping against her palm. Innocent touch turned to searing awareness in a breath. "I'm okay now."

When he spoke, steel edged his silky, smooth tone. "Alexis, if you tell me where it hurts precisely and why you whimper with such pain, then maybe I can relieve it a little. If you, however, insist on this prickly attitude, I will touch and prod you everywhere until I can figure it out. And I'm sure neither of us wants that."

"I haven't been sleeping well," she added quickly, "and it's all catching up with me. It feels like someone's taking a sledgehammer inside my head."

"Relax now," he commanded in that voice of his.

As if she could ever relax in his presence. As if that relentless peal of her nerves could ever quiet.

She had no knowledge of how long he was at it, but *God*, the man could weave magic with those fingers. In more than one way if her memories were right.

Welcome heat streaked through her temples as his clever fingers pressed just the right amount in the perfect rhythm at all the right places. Up and down, back and forth. Faster and harder. "You're really good at this," she pointed out, her voice hoarse.

"Luca always had the worst kind of headaches growing up. He would…be at the piano for days, inhales books on so many different subjects, not sleep through nights at a time, then have raging headaches for days after. It was hard to watch him struggle with it so I learned a few techniques to ease it."

Every time his fingers swooped down over her nape,

sparks tingled. Languor filled her blood. "Where were your parents?" she asked and then realized she'd never heard any of the siblings mention them. Then or now.

"My father was not fit to be called one, much less a decent human being, and our mother," his voice tempered here, "for years, she had her own problems."

"What about Antonio?"

"Antonio is old-school. He thought Luca was pretending for attention and told him to toughen up."

"You didn't?" she asked, her curiosity flaming. Not that it had ever been dormant when it came to this man.

"I knew how much Luca suffered, for all the outrageous tricks he played. I had to do something."

She opened her eyes and found the penetrating gray of his. Neck stretched over the leather seat, there was nowhere else for her gaze to land.

The white collar of his shirt was a stark contrast against the dark skin of his throat. He would feel like tempered steel and rough silk, she knew, her fingers curling around the hand rest.

Without the formal clothes, he should have looked more attainable. He didn't. It was the confidence in his eyes, the sense of authority that clung to him like a second skin.

He seemed as out of her orbit as he'd been seven years ago.

"How old were you?" She somehow managed to get back on track.

"Fourteen."

Fourteen years old and he'd been so thoughtful about his brother's pain.

Another small facet of his personality and yet all Alex felt was like she was tunneling through darkness. Her relentless awareness of his masculinity and his shabby treatment of her seven years ago only counted against him.

"Tell me about the accident," he prodded softly.

He peppered her with specific questions, asking for numerous details, about her injuries, recovery period, right down to the names of the nurses who'd attended her.

With her muscles turning into mush, Alex gave over to his deep voice, and those magical hands. Told him of the weeks she spent in the hospital, seeing Izzie's face burst into tears at the sight of her in the stark bed, of wondering if she'd have use of her hand again.

"Your hand?" He walked around her seat immediately. "What happened to your hand?"

He lifted her left hand in his bigger one and studied the crisscross of scars across the puckered skin in the back. The pithy curse that fell from his mouth almost distracted her from the gentle, almost reverent touch.

Bluntly cut square nails. Long, tapered fingers. Rough calluses. She studied his hands to her heart's content. He traced the veins on the back of her hand, sending a tingle up her arm.

"It got crushed in the impact. The nerve damage was far too extensive. But they said continued physical therapy will help."

She tried to pull her hand away, suddenly feeling self-conscious. But he didn't let go. "Was that the hardest part?"

Alexis looked down at their joined hands, her throat swelling. With his soothing tone and gentle caresses, he made her long for something that she couldn't even define.

The worst offender was mistaking that she interested him. That he was as aware of her as she was of him.

"The hospital food."

A soft smile curved his mouth, changing the entire vista of his forbidding features. Like one ray of sunlight that pierced even the thickest, densest darkness.

A carefree, laughing Leandro.

It was as novel as it was attractive. Even back then, her first impression of him had been how serious he was.

"Is Isabella like you? Strong and stubborn?"

Smiling, she nodded. "Actually, the hardest part was the sheer amount of insurance paperwork that I had to deal with. But Justin was a great help with that."

It was like she'd seen the show about predators on National Geographic. Just an infinitesimal tightening of those features—head cocking, muscles bunching in his shoulders. Regrouping before attacking. "Who is Justin?" He didn't quite meet her gaze.

"He's my friend Emma's brother. Moved back last year."

"A good friend then?"

Something in his tone tugged but the pounding in her head easing, Alex couldn't care. "We've been on a few dates this past year," she said, thinking back on how strange it had been to step out without Izzie. How hard it had been to accept Justin's help knowing that he liked her and she…she didn't feel anything like that about him.

Having known Justin for a long time, her parents, however, had all but started planning their wedding.

"A boyfriend then?" He stood up and moved behind her again, his hands moving to her head again as if they had never left.

When she looked up at him, a frown marred his brow. "Izzie likes him, too," she said, parroting her mother.

"And you, Alexis? Do you like him?" The question was silky smooth but the speed with which he asked made her heart race.

"It's hard to not like Justin. Especially when I found last year how quickly men run in the opposite direction because I come with a child in tow."

"What do you mean?"

"Emma decided I needed to get back out there and took out an ad on *Forever.com*. Forget *forever*, apparently, being a single mom means I don't even get a first date. This one creep who did contact me said it's good to have proof that I was fertile." She cringed. "Fortunately, Justin proved I wasn't quite as plague-ridden for men as I thought."

"You miss excitement in your life then?"

"Will you count it against me in this test if I say yes?" she said teasingly.

"A test?" He sounded so innocent that she laughed. "To what end?"

"To gauge my credibility as a mother and guardian before you settle money on Izzie?"

He did really laugh then. It was a deep, husky sound that wrapped around Alex like a warm blanket. "That is a cynical statement. Even an insult, I think, as it implies I care more about my money than a newly discovered daughter."

"I didn't say that," she pointed out. "I have no idea what kind of man you are, Leandro. Except for how you treated me. So if there's an insult here and there in the way I speak to you, then it's not intended."

"Then we have to learn about each other."

"Do we? Will you answer anything I ask of you?"

He smiled again and it stole through Alexis, warming her up from the inside, infusing her with a deep sense of well-being. Like one of Izzie's sweet and tight cuddles. Like the smell of the first cup of coffee in the morning. Like the crisply cold air in Central Park after a night's snowfall in winter.

"Are you bracing me with that question or yourself?"

How did he see through her so easily?

She was still chewing on that when he spoke. "Has it been hard? Doing it all on your own?"

Tension, she didn't know from where, swirled in the air all of a sudden. A million answers crowded in on her and Alex held her breath.

"For as long as I can remember, I worried about Luca

and then Valentina." Deep and low, his voice washed over her. But even more shocking was how readily he spoke of his past. "Still, only about their mental health and happiness. Not actual tangible things like their safety, finances and other things. Not to mention—"

"But that sounds like you had to grow up too fast."

He shrugged. Clearly, he hadn't seen it as a loss. "I did what anyone would have done. I could not let Luca or Valentina suffer my parents' negligence."

"Don't you regret that you missed out on a carefree, reckless kind of childhood then?"

Whatever reply came to him, he cut it off and looked down at her. "You sound wistful, Alexis. Are you sorry that you haven't lived recklessly enough?"

Pure taunt sizzled in that question.

He was thinking about that night, Alexis knew as surely as the pulsing beat of her heart. "Or the fact that having Isabella curtails you from it now?"

Refusing to take his bait, Alex looked away. Her confusion about him only rose. Made worse by her stringent awareness of him.

He'd looked after his brother and sister since he'd been a teenager. Even that week in Italy, he'd come to the villa because Valentina had slipped on some steps and twisted her ankle.

Within an hour, there he'd been—a hauntingly beautiful and masculine figure, concerned about his sister.

"Before the accident," she said, trying to cover up her confusion, "it was more a sense of never having a moment to breathe. If it wasn't the day-to-day things at the store, it was Izzie getting sick. If it wasn't Izzie, it was some health issue with my dad. If it wasn't him, then wondering about finances…" She pulled in a deep breath. "After the accident though, yes, it felt hard. And not just because of the panic attacks."

"Panic attacks? Has Isabella seen you have one?"

That he immediately thought of Izzie both warmed and alarmed Alex. "No, she hasn't. It's just fragments from the accident, that sense of my life careening out of control. I had them only a couple of times but they made me determined to ensure Izzie's future."

Not even with Emma had she admitted how much it had all become for her before the accident. And yet, sharing bits and pieces from his own past, Leandro had put her instantly at ease.

It was almost as if he'd decided to make peace with her. Did he think they could forge a friendship of some sort? Would they be like those amicable partners who shared a child?

Because as good as that sounded ideally, Alex couldn't fool herself that she could ever be just friends with Leandro. Not if she wanted to remain sane.

Even now, headache relieved, a sleepy, languorous flush claimed her.

Her jacket off her shoulders, she was awash in pure, skittering sensation.

Then those supple fingers stole under her T-shirt, pushed under the straps of her bra and pressed into the knots in her shoulders. Alex groaned, every inch of her thrumming in a molten kind of way.

It had been so long since she'd been touched by such strong, masculine hands that made her aware of her own fragility.

A desperate yearning took hold of her. She turned her cheek toward the rough hand. Rubbed it against the hair-roughened wrist. Shivers spewed everywhere.

She could just imagine those hands everywhere on her skin, teasing, taunting, drenching her in—

The utter stillness of his form, the rough texture of his

hand against her cheek, so incredibly good and yet so alien, jerked Alex back into coherence.

Breath hitching in and out roughly, she pushed off her seat.

Skin tight over angular features, Leandro stared back at her. Not a smidgen of the confusion or the stringent awareness that vibrated through every inch of her reflected in his own gaze however.

"Thanks," she said jerkily, wrapping her hands around herself. "I'm…much better."

"Are you in love with this… Justin, Alexis?" he said, without heeding the distance she'd put between them.

Senses still raw from the sensations coursing through her, shocked at how much she wanted his hands on her, a choked breath fell from her lips. The resolute lift of his chin, the implacable look in his eyes…that pushed his question to sink through. "You think I came to Italy because I'm hitching up with a man and want to fob off Izzie on you?"

Jaw tight, he wrapped his fingers around her wrist and tugged her closer. "No. As shocking as it is, it seems you're an exceptional mother and—"

Oh, the man made her so mad. "Why is it so shocking? That I had sex with you and liked it makes it impossible that I'm also a good mother? If that's the kind of attitude you're going to show around Izzie about her mother—"

He covered her mouth with his palm. Thoughts fragmented. Sensation zoomed. It was heat all over, stinging, unrelenting. From his palm, from his lean frame standing so close to her. Beneath her skin, in her muscles.

"I would never disrespect her mother in front of Isabella. And I said it the wrong way."

"Your timing sucks, that's what Valentina said to me." She had been so keen upon the previous night, she hadn't realized what that meant. "Seven years ago and now. With you…what did she mean? What was going on when we met seven years ago?"

"It is irrelevant, Alexis."

"To me, you mean?" she instantly challenged him, head cocked. "Way to put me in my place, Leandro. But this stopped being about me and you six years ago."

The question about seven years ago was a sharp reminder to Leandro of how easily Alex could distract him. Of how easily one innocent touch could morph into this craving.

"My wife had—"

Alex clutched his shirt, her knees threatening to give out under her. "*Your wife*… God, you were married?"

"*No!* I would never… No, she had passed away recently when we…met."

"How recently?"

"A month to the day that night."

A month…the leaden weight on her chest eased enough for her to breathe.

Until she met his gaze, saw the self-loathing that settled into every line of his face.

"Rosa died after a long struggle with cancer and it took me mere weeks to forget that."

Shame crawled through her insidiously, polluting her memory of that night, painting her with that same loathing she heard in his voice.

She pressed the heels of her hands to her eyes. *God, why had she asked?* "If you were the bloody saint your sister calls you, you shouldn't have come near me, you shouldn't have touched me."

"You think I didn't try?" He dragged her to him in a violent explosion of temper. "From the moment I laid eyes on you… *Maledizione!*" Fingers dug into her arms. Hard chest grazed her breasts. Her body came awake as if someone had thumped on her heart.

Excruciatingly, violently awake.

The hard length of his legs cradled hers, shaping and molding her muscles. "From the moment I saw you telling Tina not to be a spoiled, whiny brat, from the moment I saw you laugh with Luca…your face…*you haunted me.*" Fingers splayed over her jaw, he caressed every inch of her face with his eyes.

Was he remembering or did he still want her?

"Rosa suffered with cancer for three years. Through endless chemo cycles, I never even looked at another woman. I never even felt the urge.

"But every time I looked at you, there it was in your eyes. Your attraction to me, so guileless, so honest… The more I tried to stay away from the villa, the more times I found myself there. The more I told myself to leave you alone, the more I found myself near you."

Leave it alone, Alex. Every self-preserving instinct yelled at her. But she didn't heed it. "So you're saying that I asked to be hurt? That I didn't deserve a speck of the respect that you had for your wife? That I deserved to be slept with and then discarded—"

He covered her mouth with his finger. "There was no future for us. *There was no us.* Not even an affair. I did what I did to make sure you understood that."

"I would've preferred knowing that you weren't a heartless, ruthless jerk who used women and then abhorred them for wanting the same as you. I would've preferred to be treated as a person.

"I would have preferred knowing that you were grieving, that you—"

"*No*, Alexis! Do not spin theories about me. Do not make me out to be anything more than I am."

"Your arrogance in dictating to me what I should think of you is astounding, Leandro." She faced him, her heart pounding. "What scares you so much? That I might think you're a man with a conscience? That I might think you liked me and that you wanted me that night as much as I did you? That there was a connection between us that threatened all your principles?"

A muscle jumped in his clamped jaw. His head cocked, infinitesimally, as if something had come at him.

Gaze absolutely implacable, he looked at her. Slowly, Alex could see any hint of emotion driven out by his sheer, ruthless will. Could see the man of the past few hours retreat. Could feel the intangible wall rise up between them.

A shiver climbed up her spine. Like a warning to brace herself.

"What I did that night was a betrayal to Rosa. I obviously misjudged the effect of prolonged celibacy, especially when thrown in front of an irresistible temptation. I saw her waste away month after month and you...you were everything she couldn't be at the end.

"Vivacious, lively, beautiful.

"To hold you, to touch you...it's like that shot that shocks the heart." He closed his eyes, every line of his face taut. "It was pure animal lust, nothing civilized, nothing to build something on. If it wasn't you, I'm perfectly sure it would have been someone else soon."

The moment the words were out of his mouth, Leandro knew it was the utterly wrong thing to have said for the goal he had in mind.

Color leeched from her skin, leaving Alexis's features pinched. Like the lights going out of a brilliantly lit room.

Dio, the woman turned him inside out. He had destroyed his entire strategy of putting her at ease, of showing that he could be understanding and perceptive, of earning her trust with his words.

What did she want—to elevate one night of weakness to life-changing import?

No!

He couldn't let her weave fantasies about that night, couldn't risk letting her imagine romantic ideas about the future. Not the kind she obviously still believed in, even after he'd behaved like a ruthless bastard.

He was exactly what she thought him—heartless, arrogant, used to getting his own way.

Still, she held her head high and faced him square, didn't buck against his obviously cruel summation of that night.

"Will you look at Izzie like she was a symbol of your betrayal, too? Because I swear, Leandro—" She looked ferociously breathtaking, eyes flashing fire. "I won't let you come near her if you do."

Rendered mute, Leandro stared at her, amazed by the strength she showed even now.

What would it be like to possess a woman like her? To have her channel that intensity, that passion toward him? To bask in the strength of her conviction?

If his mother had possessed half that strength, would he have turned out different? Would he have had that reckless, carefree childhood that Alex mourned for him? Would he have known tender feelings?

Would he—

Dio! It was as useless as it was pathetically self-indulgent.

He was the man he was, for better or worse. But she deserved an explanation. "For years, Rosa wanted a child and we didn't conceive. When you told me about Isabella, all I could think of was her. Of how cruel it was, even to her memory that I had a child with a woman I took in a moment of insanity.

"I would never hold an innocent responsible for my lack of judgment."

Chin lifted. Shoulders squared. She had never looked so

icily cold as she did then. Whatever inner fire that made her Alexis seemed to go out of her eyes.

He felt a moment's regret about what was right for her. But like she had said, this wasn't about either of them anymore.

"No, only me, because I was a willing participant in your betrayal. Thanks for clearing that up."

She left the main cabin like a queen who had found him wanting.

It rattled him how much he wanted to follow her. How much he wanted to take her in his arms and tell her that all his disgust had been aimed at himself. That he considered her an innocent in all of this, too. That as much as he'd loathed himself, *Dio*, he'd never been able to forget her.

Even today, his self-control, his very intention in all this was threatened by all the things she made him feel.

But, at least this way, she would know what she was getting.

Because, as much as he resisted, there was only one way to be a part of his daughter's life.

He'd been prepared to marry Sophia. One woman was the same as another for the marriage he wanted. Of course, he could have lied and made his goal easier, but Leandro didn't believe in pretending things he didn't feel.

CHAPTER FIVE

FROM THE MOMENT he realized he had a daughter, Leandro had tried to imagine what he would feel a thousand times. After all, he had raised Valentina for all intents and purposes. Something novel from the emotional spectrum he'd ever experienced, he admitted that much.

But the sight of the little girl that barely came to his knees, looking up at him with those gray eyes, both curious and reticent, punched through him. It was as if he was caught in a whirlpool of emotion, tossed about by a vicious eddy that threw him from grief to anger to sheer, gut-wrenching amazement that she was his.

And loss, excruciating loss.

It had been almost close to an hour since he and Alexis had arrived at the tiny brownstone house that belonged to her parents.

Tension swirled through the air from the moment she introduced him. The Sharpes were too polite to say anything to his face, better than what Alexis had received back in his home, but their doubt filled the air. Even more powerful was their obvious anger for Alexis. She had forgotten to mention that she had come to see him against their wishes.

After an excruciatingly uncomfortable half hour, they went to visit with friends and Leandro had been able to breathe again.

Keeping to his word, he had held himself back from approaching Isabella.

But waiting had never felt so painful as he heard Alexis's firm but husky tone and Isabella's soft voice in the kitchen. He had no one to blame. Neither would he let anything nor anyone stop him from setting it to right.

He stayed on the couch, anxious like never before when Alexis and Isabella walked back into the tiny living area.

Reaching him, Isabella leveled an unabashedly curious look at him. "Mamma says you're my *papà*."

Leandro cleared his throat, found himself unable to utter a word still. Chill and heat, everything enveloped him.

"She said you guys were friends before and then fell out. Is that why you didn't come to see me before?" His gaze flew to Alexis's and held. That she hadn't filled his daughter's head with anything but the truth made his own treatment of her even more awful. "It's okay," Isabella continued, laying her small hand upon his. "My friend Sam and I fight all the time, too. Mamma says friends gotta make up after fights. You and Mamma made up?"

"*Si*...yes," he corrected himself when he saw her little frown. "We have."

"Does that mean I can tell my friends that you'll be—?"

"Izzie, sweetie," Alexis interrupted, "remember how we talked about your *papà* living all the way in Italy and us—"

"You can tell all your friends, Isabella," Leandro added, ignoring Alexis's pursed mouth. "Maybe we can even meet your friend Sam tomorrow? Would you like that?"

"Can we throw the ball around with them? Sam's dad has a really good arm."

Even as his arms ached to pull her into his embrace, even as prickling heat knocked at his eyes, Leandro consoled himself with shaking his little girl's hand. "*Si*, we can. Although it is your uncle, Luca, who's the best with a ball in the family."

A cute, heart-wrenching smile split her mouth. And Leandro's breath caught.

It was in Isabella's smile that Alexis peeked through. The effervescent joy, the confident tilt of the chin, the way it tore through him… Alexis was in his daughter where it mattered. "I have an uncle?"

"You have an uncle, an aunt and a great-*nonno* in Italy, who're all dying to meet you."

"What's a *nonno*?" Before he could answer, she tugged his hand. "Can I show you my new puzzle? Are you going to stay here? We only have three bedrooms but you can have mine. Unless you want to sleep in Mamma's room now that you're friends again?"

He laughed as her questions continued, much like the machine that threw tennis balls at a player.

"No, sweet pie, he can't stay here."

"Why not?" Both he and Isabella asked at the same time.

Alexis's smile didn't falter. "Our house is too small for you. But Brooklyn has luxury hotels that should suit your exacting tastes."

"I'm staying here, Alexis."

His heart threatening to burst out of his chest, Leandro stood up and followed his little girl to her room.

Even as he was aware of a set of molten brown eyes digging into his back, censure and curiosity and a million other questions in them.

Maybe taking Izzie on a holiday to Italy for the summer isn't such a bad idea, Alex. Izzie will get to meet the Contis and you can have a nice break.

Her dad's words from this morning still rumbled through Alex, like the after-ripples of an earthquake that had upended her world this morning.

You went when we warned you against it. Now that he's being so reasonable, what's bothering you?

This was her mother. Clenching her teeth so hard that

her jaw hurt, Alex dragged another cardboard box with canned organic beans.

The damning thing was the heartless, manipulative jerk hadn't even broached the subject of visiting Italy with her. Yet, here was her dad, the very man who'd looked at Leandro with the utmost suspicion last week, persuading her to not hold grudges and do what was best for Izzie.

Even now, her throat burned at her parents' continual, insidious hints about Leandro being a model father to Izzie. While they had never approved of a single decision of hers.

How had he done that? In just two weeks, how had he turned her own parents and even her best friend against her? And to what end?

Also, why was the man who'd wanted to be on his merry way to his waiting fiancée still here?

Marking off the cans on her inventory chart, Alex blew out a long breath. The broken A/C in the beginning of a New York summer meant the storeroom was like a sauna. Sweat poured in rivulets down the back of her neck. With her hospital bills from the myriad of treatments she had undergone still arriving every few weeks like buzzards circling a dead body, she couldn't afford to get the air-conditioning fixed now. Nor could she hire extra help to sort and stock their inventory.

Cursing, she pulled her cotton T-shirt off her back. The damn thing went straight back to sticking to her skin. Making sure that she didn't put undue strain on her left hand, she knelt in front of another box and ripped off the duct tape. She knew she was pushing herself, that this inventory could wait until next week after the long hours she had put in over the past few days.

God, she'd barely even spent any time with Izzie.

But going back home before she was exhausted meant seeing the blasted man. Seeing him meant remembering his words from the flight. Remembering meant...realizing that she'd, foolishly, hoped he would have some magnanimous reason for his behavior seven years ago. How naively unsophisticated she was in not accepting that she'd been a convenient lay and nothing else.

Until he'd said the words, until they had landed on her like poisonous darts, Alex didn't know they'd hurt so much. Didn't know that they would make her want to burrow into an emotional shell like Izzie's pet turtle and never emerge.

He'd been devoted to his wife, Alexis couldn't get over that. It said everything she'd assumed about him was wrong. Exactly opposite even.

Only when she saw him and Izzie together—Leandro, powerful and handsome and so thoroughly masculine and Izzie, tiny and smiling and his very image—did she remember the reason he was here.

Knowing that he was sleeping in the bedroom next to hers made even the little sleep she'd been getting disappear.

He should've looked incongruous in the small bed in Izzie's room, yet he looked right at home. Just as he'd slipped so easily into the role of a father.

With his utter devotion to Izzie, with his unpretentious, get-your-hands-dirty gardening skills he'd helped her mom with, with his keen attention to several issues that had to be fixed in the house and immediately arranging workers to do so...

In her parents' view, suddenly the man had gone from dishonorable stranger who'd impregnated and then ditched their reckless, good-for-nothing daughter *and more importantly*, their much-adored granddaughter to an accomplished, down-to-earth-even-though-he's-stinking-rich gentleman who could do no wrong in their eyes.

If she didn't hate him before this, Alex was sure she did now.

She attacked the second line of the stubborn tape with both hands, her temper finally fraying.

"*Alexis!*" came the thunderous growl from behind her.

Before she could react, she was hauled up from behind, viselike hands clamped tight under her arms. Awareness smoldered through her, like a current of lightning.

The moment she was upright, his grip gentled. Long fingers rested on the upper curves of her breasts. Air burned through her lungs.

Her back felt as though it would bow from the pressure of holding herself stiff.

The sheer violence of her need to feel those fingers drift down, the instant tightening of her nipples hungry for his touch, ripped through her. One step back would send her into the hard, male muscle that every inch of her wanted to feel.

God, the man was engaged to another woman. Didn't her body understand that?

Longing made her throat burn, muscles quiver, skin thrum. She didn't dare wiggle for fear of him touching her. "Let me go, Leandro," she said in a husky voice. "I'm all sweaty."

Instead of heeding her, he took a step further. The blanket of heat that surrounded her was instantaneous. The scent of him drifted down over her skin, covering every cell. Drenching her until all she breathed was him. "Not until you tell me what, *per carita*, you are doing."

As always, he sounded perfectly balanced, unruffled.

"I'm working. We can't all dance attendance on you," she snapped, and then regretted her words.

When he tried to turn her, she resisted. She couldn't face him, feeling so raw and vulnerable. She couldn't face herself if she betrayed how much she still wanted him.

Closing her eyes, she willed her breath to calm.

"Should you be pulling and pushing boxes that weigh a ton when your hand is nowhere near healed?"

"I was careful to not use my left hand."

"And what if you hurt your other hand dragging things that shouldn't be handled without the appropriate tool?"

"I can take care of myself, Leandro."

A hiss of impatient breath. "That is not up for debate. But that there are numerous things you need help with is fact, too. Especially around the store."

"You forget that I've been taking care of my parents, Izzie and the store. We don't need your help. This isn't why I asked you to come."

She heard his muttering in Italian, before she turned and looked up at him.

The clean, strong lines of his face struck her with that same fierce hunger.

For the first time since she'd laid eyes on him again, he looked truly confounded. If she wasn't battling her hyper-awareness of him and her growing, irrational temper, she would've enjoyed the look on his face.

"Why are you always so defensive? I will say this again because it does not seem to enter your stubborn mind. I do not think that you came to see me for any reason other than Isabella's welfare. And I am…glad that you did. Any man who turns away from his duty is not worth the air he breathes.

"Now, I have instructed your father to call back the manager who used to assist him at the store but full-time. My real estate agent has had some interest in the store, too."

"For one thing, I can't afford to hire staff now." Alex gritted her jaw. "And I have no plans to sell the store."

He didn't even bat an eyelid. "I have transferred some money to your account. That should help until the store is completely operational again."

God, the man had to be the most thickheaded, arrogant, high-handed specimen of the species. Didn't he realize she wanted nothing to do with him on a personal level? That her pride, which was all she had at this point, was hanging by a sheer thread? "I'm not taking money from you."

"Why not?"

"Why should I?"

He looked at her as if she were lacking brains completely. "Because I have it and you need it."

"I don't know what the hell kind of game you're playing, or what you're trying to prove. Or is that it? You get a kick out of changing how my parents see you? Your monumental ego can't stand that they think less of the mighty Leandro Conti?"

"*Cristo*, I only intend to help you. You think I like knowing that you struggled so much all these years when I should have helped?"

The guilt in his eyes stayed her for a few seconds.

"Well, I don't want your help. Is it not enough that you... you own half your country, do you also have to be good at gardening and fixing the house and a million other things?" Didn't he see how hard he was making this all for her? "You might as well label me incompetent and be done with it."

If he had ever assumed he could understand the complexities of Alexis's mind, he was wrong. A simple conversation with her was like handling a hundred Lucas and Valentinas on their worst days.

From the moment they had spoken of that night seven years ago, it was as if there was an invisible wall between them and she had retreated behind it.

Except when they were both with Isabella. That was the only time she smiled, the only time she made eye contact with him.

Dio, the only time the stubborn woman even acknowledged his presence in her house.

He hadn't been there a single night before he realized how much responsibility rested on her shoulders, how many day-to-day things Alexis handled with barely a complaint and with an efficiency that he couldn't help but admire.

Still, it was too much for one person. She had handled so much for so long alone.

It had proved easy enough to win her parents over now that he truly intended to take care of Isabella and even Alexis by association, to change their perception that he was the big bad wolf that had gobbled up their lovely daughter.

Only Alexis began to act strange. The more her parents and even her friend Emma realized his true intentions and supported him, the more withdrawn she became. A betrayed look dawned in her gaze. Now, when he was finally doing the right thing.

And the worst thing was that her mistrust was taking a toll on him. The more she dismissed him, the more stringent became his need to make her acknowledge him, and his right to be in her life.

Not just his right over Isabella. But he wanted Alexis, too.

There it was...the knot that he hadn't been able to unravel in the past week.

Look at how he had held her just now. At how violently and instantly his body had reacted to the mere graze of her slender curves against his. At how insanely powerful the urge was to touch her, to taste her, to bury his nose in the crook of her neck and breathe in the scent of her skin.

His desire for her was already out of control, threatening his plan.

When her friend Justin had visited and embraced her, all

he'd wanted to do was pull her away from the young, blond, insufferably amiable giant and tuck her away behind him.

To declare like a Neanderthal that Alexis wasn't available.

When they had laughed together over some childhood story, when he'd seen how familiar Justin was with Alexis and everything regarding her…he'd felt the most absurd sense of jealousy.

He hadn't felt possessive even about a toy in his childhood.

Teeth clenched, eyes closed, he counted to ten.

The scent of her, skin and sweat and undeniably her, it filled his lungs, his blood, unlocking every rebellious, insidiously craven indulgence his body wanted with her.

Dio, how he wanted her. Even after everything. Even today.

She would be his wife, his to possess, his to protect.

She would be in his bed, his room, his life. He could have her whenever, wherever, however he wanted, until this madness in his blood was defeated. Until every irrationally possessive clawing was satisfied. Until he was inured to this feverish desire he felt for her.

Until he could look at her and feel nothing but satisfaction that he'd done the right thing.

Beneath this war she was waging with him, Alexis was like him. At such a young age, she'd been forced into being a mother and yet it was clear that she exceled at it. She cared for everyone around her, to the detriment of her own well-being.

Now, he would look after her. Just as he had done Rosa.

She would see how good of a father he could be and would want for nothing.

They could have a marriage without drama, without the messiness of emotions. By the time the attraction between them fizzled out, they would have more children.

And then they would be bound as parents who cared about their children.

Hadn't that been his only condition when Antonio had found Rosa for him? That his new bride be someone who would love their children and devote herself to being a calm, supportive wife?

Alexis needed his strength, just as Rosa had done, only in a different way. She needed to be protected from her stubborn self first.

Only with that promise did the clamoring hunger in his blood subside.

"Alexis," he said in a composed tone, "explain to me how offering help is calling you incompetent. How trying to reassure your parents that I mean well for Isabella is," he held himself back, just, from sounding possessive about her, knowing that it would only alienate her, "...wrong."

"That's exactly the problem." Chin tilted up, her gaze flashed fire at him. Her thin T-shirt hugged the round globes of her breasts. His hands itched to touch her, trace those lush curves, to mold them. Blood hummed with a thrum as he imagined baring her to his gaze.

"You've been here barely two weeks and they worship you. They love everything you do." A choked whimper escaped her, her mouth trembling. "It's almost as if everything I've tried to do for more than a decade counts for nothing." She threw the pad in her hand against the wall, her lithe form shaking. "It's almost as if I... I count for nothing."

The sheen of moisture in her eyes punched through him, tying his insides into a knot.

Tenderness like he'd never known assailed him, releasing the fist-like tension that had been driving him this past week. He'd always been protective of those around him. It was in his nature, in his blood. And yet, nothing unmanned him as much as Alexis's tears did.

The very defiance of her meeting his gaze even as those brown eyes welled up…it was a breath-stealing sight. He wished he could capture it on paper, or in a song, like Luca would have. He wished he had words to describe how magnificently beautiful she was.

Instead, he did the one thing he'd always exceled at.

His large hands on her slender shoulders, he pulled her to him and wrapped his arms around her. Even stiff and unbending as she was, she still came. That she took the comfort he offered told him how upset she was.

"Alexis." He had never tried so hard to sound understanding, never felt such raw impatience tearing at him to fix her grief. "Tell me what bothers you and I'll fix it."

Forehead resting against his chest, she let out a slow exhale. "For once, I can't hate your arrogance, Leandro. I'd give anything if you could fix it."

Smiling, he stroked her temples. "You don't know what I can do until you try me, *cara*. You haven't been sleeping again, have you?"

"I miss him." Teary and choked, she sounded unlike the Alexis he knew. "I miss him so much."

Such unparalleled love reverberated in her tone that everything within him stilled. "Who are you taking about?"

"You'll think me the most horrible person ever."

"When have you cared about my opinion, Alexis?" he shot back, hating the thread of disquiet that coursed through him.

Just as he expected, her spine straightened. That fighting spirit returned to her eyes. "I don't. I just… It's my brother, Adrian."

Relief was a palpable thing within him. A lover would have caused problems for him. That was the only reason for it. "I didn't know you had a brother."

"He died when I was seventeen, just before he was about to start college. Oh you'd have liked him so much.

He was charming, brilliant, handsome, kind…exceled at his studies, sports. *God*, there was nothing that Adrian wasn't good at.

"I could have hated him for being their favorite, if he hadn't loved me so much. You see, unlike Adrian, I didn't excel at anything. I barely got through my classes. Mom and Dad and I never really connected… Adrian was always the buffer. When he passed away suddenly…" She wiped her eyes with the heels of her hands, much like Isabella did. "Not only were we shattered, but it felt like there was nothing connecting me to them. There were days when I wished I had died instead of him."

"*Dio*, Alexis!" The very thought unnerved Leandro on so many levels. "I'm sure your parents didn't wish that."

"No, probably not." She stepped away from him. "I have tried my level best to be a good daughter. But I… I'm not him. Seeing how happy and elated they are with everything you do, how easy you make it all, I'm sure it reminds them of him. Of how different and how better life would've been if he were alive.

"And I can't be angry with them for thinking that because it's true. I drove a very fiscally wise store toward ruin with my ideas, got pregnant at twenty and…now, I brought a myriad of problems on us with this accident."

Cristo, didn't anyone tell her that all those were not her fault? That she was braver and stronger than any woman in the same situation? Didn't she realize it was her parents' fault in measuring her against a son who was long gone?

Leandro wanted to shake her and somehow show her the image he had of her.

But finally, he understood her behavior of the past week.

Alexis was used to taking care of everyone around her, of putting everyone else's needs first. In just a week, he'd seen her handle ten different things for her mother, Isabella and even her friend Emma.

It was time for someone to remove such weight from her shoulders. And he would do it. Even if he had to manipulate that very weakness of hers.

"A small business that you think you ruined in a hard, economic climate, accolades at university you think you lack, ambition you think you don't possess." He had heard all those insidious remarks from her mother, the regretful but equally hurting statements from her father, only the awareness that he would take her away from it all had stopped him from peeling their hide. "How do they measure up against the strong, happy little girl you've been raising all these years, Alexis? Against swallowing your anger for me and coming to me when you worried about Isabella's future? I would have given anything to see my mother champion for us like you do her."

Her stunned gaze, her mouth falling open soundlessly—her shock at his words was a tangible thing in the air. Something in his chest ached at how desperate she had been to hear a compliment. To be told that she wasn't a failure.

Her disbelief slowly ebbed out of her eyes. "I...don't know what to say."

"Learn to accept my help."

She swiped at her eyes with the back of her hand and glared at him. "So nothing I just told you got through to your head?"

"Whatever I'm doing, it's so that you can breathe easy when you come to Italy with me. So that you don't worry about the store or them. They deserve better than to worry about your health and Izzie's security and about what you'll do when they're gone. They deserve that holiday they've been planning for ages."

"How do you know about their trip to Australia?"

"Your mother showed me the brochure."

That same inadequacy swirled through Alex. How had

she missed how disappointed they must be? It was something they had saved up for for so long. And because of her bills, everything had been pushed back.

She leaned her forehead against the cupboard door.

This was how she had felt when Adrian had died.

Useless, incompetent, of no good to anyone.

And now, she had bigger responsibilities and yet was worse off.

Tears scratched at her throat. "I don't know what to do. I've been trying so hard to keep everything together. I just…"

"So make it easier on yourself and them. Let me help. You've handled everything single-handedly all this while. But you don't need to anymore.

"Isn't that why you set this whole thing in motion?"

"So you want me to take your handouts and be happy about it?"

"No, I want you to get the rest you deserve so that Izzie doesn't worry about you."

"You should've talked to me first before you campaigned my parents to your side. How about if you ask instead of deciding we're coming with you?"

Autocratic wasn't enough to describe the man's attitude.

"Is this a war of wills then, Alexis? I'm proposing this so that Isabella can spend time with my family and you can recover easier, too. It won't be long before the stress you're under translates to Isabella. I could not leave everything here as is, knowing the situation."

"Stop speaking as if her very life is unstable," she protested, a lump in her throat. That sense of failure was a lead weight in her chest.

"Not unstable, no. But it is clear that the accident has made everything harder."

Which was exactly the conclusion she had come to. Yet hearing it from his mouth scraped her pride.

Of all the things, what was this compulsion to prove herself to him? Why did his opinion matter this much? Why did his concern, which she was slowly realizing was a huge part of what made Leandro, feel so personal?

"What about your wedding?"

His gaze instantly shuttered. "What about it?"

"Luca told me that your fiancée's father is pushing for a summer wedding."

If she didn't have absolute belief in his prized self-control, Alex would have thought he was close to violence. Such fury blazed in his eyes at the mention of Luca. "You have been talking to Luca?"

"He called to say hello to Izzie and yes, we chatted, a couple of times. I don't think us being there before your wedding is a good idea. The last thing I want is for your new bride or her family to treat Izzie like I was treated."

"They won't."

"What about me?"

When had he swallowed up the distance she'd put between them? Her heart raced as he gently pushed a lock of hair behind her ear. "No one will hurt you, *cara*."

"I can see the headlines now." She kept her tone casual through sheer effort, loath to betray how the idea of his wedding haunted her. The thought of him with his new bride, those hands of his caressing some unknown figure, of laying those lips on another woman, of that inscrutable gray gaze widening with desire…her lack of sleep had gotten worse since she'd seen him again.

He'd laid every concern of hers to rest and yet made her restless to her very bones.

"Leandro Conti's Love Child's Trashy Single Mom a Distinguished Guest at His Wedding to an Heiress…"

A smile broke through the austerity of his face, transforming his face into breathtaking beauty. Even white teeth flashed at her, one edge of his mouth turning up crooked.

Breath catching in her throat, Alex swallowed hard. "Reading Italian tabloids?"

Heat poured through her cheeks. She had given in and scoured for news on him. The lurid headlines and gossip that seemed to always swirl around his family explained Antonio's vulgar words to her. But what had amazed her was Leandro's lack of the same.

And she'd faced the hard truth—that he had trusted her without proof. Even before he'd seen Izzie's pictures.

That he was honorable made it so much harder for her to hate him.

"I assure you I will protect you, Alexis."

"Thanks but no thanks. I saw how you sprang to my defense when Antonio was—"

"I was in shock and you shut him up promptly. Like no one has ever done. No one will say a word to you, I promise you that."

"How can you guarantee that? There'll probably be a million guests at your wedding and they'll surely wonder who I am and I can't stand to be the object of such gossip. Not to mention being a fourth wheel between your new bride and you and your family and her family and—"

One tapered finger landed on her mouth, burning the soft flesh of her lower lip. "Will you send Izzie by herself with me then?"

She swatted his hand away. "No! I…she's a baby, Leandro and a week doesn't make you anything less than a stranger."

Her answer seemed to please him. "Then what I suggest is the only solution we have. I would like to spend time with Isabella."

"But I—"

"*Dio*, Alexis!" Impatience made his tone staccato, harsh. "No one will say anything because there will not be a wedding."

CHAPTER SIX

THERE WASN'T GOING to be a wedding.

Alex couldn't understand how the small, brusquely delivered fact could have such hold over her, even after four days.

Four days in which, somehow, she had let Leandro and her family persuade her that spending the summer with the Contis at their Lake Como villa was a good idea all around.

No sooner than she, only in possession of half her faculties, had admitted that Izzie would love to see more of him than Leandro had seen to and settled a hundred things that needed to be done.

A new manager had been hired for as long as was needed for the store. Her parents had been dispatched on a holiday to Australia as they had initially planned before Alex's accident, with no necessity overlooked. The traitors they were, they'd been more than happy to be on their way and more importantly, out of Leandro's way.

All of her insurance matters had been assigned to a lawyer hired by Leandro for the express purpose of seeing to them. Even the mortgage on her parents' house had been refinanced and the monthly payments taken care of, aided in no small financial way by him. And her and Isabella's visas to Italy taken care of with an expediency that reeked not only of the Contis' wealth but the sheer reach of their power.

It had left Alex gasping for breath one afternoon, wondering what she had invited into her life.

Tucked away in Izzie's bedroom under the guise of packing, she had buried her head between her knees. Sought escape from the feeling of her life being taken over.

Leandro had gone far and beyond anything she'd expected of him when she'd gone to him for reassurance that Izzie would be taken care of. And yet, a small thread of anxiety persisted at the speed with which he'd had their trip arranged.

Apparently, when Leandro had decided that he was very much interested in spending the summer with his daughter, he had meant it quite seriously.

If only she could get a firm grasp on herself and her reaction to his broken engagement... But he had told her nothing about his reason.

That marriage will not suit me anymore, he'd told her with a chillingly heartless calculation. Engulfed by a barrage of unwanted emotions that had hit her, she hadn't asked him any of the questions that pestered her.

For all that her worries about Izzie and her future were calmed, at least temporarily, she still wasn't sleeping well. Much as she had fought it for four days, the crux of it haunted her thoughts.

That Leandro was unattached was what made her anxious, and restless and a thousand other things she was ashamed to admit, even to herself.

It was as if a dam that held all her less than right thoughts at bay was suddenly broken and every insidiously hungry thought and desire was free to roam now.

He was everything that had attracted her back then, a thousand times more now.

Now she knew he was also honorable, that a warmth filled his gaze when he spoke of his wife, that even as he had discarded her the next morning, it had been driven by that sense of betrayal, that family and responsibility and duty were important to him.

Even as it grated, the ease and efficiency with which he'd taken over everything, it was hard not to bask in that. Hard not to feel pleasure at being looked after like that.

Hard not to take it personally.

She didn't want to want him like this.

She didn't want to fall into this trap of imagining things between them, of falling this low as to feel some kind of relief at knowing that he was unattached now. She deserved better than to want a man who thought of her as a betrayal, who tolerated her presence for the sake of his daughter.

Fortunately for her fragmenting peace of mind, she hadn't been alone with Leandro the past few days at their home. Izzie and her parents had seen to that. And on the flight, when Izzie had fallen asleep, Alex had claimed to be tired, not falsely, and retired to the rear cabin and the inviting bed.

A couple of hours later, when he sat down on the narrow bed next to her, Alex jerked into such stringent awareness that her heart ratcheted in her chest.

The solid length of his legs next to her was alien yet alluringly comforting. Musk and something so intensely Leandro coated her every breath. Slowly, he pulled her hand into his and traced the scars.

There was nothing sexual in the touch, still, it burned through her, shaking loose some strange knot of yearning.

He wasn't a tactile person, she'd noticed. Especially when it came to her, there was something very measured, very contained about his movements.

Unable to bear the tension any longer, she turned and opened her eyes.

The softly fading light in the cabin caressed the aquiline nose, the sweepingly sharp cheekbones. Softened the austere set of his mouth. Heat from his body enveloped her, churning her senses into a frenzy.

"You shouldn't be here," she whispered with not the

least bit of anger she'd wanted in her tone. Instead, she sounded husky, weak. "It's not necessary for you to touch me when Izzie's not around."

Did she imagine the soft glint to his gaze? The reverence in his touch as he traced the veins on her wrist? "I didn't realize I was taking a liberty."

"You expect me to believe you walk around touching women you barely know?" she muttered, her nose tickling against his thigh.

"You don't agree that sharing a daughter affords us a kind of intimacy, *cara*? That it binds us as much as we fight it?"

To be bound to him in any way...just the thought set her shivering.

Warm fingers moved from her hand up her arm, kneaded one shoulder and then rested on her jaw. Moved into her hair and combed through the strands. Alex fisted her hands by her side, every inch of her vibrating.

"No," she managed. "Intimacy and friendship and all such rights have to be earned. You and I...strangers who share a daughter. That you slept with me seven years ago doesn't entitle you to anything with me now."

Suddenly, his grip tightened in her hair. Not hurting but just enough to make her scalp tingle with awareness. The rough movement forced her chin up to face him. Something feral bared in his gaze, tearing at the mask of polite civility that embodied Leandro. "Such foul language from such a beautiful mouth, *cara*?"

But it was gone as fast as it came, just as his grip gentled immediately. She didn't know what to make of that momentary fracture in his facade. "It's exactly what you said."

"As far as rights are concerned," the honeyed warmth of his tone didn't hide the steel beneath, "your well-being directly affects my daughter. That means I can interfere if I think you need help.

"You lied to me. You said you were sleeping better but I heard you. I do not like that fear, that anxiety in your tone."

Her cheek tingled where his knuckles rested. Hadn't she just told him off?

"Pity then, isn't it?" She scooted on the soft cotton to get away from him and ended up even closer to the solid muscle of his thigh. "That you can't order the panic gone, that you can't order out that stress for me in that imperious way of yours."

Now, he traced the bridge of her nose, hovered over her mouth. Her pulse raced. Lungs burned.

"You sound angry, Alexis. I have never met a woman who didn't appreciate the benefits that come with my name and wealth. Will you resent me just for solving your problems? Will you resent me because I'm more interested in Isabella than you wanted?

"Or is it that you're still attracted to me?"

"Don't...presume things about me."

"I'm not presuming your racing pulse." His thumb landed at the incriminating spot on her neck. "Or hitching breath or the fact that you're tense like a bow." Long fingers stroked over the nooks and crevices of her shoulders, back and forth until she felt as though there was steel infused in her very veins. "Or that you jump like a cat every time I come near you."

"Being attracted to you doesn't mean I'm willing. I won't be a convenient itch for you to scratch while you play at being daddy for the summer. Like I was some compensation prize after your broken engagement."

"Playing at daddy?" A thread of anger spewed in his question.

"Isn't that what you're doing?"

"I assure you no, Alexis. I intend to take care of Isabella. I intend to be a proper father. If not for me, Luca and

Tina would have suffered neglect. I don't know if I made a difference even. And I will not let that be Izzie's fate."

"She's not neglected."

"But a father is important, *si*?

"Not just for the summer either. The sooner you accept that the better. I'm not grief-stricken over my broken engagement, *cara*.

"Marriage to Sophia was a business alliance. Breaking it had consequences that I'm now prepared to handle. Family comes before business, before anything else for me."

The steely resolve in his tone sent her heart thudding against her rib cage.

He wanted to be a proper father to Izzie?

Had seeing Izzie, who was truly a mirror image of him, triggered some dormant fatherly instinct and decided the matter for him?

Hadn't she read somewhere that nature made children in the image of their fathers so that they bonded with them?

Would he feel differently once he realized how hard being a parent was? How life changed because of a little girl?

"And when you marry eventually? Can you give me the reassurance that your new wife will not resent Izzie? Can you reassure me that you won't resent her for all the changes she'll bring to your life?

"I didn't give up my social life because I like being a martyr.

"I gave it up because none of the men I met would have loved Izzie like a father should. Only Justin—"

"Look at me, Alexis." His grip turned steely against her jaw, forcing her to look at him. The muscle in his jaw jumped. Gray eyes held a stormy anger. Banked, yes, but the fire showed a Leandro she didn't recognize. "My daughter already has a father. *Me*. I will not let any man take that away from me. No other man can take that place in your life."

"You've no right to tell me that I can't have another man in my life, Leandro."

"You just told me you've never met a man who would love Izzie like his own." Frustration made his tone rise, but he wrested himself under control immediately. "We both want the same thing for Isabella. And for what we want, there are not many options left to us."

Shock coursing through every vein, Alex stared at him numbly.

What the hell did he mean by that? Did he want her to move to Italy? Was he suggesting that they live together just for Izzie's sake? Or was he—

God, no! The other alternative was outrageous to even think about.

Suddenly, all Alexis wanted was to be back in her parents' tiny house with her never-ending financial problems and the store and even her fault-finding mother.

Anywhere but here, on this luxurious flight, with this man who'd taken over her life.

That same sensation of careening out of control came at her with a vicious force. "Either you're crazy or I am, because I don't think you suggested what I think you did."

He shrugged. "With Isabella's future in mind, we will come to an agreement that suits us both."

An agreement that suited them both...

"After we land, I will be gone for a week. Will you be all right at the villa? Antonio will be around."

The thought of a reprieve from Leandro and his outrageous ideas made her shudder in relief. She could deal with a hundred Antonios better than her own weakness for this man. "Yes. Of course. I understand that you have your life and commitments."

"Being here has caused too many bottlenecks in the

company, made me realize I need to delegate more. After Rosa's death, I threw myself into work. But I don't want Izzie to feel like I'm neglecting her any longer."

"Leandro?"

"Yes, Alexis?"

"You said Rosa always wanted children and couldn't conceive."

His entire, polite demeanor faded at the mere mention of his wife's name. "Yes?"

"What about you? Did you want to be a father?"

Silence had never been so fraught or so distorted for it felt like an age to Alexis before he answered.

Her stomach twisted into a knot as if her very fate depended on his answer.

"*Si.* I was ready to be a father."

Before she could absorb that, he reached for her.

Cradled her jaw with one hand and pressed his mouth to the corner of hers. Insidious heat unfurled through every nerve. Her fingers dug into his arms, toes curled as she fought the hardest battle of her life.

To not shift and cover his mouth completely. To not throw herself headlong into the need vying for life.

Lips soft and hard at once moved against her tingling skin, sending arrows of pleasure directly to the center of her sex. "You, Alexis, *are* no consolation prize or a cheap summer fling."

This time, when his hands moved over her shoulders and down her trembling body, over her waist, and hips and back up again, long fingers grazing the sides of her breasts, there was no gentleness. No comforting or soothing.

No gentling or caring.

But bold and roving and hungrily masculine and demandingly insistent. Those large hands of his touched desperately but not enough, luring her with a promise of more with his rough strokes. An exploration of the fire that burned between them the moment they touched each other.

That sinuous mouth moved an inch and an inch over, until he covered her own completely.

Such pleasure filled her that Alex groaned loudly. The sound vibrated through her bringing a threadbare rope of caution back.

"You think I would welcome advances from you two minutes after your engagement is broken? You think I'm so eager to fall back into that pattern again?"

It was every shameful thought she'd indulged in herself, and yet, she drew strength from the fact that she called him on it.

But he didn't even budge an inch. Instead, he took over the space between them. Until their legs tangled. Until her breasts grazed his chest. Until even the thought of Izzie softly snoring on the bed in the front was driven from her head.

Only he and his stroking hands and strangely intense gaze remained. Only her awareness of him remained. Only this strange intimacy that she had denied him and yet he claimed remained.

How many times had she dreamed of a moment like this over the past seven years?

One hand under her chin, he tilted it up to face him. "In seven years, I have tried, *so hard*, to forget that night. To pretend like it never happened, *si*. But I never thought such a cheap thing of you." His sigh rattled loudly in the cabin.

The reluctance in his tone made his statement all the more powerful. Made her insides into a pool of molten craving.

"I want you, *cara*. Just as I did all those years ago," he muttered it as if it was a curse. As if he had accepted defeat. "Since the moment you walked into that lounge, guns blazing."

Feral satisfaction filled every nerve, every cell.

To hear him admit that he wanted her, despite his discipline and control, a wildness, a raw sense of power filled her. She gave in to the sheer freedom of it. Just a stolen second, she told herself, before she became a mother and a daughter and a hundred other roles again.

Tremors took hold of her entire body as he continued trailing that mouth all over her face. Nose, brow, jaw, chin—it was as if he opened little portals of pleasure.

It was as if his touch could say things he couldn't. And in sensually overwhelming contrast, his big body shuddered as he took her mouth again.

Alex felt her pulse vibrate everywhere—in her neck, her heavy breasts, her shaking knees and in the wet place between her thighs.

With his hot mouth devouring hers, Leandro slammed her against himself.

Alex climbed over him like a vine, the jut of his erection a hot press against her belly. She arched against him, looped her leg around his until she was riding his thigh.

Leandro egged her on, his fingers crawling under her silk blouse. The slap of his abrasive palm against her heated flesh, the slow exploration up her skin, her nipples distended against her cotton bra, desperate for his touch.

Alex moaned, and moved over him, mindless in her pursuit of pleasure. It was when his fingers reached the seam of her bra and pushed inside that Alex realized what she was allowing.

God, she had acted just as she said she wouldn't.

A frustrated cry fell from her lips but he didn't release her.

His forehead touched hers, his breath feathered her. Lips stinging from the raw assault of his, shame permeating her, she closed her eyes.

"Do you not see the inevitability of this, Alexis? Of

how right everything is this time between us? How easily you melt in my hands, how I could make you scream with the slightest of touches? All the intimacies you'll give, all your desires, all your needs, your every breath will be mine again.

"You will be mine."

Such arrogance reverberated in his voice should have made her furious. And yet…at the core of her, she trembled at the want in it, at the intensity in it.

No one had ever wanted her like that. No one had ever put it into words like that.

With that reply, he left without glancing at her again.

Knees shaking, her sex aching for a release that wasn't coming, Alex slid to the bed. He had everything so perfectly mapped out without even telling her.

Had he truly just switched the candidate for his wife from one woman to her? Was he that heartless? Did Leandro want a future with her, just for Izzie's sake?

And if he did, *Dear God*, what was she going to do?

CHAPTER SEVEN

IN THE PROCESS of undoing his cuffs, Leandro stilled. Sounds of splashing waves accompanied by Izzie's giggles, Luca's deep laughter, Valentina's broken English and Alexis's husky warnings...it was pure cacophony at the villa. Like he'd never heard.

The afternoon sun beating down on him, he took the steps to the veranda like an eager schoolboy.

It seemed as if the entire villa was awash in a burst of sound and activity, unlike it had ever seen.

A small bicycle with training wheels and pink streamers lay against the marble pillar. An English paperback and a pink iPod lay on the bench in the garden.

Something in him flinched at the alien sounds and sights. At the sudden absence of that dark, deep silence that he'd become used to for so long.

Only now did he realize how much the silence of the past two decades had become a part of the tall pillars, the marble floors and even their very psyches. He'd thought he had made the villa a home for all three of them. But suddenly he wasn't so sure for he had never heard such joy in the air.

The scent of jasmine felt richer, the sky felt bluer, the entire world felt as if it had transitioned from a gray, bleary morning to spring sunshine.

He closed his eyes and let his hearing amplify, let the sounds wash over him. He didn't feel peaceful as he had during his marriage with Rosa, but then he didn't expect life with Izzie to be peaceful.

He'd already accepted that life with Alexis wasn't going to be peaceful.

And yet, strangely the thought excited him more than it made him uneasy.

It had taken him a week to wrap up the most urgent of his business obligations and return to their villa. He had spoken to Izzie a few times since then but every time, Alex refused to say anything except that they were doing okay.

Had he pushed her too far too soon?

He hadn't meant to confront her like that on the flight, he hadn't meant to touch her so intimately while their daughter lay asleep so close, but again, Alexis had fragmented his careful planning.

Running a hand through his hair, he strolled out into the veranda and looked at the pool. With the background of the gleaming blue of the pool, his gaze instantly found her.

Clad in a modestly cut, pink bikini, her blond hair framing her face in damp waves, Alexis sat above with her pink toes skimming the water. A serene smile touched her features as she closed her eyes and raised her face to the sun. Luca and Tina were playing with Izzie in the pool.

Two seconds, that's all he could manage before his gaze turned back to her again.

Lush and lithe, her scantily clad body was a siren's lure. He felt as if he'd been handed a treasure and didn't know where to start or what to look at.

He devoured the dips and valleys of her breasts and waist and hips, the honeyed sheen to her skin, the thick swathes of her hair like a starving man. Or a youth who was looking at a woman's body for the first time.

His hands itched to hold those lush breasts, trace that concave plane of her stomach. He would kiss and lick and taste every inch of that silky flesh. Those long legs would wrap around him as he pushed into her...

Would she scream his name like she had done seven

years ago? Would that sheer, abandoned pleasure of it send him careening toward his own release?

Dio, he hadn't gotten hard like this at the mere sight of a woman even in puberty.

As if she could sense his lustful thoughts, her elegant neck turned this way and that. And then she looked up.

Their gazes held and clashed over the distance, a pink flush suddenly seeping up her neck and cheeks. He saw the stiffness that descended in her shoulders, the vulnerability in her mouth that in turn made her spine straighten as she realized the intentions he didn't hide in his eyes.

She read him as clearly as if he had told her what he intended to do to her and with her.

Her brown gaze widened, her palm moved over her neck in a betraying gesture and then her mouth pursed. That same gaze now flashed fire at him.

With his heart pounding, he watched as she stood up in a smooth movement, like a gazelle rising from a pond. Challenge simmered in every line of her body as she walked to the lounger, picked up a tube of sun lotion and went back the pool.

Tension a live beast roaring inside him, he waited. Instantly, he realized what she was going to do. He knew she was only doing it to provoke him, to challenge him. To drive him mad. To tell him she wasn't going to fall in line so easily.

But it didn't help quiet the acrid burn in his gut.

The husky tone of her voice reached him, a mild thread outside the roaring in his ears. On cue, Luca climbed out of the pool, said something that made her laugh and put his hands on her shoulders.

Covering her breasts with her crossed hands, Alexis turned and gave Luca her back. Hands full of sunscreen, Luca undid the thin string of her bikini top, pushed it out of his way and slathered it all over her skin.

A burst of violent emotion claimed him as he looked at them transfixed.

Those elegant, artistic hands of his brother's roamed freely over the woman that belonged to him.

Skin and sinew that Leandro wanted to touch, curves that Leandro wanted to claim, laughter that he wanted to evoke…all in Luca's hands.

Sweat beaded his brow, his entire body a taut mass of frustrated desire and rampaging fury.

He had warned Luca to stay away. Of course, his brother wouldn't listen. He knew in a rational part of his mind that Luca didn't even want her. That he would not take what was Leandro's. But he would cross any line just to rile Leandro, just to push him out of his comfort zone.

Lines that neither of them could come back from…

"She pits your brother against you." Antonio's fractured English broke the grip of his anger. "I did not like that woman seven years ago and I do not trust her now. Keep your child and get rid of her."

Leandro cringed at the reckless order. "I couldn't have asked for a better mother for Isabella." Even as he committed another betrayal toward Rosa, Leandro knew it was the truth.

Rosa had been brought up traditionally, had leaned on him for strength, had been obedient, caring. If they had had children, he knew she would have bowed to Antonio's will in their upbringing.

It would have been Leandro's battle to fight.

But Alexis was like a fierce lioness.

Even as she fought her own insecurities, Alexis didn't back down, not once when it came to Isabella. "I will not separate them and fracture my family as Enzo did. She belongs with me, just as Izzie does."

"I did not think I would see the day when you would let a woman weaken you."

Dio, the last thing he wanted was to discuss Alexis with his grandfather. "You have no idea what you're talking about."

"Are you so blinded by lust that you can't see that she's manipulating you? You think she doesn't know that you stand here like a lust-crazed fool watching your shameless brother flirt with her, put his hands on her?"

A grim smile broke Leandro's mouth. Lust-crazed he might be but he was no fool. He had been right.

Alexis wasn't one to meekly fall into his plans. That he had brought her this far was only due to her insecurities and because he was ruthless when he set his mind to something. Despite her grief about her brother, despite thinking of herself as second-rate with her parents, she'd done everything for them.

The challenge of conquering her, of bending her to his will, of making her his own sizzled in his blood now. "I do not like what she just did any more than you do, but I know why she did it."

When he was through with her, she was going to wish she hadn't started it. No, scratch that.

She was going to like everything he was going to do to her. He was going to indulge himself and her, until the thought of even challenging him and his rights with her was driven from her mind.

A derisive glint entered Antonio's eyes. "I've never seen you look at a woman like that. Not even poor Rosa. This woman is not good for you. It is obvious she's after our name."

Masking the anger that filled him so easily, *so uncharacteristically*, for his grandfather had always been a man of crude words, Leandro filled his tone with cutting ice. "Rosa and Alexis are different kinds of women. Once Alexis realizes this is for the best, once she understands what I want from this marriage, it will work just fine.

"But do not speak of her in that tone, Nonno. I will not tolerate it again."

"You would go against me for a woman who slept with you after—"

Raising his hand, Leandro cut Antonio off. Let the old man see his ire. "She will be my wife. She is the mother of my child. She is your best chance at a future Conti male heir that you're so desperate for. I suggest you afford her the respect she deserves.

"Enzo let you browbeat Mamma, but I will not allow it. Whatever our private arguments, Alexis is not to hear even one of your complaints. Not if you want to see your great-grandchildren."

Chin lifting in mutiny, his grandfather glared at him. "What about the trouble Salvatore will cause with the board? He will not take kindly to you breaking your engagement to Sophia."

"Kairos Constantinou."

"That reckless Greek magnate? That's your answer?" The combined awe and horror in Antonio's voice only confirmed Leandro's decision. The Conti board needed new blood. He was tired of being the only one who had to steer it in new directions since Luca even refused to be on the board. "You thought his investment strategies were too bold in this financial climate," Antonio continued.

"Yes but Kairos proved me wrong. An alliance between us will work well." He waited for Antonio to digest it.

Kairos had grown up on the streets of Athens, built a powerful export empire, was hungry for alliances in the Old World that still looked at him and shunned him because of his background. Leandro had exactly what Kairos wanted—the Conti name that went back hundreds of years—and Kairos had what he wanted.

For all his reckless investments and hunger for power,

there was an integrity to Kairos that Leandro liked, a strength that he needed.

Already Kairos had arrived in Italy and started working on his piece of their alliance.

The threat from Salvatore was taken care of. Valentina's future was set. If only he could settle Luca's future, too. Once his alliance with Kairos was solidified, he'd have to think of it.

All that was left was for him to marry Alexis. His world would be back on its track.

"You trained me well, Nonno. Now, trust me to handle the company and the family."

After several more minutes, finally, Antonio relented. "I do trust you, Leandro. Neither will I stop protecting you and even Luca." That he left out Valentina scraped Leandro raw but that was a battle he'd learned long ago to not fight.

No matter, because soon Valentina wouldn't care that she didn't have Conti blood in her veins.

But his grandfather was nowhere near done. "Did you know this woman you trust so implicitly has been speaking with a travel agent? That she purchased two tickets back to New York in a couple of weeks? Exactly the week during which you are scheduled to travel to the Middle East on business?"

"You're playing a treacherous game, *bella*," Luca whispered in her ear as he tied back the strings of her bikini top with an efficiency that spoke volumes. "I didn't think you were the manipulative kind, playing my brother against me."

Alex cringed. Shame made her voice thin. "I'll be sad to lose you as a friend but I did what I had to do, Luca. I have to somehow fight your brother's arrogant assumptions."

"And is it so important to fight Leandro, Alex?"

"Someone has to make him learn he can't control everything." Even now, she couldn't believe the arrogance of his words, her own weakness that she hadn't even mustered a reply. "Someone needs to cut him down to size."

His laughter instantly soothed Alex's shame. She turned and as always, the words on her mouth faltered at the masculine perfection of Luca's features.

No man should have such beauty, such perfection that everything was handed over to him on a platter. That the whole world crumbled to its knees for that smile. That no woman would look past it to the man beneath, she suddenly realized.

Yet, she had always preferred Leandro's austere, almost stark beauty to Luca's overwhelming perfection.

Unlike the forbidding man whose face had become hauntingly tight at what she had done, Luca was always touching her. He did so now, framing her face with his hand.

Wicked humor shone in his jet-black eyes. "Are they still standing there?"

Alex peeked out of the corner of her vision. The dark specter of Leandro and Antonio standing over them turned her tummy into jelly. "Yes, but Luca, I'm not interested in you," she added hurriedly.

"You wound me, Alex." Pure laughter filled his words and she exhaled roughly. "What is it that my brother possesses that I don't?"

"Less cockiness in his own beauty, like a peacock, for starters," she said, raising a brow. Laughter carved dimples in his cheeks. "Not that I'm interested in Leandro either."

A sober light filled his gaze. "Resistance is futile if he's decided that he's interested, *cara*. And having seen the fury in his eyes just now, I don't think it is in question anymore."

Alarm made her question sharp. "Is that a threat to fall in line with his wishes?"

"No, *bella*." He brought her hand to his lips and kissed it. "Just a warning from a friend. I'm sure Antonio has already informed him that you bought tickets for you and Izzie to New York. I can't let him have all the odds."

Alex stepped back from him, aghast that he knew. She had made herself crazed with anxiety, cleaved herself in two before she'd decided to buy them. But just like earlier, she needed something to calm her agitation, she needed an exit strategy whether she used them or not.

"How do you know? Damn it, how does Antonio know?"

Luca shrugged. "Doesn't matter. What matters is that you've declared war on my brother by flirting with me. By buying those tickets."

"He started it. I just armed myself."

"No one's ever called me a weapon before." He preened and pouted. "I'm not sure whether to be amused or insulted."

His mock hurt expression sent her to giggles just as it did Izzie.

"Your laughter is music, *bella*, your spirit so pure," he said a wistful note to it. The jet-black of his gaze warmed for an infinitesimal moment, showing a glimpse of desperation that caught Alex's breath. "Maybe you'll prefer me instead of Leandro?"

A stinging retort rose to her lips but Alex held it back. She didn't mistake that he was attracted to her.

No, what Luca liked was the idea of what she represented to Leandro.

Shock widened her eyes as she caught a facet of the playboy that no one probably ever saw. She smiled and kissed his cheek, immensely glad to call him a friend. "Now, I know why they call you the Conti Devil."

He offered his arm and Alex linked hers around it. They started a slow walk around the exquisitely manicured lawn.

Lush greenery dotted with Japanese trees and bouquets of bougainvillea. But through every step, and every breath, Alex was aware of the presence of Leandro behind her.

She couldn't help but notice Luca carefully kept them in view of the terrace.

"That I can make you laugh is going to drive him crazy the most."

"You think so?"

"Yes, we used to compete to try to make Valentina laugh. But Leandro, you see, never had a chance to be a carefree child, to play pranks. It drove him nuts that I always won with Tina. She was this tiny, skinny thing and took ages to trust us, to get used to us. Although, it's him she goes to when she's upset, she comes to me for laughs."

Alex frowned. "Used to you?"

Luca's carefree mouth tightened and it changed the entire vista of his face. "Valentina lived with our mother until she died. When we heard of her death, Leandro brought her to live with us. It was the first time we met each other. Until then, we did not know that we had a sister."

"Leandro brought her here, not Antonio?"

"No. Antonio had his reservations about Tina. But from the moment we learned about her, Leandro wouldn't rest."

Family means everything to me, he'd said on the flight.

"How old was he?"

"Fifteen."

With every word Luca uttered, Alex's panic mounted. It felt as though something was rushing at her at breakneck speed and she was stuck in its way. Just like the truck that had crashed into her sedan. Except this time, it was her heart that could get crushed into tiny little pieces.

One kiss…she'd shared one kiss with the man and somehow her heart had already taken a beating? How had she left herself so vulnerable to his manipulations? How did she extricate herself without harming Izzie?

"Only fifteen?" she mumbled, hoping Luca would keep talking. Even as she knew that he was manipulating her in his own way.

"*Si*. Even then Leandro was set in his ways. He argued with Antonio for days, relentless in his belief that Tina belonged with us, that she have a home with us." His jet-black gaze held hers. He took Alex's hands in his and squeezed. The comfort he offered made her spine tingle with warning. "My brother will do anything to protect those he considers his, Alex. Whatever he has done or will do, he wants the best for Izzie. And you."

"But I'm not his," she whispered back. "He can't have me because he's decided it should be so."

Suddenly, Alexis understood everything she hadn't seen until now. Chills broke out on her bare skin even as the sun warmed her.

Leandro had never intended to be a stranger to Izzie. Even before they had left, he'd known that. He had accompanied her to New York knowing that he was going to bring them back here.

He'd told her nothing, let her believe that it was a burden she'd brought on him. Let her wrangle around in her own confusion and fears.

The fury in his eyes when Justin had asked Izzie when she would return, the stony gaze when Alex had mentioned bringing another man into her and Izzie's life, everything made sense now.

Chest tight, throat raw, Alex wanted to hit something.

Fingers cold on her skin, Luca stroked her shoulders, as if to calm her. As if he understood how close to the surface her temper was. "Should I tell you what else I think he's saying to Antonio, Alex?"

Forehead resting on his shoulder, for Alex felt as weak with emotion as a leaf that could be swayed by the wind, she nodded.

"I'm sure he warned Antonio to never disrespect you again. That he will banish him from his life if he ever hears him say so."

Tears knocked at her eyelids and Alex held them at bay with her last thread of will. "You've no idea what you're asking me to overlook just because he means well."

Her insecurity with her parents.

Her weakness after the accident.

Her fear that she might fail Izzie too…as she'd failed at everything else.

Leandro had learned all her fears and insecurities, while she had thought him genuinely caring, and he'd taken each one and used it all against her.

He'd caged her with good intentions and her own need to do the right thing by everyone around her.

"I know what my brother could do in his drive to do his duty. Just give him a chance, Alex. See if he's worthy of you. Do not let pride stand in your way. If you find not, I'll personally help you in your fight against him."

"And will there be a fight, Luca?"

"If you take Izzie and walk away from him? If you deprive Izzie of her own father because Leandro has his own way of doing things, because he's the most arrogant, domineering brute in the whole world?" Luca's laugh was harsh, filled with his own complaints against his brother. "Yes, *bella*." He sounded full of regret at the very prospect. "It would be a sad day if two of the most deserving people I know start tearing into each other with a child in between."

With Luca's dire-sounding prospect still ringing in her ears, Alex returned to her suite. Mind churning, she helped Izzie bathe and then picked at some fruit and olives and sipped her cold white wine. Restless to her very bones, she weaved a path through the lakefront sitting room that her suite afforded.

The vista stole her breath as it did every morning.

Luminous and blue with boats drifting lazily up and down, tiny villages glinting in the sunlight, it was a far cry from her life in Brooklyn.

But with Leandro manipulating and directing their relationship whichever way he wanted, using her own weakness against her, Alex knew the same vista, the same idyllic villa could become a gilded cage. Could choke her spirit even worse than her parents' blueprint for a perfect child had done all these years.

Finally, she called Emma.

Within minutes, she was spewing the whole sorry story into the handset, angry and outraged. And more than anything, she realized, hurt.

Had his desire for her been a pretense, too? A convenient lie to bind herself to his side? She had already betrayed how much that night seven years ago had meant to her, hadn't she? She had told him all about how curtailed her life had been after having Izzie.

The sense of betrayal was deepest in this, as if he'd taken the very thing she had handed him and carved into her.

Forget Leandro's manipulations, do you want him, Alex? Do you think he's worth taking a chance on?

Forget your house, your store, your parents and even Izzie. Think of yourself before you make a decision because this is your life.

Emma's brutally incisive questions were still racking her brain when a maid knocked at her door.

Shell-shocked and confused still, Alex mutely took the two expensive bags with designer labels.

Only when Izzie excitedly opened the bag and a beautiful, silky pink dress slipped out did she remember the party tonight.

An informal get-together of their extended family and closest friends so that they could meet Izzie, Tina had informed her last night. With shaking hands, Alex opened the velvet case.

The clipped sound of the tiny latch unhooking on the case moved through her like lightning blazed through the sky.

A delicately spun choker of diamonds set in white gold and matching earrings nestled on the navy blue velvet bed, glittering brightly in the sunlight that shafted through the windows.

Diamonds for the strongest woman I know, the curly script read.

A tingling began in her chest as she read it over and over again. Even the glittering diamonds paled in contrast to the words that moved through her like thunder and lightning.

If he'd said beautiful or smart, she would have wrote it off as another manipulation.

But calling her strong, the one thing she prided herself on, the one thing she had forced herself to be through Adrian's death and her parents' disappointment and having Izzie and her accident, it was as if he had shot an arrow direct to her heart.

As if he truly understood her.

As if he truly saw her and cherished her.

She'd been an open book to him. There was still every chance that he was manipulating her.

With his handwritten note fluttering in her hand, Alex sat on the cool tiled floor and closed her eyes.

Emma was right. With the accident and the store and Izzie and her parents' continual disappointment in her, she had forgotten something important. With or without Leandro's help, she would never do wrong by Izzie.

She loved her little girl more than anything in life.

The simple acknowledgement freed her to breathe, made her heart lighter.

For the first time in years, Alex focused on herself. On

her wants and desires. That her mind instantly fluttered to Leandro's kiss only made her smile. Her fingers rose to her lips. She could still feel his mouth on her, the insistent demand in it, the growl that had escaped him when she had tangled her tongue with his.

The way his powerful body had shuddered in supplication when she bit his lower lip, the way he had buried his mouth in her neck and whispered in Italian...

There had been no manipulation in the languid strokes of his mouth, in his desperate caresses, in those urgent whispers.

He could dress it up as duty or the right thing for Izzie or a hundred other things, but the fact was that Leandro wanted her desperately. For a man who prided himself on living by his rules and not emotions, by his duty and not desire, it was huge.

And she wanted him, she wanted to explore the heat between them, she wanted to tell him her secrets and learn his.

Was it enough to begin a relationship with?

Attraction to her and unconditional love for Izzie—could she even ask for more as a start?

Decision made, Alexis unwrapped the paper tissue around the pink dress, the whisper of its silky folds a song to her ears. Held it against herself and looked in the full-length mirror.

She would do this. She would have a relationship with Leandro, see where it took them, but it would be on her terms.

She would own her desire for him, and she would make him own that he wanted her in his life. And not for Izzie's sake or duty's sake or honor's sake.

But because he wanted her. She would have what he owed her this time, even if she had to seduce the truth out of him.

Funny that he'd armed her himself with that dress and those diamonds. He'd given her time, security and the belief that she owed it to herself to enjoy her life, even if he'd done to manipulate her.

Plugging her iPod into the speaker system, Alex turned up the volume on a Lady Gaga song and danced around with Izzie, excitement pulsing through her.

Leandro needed to learn that Alex could wrench away his control as surely as he did hers.

That this time around, Alex wouldn't settle for anything less than what she wanted.

CHAPTER EIGHT

LEANDRO MOVED THROUGH the perfectly manicured gardens and among his family and friends like a pale imitation of himself. No, an agitated, less-than-together version of himself.

The same scent of hydrangeas and jasmine that had calmed him so many times, the stone and marble villa that he had somehow wrested into a home for him, Luca and Valentina now mocked him and his very image of himself.

The disgusting and disconcerting fact was that he had rushed to her bedroom two seconds after Antonio's self-satisfied whisper about her plans. Anger and disbelief and a rope of unease had held him in its grip as he raised his hand and clutched the gleaming chrome door handle.

In a flicker of a moment, from one breath to the next, he had realized what he had been about to do.

Izzie's laughter from within the suite mocked him, scraped him.

He'd been exactly like Enzo had been so many times in one of his violent tempers.

He wouldn't have hit Alex like Enzo had done with his *mamma* that one time or spewed vitriol or called her horrible names. He knew that much. Yet that he had become so angry, so unknowing of where he was going or what he was about to do...so afraid of losing something he hadn't realized he needed.

But Leandro had never needed anything or anyone. His success with the company and being a responsible guardian to his brother and sister, they had all been driven by the needs of others.

The reminder of his father had been like a naked dip in the freezing lake that Luca had challenged him to in one of those rare moments of childhood they had enjoyed.

How had Alexis gotten under his skin? What was it about her that made him react with such violence of emotion? Why this hunger to claim her as his?

Until now, he had avoided the crowd, needing to cool his temper before he saw her. Or his brother who'd worn a smirking grin all evening as they met several of their cousins and aunts.

It was only years of meticulous habit that he now noticed the uniformed waiters and flowing champagne and Conti family members that came crawling out to see Isabella. And Alexis, of course, just like she had expected.

Because they all wanted to see the woman that had made him fall from his pedestal. They expected a stunning woman armed to the teeth with wiles and cunning. They would form a line to see his weakness, his...

But something inside him balked at calling her a weakness anymore.

With her simplicity and straightforwardness, Alexis would be a shock to all of them. She'd probably dress in a garish tank top and shorts just to insult him and his family.

He had no doubt that she would shred that dress into pieces, throw that diamond choker he'd selected himself in the rubbish bin.

"Papà...you're back." He heard Isabella's squeal behind him.

His mouth instantly curving, he turned and saw her on the marble steps. Reaching her, he picked her up while she vined those chubby arms around his neck and held him tight. Kissed him soundly on his cheek. He stayed there, suddenly realizing how much he had missed Isabella's incessant chatter in the past week. The sweet scent of her made his throat close up as it always did.

Dio, he had come so close to not knowing her...

"Did you miss me, *piccola*?"

She considered the question and he laughed again. "I had so much fun with Uncle Luca and *Zia* so not a lot, Papà." As if to mollify him, she bent closer and whispered, "You wanna know a secret?"

"*Si.* Your uncle and aunt always hide the best ones from me."

"I peeked at Mamma's special folder yesterday when she was showering."

"Mamma's special folder?" he repeated, some sleek black diary with lots of phone numbers of men she knew instantly coming to mind.

When had he become so inventively distrustful? When had every small facet of Alexis's life become this important to him?

All their lives, Antonio had in turn hated and loved Luca because he was the image of their father.

Right down to his creative pursuits and genius thinking and his looks.

Because he, like Enzo had done at a horrible price to all of them, lived so recklessly and without a direction. That he partied and drank and chased women indiscriminately.

But Luca, as far as Leandro knew, never lost it like he had this afternoon.

Luca, for all he slept with every willing woman, would never touch one in anger or distress.

Suddenly, it felt as if Leandro was the one who had inherited all of his father's disgusting traits—distrust, this sudden temper, this unease as if he was losing control of himself.

The very thought made him cold to his bones. Made him want to ship Alexis back to New York on the next

flight before she revealed sides of him he didn't want
to face.

"She has a big shelf full of those binders but she brang
only—"

"Brought," he corrected as he had seen Alexis do.

"Brought only a few here. She used to draw and write a
lot in them before the accident. Now she just opens them
and looks at them." Sadness tinged those gray eyes of hers
that were so much like his own. "Last week she thought
I was sleeping. But I wasn't and I think…she cried when
she opened them."

Alexis had been crying?

The image twisted his gut.

Izzie hugged him tighter and he knew the thought of
Alexis's tears scared her. "Papà will take care of Mamma,
Izzie. She'll never cry again, *si*?"

"*Si*," she replied, her smile wide, her eyes full of pride.

"These folders, what do they have in them, *piccola*?"
he asked, refusing to feel even a little guilt for using his
daughter as his cohort.

If there was something he could do to take away that
sadness from Alexis, he had to know.

"Lots of pictures and stories, Papà. Sometimes, she
reads them to me. But not much since her car crashed."

"Why not?"

With the attention of a gnat, Izzie tuned out his question. "Did you see these?" she added, raising her legs upward.

"New frock, *bambina*?" he inquired with the utmost affected interest while his gaze moved upward toward Alexis's bedroom.

Anxiety and something else thrummed through his
veins.

Isabella sighed that world-weary sigh of hers that made
his heart squeeze every time. That made his chest feel too

small for the laughter that roared through him. He did so now while she watched him with a bemused glance.

For his precious six-year-old, it seemed he was not only ancient but also completely out of touch with the modern world she lived in. Like how he was supposed to be buying gadgets and not stick-thin dolls for her. She was forever telling him off for not being savvy enough like Luca. Or for not installing some candy jewel game on his mobile phone.

Apparently, Leandro wasn't hip enough for his daughter. Did Alexis think so, too?

Did she wish he could flirt and charm and do all these fun things like Luca did? Did she truly prefer someone fun-loving and adventurous like Luca to him?

Her husky laughter from this afternoon with Luca played along his nerves like some jarring symphony.

Dio mio, what was she reducing him to?

"Of course I had to wear a new frock to meet all my new family," Isabella said with exaggerated patience. "It's my new pumps." She wiggled her toes again. "*Zio* Luca... *designed* Conti pumps, just for me." Pride rang through her voice, as if she understood the centuries-old legacy.

She barely let him glance at the shiny black leather before she started off again. "Although Mamma says I shouldn't expect new toys and games all the time just because you're stinking rich. Does Italian money stink, Papà?" she then asked innocently.

Laughter barreled out of his chest. His entire body shook with the impact of it and he sank to the steps with Izzie in his arms while his extended family and his closest friends stared at him as if he had grown horns.

Luca and Valentina strolled close and stood stunned, their hearts in their eyes, as if they'd never seen him laughing like that.

Had he ever? Had they been deprived of so much despite his best efforts?

While his little girl went on in that incessant way of hers. "She says it'll make me..." She scrunched her face again and by this time, Leandro was choking with laughter and tears. "... Arrogant and domi...dominairing like some people she knows."

Even Luca and Tina had joined his laughter now.

"I asked what that meant and she said I should ask you. She said you'd know best."

Leandro didn't have a memory of ever laughing like this. Of ever feeling this carefree, of this rightness in his world.

Magpie-like, Izzie went on while a sudden hush fell around the crowd that had moved toward the steps.

Leandro pushed to his feet. He put Izzie down when she wiggled.

Alexis stood at the top of the steps, a vision in the dark pink silk.

Whispers buzzed around him while his family took stock of her but she had eyes for only him.

Leandro felt like a charge of electricity had hit him straight from the sky and held him rooted to the ground.

As if he had waited all his life for this moment where he could feast on Alexis.

There was shock and disbelief and, above all, that sense of wonder, as if he'd been given a gift.

What did it mean that she had worn the dress and jewelry he had sent her? Would she ever act as he expected?

But suddenly he realized there was such profound pleasure in the unexpected with Alexis.

Her strawberry blond hair fell in lustrous waves around her shoulders, framing her distinctive features. And the scar she wore so bravely only made her even more beautiful for him.

The diamond choker he had specially commissioned for her glittered around her swan-like neck.

Slinky straps exposed tanned shoulders while the ruched neckline hinted barely at her cleavage. The silky fabric fell to her ankles molding her long legs.

Shoulders squared, hair gleaming bright, she came down the steps. Only then did he see the thigh-length slit. One toned thigh and a shapely calf winked at him.

Like an engulfing wave, want came at him, drenching him from head to toe. Blood pounded. Instinct roared. Muscles thrummed.

Challenge oozed out of every pore on that sensual body of hers. His mouth dried. And he was hard like stone.

If she meant to prance around all evening in the dress and diamonds that he had bought for her, if this was her idea of Look But Don't Touch, her idea of Privileges Revoked, then Leandro had to hand it to her.

She had devised the perfect form of revenge for his sins against her. She had also somehow taken the sails out of his anger, shaken loose the dread in his gut that she would flee one night with Izzie in hand, just because he had manipulated the truth for his purposes.

That he would wake up one day and not find her there, like he hadn't seen his mother one summer morning. That he would lose this thing, too, one of the most joyous things that had come into his life, like everything had gone before.

Because to be a father to Izzie without Alexis as his wife was just not enough anymore. And not just for Izzie's sake.

For all she bought those tickets, Alexis wouldn't flee in the night. She wouldn't leave without a fight, at least. She was not weak or cowardly.

He was no more Enzo than Alexis was his mother.

History would not repeat in his marriage, in this villa again, he told himself.

It was her way of wresting control of the situation, her way of coping when he had all but taken everything familiar away from her.

He understood her. And *Dio*, he really hoped she would understand, soon, why he had done what he had done. Or else, relief for his ever-present erection was never going to come.

Finally, she halted on the last step right in front of him. It brought her face-to-face with him. The subtle scent of her body teased him, the warmth from her body taunted.

Words came and floated away from his lips, inadequate and much too revealing of emotions he didn't understand himself. "Arrogant and domineering, *bella*? If we're going to coach her to take sides, then the war is truly on, Alexis."

She raised a brow while her eyes glittered like precious stones. "Just teaching our daughter some important facts of life, Leandro. You wouldn't want either of us to get used to this lifestyle and expect diamonds and tiaras for every little occasion now, would you? Even you couldn't buy your way out of everything. Not with the number of things I'm going to have to forgive you for."

Our daughter, she had said.

Was she going to accept what he planned for them? Or was she still going to challenge him at every turn?

He touched her then, as inevitable as his next breath. He lifted her hand and pressed his mouth to her wrist. Felt her tremble beneath his lips. Imagined trailing them over every inch of her.

Slowly, with excruciating reluctance, he returned her hand to her side.

"I would say we were even after that display at the pool this afternoon, no?"

He settled his arm around her waist and nudged her forward. She noted his possessive gesture with a raised brow but didn't say anything. "Not even close. And are you so sure it was a display?"

"Yes." He clasped her arm and pulled her to him. "A cheap ploy, too."

A hint of tease turned her voice molten. "This from the master manipulator? The control freak? The man who let me believe his daughter was a burden, a hurdle in the way of his new happiness?"

While each and every one of his guests watched with a kind of twisted fascination, she cradled his jaw and looked up at him.

As if she owned him. As if she had every right to his body and even his thoughts. As if she had shed all those insecurities and fears and become this bold, stunning creature who owned her every desire.

Heart pounding, Leandro stared at her, his hands fisting at his side. His first instinct was to shove her hand and walk away. He'd never been one for public displays of any kind. *Dio*, he hadn't even danced with Rosa in the public, or touched her this way.

He had never wanted to.

"I'm an old-fashioned man, *cara*," he warned her but it didn't carry any real threat. He sounded husky, rough. "I'll always do what I think is right." That was as far an explanation as he was willing to offer.

She traced his jawline, and then smoothed out the frown on his forehead.

Leandro held himself still, somehow. The sensation of surrendering to her touch and her words was alien yet exhilarating. "Then I'll do whatever I have to do to ensure you do not ruin any chance we have of this working. For once, I'm going to be the one in charge, Leandro, the one who'll protect this relationship. Can you handle that?"

Something danced in her eyes and he realized she understood him far better than anyone had ever done. He had done everything he could do to bring her here, to stake his claim and now she was doing the same.

Slowly the thought of denying her faded away, and stinging need rose in its place. Every other part of him waited in anticipation for her bold touch, for her daring strokes.

Cristo, would this woman ever stop surprising him? Was there any version of her that wouldn't torment and tease him?

Could there be so much fun in relinquishing control?

It both thrilled and haunted him—how much he wanted to give up the reins of their relationship to her.

"I've decided to let you make it up to me for everything you didn't tell me. But no more dresses and extravagant gifts, Leandro. You don't want to confirm your grandfather's belief that I'm for sale, do you?"

He didn't know why he couldn't suddenly tell her the truth or why with her, he acted first and then tried to rationalize his behavior to himself. Seven years ago and now. "You were right in that my family and friends here tonight will dissect every tiny detail about you and Isabella. One of them will speak to the press and there will be a furor about the Conti legacy as there is every ten years.

"I knew you wouldn't want to give them anything more to talk about."

"Meaning my usual clothes would give them something to talk about?"

"Si."

Fire flashed in her eyes. And beneath that a deep vulnerability that he would have given anything to heal. This constant battle to protect the core of what made her *her* versus the desire to use it to bind her to him, it was slowly eroding him from within. "So you're ashamed of me then?"

"No. I'm protective of you, Alexis."

She moved her hands over the diamonds, the dress, her left hand slower than the right. "So this was all to make sure there was no cheap talk about me or Izzie?"

"*Si.*"

"And the note? Was that to shore up my armor against all these people, too? To build up my confidence so that I didn't falter here tonight and humiliate you? Should I make sure I don't talk much so that I don't disappoint their image of the great Leandro Conti?"

"*Si.*"

Her head jerked as if he had slapped her, looked away and then met his gaze again with a wounded defiance. Suddenly, he felt like the lowest of low. "*Dear God,* is there anything real about you? Is there a single word or thought that comes from your heart? Do you possess one, Leandro? Or has it turned into a black lump and rotted?"

"No, Alexis." He clasped her arm before she could turn away. "Hear me. I wrote it because I thought you needed to hear it, *si*, that you needed the courage to face this crowd. But, *cara*, I also wrote it because it's the truth.

"Because it's something you should be told again and again."

Something glittered in her gaze then.

She bent toward him so suddenly that his thoughts scattered. His nostrils flared with the subtle scent of her skin and soap. "If you want this thing to work between us, if you want me to give this a chance, I need more, Leandro.

"I need more than duty and Izzie's welfare and family values. I need more than glittering jewels and designer labels and manipulative words.

"Even struggling at everything I tried, I've been a good daughter and a mom. And I always will be. With you or without you. Just Izzie's happiness is not enough for this to work.

"In this thing between us, I need to be just me, just

Alexis who's attracted to you. Who's just a little bit crazy about you. Who wants you more than she wants the next breath of air.

"So *damn it*, Leandro, give me something. Give me something that's free of your manipulation, of your duty, of what you think I need. Give me something of yourself. Or we end before we begin and it's Izzie who'll suffer."

Awash in such pure desire, eddied around by such sharp heat, Leandro was captivated by her. Drank in the unflinching honesty in her eyes, of the way she held his gaze even as her mouth trembled.

And something inside him unraveled at the stark, unabashed courage in her words.

"Pink." The word came out of him as if it was wrenched from the depths of his being, as if it was chipped off a concrete wall around his heart leaving a thundering crack behind.

"Pink?" she said then, frowning, the confidence in her eyes flickering.

He couldn't take it anymore. He couldn't stand that feeling of being ripped open with his emotions bare. He needed her taste, her scent to wash away that feeling of being stripped of his control.

So he took her mouth with a voracious greed, with little finesse. His teeth scraped against her lips as he forced her to open to him. Just as he had forced her to accept him into her life.

If there was a different way, Leandro admitted, with a sinking feeling, he didn't know how.

But Alexis opened her mouth, *Dio mio*, it was pure heaven.

Nothing existed but the sweetness of her mouth, the current of need building up inside him. The press and fit of their bodies as if they were designed for each other.

Even the thought of his friends and family seeing him

like this, undisciplined and hungry for a woman, didn't stall his raking hunger.

She fisted his shirt in her hands, her soft groan music to his famished senses. "Leandro, no, tell me—"

He tugged her lower lip with his teeth and growled. "I bought this cursed dress because it was pink. Because I remember your fixation with everything pink. Because I knew you would like it. Because I wanted the sheer pleasure of seeing you in it, because I wanted to see your pleasure in it.

"I saw it almost a month ago in a catalog on my desk, before you even came back into my life and thought of you. And this past week, I couldn't stop thinking about it, so like a schoolboy who wants to impress the girl he likes, I hunted it down to the designer store. I explained to them what it looked like, I described your size and I waited for two hours while they flew it down here from a different store in Rome.

"I have never, in my life, gone to such lengths to buy a small thing like that.

"Is that bit of madness enough for you, Alexis?"

And because he couldn't bear to see his own reflection in her eyes, because he couldn't pretend like he hadn't heard the desperation in his voice, he turned away.

Still, she stopped him. Kissed his cheek boldly. Demanded that he hold her gaze. "*Grazie*, Leandro," she said, warmth in her tone.

Why couldn't she fight him and call him a hateful man for manipulating her, for taking advantage of her situation? What courage did she possess to give of herself this way, to wrench parts of him he didn't want to give?

Such joy glittered in that brown gaze that for the first time in his life, Leandro felt truly out of his element. Her taste on his lips, her scent on his skin, that curve of her mouth, the warmth in her gaze, suddenly they were the most terrifying things he had ever beheld. Because they were both a tremendous gift and an almost unbearable burden.

For he knew now that he wasn't enough to hold those intact, knew how easily he could shatter it *and her* and then…and then he had a feeling his entire world would collapse along with it.

And he wanted neither this power nor this vulnerability that Alexis brought into his life.

CHAPTER NINE

ALEXIS'S HEART POUNDED, every sense felt amplified a thousand times as she paced the length of her room.

She hadn't been this anxious even seven years ago when she'd been naive and Leandro had been the reckless fantasy she'd indulged in.

He was still an unattainable fantasy come true but now she understood the man, what made him so irresistible to her and even better, she understood herself.

All through the long, unendurable evening, she'd been aware of Leandro's every word, every movement, of the possessive light in his gaze and his touch. It was as if there was a current that tugged and tossed them even with other people around.

And, yet, somehow, he had also been her anchor in a sea of unfamiliarity.

Every time someone had blatantly wondered at how she'd landed his interest despite her lack of high connections or illustrious career, he'd batted them away with that arrogance. Threw out casually that it was his stars that had aligned finally that Alexis had come back into his life.

That moment had stretched infinitely, Alex's heart in her throat at the genuine sentiment in his words.

Soon, with Tina's help, Alex had separated the covetous from the caring ones, the superficial hangers-on from sure but curious friends of the family. And if Tina was distracted, there was Luca.

Tears had filled her eyes at how his family soon embraced her, and Alex knew it was from Leandro that they took their cue.

So strange that she'd received what she had always craved for, from the man who manipulated her into accepting it.

Now, it was past midnight and Izzie was out for the night after thoroughly enjoying being the center of attention. And she knew Leandro would be here any second.

She had all but issued an invitation. But acting the confident aggressor who wouldn't back down was easy when it was all words and safe kisses. When they were surrounded by a hundred other people.

Now, now she trod a path on the thick carpet, her nerves stretched to the hilt. She was wondering if she should just change into her pajamas and wait for him or remain in her dress and brazenly go to him when she heard the door open.

Nape prickling, chest tight with ache, she turned.

Leandro stood leaning against the door just like he had that first night. His jacket was discarded, hair rumpled. But this time, there was no fury, no distrust, no inscrutability. There was only a fire and she knew he was going to set her aflame tonight, demand everything she had to give, bend her will to his.

Just because she'd demanded he give her a tiny part of him.

"Am I allowed in here, Alexis?" Stark longing pinched those features, making him look sharper, harsher. "Have I paid the toll to be in your room?"

She stared at him, heart in her throat. A dangerous light glinted in his eyes as he pushed off the door. Tension swathed the room. "Toll, Leandro?" Unease fluttered through her gut, knotting it until fierce anger came to her aid. "Is that how you still see this? After everything I've said to you, will you still call this some sort of trade between us?"

He shrugged and approached her, something predatory in his very gait. "I'm trying to understand if I've paid enough to touch you, to be inside you."

Alex wanted to howl and rage and scratch that arrogance off his face. Wanted to throw those hurtful words back at him. She wanted to take Izzie and walk right out of his life. She wanted to—

No, she wouldn't give up this easily. There had been such vulnerability, such desperation in his tone when he had told her about that dress. She pressed her hand to her stomach, felt the silk under her hand and slowly, a thread of her courage, her determination returned.

He couldn't stand needing her like this, couldn't bear that she'd ripped that invulnerability he believed he possessed. So she played his game and dared him. "I want this as much as you do."

His head jerked toward her, his gaze drinking her in. "Izzie won't wake up again tonight, will she?"

Without waiting for her answer, he crossed to the connecting door, looked through it and then locked it.

The sound of the latch clicking magnified in the fraught silence. Turning around, he undid the cuffs of his shirt and pushed them back. Long fingers moved to the buttons on his white shirt then. With a casualness that only betrayed his need to be in control, he unbuttoned it all the way, pulled it out of his trousers and shrugged it off.

Alexis's pulse raced, pounded.

The shirt slithered to the ground soundlessly while moonlight bathed olive-gold skin stretched taut over contoured muscles. A smattering of hair covered his chest, a line of it disappearing down his taut abdomen. Her chest fell and rose at the evidence of his arousal.

Possessiveness streamed through Alex. She wanted to touch him and stroke him and see more of what he hid beneath that facade. She wanted all of Leandro.

"Come here then, *cara*." He pushed off the door and her entire body vibrated as if in tune to him. "Let us see how good our understanding is with each other, how many liberties you'll allow me before you stop me."

"Do you think you can scare me away with those words?" He was the only man she'd ever wanted this intimate pleasure with. The only one who'd made her believe she was bold enough, worthy enough for everything. "You think this is a punishment?"

He reached her and pulled her to him. Pressed a kiss to the back of her hand. His tongue flicked the veins on her wrist. Waves of heat engulfed her as he trailed that wicked mouth up her arm.

Everywhere he touched, pleasure burst forth.

He was as much as prisoner to this fire between them as she was.

Like a mass of clay waiting to be molded by a master sculptor, she went willingly into his hands, gave herself over with complete trust.

"You're a little scared, *tesoro*. Admit it."

She laughed as he turned her around. "No, Leandro. I trust you implicitly."

She heard his heated hiss before he licked the sensitive curve of her neck.

Her knees bumped the high bed and to her back stood Leandro. Their bare feet touched, the buckle of his belt dug into her backbone. His wide shoulders framed hers. Every inch of his rock-hard body imprinted against her shuddering muscles.

Hands on her hips, he kneaded her muscles, stroked them up and down her sides, grazing the sides of her breasts with his palms. Currents swept downward as her nipples tightened, turned into knots of need with a direct connection to the pulse between her legs.

But he didn't touch her where she wanted even as his mouth kissed her back, licking and nipping.

She arched and slammed back into him as his teeth dug into a spot on her shoulder. His erection nestled against her buttocks and lengthened, erotic heat spewing into her muscles. Alex burned to the tips of her fingers, wanting to touch that rigid length.

Her mouth dried with anticipation, of feeling that velvet heat pound through her aching sex.

She heard his curse and rough rasp in Italian when she ground herself against him wantonly. There was no fear when it was this man. No shame in this need that only he fueled within her.

"Should I take you like this, Alexis?" Something she had never associated with Leandro, a feral rawness, a wild heat reverberated in his voice. "Should I bend you over and sheath myself in you, *cara*? I have fantasized about it, I have spilled into my own hands like a schoolboy imagining you like this, *bella*. Should I possess you like I have never taken another woman? That's what you want of me, *si*?

"You want what I've never given anyone else. You want what I don't have to give."

"Yes. I want your darkest fantasy, Leandro."

Reaching behind, Alex plunged her hands in his hair. Reduced the distance between them even more. Her breasts pouted in the air, desperate for his touch. "So stop testing me and tormenting yourself, Leandro."

Her heart pounded in utter contrast to the insouciance in her tone. To take her like that, he meant to deny her the pleasure of touching him, the pleasure of making love to him. He meant to strip this intimacy of tenderness. But if this was what he needed to learn that she wouldn't break, then so be it. "Whatever you want, do it soon. It's been seven long years since anyone touched me. Seven years since I've known this pleasure…and God, I need it more than I need air right now."

Sulky and demanding and utterly sensuous, she couldn't believe that was her.

But unlike him, Alexis reveled in the current that thrummed through her, in this feeling of being so sharply attuned to another person.

"You have not been with another man." His shock and disbelief coated the air.

"I've never wanted another man like I want you. Then or now," she said simply. "Do you still not get it, Leandro? You make me want to risk everything. You make me want to live."

Something reverent fell from his lips as he held her tight against him.

She felt the breezy air from the windows on her puckering nipples and bare flesh before she heard the rip of the silk. "Wait, no…" she cried but already the silk was pooling at her feet.

Breath crashing over her, she shuddered, told herself it didn't matter. The dress might be beyond repair but what it represented was enough for her.

One finger traced the ridge of her spine as he whispered at her ears. "I will buy you a thousand dresses, Alexis," gravel-rough, his voice was a sultry caress just on its own, "and then rip them all off you. By the time I'm through with you, you won't even think of another man, much less ask him to put his hands on you."

With that heated promise, he moved his hands around and cupped her breasts. Rough and abrasive, the sensation was beyond erotic. Alex moaned and pushed herself into those hands. His fingers pinched the needy nubs, sending arrows of wet heat to her sex. "Please…" she moaned, trying to turn in his arms, needing more desperately. Thighs trembled, knees shook as his touch became rougher, her nipples turning into turgid points of pleasure and pain.

But he didn't let her turn. "Please what…Alexis? Should I stop? Is this too much for you to bear?"

"Not enough," she groaned. For the life of her, she couldn't stop begging.

"Should I take these lovely breasts in my mouth, *cara*? Should I tangle my tongue on these tight buds and suckle? Should I use my teeth on them?"

"Yes, please, God, yes," she muttered, quaking from head to toe.

"Maybe if you please me, *bella*," he offered, his words full of retribution and Alex wanted to kill him right there.

He moved his hand down the concave plane of her stomach, pushed his fingers into her thong. Deliberate and torturous, he traced the crease of her folds with exquisite pressure.

Breath was fire in her throat. "Damn it, Leandro… Will you kill me?"

His delicious laughter played along her very nerves. And then he flicked the swollen bundle screaming for his attention.

Alex jerked as he rubbed it between his forefinger and thumb, a groan clawing its way out of her throat. Fever took over her lower body and she rocked herself against his fingers instinctively.

Threw her head back against him and whimpered as pleasure edged closer but still remained elusive.

"Widen your legs for me, *bella*," he commanded.

Thighs trembling, she did.

She had no mind of her own, no will of her own. She would have gone down on her knees and tasted him if he willed it of her in that moment.

Her thong out of the way, his fingers found her aching sex again. "*Dio*, you're so wet for me. So hot for me. Raise your knee," he asked again and when she did, he plunged first one and then another finger into her wet core.

His other hand stroked her bare buttocks, moved up and down her spine.

Fire. Need. Desire. She had everything and nothing.

Alex became a mass of a million different sensations as he stroked in and out and his thumb pressed on her clitoris.

Fine droplets of sweat beaded all over, her own skin was a prison. Whorls of pleasure gathered in momentum and intensity, threatening to break her into a thousand pieces if relief didn't come soon. The world narrowed to her sensitive flesh and his fingers and the blinding pleasure of both.

Throat dried. Nerves screamed.

"Come for me, *mia cara*," he persuaded her, rough and husky and bit down on her shoulder.

Tension corkscrewed through her belly and tightened and tightened until her climax beat down on her in relentless waves. Alex threw her head back against his shoulder and let out a deep keening cry that sounded erotic to her own ears. Her pelvic muscles contracted, released, spasmed, still his fingers stroked her. On and on it went until she didn't know where or what she was. Until she was only fragments of sensation and pleasure.

She fell against him, only upright because he was holding her.

His hands moved the damp swathe of her hair from her neck and he flicked her skin with his tongue, whispering soothing words as if she was a distraught filly. "*Dio*, you come like thunder streaks the sky, you taste like lightning in the air..." She felt his shudder at her back, the rigid press of his erection against her butt. "I never stood a chance against you, *bella*."

The desperate hunger in his tone woke Alex from the stupor of her pleasure.

Determined to have whatever he gave her, swallowing

down her self-consciousness, Alex anchored herself on the arm around her midriff, and started to bend forward.

Instantly, he stiffened around her, stopping her from moving. "Leandro?"

Whatever his dark threat, whatever he'd forced himself to say, to consider, whatever strategy he employed to keep Alexis in her place and his roiling emotions in theirs, Leandro knew he failed.

That she'd undone him.

He already felt as if he'd cheated himself of the sight of her unraveling, of seeing those gorgeous eyes widen and flash in pleasure, of that sensuous mouth softening. Of being drenched in the passion of her cry.

So before the tremors of her orgasm had subsided, even before she had caught her breath, he turned her around, desperate to see her.

She hung on to him like a limpid doll, eyelids drooping down, pink flush staining her cheeks and damp neck, her naked body bowed in the aftermath of her release.

High and pouty, her breasts were a languid invitation, the flare of her hips, the lithe length of her thighs a sensual feast.

Desire and tenderness and every emotion he'd never experienced buffeted him from all sides. How had he even assumed he could separate sex and emotion, especially when it was Alexis?

How could he be in control when she eroded it so easily? How could he hold himself back when she stole all of him by giving everything of hers?

Hands on her hips, he lifted her onto the bed. He shed his trousers and boxers and climbed up over her.

Feasted his gaze all over her damp, trembling body.

Doe-like eyes fluttered open and then widened slightly. "I can see you," she said with a smile. "And touch you. I've had dreamed so many times of stroking my hands over you, of learning every inch of you. Of seeing your eyes widen in desperate need. Of you smiling at me, of knowing that you revel in this attraction between us as much as I do."

"I do, *bella*," he admitted hoarsely. He bent his head and surrendered to this woman. "Touch me, Alexis. All you want."

Pushing herself onto her elbow, she reached out instantly. Fingers fell on his shoulders and fluttered down his collarbone.

Feather-soft caresses that burned him. Light strokes that learned him.

Traced the ridge of his chest. Moved in maddening circles that made his throat dry.

"Leandro?"

"Si, mia cara?" he said breathless and still beneath her tentative touch, pulse thundering under the surface, senses screaming for more.

A fingernail raked his nipple. His breath hissed out of him. "Why does the press call you a saint?"

"The press is not always truthful, *bella*."

"But they call Luca the devil and I know he is one when he sets his mind to it." Now her finger moved over his abdomen, traced the roped ridge of muscle there and moved lower.

Grasping her wrist, he pushed it up over her head. With her other hand, she smoothed his brow, plunged her hands into his hair and tugged. Mouth against his, she pleaded with her lips.

She didn't demand like he had done, she simply gave of herself. And made him give of himself to her.

"After the night we shared, I stayed away from women for a long time."

"How long?" she whispered, pressing her hot little mouth to his pectorals.

"Does it matter?"

"To me, yes." Now, her tongue came out, licking him as if he was her favorite dessert.

He fisted his hands on the sheets, desire a live beast inside him. "Alexis…" he groaned, and held her hair in a punishing grip.

As if she understood his unspoken command perfectly, as if she was tuned in to every dark fantasy he had ever had of her, she grazed his nipple with her teeth. When she pursed her mouth and sucked on his skin, Leandro jerked, his erection drawing tight against his belly.

Dio, he wanted her on her knees, that pert mouth around his rigid length. He wanted all the pleasures with Alexis that he'd never allowed himself before.

Her mouth reached his abdomen now. Steel would have more give than his muscles then. "Do you still want me to believe I was one of many?" she whispered against his skin. "That I was just a convenient lay?"

"*No*…my father…was indiscriminate with any number of women, abusive of my mother in ways I can't even bear to mention. I promised myself a long time ago that I would never become like him." He forced the words out wondering if they would bring back a little sanity. "After I was with you…that next morning, I realized you had been a virgin. That I had taken you like that, with such little tenderness, against the wall, that even your gasp of pain couldn't penetrate the haze of my desire…"

A hard, inflaming kiss that delivered the depth of her want on his lips. It soothed and yet claimed. "But that pain was momentary, Leandro…nothing compared to what I felt after. Nothing compared to what you made me feel."

He closed his eyes, the memory haunting him even now. "I couldn't bear to look at myself. I couldn't stand to think I had been so reckless with my hunger. So mindless.

"And I abhor befriending women, letting them think I

was interested when I had no intention of ever marrying, just for sex. So I never touched another woman again."

Something akin to wonder crossed her face as she cradled his cheek. "Seven years, Leandro?"

The implicit trust in her gaze, the pure pleasure in the curve of her mouth felt like a gift, one he had never received before. "Any release I needed, my hands provided it."

Even as she stared back at him like a queen, gloriously naked, color suffused her cheeks at that. "Then it's true. I have toppled the saint from his pedestal," she whispered with a satisfied smile before she claimed his mouth.

Soft and tentative, she slanted her lips this way and that, looking for that perfect fit. Swiped her tongue over the seam of his lips.

He pushed his hand through the silky curtain of her hair and held her there, awash in the heated seduction of her mouth. But he needed more. Soon, he took over the kiss. Dueled his tongue with her tentative one. Scraped his teeth across her lush lower lip. Sucked it into his mouth.

He explored and ravaged that soft mouth so thoroughly that her whimper raced along his spine.

But it wasn't enough. *Dio,* nothing was going to be enough except utter possession. And complete surrender.

He pushed her onto her back and covered her body with his. Inch by inch, skin to skin, hardness against soft curves, he settled over her lithe body.

A perfect fit, as if they were made for each other.

As if there was magic in the room. Something beyond passion and pleasure. Beyond the frantic beats of their hearts and the sweat-slicked friction of their skin.

There was a raw intimacy, a closeness with Alexis that he vowed to never lose.

Alex's jagged growl joined his as her breasts rubbed his chest, as she brought her knees up and his thick shaft settled against her womanhood. He jerked at the heated invitation of her sex, slick against his. Her arms vined around his neck, fingers plunging into his hair and scraping. Softness settling against his hardness in all the right ways.

She was made for him, the thought circled him.

"Leandro, please, I want to touch you... I want to—"

"No, *cara*. I can't...wait anymore."

Pushing her thighs wide with his hips, rough hands holding her down for him, he entered her in one slick thrust and sheathed himself in her fully.

A gasp wrenched out of her as her sex stretched and closed over him like a tight fist. Every muscle in him screamed for movement, for friction, sweat gathered on his forehead. Leandro buried his mouth in the crook of her neck and counted his breaths.

Only then did he realize the tension in Alex's body, the punishing grip of her fingers on his shoulders. The thought of hurting her, *again*, cleaved him in two.

"Alexis, *mia cara*," he said, her name a prayer on his lips, "did I hurt you?" Had he been rough in his desperation?

Slowly, she relaxed under him, her breath blowing warmly against his shoulder blades. "No...it just feels unfamiliar and strange."

Her skin tasted like summer to his lips. "Good strange?" he somehow managed through the shrieking demands of his body.

"Overwhelmingly good, achingly...intimate." Her words mirrored his thoughts in a moment of pure perfection. She glanced at him and then away as if she needed to hide her expression from him. "Don't you think so?"

He smiled against her trembling mouth. "You think me capable of thinking, *cara*?"

After a moment, she found his gaze again. Kissed the corner of his mouth.

Slowly, her hands drifted down his back, cupped his buttocks and then she wiggled her hips under him. Liquid fire surged through every nerve ending. "I like when you can't think, Leandro."

It was all the sign he needed.

And then he was thrusting deep and hard inside her, breath balling up in his throat and she met him thrust to thrust, raking her fingers over his back, urging him on and on with her whimpers and moans.

Hands on her hips, he tilted her up for him and pistoned in and out, deeper and faster.

The slap of flesh, the pounding of their hearts, the damp whisper of their skin…

There was nothing civilized, nothing even remotely like self-control left in him anymore. Only the mind-numbing pleasure rushing at him mattered.

In the blink of a breath, he moved his hand and tugged the center of her slick sex with his fingers.

With a whimper, Alex bowed and bucked and fell apart around him and the convulsions of her body sent Leandro careening toward his own release.

Pleasure splintered him into a thousand pieces, slammed his heart awake as if it had merely been a functioning organ until now. His very breath a fire in the back of his throat, Leandro let out a guttural grunt at the surfeit of sensation.

Alex's hands came around him and held him hard as he fell from the dizzying pleasure.

And Leandro knew that he'd never been more vulnerable in his entire life. Knew why he'd fought and resisted this rushing fate from the moment he'd seen her again.

Not when he'd discovered the abuse his father had heaped upon his mother. Not when his mother had walked out and he had hugged a sobbing Luca and had taken on the mantle of his family and business. Not when Rosa had died and he had suddenly felt anchorless.

It seemed as if there were no coping strategies left. No automatic mechanisms that his mind could conjure to lift away the strange weight on his soul, the fever in his blood.

Alexis had burrowed herself under his skin, into his heart and if he lost her, he had a feeling his world was never going to be the same again.

CHAPTER TEN

"Alexis?"

Burrowing deeper into the warmth of his body, Alex purred. Or at least that's what the sound that escaped her throat sounded like.

"Wake up, *tesoro*."

A deep languor claimed every sated muscle, every sensitive nerve ending. Leandro had carried her to the en suite and washed her. A rainfall shower that she hadn't known existed, purple marble tiled bathroom and Leandro's roving hands that had persuaded and pushed her to another release—the erotic sounds from her own mouth were going to haunt her every time she went in there.

Her sex felt swollen and pulsed between her legs, her muscles sore in the most delicious sort of way.

Mind numb with a profound sense of well-being, she took her own time before she remembered he'd said her name. "Hmm?" she answered back lazily, tossing about on the bed.

"Stop wiggling around and stay still." Large hands, capable of heart-wrenching tenderness, gripped her. "I can't think if you keep doing that. Or I can think of only one thing."

As if he didn't trust her to listen, Leandro himself shifted behind her.

His arm went around her waist and rested snug between her breasts, the long T-shirt she'd donned after their shower no barrier. Somehow, she had convinced him she needed the T-shirt, not completely comfortable with her nudity yet.

He was another issue altogether. The rough velvet of his skin was a visual and sensual feast she couldn't get enough of.

As if there was an embedded chip that reacted to his touch, her breasts became heavy, nipples sprang to peaks.

One of his legs rested between her thighs and she could already feel him hardening against her again. Her head rested on his hand, his hands combed through her still damp hair.

Need slowly uncoiled within her again. She traced his leg with her foot, a languid invitation. "Something wrong with that?"

He pushed away her foot and slapped her on her bum. "Behave, *cara*."

She grabbed his hand and pressed a kiss to his rough palm. "Sorry, I forgot, you're ancient and decrepit. This last session probably wiped you out." She made a regretful sound as she moved a palm up and down his forearm. God, how she loved the silky rasp of his hair-roughened arm against hers. "I won't see action again for a while, will I?"

The words had barely left her mouth when he pushed up her T-shirt, lifted her leg and entered her from behind.

The shock of his invasion made the pleasure sharper and a desperate cry wrenched from the depths of her soul. She clutched his forearm and hitched out a hard breath.

"Any complaints now, *cara*?" he asked at her ear, his breath a rattling rumble.

"God, no," Alex whimpered as he tested their fit. The sensation was exquisite, like a lick of fire traversed down her spine, lighting every nerve ending on fire.

He felt even deeper like this, as though he was a part of her that she never wanted to lose.

"Take off your T-shirt," he growled then. With arms

that could barely hold up, Alex managed to roll the thin cotton up and over her head.

The moment she did, he slid his hand under her head, turned her so that her torso faced him. "One more time, *mia cara*." Dark and deep, his command sent shivers through her.

Alex groaned, every inch of her supersensitive. "Enough, Leandro, please."

He shook his head, his fingers rubbing her lower lip. When he pushed his finger into her mouth, she sucked on it. Wet heat rushed between her legs, and she writhed restlessly against him.

The dark sensuality of his demands was as revealing of the man as they were of her.

Such passion he leashed, such need he'd denied for so long, Alexis couldn't help but feel as if only she had unlocked it. Only she that all his desires belonged to.

Only she that could make all his fantasies come true.

"Yes, *mia cara*. I need to hear your scream, again." His eyes with a deeply possessive heat. "It's never going to be enough with you, *bella*."

Her gaze collided with his, excitement and something else a pulsating drum in her ears.

Without breaking her gaze, he bent that dark, arrogant head and took her nipple in his mouth. Soft lips suckled in that persistent rhythm that he'd discovered she liked until a flood of fire filled every inch of her.

And then he was moving within her even as his teeth grazed the hard knot, their flesh more joined than even before.

Control and inhibitions were dust beneath the thunderous roar of pleasure and the darkly sensual net of intimacy. They danced to a primal, age-old rhythm, instincts already honed to each other's needs and wants, hearts pounding together, skin slicked with sweat.

Release came upon them together in a violent cacophony of such pleasure that Alex thought she had died under the onslaught of it and became born again anew in Leandro's arms.

After what felt like an eternity of heaven, Leandro spoke into the darkness. The sheets were blissfully cool against her skin. And behind her, Leandro a fortress of warmth.

"Tell me about these folders that are full of drawings and stories."

Alex stiffened, hitched a much-needed breath. She clicked on the night lamp and turned toward him. "How do you know about that?" She sounded defensive, but she didn't care. "It was horrible of Antonio to snoop into my private matters. For you to do that is just plain crossing so many bloody lines. Don't manipulate me—"

"Izzie told me."

She tried to move away from him but his grip only tightened. "Because you prodded her?" she snarled. "Will you use her now to get your way?"

"*No.* She sounded very upset that she found you crying over one of them when you thought she was sleeping."

"Oh…" Dismay and a sense of failure swirled through Alex. "I should've been more careful. I hadn't realized… God, she must have been so scared. What did—?"

"Shh…calm down, *tesoro.* Izzie is just like you, strong and resilient. I reassured her that I would take care of her *mamma.*"

The wild beat of her heart calmed as Alex glanced into Leandro's gray eyes. She bit back the instant, defensive retort that sprang to her lips. It was his instinct to be protective, true. It didn't mean that he didn't care for her, just a little.

She couldn't believe him heartless anymore, not after

what they had shared. Not now when she understood what had made him so rigidly protective of those around him.

Something in her ached at the thought of him losing his innocence at such a young age, of him taking over responsibility for Luca and Valentina.

How would there be anything left for his own indulgence? Would he even know his own heart when it had always been buried under such weight?

"Thanks for reassuring her," she said.

Something warm filtered through his gray eyes and he laced their fingers together. "Should I thank you for raising such a wonderfully strong girl? We're a team now, *si*?"

She nodded, liking the sound of that.

The kiss he pressed to the back of her hand was tender, almost reverent. "So…what do I have to do to have the privilege of seeing the contents of these folders?"

"How do you know it's a privilege?" she retorted, keeping it casual.

Sharing those stories was like giving him a piece of her heart, the most precious, guarded part. So much of her sense of self was tied to them.

What if he thought they were rubbish like her parents had done? Or what if he used them and their value to her to manipulate her?

Alex didn't think she could bear it if he did that. There would be no coming back from that, even for Izzie's sake. It was better to keep that part to herself as she'd always done.

That way lay safety. For all of them.

"Izzie says they are fantastic. I believe her."

"Izzie is six years old. And they are very private. Only one person's seen them besides Izzie."

Instantly, he scowled. "Justin?"

Alex smothered a smile, knowing it would only rile him further. He sounded so fiercely jealous and her heart did a skip. *God*, how pathetic was she. "No, Adrian," she answered. "My parents thought it was an utter waste of time when I showed them once."

"Your parents are idiots, *bella*."

"Hey!" She swatted him on his shoulder. "I'd just gotten an F in math, they discovered Adrian pretty much did my science project from start to finish *and* they had been called to a meeting with the teacher to discuss my lack of *application to academics*. And then they found out I had pages and pages of these…doodles," Alex repeated her mother's word, though a part of her still hurt at the denigration. "They didn't know what to do with me."

"So tell me, what did Adrian think of them?"

How did he always know to ask the right question?

"He loved them and told me I should never stop. Never lose my pleasure in them. He had all these grand plans of becoming my agent and selling them and used to beg if he could live off me when I became a famed, big-name author." Tears filled her eyes, just remembering his goofy smile and his tight hugs. And his easy acceptance of all her flaws and weird quirks. "He was just being kind but I loved him even more for that."

"Wait, so other than Adrian, you've never shared them with anyone? Never wondered if they should be shared with people, if they would bring pleasure and joy to someone else?"

Alex shrugged. "I told you they're not important."

"Leave it to me to decide that," he growled back at her. In utter contrast, he cupped her cheek with such tenderness and kissed her mouth. "Why were you crying, *bella*?"

She lowered her eyes, her insecurities and her love of those drawings roping together into a twisted knot. "I was just probably feeling emotional. You already know that the accident was bad and not just physically."

"Will you lie after telling me we have to do better with each other, Alexis?"

Alex sighed and pulled up her left hand. She could never share them with him but maybe speaking of her loss would lessen the pain of it?

"I'm left-handed, Leandro. For years, those drawings and stories were my only escape, my only relief from the pressure I felt at not being brilliant like Adrian. Even from the grief of losing him.

"Now, I can't even hold a pencil properly for more than a minute, much less draw anything. It feels like the one thing I enjoy so much—" The one thing she thought defined her, the one thing she had built her entire identity around, "—has been snatched away from me."

As if she was now truly nothing, just as her mother had said for all those years.

Her tears slipped from her eyes, and Alex hid her face in his neck, refusing to let him see them.

She felt so small in that moment, like that little girl who had forever waited for her parents to tell her that she was loved just as she was.

But at least now, she had accepted that no one would. That her own acceptance of herself had to be enough. There was relief, painful but still there, in that truth.

Soundlessly, he wrapped those corded arms of his around her and squeezed her tight. "We'll see world-class specialists, *cara*. We'll do whatever it takes. It'll come back, you will see. Whatever exercises they prescribe, you'll do them with me from now on." Authority clipped his words, making it a harsh command. "No more lifting things or—"

Instantly, her hackles rose. "I'm not an imbecile, Leandro. I've been doing everything I was told to."

"You will indulge me. In the meanwhile, you can show me some of those lovely folders, *si*?" Pure mischief glinted in the gray eyes and the serious mouth, transforming his entire face. He looked younger, carefree in a way she'd never seen him. "I think it's important to share them with me so that you don't feel like you're alone—"

Alex thumped him hard on his shoulder. "You're a horrible, manipulative man, do you know that? You just can't help it, can you?"

Laughing, he fell back against the bed, and took her with him. Alex lay sprawled over him, her legs tangled with his, her breasts crushed against his muscles. It felt so natural to lie with him like this, so effortlessly easy.

"Maybe I'll have to withhold other things from you until you share them with me then."

Share them with me...

He was asking to know a part of her, showing interest in the thing that mattered to no one except her. Only Adrian had ever done that.

A matter, for all Leandro knew, that didn't give him any advantage in this relationship of theirs. Hope yawned in her entire being, an incandescent flicker that was as good as imagining that she, only Alexis, and not the idea of the mother of his child, held his interest now, without his sense of duty chaining him to her.

"Let's see about that," Alex challenged before sliding over him and straddling him.

She gasped as she felt him hardening and lengthening against her core, just where she needed. She fisted her hand around the base, and the feral growl that fell from his mouth filled her with a satisfaction unlike she had ever known.

Rising up on her knees, she took him into her body and then there were no challenges between them, no withholding, nothing but mutual pleasure.

Alex finished her swim in the infinity pool and rubbed down her arms and legs. The Italian sun was at its peak but she lingered at the covered stone patio deck for another few minutes.

The scent of olive trees and the spice garden to the side of the villa that she had learned Leandro tended to personally permeated the air.

Among all of Leandro's estates and she had toured a mind-gaping number of them this past week with him and Izzie, she liked Villa de Conti the best.

And not just because of the spectacular view Lake Como offered either. There was a peace, a kind of quiet here in the villa that she didn't see elsewhere. A sense of happiness among the three siblings, of what they had built together after the disastrous, it seemed, almost destructive consequences of their parents' marriage.

Even as Valentina sometimes rebelled at his dictates and Luca, quite recklessly, provoked Leandro, just for the fun of it—the devil—over the past few weeks Alex had realized any happiness they had found, the love they shared was because of Leandro.

In the name of duty he did it, but the fact that he would give anything for their happiness warmed Alex's heart.

Also, Valentina lived here and they had become fast friends again. Even Luca dropped by every few days and somehow Alex felt as if she was as much a part of their family now as Izzie was.

Or perhaps it was the absence of Leandro's grandfather, Antonio.

The old man hadn't said one word to her again, hadn't even approached her. Only looked at her with a cutting hostility but Alex told herself she didn't need his approval.

She knew, however, that Antonio was still a large part of Leandro's life. He seemed to be the closest to a friend and mentor Leandro had. But something about him didn't sit well with Alex.

She hoped it was just her reaction to the old man not liking her and making it very obvious.

Grabbing a robe from the lounger, Alex pulled it on and

headed for her bedroom. Izzie was out with Valentina and the afternoon stretched ahead of her.

Alex showered and dressed.

Settling in the shade in the sun-drenched terrace, she dialed her parents' home number, eager to hear how their trip went. When an automated voice told her that the line was disconnected, she called her mom's cell instead.

It took her mom barely five minutes to cut across Alex's questions and blurt out her excitement.

Her parents had sold the store to an interested buyer who had offered them loads of money for the prime location.

Alex made all the necessary comments, faked excitement she didn't feel.

How many times had she tried to get a refinance for their house with the store as a guarantee? And yet someone had spent a bucketload of money on it.

But the weight on her chest refused to melt away as she went through the day. Something about her parents' sudden bout of good fortune made her uneasy.

Or was it just her attachment to the store, she doubted herself again. Was it just that things were changing too rapidly for her peace of mind or was it something else?

Days passed by in a blur as Alex tried to hold on to the wave of change that rocked through her life.

Only nights spent between the sheets with Leandro made her feel together again. Only by laying against his warm chest and hard body could she retain a sense of herself, could hold the reins of her life.

Outside of it, the weight returned to her chest.

Her parents' selling the store.

Valentina not only meeting the enigmatic Kairos Constantinou, but within three weeks of meeting her, Kairos proposing marriage to her.

The rapid-fire argument she had caught between Leandro and Luca over Kairos.

That vague sense of unease returned a hundredfold and Alex struggled with it for days.

It felt like a dark portent, like a choice was rushing at her that she didn't want to make. As if the sense of well-being and wonder she had discovered with Leandro would be ripped away at any moment.

The sounds of revelry from the gardens that floated up through the windows and the balconies, of snippets of Italian and Greek, of the sultry jazz tune that Kairos and Valentina were dancing to, the intensely lush colors of the summer—jasmine and rose, and the scent of wild orchids that decorated each table…

Everything faded as Leandro straightened from the vanity sink and his gaze fell on the wrapper half peeking out of the wastebasket.

He'd almost missed it and if not for the word flashing at him like a neon sign he would have thought nothing of it.

Half of that phrase winked at him as if playing peekaboo with his already somber mood.

Fingers turning as cold as the gold-tinted marble, he stared at it. It seemed as if he was being petrified from the inside out, such was the stillness inside him.

He didn't know how long he stood like that, looking at it, but unmoving. And then shattering that stillness, laying waste to that stony silence inside him came a howl from his throat that should have quaked the very foundation of the centuries-old villa he stood in.

It propelled him into action, and he bent his knees, and pulled out the wrapper gingerly, as if it was a bomb that could detonate at any moment and decimate his suddenly fragile life.

Breath ballooned up in his chest, crushing his lungs as he read the script on the wrapper.

Someone had taken a pregnancy test.

And since this was Alexis's bedroom, the bedroom in which he had made love to her in the past six weeks, he had little doubt who. He had forgotten to use protection that first night after the party.

And after that, Alexis had told him they would have to use condoms until she went back on the pill.

He had bitten off his retort countless times about how they wouldn't need it if they just got married, like he wanted to.

Her mouth falling open, she had looked at him in disbelief. "Married? You want more kids?" she had said, as if the very prospect was scary.

"*Si.* Where did you think this is leading?" he'd thrown back at her curtly, frustration turning his temper ragged.

"Marriage is a big step," she'd countered then. "And I can't even think about more kids now."

He'd barely held back the snarl that rose to his lips. "You would have us continue in this vein, sneaking into bed at night and into closets during the day? For how many days do you think you can fool Isabella?"

For how many more days would she torture him this way?

For days, there had been a compulsion in his blood, a pulsing throb under his skin that he needed to secure their future. That he needed to bind Alexis to him in any way he could.

But she had told him not to rush her, that she was enjoying their learning each other, enjoying the freedom of being his lover without the restrictions and confines of marriage.

Maledizione! He should have dragged her to the church by the hair after that statement.

But no!

Vulnerable in a way he'd never been before, having no experience of this confusion within, he had let her set the tone for their relationship.

After all, he'd manipulated her thoroughly, hadn't he?

It was the only thing she'd ever asked of him. That they take it slow.

He understood the word *sucker* that Luca used for some of his friends.

He had thought to make her happy, to gain her trust. He'd taken her to the opera and when she had challenged him, he'd watched a marathon of some cult TV show because she'd called him a traditional, stick-up-his-ass, starchy brute.

He made love to her in the night in her room, like some illicit lover, because she insisted on not confusing their daughter before matters were settled between them.

Dio, she hadn't even come into his room once. Hadn't let him take her in his bed. She didn't let him wake up with her in the morning, shuffling him out of her room at dawn because she thought Izzie would wander in.

And now to find this…

The test, where was the test…he went to his knees. With shaking fingers, he upended the basket.

Maybe it wasn't positive, the vulnerable, emotionally weak part of him piped up. *Maybe that's why she hadn't even mentioned it. Maybe he was making a big issue out of—*

And the plastic, rectangular tube lay faceup on the white marble, the answer winking up at him.

She was pregnant!

Alexis was pregnant. With his child. Again.

And she hadn't told him.

Cold chill infiltrated Leandro's skin, clamped his very bones.

She hadn't said a word all day.

He had seen her at the lavish breakfast he had arranged in Kairos and Valentina's honor just for family. She had sat next to him, a little bit lost, until Luca had prodded her.

He did that always, Leandro had realized irritably. Made Alexis smile and laugh. Looked after her in a way he'd never seen Luca do before with another woman.

After the breakfast, they had both gone their separate ways, a hundred things on his mind about the engagement party tonight.

Until he had come upon her, here in this bedroom and asked her point-blank if something was bothering her. If there was something he could fix for her.

She had fed him a white lie that she was anxious about her dad's health.

Too afraid to examine his own spiraling anxiety about her continued refusal, he had accepted her answer.

Had made love to her in that very bed while the entirety of his family and three hundred members of Italian society had been arriving on his estate. Stroked and tasted and touched every inch of her until his name was a litany on her lips.

Because only there could he strip her defenses, only when she was naked and writhing beneath him, only when he drove away everything else with his hands and mouth and touch, did Alexis belong to him completely, mind, body and soul.

All last week, she had been curt, a little distracted, even with Izzie. Even Valentina, as self-involved as she'd been, had commented on Alex's appetite.

Which meant Alexis had known, or at least guessed, the truth before this morning.

With a growl, he pushed away the basket, threw the test on the floor.

Hurt and pain were like twin spikes in his sides, stealing his very rationality. Shredding that sense of control he had always needed to handle his world.

Why hide the truth from him this time? What did she fear? Or had she decided she didn't want to be with him after all?

I would like to visit New York for a couple of weeks, she had said just yesterday, throwing him for a loop.

Why? Why go to New York now?

Why was she pulling away from him?

And what could he do to stop her?

CHAPTER ELEVEN

IT WAS ALMOST dawn and she still hadn't come to him, still hadn't told him. And for the first time since that night when he had made love to her, Leandro kept himself away from her bedroom.

The party had come to an end hours ago and the dense silence, the pitch-dark of the night, suited his somber mood. Somehow, he'd held on to his control. His jaw should have turned to concrete hours ago for the way he'd gritted his teeth and greeted everyone.

His face should have turned to brittle glass for the happiness and normalcy he'd had to fake.

His blood should have chilled to ice at the sight of Alexis in a navy blue silk dress that hugged her curves so gloriously. She had looked strained though he was the only one who noticed.

Like him, she hadn't wanted to mar the happiness of Valentina's big night.

If he went to her, he would weaken.

If he touched her, if he lost himself in the sensuality of her body, he wouldn't care about why she was avoiding him.

If he took her and moved inside her, the hurt wouldn't lessen when he was done.

Because he would still be outside of the wall she'd erected between them.

It was nothing but a madness and Leandro was through with being this mad, this out of control.

He had to do something to shred this fear. He had to take action.

Only action, only setting things right had always saved him. Had stopped him from crumbling. Had enabled him to take care of Luca and Valentina.

And the right thing was that Alexis belonged with him just as Isabella did.

She was his and he wouldn't let her go.

He reached his study and slammed the door shut behind him.

Countless times, he had come in here, to swallow his tears. To bury his fears. To shore up his courage so that he could act like an adult when he had barely been one.

Here was where he had lost his innocence and discovered that the man who should have protected them all was an animal instead.

Here was where he had threatened Enzo after he had raised his hand at their mother.

Here was where he had hugged Luca when they'd discovered the horrible truth their mother swallowed.

Here was where he had argued with Antonio, for days, about the rightness of bringing Valentina home.

A growl rumbled through him at the thought of losing Alexis, too.

He had just poured a generous measure of whiskey, something else he'd never indulged in as a rule, when the door opened behind him.

Even in that moment, his breath hitched in his throat, hope flared.

Antonio stood at the door and Leandro turned away from his grandfather's shrewd gaze. He didn't want anyone to see him like this.

Not when he didn't understand himself.

"Drinking, Leandro?" Antonio's challenge was instant,

dry and carried the weight of a thousand questions. Enzo had not only been an alcoholic but an abusive one.

All of them, even Antonio, had felt the effects of that.

Leandro threw back the whiskey in a reckless gesture. It seemed he was finally coming apart at the seams and he hadn't even realized that he had been holding so tight. That his complacency and his control were this flimsy.

The fiery slide of the whiskey against his throat and chest blunted the edge of his roiling emotions. Just. He faced Antonio and shrugged. "Maybe I have earned the right, Nonno?"

Antonio's cane was a harsh rap against the gleaming marble floor. "Maybe you have become weak."

Leandro remained silent, hating to agree with Antonio.

"That woman, what has she done now?"

Brittle laughter escaped Leandro's mouth. Apparently, the only absolute in his shifting world was Antonio's black prejudice of Alexis.

"She is pregnant."

A fierce kind of joy lit up Antonio's old eyes, so raw that Leandro looked away. He thumped Leandro on the shoulder, the force of it no less for his frail body.

"Marry her soon," he declared as if that hadn't been a foregone conclusion from the moment Leandro had seen that Alexis needed him just as much as Isabella did.

Why couldn't she accept it when Leandro offered her everything?

"The Conti heir cannot be a *bastardo*—"

"You do not know if it is a boy, Nonno, and she has not told me."

Antonio missed a beat. "You think she will use this to manipulate you?"

"Alexis doesn't have a manipulative bone in her body."

"Then why does it—" Antonio stared at Leandro, then

frowned as if he couldn't fathom the import of this. "This matters to you? That she has not informed you?"

Leandro drove his shaking fingers through his hair. Trust his grandfather to arrive at the crux of it so easily. "*Si*, it does. It means I still do not have her trust. It means she still has not accepted that we must marry."

It means that he still did not have her heart. And that clawed through him.

Something dawned in Antonio's gaze. Whatever it was, Leandro didn't like it one bit. "She leads you by your manhood, she refuses to marry you and now…she plays with your emotions. I knew this would happen."

Running a shaking hand over his nape, Leandro bit back his stinging retort.

The sounds of a file slapping the mahogany desk brought his head up.

A grim sort of triumph danced in Antonio's eyes.

"What is that?" Leandro inquired.

"Read it for yourself."

A small insignia on the top right corner of the file was Leandro's first clue—a highly expensive Milanese private investigations firm.

A passport-size picture of Alexis, maybe eight or nine years old, that naive but defiant tilt to her chin, his second clue.

Pages and pages of information on Alexis from school grades to jobs, including the time she and her friends had received a mark on their juvenile record for some minor shoplifting. When she had been fired from a job at an accounting firm when she'd been eighteen—the year after her brother's death, he remembered.

Facts even he didn't know about her pregnancy. The loan on her store that had been almost defaulted. And then details about the accident and her recovery.

Nausea barreled up Leandro's chest and filled his throat.

"What in hell is this?" The question was rhetorical yet he couldn't wrap his mind around it.

"It's a report that I had that firm put together a week after that woman stormed into our home. That shoplifting record, those bad investments, and this accident recently... it is not a hard story to put together.

"I can find a lawyer in two minutes who will label her an incompetent mother. And your children will be yours."

"I will not separate my children from their mother. I need her in my life, Antonio."

Leandro's stark statement echoed around them while Antonio's mouth tightened. But he did not care. *Dio*, he did not care about anything.

For the first time in his life, he wanted, *no, desperately needed*, something to even go on. He wanted Alexis's heart, he wanted to be loved by this strong woman, he wanted to bask in the generosity of her laughter and passion. He wanted to go to bed with her through countless dark nights and wake up with her to a million sunrises. He wanted to help her heal and see her soar...

Yet he did not know how to keep her from slipping away from him.

She was. *Dio, she was.*

"I could not hurt her with this, Nonno. I could not forgive myself if I hurt her."

"Then use it in my name. Use it to scare her, use it to bind her to you."

Leandro jerked away from the table.

It was so diabolical and yet simple.

Antonio could force her hand with this very file. Even a whisper of a separation from Isabella would send Alexis into his arms. Leandro could reassure her it was not true, but persuade her to the altar with him. And she would be Leandro's forever.

Once Alexis gave her commitment, once she vowed

herself to him in marriage, there would be no going back, whatever way she'd arrived there.

She would be that perfect, adoring wife, her loyalty toward him and their family absolute. He knew that as well as he knew his own mind.

A life with Alexis and Isabella and his unborn child, just as it should be, versus this anxiety, this confusion about her feelings, this desperate chasm that he couldn't fill no matter what he did.

If he used it, Alexis would be shattered. It was the worst thing he could aim at her, even in the guise of Antonio, the worst that she believed of herself.

But if he didn't…what if she never agreed to marry him? What if after everything Leandro had done, he wasn't enough?

He could have the only woman he'd ever wanted in his life this badly.

What, per carita, was he waiting for?

Alex felt every passing second like a net was drawing in closer around her. Soon it would choke her if she didn't tell Leandro about the pregnancy. The terrifying anxiety she had felt at seeing the test positive had calmed now, but not the fear of the oncoming fate.

She hated cheating him of this news every passing second, especially as she knew how elated he would be.

A big, loving family, he wanted it. He wanted everything he and Luca and Valentina hadn't had growing up. He would shower this baby with just as much love as he did Isabella. He had so much love to give, and yet, would he open himself up to feeling anything remotely like that for Alex herself?

Again and again, he talked of duty, of what an exceptional mother she was, of giving Isabella security, of the rightness of all of them together…

And nothing about her and him…

Nothing about why he wanted her with a desperate intensity every night, about the raw fear she saw in his eyes when he didn't think she was looking at him, about the urgency and anger she sensed gathering in him every time she postponed their talk of future…

Would he ever learn that he had to risk his heart to have and hold hers? Would it all be her capitulation but none of his? Would he only manipulate her again and again, like he'd already done with her parents' store?

For one question of Luca and five minutes of his time had told her that some offshore branch of Conti Luxury Goods had acquired a tiny health food store in Brooklyn.

Why, why did he need to buy their store and offer that exaggerated price for it?

Was it just to retain control of this situation between them? To arm himself against her?

So every time she had gathered courage yesterday, every time she had firmly put her reasons for not jumping into marriage, fear eroded her courage.

That she would let him persuade her, that he would forever bind her to him without ever opening his heart to her, that she would forever wonder if it was something to do with her that stopped him from loving her… Alex didn't want to live like that.

She didn't want to spend the rest of her life like she'd done for so long. Craving her parents' approval and attention but never receiving it, calling herself inadequate and not being able to help it, forcing herself at things that she'd never been good at and failing…

On and on, the cycle would go on…

God, it would be a thousand times worse with Leandro, for she wanted more from Leandro than she'd ever wanted from anyone else.

She wanted him to want her because he couldn't live

without her. Because he loved her, just as much as she loved him. She wanted him to be desperate for her, just as she was.

Bloodthirsty of her, true, but how could she live with anything else?

When she knew walking away from him would shatter her into a thousand different pieces.

The morning had started out horrible with nausea churning through Alex's stomach. She had barely slept, waiting and wondering if Leandro would come to her.

When somewhere around dawn, she'd realized he wasn't going to, she had cried herself to sleep. The tears felt both like a burden and a relief for she was no closer to deciding what she wanted to do.

She'd desperately wanted to go find him, to sink into his embrace, to tell him how much she loved him. But what would he say? What if he only took advantage of it?

What if he turned the biggest truth of her life into another weakness?

She emptied her glass of orange juice and decided to take Izzie out for a walk when Luca walked onto the terrace, a grim expression on his face.

Fear was a fist in her throat for Alex knew, instantly, that something was very wrong.

Luca threw a file on the table. "I promised I would help." There was no warmth or charm in his tone. A nerve flicked violently in his temple while that laughing mouth set into a hard, cruel curve.

It was such a change in his demeanor that it took her a few seconds to focus on the file.

Like a snake uncoiling, ready to strike and sink poison, it stared back at her. "What is it, Luca?"

"A file, *cara*." His tone tempered and perversely, it

made her throat raw. "About you. To prove that you're an incompetent mother."

Alex jerked so hard that she'd have toppled off the chair if not for Luca's hand behind her. Her heart thumped in her chest, a loud rushing in her ears made her head spin. The nausea she'd felt this morning returned a hundredfold.

She gripped the edge of the breakfast table, looking for an anchor in her drowning world.

Incompetent…the word was a like a burn mark on her skin, festering and deep and painful. More so than all the pain she'd suffered in the accident.

More so than all the years of tears and deprecation and grief she had suffered at her parents' hands.

With shaking hands, she opened the file. Watched pages and pages of her life distilled into hard little facts. Stripped of her insecurities and fears. Reducing her entire life into one dimension.

Disorganized. Years of her chaotic nature, her rebellion against being compared to Adrian's obsessively organized life.

Poor financial straits. Years of having slaved over the store and the house and nothing to show in return. Apparently, no loans at least, thanks to Leandro.

Panic attacks. Incomplete use of one hand.

No career prospects.

Doubt was a pit of thorns that she tumbled into, mocking her, scraping her.

It was every horrible thing her mother had insinuated over the years and every fear she had made herself sick over again and again.

Alexis bent her head to the table, and pulled in a deep breath to keep the grief rising through her at bay.

No, she refused to be reduced, refused to let her pain, her fears, her very life, be reduced to such cold, hard facts.

This wasn't even about her.

She wasn't a failure. Not the woman who took what she wanted seven years ago. Not the woman who had a daughter and raised her against all odds. Not the woman who dared set the rules with a man as ruthless and autocratic as Leandro.

She dashed away the tears before they could spill. Rage was a feral thing inside her and she let it roam freely. She stood up and faced Luca. "Do you know who commissioned this?"

Please, let it not be Leandro, she prayed frantically.

If he'd done this, she could never forgive him. There'd be nothing but ashes left.

"Antonio." Relief battered her. "A chartered flight leaves in three hours. It is best if you take Izzie and leave."

"You think Leandro will use this against me." Horror seeped into her words.

"I have stopped guessing the lengths to which my brother will go to ensure what he thinks is right. He's done it for too long and knows nothing else." The impact of Luca's fist on the table rocked through Alexis. "Maybe I was wrong and there's no hope for—"

A fist to his mouth threw Luca back. Loud and vicious, his pithy curse rent the air. Heart rapping against her rib cage, Alex pushed her chair back and stood up.

Shock buffeted her as she realized it was Leandro that had thrown the punch at Luca.

Knuckles bruised, mouth tightened into a thin line, gray eyes blazing with fury, it was Leandro like she'd never seen before.

When he moved toward a barely upright Luca again, Alex planted herself in front of him. "Stop it, Leandro. What the hell is wrong with you?"

Something swept across Leandro's face then, a black, glittering shadow that sent ripples of alarm up and down her skin. "He not only advises you but aids you to run away, with Isabella in tow, and I should forgive him?"

"He aids me because he has lost hope for you. Because he thinks—" her chest was so tight, "—that you're an unfeeling brute who would manipulate me into spending my life with you without earning it, without even deserving it."

That arrogant head of his reared back as if she had slapped him. That sensuously wicked mouth that had licked and caressed her to rapture flinched. But Alex felt no satisfaction in hurting him, in piercing that steely invulnerability of his.

How could she when her gut was twisted into a painful knot, when her heart thudded in fear of a future that could very well be ruined?

Luca's harsh, pain-filled laughter surrounded them. He stepped forward now, past Alex, as if challenging, almost inviting, Leandro to take another swing at him. "Our parents have ruined him, too, *cara*. You are a fool to trust him."

The contempt in his tone left a jarring reminder even after he left.

A bleakness touched Leandro's gray gaze even as it swept over Alex in that hungry way of his. "Have you decided I do not deserve to know that I'm to be a father again?"

He didn't demand in a fury or betrayal but as if he'd already lost her. As if she'd hurt him immeasurably by not sharing it with him. "It's not something I could hide from you long."

"But you did not share it with me in happiness. That is telling enough."

"I hated not telling you every moment. I hated depriving us of the joy of it…but *God*, Leandro, you manipulate everything around you, arrange everyone's lives." Tears she'd held back fell out of her eyes. "I trusted you, always and you…

"Is he right, Leandro? Would you have used that file against…me?" Her voice broke, throat full of needles. "Did you consider it?"

His strength and heat surrounded her, and Alex almost leaned into him, driven by deep need and instinct. When he spoke, he sounded as if his own throat was full of gravel. "I considered it. For all of five minutes.

"I was desperate, *bella*, I could feel you slipping away from me this past week. And then you wouldn't look me in the eyes, you hide this news from me."

He rubbed the heel of his hand over his eyes, the vulnerability of the gesture tugging at Alex even now.

"Because you made me doubt everything. You bought my parents' store and didn't say a word to me. You talked of marriage and duty and family but not of us. Not once.

"I couldn't live like that again. Not when I discovered how…

"Not for Izzie, not for this baby. I couldn't settle for something less again. Not from you, of all the people in the world. I deserve to spend my life with someone who loves me, Leandro."

"Are you leaving me then, Alexis?"

The stiffness in her spine relented, the rigidness of her muscles melted and Alex struggled to regulate her long exhale.

For in that tiny question, she discovered a universe of meaning.

The old Leandro wouldn't have asked such a desperate question. As if it was all beyond him now. He would have never accepted defeat when he could move mountains and rearrange landscapes for his purpose.

His pain in those words and the relief it provoked was a

tiny, threadbare bridge between the chasm that had opened up between them over the past week.

Hope flickered in her chest.

Heart in throat, every inch of her skin hyper-aware of him, Alex stared back at him. Refused to even betray her heart by the flicker of an eyelid. "If I do take Luca's help and leave, it's your own fault.

"If you lose the right to be Izzie's father, if you lose this joy that we could've had…" she swallowed away the words that rose to her lips, "then it is all your fault.

"It is your own refusal to open up your heart to me, your own stubborn, arrogant belief in thinking you know best, your bloody incapability to feel anything, that would ruin the best thing that's come into your life."

The silence clattered with the beat of some bird's wings across the blue sky, with the soft hum of a lawn mower somewhere, the world puttering on its humdrum way while her heart stuttered in her chest.

"You think me unfeeling, *mia cara*? To attack my own brother like an animal, you think I'm not weak? You think it doesn't terrify me at this moment that there is nothing I can do to stop my very life from falling apart? You think it didn't disgust me that I considered even letting you see that file?

"My heart is not mine anymore.

"My fate is not mine anymore.

"I have been rendered into nothing at your hands, *tesoro*. I'm nothing without your love."

And just like that, the man she loved with every fiber of her being went on his knees.

That stunning, honorable man raised his head toward her and spoke the words she'd been dying to hear with every breath in her. "All my life, I have tried to control and master every emotion. I lived only to make sure no one ever hurt me and Luca and Valentina, without ever risking anything… I didn't even realize what I missed until I met you.

"You…you make me risk everything, *bella*. To place my happiness in your hands, to trust myself into your hands, it terrifies me.

"But I love you so much, *mia cara*. If you give me one chance, I will change. And I will love. And I will risk everything I have again and again to prove I'm worthy of the woman I love more than anything else."

The woman I love more than anything else…

Tears filled and overflowed from Alex's eyes at the pure supplication in Leandro's words.

Her trust in him soared on wings, her entire being felt as if she could float away on a cloud of happiness.

She fell to her knees in front of him and took his mouth with hers. He tasted of passion and thirst and hunger that could never be sated, and of love.

Of unconditional love, of utter acceptance, of deep, abiding trust.

Frantic words in Italian caressed her skin as he pressed kisses to every inch of her face, as he wrapped his strong arms around her and held her tight. His anxiety spoke in his shaking fingers, in his tight grip.

In the shudder that went through him when he said roughly, "*Per piacere, bella,* tell me you're not leaving me. Tell me you'll stay and love me. Tell me you'll let me be a part of your life, *cara*.

"I would take nothing that you do not want to give, Alexis. Never again."

"I love you, Leandro, so much." Alex buried her mouth in his neck, breathed in the taste and scent of him. "I would have killed you if you had used that against me. I'd have—"

"Shh…*mia cara*. They are all lies, you know that, don't you? If anything, I'm the one incompetent to love you. I'm the one who's not worthy of you and Izzie and this baby."

He pulled her to him right there until she sat in the cradle of his thighs, and his hand found her stomach.

"I hate him, Leandro," she said snuggling into his warmth. "I'll never forgive him for putting such idea in your head."

With gentle fingers, he clasped her chin, understanding her. "He's old and set in his ways, *cara*."

Fear made her words sharp, harsh. "What if you had lost me because of his horrible advice? What if we had lost all this?"

"You know what I see when I look at him, Alexis?

"Myself, if you hadn't come along. He has been through grief and loss and such pain to be hardened by it all, *bella*. He tried to do right by Luca and me in his own way.

"If nothing else, I have to keep him around the family as a reminder of what I could become if—"

"You're generous and kind and honorable, Leandro." Alex turned around in his arms and pressed her forehead to his. "You're the man I love. You would never become like that. You could never hurt anyone you love like that."

Her belief in him unmanned Leandro, her love for him shook him. "But I already have, Alexis." A shiver ran through him and Alex turned and embraced him again.

"What do you mean?"

Leandro hid his face in her shoulder, fear fisting his gut. How foolish he had been in thinking he could arrange and assure everyone's happiness around him. When his own wasn't in his hands. "Luca hates me. And Tina… *Dio*, Tina's entire happiness hinges on the fact that the bet I made is right."

"You set up Kairos with her, didn't you?" Alex asked, her perceptive gaze settling on him.

"I did. I couldn't risk Antonio threatening to tell her that she's not a Conti. If she was married, if she wasn't one anymore, I thought she would not care. Luca thinks, rightly, that I have gambled with her happiness.

"If she discovers it, she will never forgive me. And I will lose her."

Alex caressed the clenched muscles in his back, clasped her arms around Leandro tight. She understood Luca's anger now, and the underlying fear. But she couldn't let the man she loved suffer. Pressing her mouth to his temple, she lifted his chin. "You did it with the right intentions. You did it because you love her so much.

"She'll understand one day, Leandro. Because she loves you. Just as I understood what you did with me."

The trust in her eyes, the fierceness of her embrace, Leandro realized for the first time in his life that he wasn't alone anymore. That he didn't have to bear the burden by himself. That Alexis would seek to protect him just as he would do with her.

The depth of her love filled him with a quiet strength. He brushed his lips against hers, sensing a hole he hadn't even known inside fill. "Promise me that you will spend eternity with me."

With a kiss, Alex agreed.

EPILOGUE

Ten Years Later

LEANDRO STOOD LEANING against the wall by the entrance to the small bookstore while cold November rain and sleet pounded the streets of Seattle.

A fire burned brightly in the stone hearth on the far corner, its hissing sparks and flames adding to his wife's spooky storytelling abilities.

His mouth curved as she reached the part where the magical squirrel reached the dark cave she had to venture into.

High and low, deep and bass, she modulated her voice to match the ferocious tiger and the shaking squirrel while the group of children surrounding her wore matching reactions of wonder and shock and anticipation. Some smiled with a knowing look for they knew what came next, some shuddered for they were hearing the story for the first time.

His ten-year-old Violetta and six-year-old Chiara watched Alexis with wide eyes and wider mouths as if they couldn't believe that their *mamma* could be this entertainer extraordinaire who authored such magical, elaborate stories.

It had taken him eighteen torturous, agonizing months to win Alexis's trust, to receive the last piece of her heart, to see the stories she had written and drawn pictures around for so long.

The innocence hidden in the stories despite the treacherous adventures, her particular gift of transforming the average, the downtrodden, the underdog into tremendous heroes meant her success after being published had been meteoric.

And Leandro had cherished every moment of this journey with her, was humbled every day that this brilliant woman was his in every way that mattered.

He wasn't sure Chiara even understood that Alexis was such a famous children's books author.

To her and his other girls, she was just their loving, adorable and, in Izzie's case recently, a little strict *mamma*.

Remembering his teenage troublemaker, Leandro turned. At sixteen, his eldest was already giving him minor heart attacks with her rebellious streak. She hid in one of the back aisles chatting with a boy and throwing him warning glances to not even acknowledge her.

Turning around, Leandro smiled widely.

He wouldn't admit it to her even at the pain of death but he loved Izzie for exactly what she was, even as she drove him up the wall every other day with her tricks. He loved all his girls as different as they were for they were all pieces of his heart.

Something Antonio still couldn't grasp after all these years. Just remembering Antonio's crushing disappointment when Chiara had been born made Leandro chortle even now.

That the Conti male heir he so desperately wanted, that he wanted to groom, was Luca's son was a bitter pill he still couldn't seem to swallow.

He straightened from the door to the sound of thunderous applause from a bunch of tiny hands. Alex stood up from the stool but waited patiently as some kids asked her to sign their books and some just asked about the magical squirrel's next adventure.

Violetta ran toward Izzie and Chiara followed while his wife made her way toward him.

The moment she reached him, Leandro took her mouth in a fast, hard kiss. Cheeks staining pink, Alex pushed at him. "Bookstore, Leandro, and children, remember?"

His hands on her hips, Leandro dragged her to his side and locked her there. It had been three months of Alexis's book tour with his entire family. Of Chiara crashing into their bed because she didn't like her bed, of Isabella hating her life and Violetta following her little sister.

"I can't help it, *mia cara*. It's going to be hell once we get to the hotel again."

Alex elbowed him in the ribs. "You're the one who wanted a big family, remember?"

"Yes, but I thought they would all be saints like me. But they are like you—"

This time, it was she that pressed her mouth to his.

Dio, his hunger for this woman would never abate and he liked it just like that. "Take me home then, won't you, Leandro? To our big bed and endless privacy and to those long nights." Wicked laughter made her eyes shine. "Maybe we can fob them off on their *Zia* and have a fourth honeymoon." She swiped her tongue over his lips in a languid invitation and then drew back. "That is, if you're up to it."

Leandro pressed her hips until she could feel the rigid length of him. "I'm always up for you, *bella*," he said nuzzling her hair.

Pink stained his wife's cheeks, a soft gasp fluttered out and he fell in love just a little more. Every day, he fell a little more, the magic of it filling his every breath.

"I love you, Leandro." She never let him forget it.

Through day and night, joy and sorrow, Alexis never let him forget that he was loved.

"*Ti amo*, Alexis," he whispered back, his heart bursting to full.

* * * * *

LET'S TALK

Romance

For exclusive extracts, competitions
and special offers, find us online:

f facebook.com/millsandboon

🐦 @MillsandBoon

📷 @MillsandBoonUK

Get in touch on 01413 063232